Right Place, Right Time

Ali McNamara

Right Place, Right Time

BLOOMSBURY PUBLISHING

LONDON • OXFORD • NEW YORK • NEW DELHI • SYDNEY

BLOOMSBURY PUBLISHING
Bloomsbury Publishing Plc
50 Bedford Square, London, WC1B 3DP, UK
Bloomsbury Publishing Ireland Limited,
29 Earlsfort Terrace, Dublin 2, D02 AY28, Ireland

BLOOMSBURY, BLOOMSBURY PUBLISHING and the Diana logo
are trademarks of Bloomsbury Publishing Plc

First published in Great Britain 2025

A catalogue record for this book is available from the British Library

ISBN: PB: 978-1-5266-8618-3; EBOOK: 978-1-5266-8702-9; EPDF: 978-1-5266-8703-6

2 4 6 8 10 9 7 5 3 1

Typeset by Integra Software Services Pvt. Ltd.
Printed and bound in Great Britain by CPI Group (UK) Ltd, Croydon CR0 4YY

To find out more about our authors and books visit www.bloomsbury.com
and sign up for our newsletters
For product-safety-related questions contact productsafety@bloomsbury.com

The time you enjoy wasting is not wasted time
– Bertrand Russell

1

Cambridge. 29 February 2024

'You can do this,' I tell myself determinedly, as I glance in the ornate silver mirror that hangs on the wall of my shop. For my meeting today I've chosen to wear a long green velvet coat and a bright art nouveau scarf that I recently bought from my friend Luca's vintage-clothes shop. I've pinned my long hair up in a messy bun, and I hope I'm giving off just the right sort of vibe to land one of the biggest jobs I've taken on since I began running my grandparents' shop – Rainy Day Antiques.

I lock up the shop and head across Clockmaker Court, a historic circular court in the centre of Cambridge, originally built in Tudor times, that now contains a mixture of shops and residential buildings.

'Happy birthday, Eve!' a cheery voice calls from the coffee shop as I pass.

I stop and turn back to acknowledge the good wishes. 'Thank you, Harriet. It's good of you to remember.'

'How could we forget?' Harriet's husband, Rocky, says cheerfully. 'I've baked a cake especially. I thought we could all have a slice when everyone has shut up their shops tonight and then go for quick drink to celebrate?'

'Oh, Rocky, you shouldn't have,' I say, touched by his kind gesture. 'Wait, what do you mean everyone? Do you all know it's my birthday today?'

Harriet nods eagerly. 'Of course we do! When you only get a birthday every four years you have to celebrate! Pop back just after five and we'll raise a toast to you.'

I turn and look at the rest of the shops that surround me and I'm surprised to see all my fellow shopkeepers have come to their open doorways and windows.

'Happy birthday, Eve!' Orla calls from her holistic shop full of crystals, tarot cards and the like. 'Would you like me to read your cards later and see what the future has in store for you?' Orla's green eyes sparkle against her pale Celtic skin.

'Maybe!' I reply as enthusiastically as I can. Orla regularly offers to do this for me and I'm usually quite adept at finding a reason why it's not quite the right time. I know how accurate Orla can be with her readings, but there's parts of my life I'd much rather not be reminded of if I can help it.

'Happy birthday, my darling!' Luca waves from the doorway of his shop, where behind him rail upon rail of vintage clothes hang, interspersed with antique hats, jewellery and bags. 'You didn't think we'd forgotten, did you?'

'Of course not. But it's difficult enough for people to remember your birthday when you have one every year, let alone when you only have one every four. I'm touched you all remembered – really, I am.' I look around at their smiling faces, and, as they've done so often over the years,

Clockmaker Court and the people within it lift my heart and soothe my soul.

'Ben even said he'd try to pop by,' Harriet tells me. 'Even though he doesn't usually open on a Thursday.'

Ben is a lovely but quite elderly gentleman who also owns one of the shops in Clockmaker Court. Recently he's only been opening his shop, which sells antique maps, coins and bank notes, for three days a week. The rest of us always marvel at how he's able to make a profit with these reduced opening times and some of us have even offered to mind his shop for him when he can't make it in. But Ben always insists he makes enough to live comfortably and within his means, and that's all he needs now in what he likes to call his twilight years.

'Then I am truly honoured,' I say, turning around to smile at them all. 'Thank you. I'll make sure I'm back for around five o'clock.'

'Have you shut your shop?' Orla asks, looking behind me at Rainy Day Antiques. 'I could have watched it for you. None of us are ever going to be rushed off our feet at the end of February now, are we?'

'I appreciate the offer, Orla. But I'm hoping shutting the shop is going to be worth it today. I'm off to look at a big house clearance.'

'Oh, really?' Rocky asks. 'Where?'

'It's a large house in Grantchester. It's a lot bigger than the usual houses I clear, but the owner recently passed away and, apparently, he specifically requested that I perform his house clearance.'

'Ooh, sounds exciting,' Luca says. 'You'll let me in on any gorgeous vintage pieces, won't you? You know, any stunning twenties flapper dresses, tiaras, that kind of thing.'

3

'Of course! I always do. I doubt there will be any tiaras this time, but if I do see any, you'll be the first to know!'

Luca winks.

'Right, I'd better go. I guess I'll see you all later, then?'

'You will indeed, my love!' Harriet calls, as the others all smile and wave.

I leave the calm and quiet of Clockmaker Court, which has barely changed over the four hundred plus years it's stood in the centre of Cambridge. Its half-clad buildings, covered in dark timbers over uneven whitewashed walls, would look more at home in a Shakespearean play than in modern-day England, and I step out onto King's Parade, one of the major tourist areas in Cambridge. Even though it's February and there's a distinct chill in the air, there are still a fair few visitors wandering around, either taking photos, browsing the many small independent shops that run along one side of the road, or staring up at the dramatic gothic façade of King's College Chapel – the huge building that not only dominates this part of Cambridge, but is also one of the most well-known and photographed buildings in the city.

If it were a warmer day in springtime, I might have walked alongside the river across the meadows to Grantchester – a lovely walk on a pleasant day. But it's a cold winter afternoon and sadly I don't have that much time to spare. My appointment to view the house is at three o'clock and I still need to pop to WHSmith, which is on the other side of the market square in Cambridge, to pick up a new notebook.

When I do house clearances, I like to log everything of interest in a hardback notebook – I could use the notes app on my phone, but I'm a bit old-fashioned and I like to write everything down by hand. So before I begin to walk across town towards the bus station at Drummer Street – the number eighteen bus only takes between ten and fifteen minutes to get to Grantchester, so I should arrive in plenty of time – I do just that, buying my favourite brand of notebook with soft, lined pages and, on this occasion, a bright red cover. Then I set off across the town towards the bus station.

The number eighteen bus is already in its bay when I arrive, so I climb aboard and pay my fare. Then I find a seat upstairs and wait for the bus to depart.

From the upstairs window I can see people walking the paths that lead through the trees and across the grass of Jesus Green – a large park that links the two shopping districts of Cambridge. In the summer, the green is filled with people picnicking and students lolling around on the grass in between lectures. But today, it's just people hurrying about their business. All of them bundled up from the cold, not wanting to be outside too long, and as I watch them, I wonder how many people have walked those same paths before them over the years. Cambridge has such a rich history – there's so much more to the city than the grand universities with their many students, the thousands of tourists who flock here every year to go punting down the river, and the hundreds of bicycles either being ridden around the ancient streets or chained to the railings while their owners attend a university lecture in a nearby building.

I've always enjoyed thinking about the history of any place I visit or live in. I find myself wondering about the people who lived and worked there before me. I want to know more about the stories that unfolded within buildings and behind closed doors. It's the same with the antiques in my shop. Most of them belonged to various owners over the years and usually resided in many different homes. I love trying to figure out their background and their stories. In fact, I pride myself on being able to give most of the objects in my shop some sort of provenance, which is always written on a little white card next to their price tag. I call it giving them their own story and my customers really seem to love it.

Of my many success stories, I once traced the history of an antique teddy bear back over several owners. The bear lived quite the life and travelled with its owners all over the world, only for me to rescue it from a wet car-boot sale one Sunday morning, where it was being used to demonstrate a baby's high chair that was for sale. In the end, I couldn't bring myself to sell the bear so I called him Bill, after my grandfather, and he still resides behind the counter in my shop, watching over the customers who come in to browse and hopefully make a purchase.

The bus finally pulls away from the station and as I watch the familiar streets of Cambridge pass by, I think about my little shop in Clockmaker Court.

I never set out to own an antiques shop. Rainy Day Antiques was owned from its inception by my grandparents, Sarah and William. Before that, the shop was run by my great-great aunt as a dressmaker's.

I always loved visiting my grandparents when I was young, and helping them out in their shop. I think my love of history must have grown from witnessing their enthusiasm for antiques and listening to their stories of how they obtained their items to sell. Unforeseen circumstances in my life led me to working in the shop alongside them when I was younger, with me eventually taking on the running of the shop when my grandfather passed away and my grandmother decided to take a back seat. It was a difficult time for both of us, and, when she sadly passed a few years later, I fully took over the ailing business, determined to make it profitable once more.

Performing house clearances was my idea, a way to procure items for the shop at a lower margin than buying them at auction or car-boot sales as my grandparents had favoured. I managed to come to an arrangement with a large local auction house – they would take on any larger clearances that I was offered and I couldn't handle, and if they received a property too small for them to bother with, they would pass the details on to me to take care of. This mutual relationship has been working well for both of us over the last few years.

The bus arrives in Grantchester – a small, picturesque village just outside of Cambridge. I hop off at the bus stop in the centre of the village and walk the rest of the way to the house on the outskirts. *Past Times House*, a slate sign declares on the sandy-coloured brick wall that surrounds the property. Next to the sign are a pair of black wrought-iron gates, one of which has been left open – presumably for me.

I walk through the gates and up a long gravel driveway. The large stately-looking house at the end of the drive has been built in the same sandy-coloured brick as the wall that surrounds it. I date the house immediately as Georgian. The symmetrical architecture, the long sash windows with white panels, each containing smaller panes of glass, and the no-nonsense black front door give it away as dating from the eighteenth to the nineteenth century. But for all its sleek lines and precise, neat architecture, the house manages to look warm and inviting as it watches silently over the gardens and pathways that surround it.

House clearances are always a difficult part of my job and I never know quite what I might find when I turn up at a house, usually to meet a recently bereaved relative.

They normally fall into two camps. The first group just want the house cleared as quickly as possible; they don't really care what happens to their relative's possessions, only that they need it to happen fast so they can prepare the house to be sold. The second haven't quite come to terms with what's happened yet and can hardly face the thought of removing their loved one's possessions from their home. I have to tread super carefully with the second group – one wrong word and the whole process immediately stalls until the relative can bring themselves to begin it all again.

Today I don't know which group the grandson I'm meeting will be in. We've only had brief contact over email so far. Apparently, his grandfather specifically requested that Rainy Day Antiques perform the clearance of his house and possessions. As I told the others earlier, this house is a lot bigger than the ones I usually take on, so why he specifically wanted my little shop, I have no clue. Perhaps he'd visited the shop before, or knew of our reputation in the area.

Whatever the reason, I'm here now. I'm about to rattle the brass knocker at the side of the elegant front door when, to my surprise, the door swings open.

'Oh, hello,' I say brightly to the person in front of me. 'I have an appointment to view the house this afternoon for a possible house clearance?'

As I look up at the slightly dishevelled-looking man in front of me, I'm doubtful this is who I'm supposed to be meeting. If this is the grandson of the owner, he's not what I'm expecting at all. He was very eloquent over email – formal, even. Here he looks a bit … well, scruffy is the only way I can describe him. He's wearing blue jeans that look a bit tatty, a white T-shirt with a black emblem emblazoned across the front, a battered well-worn leather jacket, and black boots with far too many buckles than are necessary to fasten any shoe. And as his tanned face stares quizzically at me, I get the feeling he has no idea what I'm talking about.

'Are you Eve?' he says in a deep, gravelly voice, making me jump a little inside. The bright eyes that look me up and down are a piercing shade of sapphire blue.

'Yes, that's me,' I say hurriedly, wondering why my insides are suddenly wobbling a little. 'I'm here to look at the interiors for a possible house clearance?'

'Come on in,' he says casually, taking a step back to let me through the door. 'Pleased to meet you, Eve. My name is Adam.'

2

I stare at him for a moment, wondering if he's joking with me. He looks the type that doesn't take life too seriously.

'Oh,' I say carefully, wondering if my initial thoughts were right. 'I thought I was here to meet with an Alexander Darcy?'

'Yeah, that's me,' he says with a glint in his eye. 'When I found out your name was Eve, I thought you'd think the house clearance was a wind-up if I said my name was Adam, so I said it was Alexander instead. Same initial in my email address.'

'Oh, right …' I'm still a bit confused, and, if I'm honest, a little taken aback too. I just hadn't expected to be greeted by anyone like Adam today. He's confident and relaxed. Everything I'm not right now. But I still don't quite see why you'd pretend to be someone different?'

'Adam and Eve? Surely I don't need to explain that to you, do I?' He raises his dark eyebrows at me, while a lopsided grin appears on his face. Then he tilts his head to one side awaiting my reply.

I see, so it's like that, is it? I have a joker on my hands … I have a feeling that how I respond to this could make or break our professional relationship, and as a result, the success of the house clearance.

'Perhaps you'd prefer it if I referred to you as *Mr* Darcy instead?' I say innocently, hoping he'll respond well to playing him at his own game.

But Adam just blinks steadily back at me.

'You know, with the age of the house and all,' I add, hoping I haven't gone too far. 'And you appearing to be the lord of the manor?'

Adam doesn't respond. He simply watches me from the same position, leaning casually up against the door frame of the house.

'Because this is a Georgian house,' I hurriedly explain, wishing I never started this. 'And—'

'I know who Mr Darcy is,' he says firmly, breaking his silence. 'You are, I assume, referring to the Jane Austen character Fitzwilliam Darcy from the novel *Pride and Prejudice*?'

Oh, God. Did I go too far? Have I blown this deal before I've even set foot inside the house? He doesn't look too happy …

But then, to my enormous relief, Adam smiles again. 'Touché,' he says. 'I like your style, Eve.'

'Perhaps we should start again,' I say, smiling back at him. 'My name is Eve Sinclair from Rainy Day Antiques, and I'm very pleased to meet you.' I formally hold out my hand for him to shake.

Adam takes my hand, but he doesn't shake it. Instead he holds my fingertips and takes a long bow. 'Adam Darcy at your service, madam. Won't you please come into my humble abode.' He gestures behind him into the house.

As I follow Adam into the large entrance hall, I take a quick look at my watch. I must be back in Clockmaker Court by five; I can't let the others down when they've gone to so much effort for me. But I have a feeling after our initial conversation that this visit might not be quite as simple as I originally hoped.

'Adam and Eve, though?' Adam says, closing the door behind me. 'I mean, what are the chances of that?' As he smiles, I notice two dimples appear through the dark stubble that covers his cheeks and his square jaw.

'I guess it had to happen sometime,' I reply brightly. I've decided the only way to deal with Adam, and to actually get to look around this house properly and get back to the court by five, is to play along with his fun. 'Are you saying you've never met anyone called Eve before?'

He considers this for a moment. 'Don't think I have, no.'

'I've met plenty of Adams,' I say quickly, not actually remembering if I have or not. 'It's quite a common name among men of your age.'

Adam tips his head back and laughs loudly. 'Well, that put me in my place!' he says, still smiling.

I didn't mean that as an insult at all and I'm about to apologise when he asks, 'How old do you think I am?'

Even though Adam is dressed in quite a young, casual way, the lines at the side of his eyes and across his forehead suggest otherwise.

'Hmm ... forty, maybe?' I know this sort of question never ends well.

'Very good. I am indeed forty. Forty today, actually.'

'You're a leap-year baby,' I say before I've thought it through.

'I am.' He looks suspiciously at me. 'Most people would say happy birthday if I told them it was my birthday today. They wouldn't immediately think of the leap-year thing unless ...'

'Unless?' I ask innocently.

'Unless they were one too … is it your birthday today, by any chance?'

'It is, actually. But I'm not as old as you.'

Again, Adam grins. Nothing seems to annoy him.

'Dare I ask just how old *you* are then, Eve? Do not ask me to guess. You never guess a woman's age – it's always asking for trouble.'

'I'm thirty-six today,' I tell him.

'Really? Then many happy returns to you.'

'And a very happy birthday to you too,' I reply awkwardly. I glance around me. 'Should we take a look at the house now?'

'Of course. I thought you'd never ask. Where would you like to start?'

Over the next half an hour or so, Adam leads me around the large house, which although old-fashioned and traditionally furnished, is immaculately kept. As we walk, I spy various antiques and valuable items that I know I'll be able to make a profit with if I play this right, so I hurriedly scribble notes in my book as we go from room to room, which for some reason Adam seems to find amusing.

'What are you writing about?' he asks as we pause in the dining room. 'I mean, I know you're making note of anything valuable, but what's all the detail about?'

'I don't just deal in values when it comes to an object. I like to write down what I think its provenance will be – where it might have come from originally,' I add, noting down a pair of pretty-looking candlesticks carved in wood, likely oak, rather than the usual silver so often seen in this type of property.

'I know what provenance means.' Adam doesn't sound at all irritated. 'I'm not quite the idiot you think I am.'

'I don't think you're an idiot,' I say hurriedly, horrified if that's the impression I've given him. 'Whatever gave you that idea?'

Adam smiles. 'Nothing … Glad to hear it. So what else do you write about in your little notebook?' Adam is leaning casually against what's likely quite an expensive Queen Anne chest of drawers. Seeing him treating this beautifully crafted piece of furniture in this way while he folds his arms in front of him is irking me greatly. But I try desperately to put it to the back of my mind and concentrate on the job in hand.

'After I've noted a possible value to a piece, and its likely provenance, I write down what its history might be – which helps me date the item,' I add, hoping this makes sense. I actually do a lot more than that, but it doesn't seem necessary to tell Adam that right now. He'd probably only find that amusing too.

'Right, I see,' he says, nodding. 'You go into a lot of detail, then?'

'I like to – yes.' I can stand it no longer. 'Can I just say that chest of drawers you're leaning against could be worth quite a lot of money.'

Adam stands up and looks down at the chest of drawers. 'Really?'

I nod.

'Best not lean against it then, had I?' He winks at me. I quickly turn away to look at a painting hanging over the fireplace and I'm surprised to find my cheeks feel flushed.

'If it helps you at all, it was only my grandfather who lived here,' Adam says while I continue examining the painting. 'He passed away at the end of last year. My grandmother passed away many years ago. So it was just the old fella rattling around here on his own in recent times.'

'I'm sorry to hear that,' I say, turning back from the excellent oil painting of Trinity College in Cambridge that I know I'll be able to sell easily in the shop.

'Yeah, well, he was ninety-five, so he'd reached a good age.'

'That is good. There's a chap who has a shop near to mine – he's about ninety. I just hope I'm in as good a shape as him if I ever reach that age.'

Adam holds my gaze and smiles, so I hurriedly scribble something about the painting in my notebook.

'Unfortunately, it took me a while to get back here so I could begin sorting the house. I'm the executor of his will. Have you ever been an executor of a will? There's so much paperwork and forms to fill in.' Adam pulls a pained expression, as if paperwork is the worst thing in the world. 'There's so many better ways I could be spending my time. But I guess it has to be done.'

I find myself wondering in what ways he might spend his time. But I quickly shake that thought away. *Concentrate on the task in hand, Eve!*

'I was the executor on my grandmother's will,' I tell him. 'She passed away a few years ago now, and before that I helped out a lot with my grandfather's estate when he passed.'

'Then you'll know what a pain it is,' Adam says, nodding.

'Someone has to do it,' I reply diplomatically. 'It is a lot of work, but you don't really mind too much if you cared for the person who died.'

'That's true.' Adam agrees. 'In my case, there was no one else. There's only me left now.'

Again I want to ask more, but I stop myself. I have to get back to the court by five, I must press on with the rest of the house.

But as we move on to the next room, I can't help wondering what's happened to the rest of Adam's family. I know from personal experience how it feels to be the last one. But I'm also aware that not everyone wants to share every part of their lives, especially with strangers.

'You said before you'd only just been able to get here to arrange the clearance of the house. Do you live far away, then?' I ask as I examine a large china cabinet full of interesting bits and pieces – I've already spotted some Beswick horses and some Royal Doulton figurines, and oddly among the more traditional and valuable items – a china fruit bowl filled with glazed red and green apples.

'I'm live in London most of the time, but I don't really have much of a permanent base because I'm away a lot.'

'What do you do?' I look around the rest of the room. I'm playing for more time in the beautiful drawing room we've just entered. There is so much here I'm interested in – as well as the china, there's more paintings and some beautiful art nouveau furniture. But I'm beginning to wonder if this house clearance is going to be too big for me to cope with after all. My shop is only small; I will have to put some of this in storage until I have the room to sell it in the shop – either that or list it online for sale.

'I work in music,' Adam says. 'So I travel quite a bit.'

'Oh, yes, what sort of music?' I say a little absent-mindedly as I open up one of the cabinet doors, turn over a china dog and look at the maker's mark underneath.

'Can't you tell?'

I put the dog down and turn to look at Adam. He's standing with his legs apart, and his arms and hands out to the side, as if he's asking me to guess.

'Er … pop music?'

'Er, no! Rock 'n' roll, baby!'

'Oh … yes, of course.'

Adam's eyes narrow. 'Do you like music?'

'Yes. Who doesn't?'

'What sort?'

I really hate small talk. I just want to get to more of the lovely things this house contains. But I know it has to be done. Building a rapport with the client is essential to negotiating a good price.

'Erm, eighties and nineties music mostly.'

Adam nods. 'Vintage – makes sense. Any particular artists?'

'No, not really.'

Adam pulls a face.

'Why, what does it matter?'

Adam looks wounded. 'The fact you've even asked that tells me so much about you as a person.'

Don't bite. Don't bite! That's what he wants. I've only known him for about forty minutes, but I can tell Adam enjoys winding people up for his own amusement.

'I'm guessing you like rock music?' I answer as politely as I can.

'I don't *like* rock music – I *live* rock music!' he says without a hint of irony.

'Indeed. Music is your job and your passion, I get it. I feel the same about antiques.'

Adam grins now.

'And why is *that* funny?' I ask calmly, but I'm beginning to feel myself getting riled up. *You're biting, Eve*, I warn myself. *Be careful!*

Adam shrugs. 'I would hardly compare the two.'

'I would,' I say, standing my ground this time when it comes to my own passion. I look him straight in the eye. 'I think they are both *very* similar, actually.'

'Go on.' Adam looks intrigued. 'You need to explain now you've put that statement out there.'

'Right then, I will,' I reply defiantly. I think for a moment. 'As you've probably guessed by now, I adore all things vintage and antique. Like I said a few minutes ago, I also love discovering items from the past and finding out that particular item's backstory. Every object has a story, from who it's belonged to, to the houses it's lived in. I love discovering what that story is, sharing it with others, and then eventually placing that item in a new home so it can begin a new story with a new family.'

'That's actually quite poetic,' Adam says, looking surprised.

'Whereas you clearly love music,' I continue. 'From the look of you and your T-shirt, I'd say you have a particular love of classic eighties rock music. Although you're just a bit young to remember it when it actually happened, so you dress like you were there instead. So in the same way as I love items from the past, you love music from the past. We've both chosen to work with our passion in life, and we'd both probably quite like to go back and witness past history too – but for very different reasons. So, although it's not the same by any means, our passion is actually very similar.'

Adam stares at me. Then he grins.

'That is very astute of you,' he says. 'And scarily accurate too. I work as a roadie for a band. Actually, quite a lot of bands, depending on who is touring at the time.'

'Do you enjoy it?'

'Yeah, I do. I'm probably getting a bit old for it now, to be honest.'

'Forty isn't old.'

'In music it is – unless you're the Rolling Stones, of course, and then I'd be a baby.'

I smile at him.

'I sold a Rolling Stones album once,' I say, assuming he will like this reference. 'Not through my shop, but at auction. It was signed by Mick Jagger.'

'Nice. Made a fair bit, I bet.'

'Yeah, it was a good little profit.'

'So, what do you think about my grandfather's stuff,' Adam says, looking around the drawing room. 'Do you see a good little profit in this house?'

'Some of it.' Even though I need to make a profit from house clearances, I'm always honest about valuations. 'It's a little larger a project than I'm used to, to be completely honest. I usually take on much smaller clearances.'

'Yeah, that's what I thought when I looked you up. But my grandfather was insistent in his requests that you do the clearance and sell the contents of his house.'

'I've been wondering about that – do you know why?' I ask, closing up my notebook.

'I've no idea. I only arrived here earlier today myself. I've been dealing with all the paperwork and stuff from London. He just said it must be Rainy Day Antiques in Clockmaker Court in Cambridge.'

'Perhaps he used to visit the shop when my grandparents were alive? They owned the shop before me.'

'Perhaps. I really don't know. Would you like a cup of tea or coffee maybe?' Adam says, looking around, and

I wonder if he even knows where the kitchen is. 'Sorry, I should have offered you one when you arrived.'

'I'd say yes, but if you only arrived today is there actually anything in the kitchen?'

'Another very astute and likely correct observation!' Adam says, grinning. 'What about a birthday drink, then? We can hash out the finer points of how this all works. There's a couple of good pubs here, that I do know.'

'Erm … shall we finish looking around the house first?' I don't want to offend him by declining his offer, but I know time is ticking away.

'Yes, of course. You lead the way.'

'So, give it to me. What's your expert opinion?' Adam asks as we finish our tour of the house in a room that's a cross between a library and a study. The walls are lined with shelves of books and there's a large walnut writing desk at one end of the room. 'Has my grandfather left me a pile of gold within this house or a crock of shi … sorry, rubbish?'

'There are definitely some items that I'd be happy to take off your hands and some items that might have more sentimental value, but which I could still sell if you'd like me to take them too. Your grandfather had a good eye and there's some very interesting pieces here.'

'Interesting and valuable?'

'They're only valuable if someone else wants to buy them,' I reply carefully. 'It's very subjective.'

'True … again, a good comparison between our two worlds. Music is only profitable if people want to buy your records and pay to watch you in concert.'

'Indeed.' I look around the room. 'Take for instance that grandfather clock over there. I think it's beautiful — the carving on the door in particular is very well done and also very unusual. But grandfather clocks are really difficult to sell these days, because most people don't have houses big enough to put them in. That doesn't mean I won't try to sell it, though. You just never know when the right buyer might pop their head around the shop door looking for exactly what you have. And that cabinet on the wall by the window. It's filled with all sorts of action figures and stuff from comics. Not exactly antiques, and I have to admit I don't know all that much about that kind of thing. But I know it's becoming more collectable all the time.'

I turn back to Adam and find that he's silently watching me.

'Is everything all right?' I ask, wondering if he's OK.

'Yes, I was just thinking about that cabinet. I always wanted to play with some of those figures when I was a child, but I was never allowed to. They were my grandfather's pride and joy.'

'I can leave them if you like? If they have sentimental value?'

'No, take them,' he says abruptly. 'It's fine.'

'Would you like me to take all these books too?' I ask quickly, hoping I've not upset him. 'I can't house them in my shop, but I know a dealer who could probably sell them on. It's a shame – we used to have a lovely second-hand bookshop next door to my antiques shop. But they closed down last year and no one has taken on the shop since.'

'No,' Adam says sharply again. His manner has been so relaxed until now that I wonder what's made it change. 'I'd like to keep them.'

'Sure, not a problem. There's quite a lot, isn't there? Do you have room for—'

'I'll make room if I have to,' Adam says shortly.

'Like I said, not a problem.' I glance down at my notebook.

'Sorry. The books remind me of happier times, that's all. Happier times long gone …' He gives a little shake of his head as though he's clearing away those memories. 'How about we get that drink now?' he asks, sounding much more like his usual self again. 'I could do with a pint. Who knew antiques were such thirsty work?'

I can't help wondering what he means by 'happier times long gone', but it's really not my business so I glance at my watch. 'Perhaps just a quick drink?' I agree to be convivial. After all, the deal isn't 100 per cent completed yet – we still haven't talked money. 'I do have to be back at my shop for five, though.'

'Do you have staff that finish then?' Adam asks as we begin to walk towards the front door.

'No, it's just me today. It's actually the other shopkeepers in Clockmaker Court – they're putting something on for my birthday.' I feel embarrassed telling him. 'It's nothing much, but there's going to be a cake and I think a few drinks afterwards. I can't let them down.'

Adam nods. 'Lucky you, to have people that care it's your birthday. It sounds cool.'

'Are you doing anything for yours?' I find myself asking. Even though I pretend my birthday isn't something I'm overly bothered about, when you only get a proper birthday every four years, I know that actually you care very much about marking it.

'No, not tonight.' Adam shrugs dismissively. 'I don't know anyone here – only you now, of course – all my mates are in London.' He pauses for a moment. 'We plan to go out next weekend – you know, for a really big night out.'

He doesn't look quite as convinced about this statement as his words suggest.

My idea of a good night these days is settling down on my sofa with a blanket, a box of chocolates and a good book. The luxury of being left to read undisturbed for several hours far outweighing any temporary high alcohol might give me.

But I don't tell Adam this.

'Are you heading back to London tonight, then?' I ask instead.

'Nope, I'm staying here. Probably heading back tomorrow.'

Before I know what I'm doing, my mouth – despite trying to teach it over the years to always listen to my head first – says, 'Why don't you come into town and join us for a few drinks? I can't have a fellow leap-year baby on his own on our special day.'

I don't know if I'm more shocked by the fact I've actually said this, or the fact that Adam looks delighted by my invitation.

'If you're sure I wouldn't be crashing your celebration?'

'No, of course not. I mean I'm sure it won't be the kind of thing you're used to. The pub we usually go to is pretty quiet and—'

'I'd love to,' Adam says firmly before I can change my mind. 'You can tell me more about your antiques business and how you got into it all. I'm sure your story will be just as interesting as some of the items you sell in your shop.'

Interesting is not the word I'd use to describe my story, I think to myself as I wait in the hallway for Adam to lock up the house and accompany me back to Clockmaker Court. *But the chances of me telling my story to you – a virtual stranger – is about as likely as me finding a lost Van Gogh in the attic of this house.*

3

Adam and I walk out of Past Times House with me assuming we are going to catch the bus back into town. But when Adam says he has transport, I accept his offer of a lift and wait for him in front of the house by a row of apple trees.

'What's that?' I say, not hiding my disdain as he reappears, not in a car as I had assumed, but proudly pushing a motorbike. I gaze in horror at the contraption in front of me – I don't know much about motorbikes, but this one looks a beast of a thing.

'It's a vintage Suzuki,' Adam replies, still smiling proudly at the red–and–white bike. 'Isn't she gorgeous?' He looks up at my horrified expression and frowns. 'Oh … did you think I meant a car?'

'Yes, yes, I did. Most sensible people would.'

'I guess I'm not that sensible, then!' Adam says, beginning to prep the bike.

'Look, no offence, but I can't go on that thing.'

'Why not? I ride it all the time.'

'Because … I don't have a helmet,' I say in a stroke of genius.

'That's all right.' Adam reaches around to the back of the bike and opens up one of the panniers. 'I usually carry a spare in case I give someone a lift.' He passes me a ruby-red helmet and then expertly pulls his own jet-black helmet over his head.

'But … is it safe?' I ask, still holding the helmet at arm's length. I don't know how I'm going to get out of this without seeming like a wimp in front of Adam.

'It will be if you put that helmet on. Your coat isn't perfect, but it's quite thick so it will help.'

'Help what?' I ask, looking down at my coat.

'In case you fall off. You should always wear something with a lot of padding when you're riding a motorbike – like I said, it's not ideal, but it's better than nothing.' Adam has already pulled on a black leather motorbike jacket. 'You're not *scared*, are you?' he asks, grinning at me. 'You can get the bus back if you like and I'll meet you there.' He reaches for the red helmet.

'No. Of course I'm not scared.' I pull the helmet back towards me. But I can't help staring at the bike.

'Most people are a little apprehensive when it's their first time,' Adam says kindly. 'It's nothing unusual. I assume this is your first time?'

'How did you guess?' I shove the helmet on my head and attempt to tighten the strap.

'Here, let me help you.' Adam takes a step closer to me and I have no choice but to let him assist me.

I really don't know where to look while Adam expertly adjusts the strap under my chin. I don't want to look at the motorbike, but, similarly, I don't want to look at Adam when he's quite this close, either – it seems far too inti-mate. But Adam is definitely the lesser of two evils right now, so I have no choice. This close, I can see every bit of stubble on his face, and every line, which, rather than just being a result of ageing as I first thought, actually seems to have developed as a result of Adam smiling so much.

While Adam is tightening the strap, he glances away from my chin up into my eyes.

'Don't look so worried,' he says, smiling in that annoyingly relaxed way he has. 'I won't let anything happen to you.' He finishes tightening the strap under my chin and then he steps away. 'You look great,' he says admiringly. 'Like you've been riding bikes all your life. Motorbikes, that is – not penny farthings! It's my attempt at an antique joke,' he adds when I don't laugh.

'I know.'

'Tough crowd! Right.' He expertly swings one leg over the top of the bike. 'You do the same, then you hold on to me, OK? Whatever you do, don't let go.'

'Don't worry, I'm not going to fall off and sue you.'

'No, it's not that,' he says, as I not-quite-so-expertly climb onto the bike behind him and hesitantly put my arms around his waist. 'I won't be able to find anyone else at short notice to clear my grandfather's house if anything was to happen to you!' He turns around and grins. 'So I kind of need to keep you alive!' Then he winks before he pulls his visor down over his eyes and does the same to mine.

'Ready?' he asks in a muffled voice.

'Ready,' I reply, trying to sound relaxed and unconcerned about what's about to happen.

'Hold on tight now.'

I tighten my grip on his waist as Adam starts up the bike, then, with a roar of the engine, we pull away from the house and head down the long drive towards the gate.

The ride back into Cambridge is nowhere near as bad as I feared it might be. Even though I keep my eyes tightly shut for the first minute or so, once I dare to open them, I realise there's actually something quite freeing about being on a motorbike that I never really considered before. After I get used to holding onto Adam's waist, and I stop gripping him quite so tightly, I find I actually quite enjoy our journey together. We could be riding through a series of the picture postcards that are for sale outside many of the tourist shops in Cambridge. First we ride through the quaint streets of Grantchester, with its pretty thatched cottages and houses frozen in time, then back into the city, past the college sports grounds, over the river, past some of the famous universities and the Fitzwilliam Museum, and then finally back into Clockmaker Court.

The others are already waiting for us as we walk the last part of our journey, with Adam pushing his motorbike along the pedestrian-only street of King's Parade. Their faces are a mixture of surprise and amusement as I quickly explain the situation, and why Adam is here with me. I know what they're thinking as we gather in the café to share some of Rocky's homemade birthday cake, but, to their credit, no one makes any jokes about me bringing a plus-one to the party or anything like that. They all know me well enough by now to know this is purely a business arrangement and nothing more. But I can't help notice some of the females in our gathering casting admiring glances in Adam's direction. Luca, too, seems particularly smitten by our unexpected guest.

After everyone sings 'Happy Birthday' to both me and to Adam, a few of us depart to our local pub, The Timekeeper, for some after-work drinks.

I love The Timekeeper – it's a traditional old-fashioned pub, but slap bang in the centre of Cambridge. Antique brass and copperware hang from the dark wood timbers, and in between, on the uneven whitewashed walls, old paintings and black-and-white photographs tell tales of times gone by. Apparently, servicemen and -women from both Britain and the US used to frequent the pub during the Second World War, and some of the photographs reflect this, showing service personnel both enjoying a drink in their down time, and, more formally, in front of aircraft and on manoeuvres at the local Duxford airfield.

'I might have to start doing house clearances if that's what you find on them,' Luca says, looking admiringly in Adam's direction once more as we stand at the old-fashioned bar together waiting to order our latest round of drinks. He smooths his hand over his dark, immaculately arranged hair.

I follow Luca's gaze. 'Not *your* usual type, Luca,' I tell him, quickly turning my head back to the bar. 'I thought you liked a well-kept man?'

'Nothing wrong with a bit of rough, my darling,' Luca says, his dark Italian eyes glinting mischievously. 'Even you must be able to appreciate that.'

'I'd hardly call Adam rough,' I say, for some reason feeling the need to defend him. 'He's just a bit rock and roll.'

I feel Luca's eyes upon me.

'What?' I ask. 'Why are you looking at me like that?'

'*Rock* and *roll*?' Luca says, rolling his Rs dramatically. 'What do you know of rock and roll? Wedgwood and Doulton, perhaps?'

I pull a wry face. 'He's a comedian now! My life isn't all antiques, you know?'

I've known Luca long enough to understand when he's teasing me. Other than Orla, our newest and youngest member of Clockmaker Court, Luca and I are two of the younger shopkeepers in the court. When I first arrived here to help my grandparents with their shop, we immediately formed a friendship. There were quite a few of us back then, but that was in the good old days before Covid, Brexit and the country's economic instability that sadly led to many of our fellow shopkeepers both in Clockmaker Court and the rest of Cambridge closing their independently run stores.

But, fortunately, some of us in Clockmaker Court managed to survive. We'd been able to keep our heads above water because many of us owned the building our shop was in, so we didn't have to pay any additional rent. Most lived above their shops, but I was lucky enough to live elsewhere in Cambridge, in an old terraced house my grandparents lived in before me, so I earned extra cash from renting the top floor of my shop out to a local accountancy firm.

Of the twelve buildings in Clockmaker Court, currently five of them are still trading as shops. Just last year the shop next to me – an antique bookshop – closed down when Gerald, the owner, passed away. I still have hope someone might take on the shop, but so far no one has come forward.

So although we are all a tight-knit bunch in Clockmaker Court, and we get on really well, Luca, with his Italian charm and optimistic outlook on life, is secretly one of my favourites.

Luca grins at me. 'OK, maybe antiques are not your *whole* life, but, you have to admit, they are an awfully large part of it.'

One of the bar staff finally comes over and we place our order. We wait while they pour our drinks and then Luca helps me carry them over to our table.

We hand all the drinks out, with Ben nodding his gratitude from his armchair in the corner as I place his glass of rum in front of him. Then, finally, I sit down in my wooden chair between Rocky and Luca, with Harriet, Orla and Adam all on the other side of the table.

'What have you got there?' Rocky asks, looking with interest at my drink.

'It's an apple juice cocktail. There's a cocktail menu on the bar – it's half price before seven. I don't know why, I just fancied it for a change.'

'Non-alcoholic?' Rocky asks, smiling.

'Not quite – there's vodka in there somewhere.'

Rocky winks.

'We were just discussing Clockmaker Court with Adam,' Harriet says, lifting up her own glass. 'He's quite fascinated by its history, aren't you, Adam?'

'I am indeed,' Adam says, smiling at me across the table. 'You never told me quite how old your shop is, Eve.'

'Oh!' Orla suddenly gestures excitedly between Adam and me. 'Your names – I've just realised, they're Adam and Eve!'

'Orla, darling, how could you only just have noticed that?' Luca asks, his eyes wide. 'We were all open-mouthed when Eve introduced him – and not just because of your name, Adam,' he adds suggestively.

Adam takes this all in his stride. 'Thank you! Eve didn't seem to think it was anything unusual.'

As if we are at a tennis match, all heads turn back to me in unison.

I'm just taking a sip of my drink, so I hurriedly swallow and put my glass down.

'What?' I ask. 'It's not *that* unusual, is it?'

'I should read your cards.' Orla looks between us. 'Both of you.'

'Cards?' Adam asks, looking confused.

'Orla reads tarot cards,' I say.

'Not only tarot. I do angel cards too. I'm very good.'

Adam nods. 'I'm sure you are. Have you not had a reading then, Eve?' he asks innocently. 'It sounds like you should sometime?' He raises his eyebrows at me and I know he's trying to wind me up as usual.

'I will someday,' I reply diplomatically. 'When the time is right. Perhaps you might like a reading, though, if Orla is keen to do one for you?' I smile at him, blinking slowly so he's in no doubt I'm aware just what he's doing.

'Sure, why not?' Adam shrugs. 'I'd welcome knowing what my future might bring. I'm not scared.'

'Er ... neither am I!' I quickly say. 'I just said that it isn't an appropriate time right now.' The truth is it's never going to be an appropriate time, but I'm not going to let Adam know that.

'Uh-huh ...' Adam says, raising his eyebrows again.

I suddenly realise the rest of the table are watching our exchange intently. As I turn away from Adam to look at them, they all hurriedly pick up their drinks and begin innocently sipping on them.

'I could do it now if you like?' Orla says. She pulls a pack of tarot cards from her bag. 'I always carry my cards with me and there's a free table over there. No one else need overhear.'

'Why not?' Adam says, holding out his hand to Orla.

'Grand!' Orla takes his hand and shakes it. They both stand up and go over to the small empty table in the corner of the room. Adam throws me a triumphant look as he walks past me.

'He's very nice, isn't he, Adam?' Harriet says, watching the two of them sit down opposite each other. 'What a life he's had, travelling the world with all these bands. It sounds incredibly exciting.'

'You've found out a lot about him in the few minutes I was gone!' I say, smiling at Harriet. Harriet is well known for being the gossip of Clockmaker Court, and makes it her business to know everything about everyone.

'If you ask the right questions, you can learn a lot about a person in five minutes,' Harriet replies knowingly.

'She's right,' Rocky says. 'I've never known anyone to find out someone's life history as quickly as my Harriet can.'

'Thanks, love.' Harriet smiles lovingly as him.

'We called that a busybody in my day,' Ben says from his comfortable armchair at the end of the table. 'Or just plain nosey.'

'Nonsense, Ben,' Harriet says briskly. 'Just because you don't choose to engage with your customers, doesn't mean I'm nosey for doing so. It helps to build a rapport with them.'

'I don't need to build a rapport with someone to sell them a map or a thruppenny bit,' Ben says, lifting up his glass of rum. 'In fact, most of my customers would be put off if I tried to engage them in too much conversation. I find they prefer to browse in peace and quiet.'

I like Ben. He never says a lot, but when he does speak, it is always short and to the point. His shop is a few doors down from mine, and we will often pass antiques and customers on to each other if they are more suited to the other one's shop.

None of us know how old Ben actually is, and he makes it quite difficult to guess. He has kind, dark brown eyes that look piercingly right through you if he feels you've said something silly. He's tall, but these days walks a little hunched over. His movements are often stiff and slow, but he's able to get about with the use of an elegant Derby walking stick with a curved wooden handle. His dark skin has aged well, and, if it wasn't for his head of tightly curled white hair, he would probably look much younger. He knew my grandparents before me, and when I first took over Rainy Day Antiques and needed advice about anything either to do with the shop or the wider antiques community, he was extremely helpful.

'Well, running a café and bakery is a lot different than selling old maps and coins,' Harriet says haughtily. But I knew she would never stay cross with him for long. We all have a soft spot for Ben.

'It is that,' Ben says, nodding agreeably.

I glance over at Adam and Orla. They are already deep into the reading, both looking intently at the cards Orla has dealt on the table.

'Don't you be worrying about them two, young Eve,' Ben says, seeing me. 'What will be, will be.'

I smile at him. 'I'm not worried, Ben. I just want to make sure Orla doesn't tell Adam anything to make my house clearance fall through.'

'Any vintage clothes?' Luca asks hopefully.

'Not that I've seen. But we didn't really go in any wardrobes.'

'Shame.'

'No maps or coins either,' I tell Ben. 'Sorry.'

Ben doesn't seem all that bothered. 'Not in the house anyway,' he says oddly.

'I guess there might be some outbuildings I haven't investigated yet.'

Ben shakes his head. 'No, not there either.'

I'm about to ask him what he means when there's a slight commotion across the room. Adam has scraped his chair back from the table and is standing up, staring suspiciously at Orla.

'How could you possibly know that?' we hear him ask.

Orla doesn't look at all ruffled by Adam's outburst.

'Please, Adam, sit down,' she says calmly. 'There is nothing to be afraid of.'

Adam glances across at our table, then reluctantly he sits again, and I can't help notice he looks a little pale.

'Ooh, what do you think Orla has seen in the cards?' Luca asks, his eyes wide.

'That's between the two of them,' Ben says firmly. 'I don't think we should speculate.'

Harriet, who is already leaning forward ready to gossip, sits back in her chair looking a little deflated.

'I agree,' I tell Ben.

After a few more minutes, Adam comes back over to our table. The colour has returned to his cheeks and he seems his usual confident self once more. 'Well, that was … *interesting*,' he says, sitting down.

I can tell Harriet is desperate to ask him more, but she restrains herself.

'Were you happy with Orla's reading?' I ask tactfully.

'Er … I'm not sure happy is the right word,' Adam says, lifting his pint of beer. 'Orla is extremely good, though. Very accurate. She wants to know if you'll go over for a reading now, Eve.'

I look back over at the table where Orla is sitting shuffling her cards.

'No, I don't think so.'

'Why not? It's just a bit of fun.'

'It didn't look like fun when you jumped up from the table just now. You looked as white as a sheet!'

'I was just playing along, you know?' Adam says casually.

Adam seems to do everything casually and with apparent ease. It's incredibly frustrating to someone like me. I feel like I'm constantly trying hard at everything I do in life. Adam has only known my fellow Clockmaker Court shopkeepers for an hour or two and already he seems right at home with all of them, as they equally do with him.

'Oh really? It didn't look like that to me.'

Adam shrugs good-naturedly. 'Maybe I'm a good actor?'

'Why don't you let Orla read your cards, Eve?' Harriet says encouragingly. 'She's read all ours, hasn't she?' She looks around at all the others.

'Not mine she hasn't,' Ben says stoutly. 'I don't need a pack of cards to tell me my future.'

'Why doesn't that surprise me, Ben?' Harriet raises her eyebrows. 'Orla loves to read for us and she's very accurate, isn't she, Rocky?'

Rocky nods. It is rare for him not to agree with something Harriet says. I get the feeling it is just easier that way.

'Just leave the poor girl alone, Harriet,' Ben says, coming to my rescue. 'If she doesn't want to, she doesn't have to. In the same way as I don't always eat the cake you insist on passing on to me when it's a bit too stale to sell in your shop. It doesn't mean I don't appreciate the offer. I just choose not to eat it every time.'

'You don't always eat it?' Harriet asks, looking shocked.

Ben shakes his head. 'Like I said, I appreciate you trying to look out for me. But it's my choice what I do with the offer when it's presented. In the same way as it's Eve's choice whether she has a reading or not.'

I think this is the most I've ever heard Ben say in one go.

'Thanks, Ben,' I say gratefully. I look over at Orla, assuming she's still waiting at the table. But to my surprise, I see she's already packed up her cards and is heading back over to us.

'I'm sorry, Orla,' I tell her as she sits back down in her seat beside Harriet. 'I will let you read my cards one day.'

Orla nods serenely. 'When the time is right.'

'So, Adam, what are you going to do with your grandfather's house when it's been cleared by our Eve?' Ben asks.

'Nothing exciting – just sell it, I hope,' Adam says. 'Maybe I'll be able to put a deposit down on somewhere in London then. Currently I rent.'

'George wouldn't have wanted you to keep that big old house, I'm sure,' Ben says. 'He wasn't the biggest fan of it.'

'You knew my grandfather?' Adam asks, looking surprised.

'Oh, yes, George used to come to Clockmaker Court quite a lot when the old bookstore was there. He loved to read. We had many chats over the years attempting to put the world to rights.'

'Did he go in Rainy Day Antiques too?' I ask, wondering if this is the answer to our mystery.

'Yes, I believe so. George had a great fondness for both shops. He used to spend a lot of his time in Clockmaker Court when he was a child.'

'Why when he was a child?'

'The bookshop sold comic books before comic books were as popular as they are today. George loved to come and browse through them.'

'So you knew George when he was young?' I ask, surprised to hear this.

'I did. We were friends a long time.'

'You were at his funeral, weren't you?' Adam asks Ben. 'I thought I recognised you.'

'I was.'

'I'm sorry I didn't remember you before.'

'There were a lot of people there that day,' Ben says, picking up his drink again. 'George was well known and well respected in the area.'

Adam smiles. 'That's good to know. It's funny you mentioned comics, because we found a whole cabinet full of comic-book stuff in the house, didn't we, Eve?'

I nod. 'Yes, we did. That explains why now; it seemed a bit at odds to everything else he had in the house. It also might explain why your grandfather wanted me to do his house clearance if he knew this court well.'

'Yes, I suppose that could be it,' Adam says thoughtfully. 'You know, Eve, I'm more than happy for you to clear the house, if you want to take the job?'

'Yes, I'd like that. I'd like it very much.'

'Great, when can you start?'

'Next week, perhaps? It would be better for me if I could come for a few evenings and sort through everything first, then I don't have to close the shop.'

'I don't suppose you could possibly do it this weekend?' Adam says, looking apologetic. 'I know it's short notice, but I have to head back to London by Monday evening at the latest. If you could manage to do it over this weekend, then I could help you.'

'I do have extra help in the shop over the weekends. But it's our busiest time – it wouldn't be fair to leave him on his own both days.'

'Barney is perfectly capable,' Orla says. 'We can all keep an eye out for him and help him if he gets too busy, can't we?' She looks to the others for support.

'Yes, of course we can,' Luca says encouragingly. 'If it means you get help in what sounds like a quite big job from what you've told me. Two pairs of hands are always going to be better than one. And Adam looks like he could bring the muscle...' He winks at Adam.

Adam takes it all in his stride, and just flexes one of his biceps at Luca.

'Barney is like your Saturday staff, is he?' Adam asks me.

'He's a bit more than that. He also helps me out when I'm busy or if I can't be in the shop myself. He works part-time as an assistant in the Cavendish Laboratory – that's a science laboratory at the university – and part-time with me.' I look at the others. 'If you're all sure? I mean, I don't want to put you out.'

'Eve, you'd do the same for us, wouldn't you?' Rocky asks.

'Of course.'

'Then it's all sorted,' Harriet says briskly. 'You will clear the house with Adam helping you both Saturday and Sunday, and we'll assist Barney, should he need our help.'

I smile gratefully at them all. 'Thank you.' Then I turn to Adam. 'Looks like it's this weekend then. My little van isn't big enough to carry everything from the house, that's for sure. I'll hire a larger van for a couple of days.'

'You have your own transport then?' Adam asks. 'Only when you came on the bus today, I assumed you hadn't.'

'That's because I much prefer to use public transport or to walk. Plus, there's nowhere to park in central Cambridge, not that won't cost me an arm and a leg anyway. So I keep my van in a locked garage I rent near my home. I store some of my stock there too.'

'Nice. Where do you live, over the shop?'

I'm not used to someone asking me so many questions – not personal ones anyway. People usually aren't that interested in me – present company excepted.

'No, I have a little house not far from the shop.'

'Eve's house is gorgeous,' Orla says keenly. 'I adore it so much. Some of us live over our shops. But Eve owns her little home.'

'I'm just lucky my grandparents left me the house,' I say for Adam's benefit.

'Grandparents come in handy, eh?' Adam says. 'Well, I definitely won't be living in my grandparents' home. Nope, as soon as it's sold, it's straight back to London for me.'

'The sooner we get it cleared, the better, then!' I say. 'Then you can go back to your life in London and I can get on with selling all your grandfather's treasures.'

But as I'm about to find out, the best-laid plans have a habit of not turning out quite how you expected …

4

'Blimey,' Adam says as I open up the back of the hire van on Saturday morning to reveal neat rows of cardboard boxes and protective paper. 'It looks like a professional removals company you're running here.'

'It is a professional company, thank you,' I say, climbing up into the vehicle I've rented from Cox's van rental in Cambridge, and I get ready to pass him down all the packing supplies. 'I have done this before, you know?'

That was a bit of a white lie. I have never taken on a house clearance quite as big or as valuable as this one is going to be. But what I do have is confidence that we'll be able to get the majority of the house packed up with a couple of days of hard work.

I was a little hesitant when Adam offered to help me with the packing – I'm used to doing that part on my own. But I quickly realised it was going to be impossible to get the house cleared completely within two days if I didn't have help, and other than Barney, who is in charge of the shop for the weekend, I don't have anyone else. So Adam will have to do.

Adam helps me carry the boxes and paper into the hall-way of the house, and we stack them neatly at the bottom of the staircase that curves elegantly up to the second floor.

Today Adam is wearing jeans again – black ones this time – along with a long-sleeved black T-shirt advertising the band Metallica, and a plaid green-and-black shirt. He has the same amount of stubble as yesterday and I find myself wondering if he keeps it that length at all times, and, if so, how? Is there a special razor that men use to achieve the perfect length of stubble?

'Where do you want to start?' he asks, pushing the sleeves of his shirt up his forearms in a determined fashion.

'Hmm?' I ask absent-mindedly, still thinking about razors.

'Where do you want to get going?'

'Oh, right yes. How about in one of the bedrooms?' I say, looking up the staircase.

Adam doesn't answer, so I glance back at him – he's grinning. I immediately understand his amusement at my answer, but I choose not to react to it.

'*Because* there's less stuff in them, and it will feel like we're making more progress than if we start down here on the bigger rooms.'

Adam's amused face drops a little.

'Look, we've got a lot of stuff to get through today,' I tell him kindly. 'There's not going to be a lot of time for joking around.'

'You're in charge of course,' Adam says, saluting. 'But there might be room for both? It might keep our spirits up.'

'Anything that gets you filling all these boxes with more speed might be worth a shot, I suppose.' I pick up a couple of the boxes and some sheets of paper, and then I begin to climb the stairs. 'Well, what are you waiting for?' I ask, turning back, but I can't help smiling.

'Nothing, sir!' Adam says, looking delighted. 'I'm right behind you.'

We make quick progress with the bedrooms. I carefully wrap up anything I'm taking for the shop that's precious or delicate, while Adam puts everything else into cardboard boxes labelled *Personal*, *Sell*, *Donate*, et cetera. Then we move on to some of the downstairs rooms.

While we're carrying some of the full boxes through the house to stack in the hall, the doorbell rings.

'Are you expecting anyone?' I ask.

Adam nods. He puts down his box and hurries towards the entrance.

'Great!' he says, opening the door. I can't see who's there because the door is blocking them. But Adam pulls his wallet from his back pocket and produces some notes. Then he hands them to whoever is on the other side of the door, and in return is given three pizza boxes. 'Cheers!' he says, before kicking the door closed with his foot and spinning around. 'Voila! Luncheon is served!'

'You really didn't have to do that,' I say, putting my box down on top of his. 'Kind though it is.'

'What were we going to have for lunch, then? There's nothing in the kitchen. Believe me, I've looked.'

'I've actually brought my own.'

'Oh, so you won't have any of this delicious pizza, then?' Adam closes his eyes and pretends to savour the aroma above the boxes.

Again I have to smile. Annoyingly, his constant quips and carefree attitude are actually starting to grow on me. 'That depends on what you've ordered. If it's only pepperoni, then I'm out.'

Adam grins as he carries the boxes towards the kitchen. 'Come this way ... and we'll see if I was right with my guess.'

I follow him through to the kitchen where we both wash our hands, drying them on some clean hand towels I find in one of the kitchen drawers.

'Shall we perch in here?' Adam asks, gesturing to two bar stools at the end of one of the kitchen worktops. 'The dining room seems a bit formal for pizza.'

'Yes, let's.'

'Drink?' Adam opens up the fridge. 'I took the liberty of getting some in.'

'I'll take a water, please,' I say, looking at the selection he's chosen. 'Sparkling.'

Adam nods and pulls out a bottle of sparkling water for me, and a can of Appletiser for him. 'I haven't had Appletiser for years,' he says, carrying the drinks over to the counter and putting them down next to the pizzas. 'But for some reason I just fancied it some. Right.' He lifts the lids of the boxes one by one. 'Like I said, I took a guess. We have a veggie supreme in case you're a vegetarian, the classic Hawaiian – ham and pineapple – and a plain Margherita in case I got it all completely wrong.' He looks hopefully up at me.

'I'm not a vegetarian, but they all look lovely. Thank you.'

'But they're not your favourite, though, right?' Adam asks.

'Not my favourite, but I'll happily eat any of them.' I reach for one of the plates Adam has put out and help myself to a slice of veggie supreme.

'What is then?' Adam helps himself to a slice of Hawaiian and a slice of Margherita. 'Your favourite, I mean.'

'Tuna and olive.'

'Tuna!' Adam says, screwing his face up. 'On a pizza?'

'Yes, I happen to like tuna. And some would say that putting pineapple on a pizza is equally as bad.'

'Don't you like pineapple, then?'

'I didn't say *I* didn't like it. Just that some people think it's wrong.'

Adam smiles.

'Have I said something funny?' I ask.

'No, not at all. I just like the way you defend yourself and what you believe in.'

'Oh … well, thanks, I guess. It was just a pizza.'

'I know, but I like your passion for defending the small stuff.'

'That's because the small stuff is often just as important as the big.'

I open my bottle of water and take a sip. Adam watches me, doing that thing he often does when he studies my face really intently, but doesn't say anything.

'Why don't you tell me about you?' I ask quickly. I can't put my finger on it – it's not that I'm unnerved by his behaviour, it's just a little odd when he does this. 'When I was at the bar with Luca last night, you were telling the others all about your exciting life.'

'I wouldn't call it exciting, really.'

'What would you call it, then?'

'Unusual, maybe. Different, perhaps?'

'Different how?'

'I'm travelling nearly all the time,' Adam says, thinking for a moment. 'Constantly on the road. Bands live a funny, nocturnal sort of life and their roadies are similar – just not as famous or well paid!'

'Don't you enjoy it, then?'

'Yes … well, I did. When I was younger it seemed like a great job. You get to travel around – not only this country, but if you're lucky, the world. You get to stay in some wonderful hotels if you're on the road with a successful band, and the lifestyle can be pretty good.' He smiles fondly. 'But I've never felt the same about the industry since …'

He pauses as if he's remembering something and I can't help wondering what. He suddenly looks incredibly sad and I'm surprised when I feel something jolt sharply inside me. As if we've shared the same memory, the same pain.

'Let's just say I'd like to move away from the industry now,' Adam says, suddenly snapping back into the present. 'If I'm honest, I'm probably getting a bit too old these days for the rock 'n' roll lifestyle. Even if my look does suggest otherwise!'

He gestures to himself and grins, but his amused expression is quickly replaced by an anxious one as he looks up at me. 'But I don't know any other life than this one.'

'Haven't you ever done anything else? No other jobs?' I ask, surprised again by the effect his honesty is having on me. I can see beyond his confident, slightly brash exterior right now, and there's a vulnerability I didn't expect.

'Not really. I was already in a band at eighteen, so I didn't go to uni. I dropped out of education after my A levels because the band got signed to a big record label, and we thought we were about to hit the big time and become famous.' He rolls his eyes. 'Little did we know. We were only together for about three years and during that time we never made much of a dent in the UK charts. Various things led to our break-up in 2005 and we went our separate ways. A few years later, I got my first job working on another, much more successful band's UK tour and that was it – touring became my life and it's what I've done ever since. I'm more management now, rather than simply muscle.'

'That makes sense,' I say, not thinking.

'Thanks.' Adam grimaces.

'Oh, sorry,' I say hurriedly, realising how that must sound. 'I really didn't mean it like that. I meant with your age – it makes sense for you to be in more of a managerial role. Honestly,' I insist, when Adam looks like he doesn't believe me.

'All right,' Adam says, after apparently studying my face again. *What is he doing – reading my mind or something?*

'So, what about you then?' he asks. 'Have you always been involved in antiques? You said yesterday it was your passion in life.'

'Yes, it is, now. But it wasn't always that way. I went to university and studied history because I wanted to be a social historian, not own an antiques shop.'

'What's a *social* historian?'

'It's learning more about *how* people lived in the past, rather than the events of history. I've always been interested in the stories of normal people's lives, rather than politics and wars.'

'I get it.'

'That's the most interesting part of the antiques business, wondering where an item has originated from, who has owned it before, where it's lived, what it's seen. Like I told you before, I like to give my objects their own story.'

'You talk like these things are alive.'

'Everything and everyone has a story.'

'Even you?'

'Perhaps.' I take a careful bite of my pizza to prevent me having to say more.

'So what are you going to say about my grandfather's things?' Adam lifts another slice of pizza from the box.

'It depends very much on what you tell me,' I say when I've finished chewing. 'What do you know about him and the rest of your family? Was he your paternal grandfather?'

'No, my mum's dad.'

'Were you close?'

Adam shrugs. 'Not really. Even though I came to live here with him when I was a child, he was always too busy to pay me much attention. He wasn't really a hands-on grandfather, if you know what I mean?'

I didn't. My grandparents and I had been very close.

'How long did you live here for?'

Adam thinks. 'About five years, maybe. I went to boarding school when I was quite young, so I only spent holidays here, really.'

'*You* went to boarding school?' I ask in surprise.

'Yes, what's so strange about that?'

'Nothing, nothing at all. You just don't seem the type.'

'What type is that, then? Upper crust and snooty? That's very judgemental of you.' He gives me a reproving look.

I'm about to apologise when I realise he's trying to wind me up as usual.

'Ha ha,' I say flatly, shaking my head. 'You're hilarious.'

'Aren't I?' Adam grins. 'Sorry, I couldn't help it. Your face was a picture.'

'Jokes aside,' I say, trying to bring our conversation back on track. 'Why did you come and live here with your grandfather?'

'My mum passed away when I was seven, and my dad upped and left a few years later. I had no choice.'

'Oh, I'm sorry to hear that.' I'm surprised, shocked even, to hear that Adam has gone through this sort of trauma in his younger years.

'Yeah, well, it is what it is,' Adam says, far too matter-of-factly. 'Mum died of cancer and Dad couldn't cope. He walked out one day and never came back. So my grandfather had to look after me. His idea of that was sending me away to boarding school.'

I just nod. Underneath his apparent bravado, I can see this is clearly not an easy topic for Adam to talk about. For once, something we both have in common.

'So you can understand why I don't have many happy memories of this house and I just want to sell it as quickly as possible.' He takes a long sip of his drink and looks out of the kitchen window.

'Of course,' I say, then hesitate, debating whether I should say what I want to. 'You must have had some good times here, though? Perhaps just one or two better memories when your mum was alive? It seems a shame to cast a dark cloud over *all* your memories of living here.'

Adam looks at me and I wonder for a moment if he's about to tell me to mind my own business. But instead he appears to consider my question.

'I do have one good memory,' he says, remembering. 'When we'd come to visit my grandfather, my mum would take me into the library and read to me.' He smiles wistfully. 'They were happy times.'

I smile too. 'There's quite a collection in there. What sort of books did he have back then?'

'Oh, all sorts. Similar to what's there now, I suppose. There were encyclopaedias and classical fiction. But there was also quite a big children's section that my mother would always choose a book from to read to me.'

'Did you have any brothers or sisters?' I ask.

'No, it was just me – only child.'

'So your grandfather must have got those books in just for you?' I say.

Adam considers this. 'Yes, I suppose he must. I'd never really thought about it like that.' He looks at me. 'Thank you, Eve. You've given me a happy memory of this place. When before, all I had were tortured ones, of missing my parents and living with a grumpy old man.'

'No problem.' I'm genuinely happy for him. 'Is that why you don't want to part with the books in the library? Because your mother would read them with you?'

Adam nods. 'Yes, I have so few memories of her that those are special ones.'

'I completely understand.' I mean every word.

'I can see that,' Adam says, his gaze again lingering on me for just a moment longer than necessary.

'Now, going back to your grandfather's story,' I say hurriedly, uncomfortable once more with this level of intimacy. 'Do you know if your grandfather bought this house himself or did he inherit it?'

'He inherited it from my great-grandfather, I believe,' Adam says, and I get the feeling he's happy to get back to the matter in hand too. 'I don't think my grandfather could have afforded to buy a house like this on his wages alone – he worked in banking, but he was only a bank manager, and my grandmother, Lily, she worked at one of the universities as a secretary if I remember rightly.'

'Your grandmother passed away before you went to live with grandfather?'

'Yes.'

I think for a moment. 'Do you know what your great-grandfather did? He must have had a good job to have afforded a house like this.'

'He was a professor at one of the universities. I think he worked at the Cavendish Laboratory for a while. When you said your assistant worked there, the name rang a bell. I'm pretty sure that's where my great-grandfather worked too.'

'The Cavendish Laboratory specialises in physics. He must have been a professor of physics at the university.'

'Possibly, I'm afraid I don't actually know. God, that's awful, isn't it?'

'Most people couldn't tell you what their great-grandparents did for a living.'

'I bet you know what your great-grandparents did, don't you?' Adam smiles knowingly.

'I do, actually. My maternal ones anyway. My great-grandmother, Dotty, was one of the first female engineers at RAF Duxford in the Second World War, and my great-grandfather, Harry, was a US serviceman, who was stationed here in Cambridge at the same time.'

'Cool. Did they become sweethearts and get married after the war?'

'Not exactly.'

'What happened then? They must have stayed together or you wouldn't be here now? Wait.' Adam pretends to look shocked. 'She didn't get pregnant, did she, by a GI Joe?'

'She did get pregnant before they were married,' I tell him calmly, not rising to the bait. 'But there was a wedding shortly afterwards – if it makes you feel better?'

Adam smiles. 'Thank you, yes, it does.'

'After the war, Harry left America and came to live here in the UK. He brought my grandmother, Sarah, up himself, with a little help from my great-aunt Amelia.'

'What happened to Dotty?'

'She died,' I say quickly. 'When my grandmother was very young.'

'Oh, that's very sad,' Adam says, looking like he genuinely means it.

'Yes, it was. Dotty went missing during the war. No one knows exactly what happened to her, but, eventually, when she didn't return home, she was presumed dead.'

'Christ, and she had a young child too?'

'My grandmother, yes.'

'And no one in your family ever found out exactly what happened to her?' Adam seems genuinely interested, so I'm happy to talk about this with him.

'No, she's a bit of an enigma within the family. Some people think she might have just up and left, but others think she must have been killed.'

'So, it's a bit of a mystery then, what happened to her?'

'It certainly is. But I guess we'll never know now.'

'I bet that really irks you?' Adam says, tilting his head to one side. 'A mystery in your family you can't solve. It's like one of your antiques you can't give its full story to.'

'I don't think you can compare my great-grandmother's disappearance with an antique!'

Adam pulls a disapproving face. 'Even I wouldn't do that. But it does bother you, though, doesn't it, this mystery?'

'A bit.'

Adam raises his eyebrows.

'OK, a lot. But there's not much I can do now to try to solve it. It all happened eighty years ago. I've been told I look a bit like her, though.'

'Really, you must have seen photos of her?'

'A few. I can't say I see the resemblance. But everyone else seems to.'

'Amazing. Well, I hate to disappoint, but I'm sure my family history will seem very dull compared to yours.'

'You might be surprised. Do you know if there are any documents in the house that would tell us anything more about your family? Or photograph albums, perhaps.'

'Why do you want them?'

'I just like to get a picture of where the items I'm going to sell have originated from. I don't need to see the house deeds or anything. But sometimes invoices or bills for expensive items are kept, and they help me a lot with both valuation and provenance. And a photograph album showing people with their furniture, or their precious objects, can tell you so much.'

'Right, er … there might be something in my grandfather's study – his name was George, by the way.'

'Yes, Ben said last night.'

'Oh, so he did, you're right. And my great-grandfather was Archie – I do know that much.'

'Good.'

'If we don't find anything in the study, it might be worth trying the attic. There could be boxes up there we've not even thought about yet.'

'Great idea. We'll try the study first though. I do love a good rummage in an attic!'

Adam looks at me with a puzzled expression. 'Really? Aren't they usually dusty old places full of junk in my experience.'

'Trust me. An attic is not always where the most valuable items are found, but it's often where the most interesting treasures are hidden.'

5

'Are you coming up?' Adam asks from the top of the staircase that magically appeared from the attic once we opened up a little trapdoor in the ceiling. 'Or do you want me to start passing boxes down to you?'

After we finished lunch, we looked through Adam's grandfather's study. Adam said he was keeping all the books that lined the walls, so other than the rather large grandfather clock, an oak writing desk, a couple of interesting paintings and the cabinet full of action figures and comic books, there wasn't too much of interest to me. We looked inside the desk, where there was a lot of paperwork, but, again, nothing of interest, so we climbed the stairs again and made a beeline for the attic. Adam seemed a bit hesitant at first, but once he found the light switch and he could see properly, he described it as quite a spacious area, which to my enormous relief didn't appear to be packed to the rafters with junk, as many attics and lofts are.

'How much is there?'

'Other than a lot of boxes, there's some suitcases and a few bits of old furniture.'

'We may as well get it down, then. It's all got to be sorted.'

Adam begins to pass the contents of the attic down to me.

'You don't have to go through all this, you know?' he says when we've been emptying the attic for about ten minutes. 'You're really only here for the good stuff, I know that. It's up to me to sort through all this junk and see what might be important.'

'Not at all,' I say. 'Anything we find could be of interest to me. Yes, I need to make a profit for my business on some things. But I'm also looking for interesting items that might not be worth as much, but could have a fascinating history.' I reach up to take an old vintage suitcase from him. 'Whoa, that's a heavy one. I assumed it would be empty.'

'Sorry,' Adam says, looking apologetically down from the attic opening. 'I probably should have said. This next case is pretty heavy too.'

I take the second suitcase from him, but this time it really is heavy so I don't quite get hold of it properly. It falls from my hands onto the floor next to me and the lid flies open.

'Are you OK?' Adam asks, poking his head out from the attic entrance.

'Yes, I'm fine. Sorry about that. Oh, there's some photos.' I bend down and lift up a couple of the pictures that have fallen from the case. 'In fact, it looks like this whole case is full of old photos and albums.'

Adam climbs down the ladder and peers inside the case with me. 'I don't know about you, but I could do with a break from that attic for a bit – it's very musty up there. Why don't we take a look through these for a while? Maybe they're just what you're looking for to tell you more about my grandfather?'

We sit on the floor either side of the suitcase and begin pulling out bunches of photos tied together with ribbon and string, and old photograph albums with leather covers and thick black pages displaying a mix of black-and-white and colour prints.

Luckily for us, the backs of many of the photos have been written on in black ink with dates and names.

'I think this must be a photo of your grandfather outside his bank,' I say, handing him a photo of a smart-looking man in a suit standing outside the Lloyd's bank building in Sidney Street, one of the main shopping thoroughfares in Cambridge. 'It says *George, June 1974.*'

'Yes, that's him,' Adam says, looking at the photo. 'I remember him still looking a bit like that in the late eighties, early nineties – slightly smaller flares on his trousers by then, though! They're some humdingers, aren't they?'

We both smile at the man. While the rest of his brown suit is smart and tailored, the matching flared trousers overhanging his brown lace-up shoes would easily date the photo for us, even if this information wasn't helpfully noted on the back.

'These are from my grandparents' wedding day,' Adam says, passing me an open album.

I look down at the photos and see a young couple looking extremely happy in front of a church. Underneath the photos, in neat handwriting, is written *Lily and George, Wedding Day, June 1952.*

'My mother was born two years after that in 1954,' Adam says. 'She was thirty when she had me.'

We continue looking through the photos and see more of Adam's family.

'Is this you with your mother?' I ask when I spy a photo titled *Susan and Adam, Easter 1984.* 'You don't look very old there – a couple of months maybe?'

Adam takes the photo album from me and gazes longingly at it.

'Yes, that's her.' He runs his finger gently across the photo. 'I've never seen this before.'

'I'm pleased I made you go up into the attic now,' I say quietly. 'I was feeling a bit guilty when you were lugging all those boxes down.'

Adam lifts the photo from the album. 'I'm going to keep this,' he says, still looking at it. 'Maybe get a frame for it too.'

'I think that's a lovely idea. Perhaps there's some more buried in here you can put aside to frame.' I look at the album again. 'Oh, what's this?'

Hidden behind the photo of Adam's mother, there seems to be another photo – but it's much larger than the others, so I can only see part of it. 'I think there's another, bigger photo hidden behind these others,' I say. 'Look, it's trapped between the two pieces of paper that make up the page.'

We begin to remove the other photos – carefully so we don't damage them – and, piece by piece, as though we are doing a jigsaw in reverse, a new photo begins to reveal itself.

'Ooh, who's this?' I ask as we pull the photo from its hiding place. This man looks a little like George did in his bank photo, but, this time, instead of a loose brown suit with flared trousers, the man is wearing a top hat, a black tailcoat, a waistcoat with a pocket watch, and some striped trousers. 'Is it your grandfather in fancy dress, do you think?'

'It does look a bit like him, I suppose. But, no, this is someone different. I think this might be my great-grandfather. Wait.' He goes back to a previous pile of photos and finds a black-and-white photo of a man in a smart 1940s-style suit along with a dapper-looking trilby hat perched jauntily on his head. He reads the back of the picture. '*Archie, Cambridge, 1939.* He was actually Archibald Darcy – I do know that much about my great-grandfather. Do you know where this was taken in Cambridge?'

I take the photo from him. Alongside the old cars and the familiar sight of gowned students riding bicycles, I recognise one of the many famous buildings Cambridge possesses. 'He's in front of the Senate House,' I say. 'You've probably seen it on King's Parade. It's where the students' graduation ceremonies are held every year.'

I hold the 1939 photo next to the one that was hidden in the album. 'It looks very much like the same man in the two photos, doesn't it? But how can it be? Even though it's taken in exactly the same place as the previous photo, there's a horse and carriage in the larger one, and all the people in the background are dressed like Victorians. Perhaps it's another relative of yours?'

'Maybe, but the guy in this Victorian photo looks the spitting image of my great-grandfather in the wartime one, doesn't he?'

'Yes, he really does. Perhaps it's his father, so your great-great-grandfather? Actually, he must be even further back than that if he's from the Victorian times.'

'Does it have anything written on the back of that photo like some of the others do?' Adam asks.

I turn the photo over. 'It says *Archie, Cambridge, 1850.*' I look at Adam. 'That can't be right, though? Are there two Archies in your family, do you know? Is Archibald a family name passed down through the generations?'

'I don't think so,' Adam says, taking the photographs from me and comparing them. 'And definitely not two Archies who look exactly the same. Someone must have got it wrong. Maybe he *is* in fancy dress?'

'That wouldn't explain the horse and cart next to him, and all the other people in Victorian clothing in the background, would it? And here's another odd thing – I'm not sure photography was even invented by 1850. Even if it was, it wouldn't have been a common thing, and I highly doubt there would have been a photographer roaming the streets of Cambridge in 1850 using a portable camera – even an early prototype – and the end results would never have been as clear and sharp as this photo is.'

'But why would someone write 1850 if it wasn't?' Adam asks. 'It doesn't make sense?'

'Maybe your great-grandfather liked recreating scenes from different eras through Cambridge for some reason? Was he a bit of an eccentric, do you know?'

'Not that I know of. But then I don't know all that much about him, to be fair.'

'I wonder if there are more hidden photos in the album?' I say hopefully, turning the page over. To my delight, yet again behind some other smaller photos, we find another larger picture hidden between the two layers of the thick black page. 'It's exactly the same size as the last one,' I tell Adam as I gradually uncover the picture bit by bit. 'And it looks like the same man again.'

'Where is he this time?' Adam asks.

'It's Cambridge again. Down by the river – he looks like he's about to go punting.' Our mysterious Archie is this time wearing a striped blazer, a straw boater and pale trousers in the black-and-white photo. In his hand he's holding a long punting pole. 'He looks like he's wearing twenties clothing this time. But it's definitely him again.'

'How can you tell?' Adam looks at the latest photo.

'Look just here,' I say, pointing at Archie's face. 'He has a mole on his cheek. You could see it in the Victorian photo too. You can't quite make it out in the 1939 photo because it's much smaller, but on these big ones you can.'

'Well spotted. You must have good eyesight; I can hardly see it.'

'It's definitely there. I'm convinced this is the same man. Does it say anything on the back this time?'

Adam turns over the photo. *'Archie, The Backs, Cambridge, 1928.* What's the Backs?''

'The Backs is what we call the river here in Cambridge where it runs along the back of the universities,' I say.

Adam nods. 'It looks real enough once more. But why take photos of yourself in all these different outfits? And why go to the trouble to mock up the backgrounds too. I mean, look at the girls in the punt behind him on this photo – they look just like flapper girls, don't they?'

'Their outfits are pretty accurate, yes, with their cloche hats and short hair. I should show these to Luca – he'd soon tell us if they are genuine outfits or not.'

'Are there any more hidden photos?' Adam asks. 'Or is this it?'

We look through some more of the albums and find another four hidden photos – all taken from different eras, but all featuring the same man who, without doubt, looks exactly like Adam's great-grandfather, Archie.

'That's six altogether,' I say, laying them all out next to each other. 'There's something else that's just occurred to me.'

'What's that?' Adam asks, still looking over the photos.

'If these photos are all of Archie, I wonder if it's also the same person taking them?'

'You mean the person holding the camera?'

'Yes. Someone had to be taking the photos. Even if this is a hobby that your great-grandfather had, recreating different time periods for photographs, he must have had an accomplice. The selfie certainly wasn't invented until mobile phones became popular, and there weren't cameras around in the forties that could take a timed photo without a photographer.'

'But why go to so much effort and then hide all the photos away in the albums like this if they were just a bit of fun?' Adam looks over the photos again.

'I don't know. Perhaps he was embarrassed by them for some reason?'

'And why are they all so big, when all the other photos of Archie are smaller? I'm sure it wasn't common to get … what …' Adam lifts one of the photos up. 'A4-size photos as standard back then?'

'Unless they were printed out by someone with their own photographic studio, or even just a darkroom,' I reply, thinking about this. 'If someone had access to their own developing process, the results could have been as large as they wanted them to be.'

'True, I suppose.' Adam sighs. 'I guess we'll never know now.'

'Well, I'm sure he had fun taking the photos. I told you attics could be interesting places, didn't I? I guess we ought to get on with sorting through your grandfather's things, though – time is getting on.'

'Yes, I suppose we had.' Adam glances at his watch. 'But I could sit quite happily looking through these old photos all afternoon. I've never seen them before. Look at this one, for instance.' He lifts another photo from a pile. 'This is Archie again. It says on the back he's in 1940 this time, which makes more sense. Cambridge again, and he's with a woman.'

'Is it his wife?'

'Nope, this one is his wife.' Adam reaches for another photo. 'See – *Archie and Violet, 1928*. It's their wedding day.'

I take the wedding photo from him and see the now familiar, but much younger, face of Archie smiling back at me with his new bride on his arm. 'This is taken the same year as the punting one is supposed to be, yet Archie looks a lot younger in this photo than in the one taken by the river. How can that be?'

Adam shrugs. 'You tell me?'

'And this wedding photo is nowhere near the quality of the other photos of Archie we've found. It's much more sepia-toned and fuzzy than the others.'

'The photo I have here looks quite formal,' Adam says, looking at the first photo again. 'Archie standing side by side with a woman, in front of an aeroplane of all things. He's wearing a suit, but she is wearing some sort of uniform.' He squints as he examines the photo in more detail. 'Funny, she looks a bit like you, actually.' Adam passes me the photo and I glance at it. Then, like Adam, I take a closer look. He continues to speak. 'It says on the back her name is Dorothy.'

'Dotty,' I say at the same time.

He looks at me. 'What do you mean Dotty? It says *Dorothy and Archie* on the back. *RAF Duxford, Cambridge, 1940.*'

'Don't you remember?' I ask, my heart racing. 'I told you that my great-grandmother was stationed at RAF Duxford in the Second World War; her nickname was Dotty, but her full name was *Dorothy* ...'

6

Adam steadily blinks at me while he tries to process what I've just said.

'Are you suggesting that this is a photograph of *my* great-grandfather and *your* great-grandmother?' he asks, his eyes now wide. 'It can't be … can it?'

'I know, it sounds crazy, but I'm sure this is her. I have seen a few photos before and even you said she looked a bit like me.'

Adam takes hold of the photo again and studies it. 'She *does* look like you. What are the odds they both knew each other?'

'Bit crazy, isn't it?'

'Too right considering *we've* only just met. So this really is your great-grandmother?' He looks up at me.

'It is.'

'We definitely know this is my great-grandfather, because the other photos say Archibald Darcy on the back and there's the newspaper clippings too.'

'What newspaper clippings?'

Adam reaches behind him and pulls an old scrapbook out of the suitcase. 'Here, I had a quick flick through when we were first looking at the photos.'

He passes me the scrapbook and I open the front cover. Inside are pages of newspaper clippings, mainly from the 1930s and 1940s.

Professor Archibald Darcy – a clipping from the *Cambridge Daily News* states – *of the Cavendish Laboratory, Cambridge, welcomes new students at the beginning of the Michaelmas Term.* And there's a photo of Archie in a tweed suit, a long gown and a mortar board.

Professor Archibald Darcy opens the new wing of the Cavendish Laboratory. Professor Archibald Darcy on why Cambridge University is the best in the world for the study of Physics – and it goes on, with clipping after clipping from mainly local newspapers, until the surprising headline in *The Times* newspaper of *Professor Archibald Darcy, formally of the Cavendish Laboratory in Cambridge, goes missing.*

'Have you seen this?' I ask Adam as I tap the page. 'It says your great-grandfather went missing in 1945. Did you know?'

'It does ring a bell,' Adam says, screwing up his face trying to remember. 'Someone might have mentioned it to me at some stage – I can't really recall. What else does it say?'

'Professor Archibald Darcy has been reported as missing by his wife, Violet. The professor was last seen leaving the university grounds on Thursday. Cambridge police are investigating the matter, but there are currently not thought to be suspicious circumstances surrounding the professor's disappearance.'

'Can I see?' Adam has a quick read, then looks back through a few pages of the album. 'It says on this newspaper clipping that he resigned from the Cavendish Laboratory in 1940, but they didn't know what he was going on to do.'

'Bit odd, isn't it?' I ask. 'He left a distinguished and I imagine well-paid job that was clearly very well respected

64

both within the university and the city, and then a few years later he disappeared?'

'I don't know – these things happen, don't they?' Adam says, clearly not quite as intrigued by the possible mystery as I am. 'Perhaps he had a breakdown or something, and went off the rails for a bit. It was wartime after all. Today we'd be more likely to recognise it as mental illness and he'd be given help. But back then it was either covered up or just not diagnosed as such.'

I shouldn't be, but I'm surprised at Adam's empathetic and informed reaction.

'What?' he asks, making me jump as I realise I've been simply gazing at him while I think.

'Nothing … I'm just trying to think what this could all mean?'

'Maybe it's as simple as they knew each other back then and it's just coincidence that we've bumped into each other now all these years later? They both lived in Cambridge then, didn't they? I doubt Cambridge was as big a city in the forties as it is now.'

'Perhaps …' I reply to be polite, but I'm not happy with this explanation. I want to know why and how they knew each other. Whereas Adam just seems happy to let it go. As always, he seems relaxed and chilled about this new discovery, whereas I want to get to the bottom of the mystery. 'You don't suppose …' I say casually.

'I don't suppose what?' Adam asks.

'You don't suppose they might have had an affair or something like that? I mean, the photo in itself wouldn't suggest that – it is quite a formal composition. But the fact it was hidden away in this photograph album suggests there might be more to it?'

Adam grins. 'I thought that too, but I thought you might take offence if I suggested your great-grandmother had had an affair. She seems like quite the folklore hero within your family.'

'I didn't say she was that. Just that no one knew exactly what happened to her.'

'So you think she could have had an affair and then disappeared?'

I don't want to think that, but I have to admit it's a possibility.

'Perhaps. But would she really leave her young child? I'm not a mother, but I could only imagine what a wrench that would be. I can't see her just upping and leaving her daughter over an affair, especially not back then.'

'True.'

'What about your great-grandfather – would he be capable of having an affair?'

'I have no idea, I never met him. Most of what I know about him I've discovered today with you. As far as I'm aware, he was happily married to his wife, Violet.'

'I guess we can never truly know, and really, what does it matter now? It makes no difference to us, does it?'

'Unless we are distantly related, of course?' Adam says, raising an eyebrow.

I stare at him for a moment, but I don't have time to work out why the thought of that possibility makes me panic so, because my rational brain kicks in.

'Impossible. Dotty only had one child – my grandmother.'

'So … it's possible she was Archie's child. *If* they did have an affair.'

'But my grandmother was born in 1943. That photo of them together was taken in 1940.'

'Affairs can go on for some time.'

'I've seen my grandmother's birth certificate. I saw everything when she died. My great-grandfather was called Harrison; Harry was definitely listed as her father.'

'OK, fair enough,' Adam says, shrugging. 'We'll go with it's highly unlikely we're related.'

'What do you mean *unlikely*? Are you saying Dotty lied on my grandmother's birth certificate? Why would she do that? Do you want us to be related?'

'No, I most certainly do not,' he says quickly. 'Do you?'

'No, of course not.'

We sit on the floor in silence for a few seconds. Both of us thinking this through.

'Do you think that's why my grandfather asked you to do his house clearance?' Adam asks, breaking the silence. 'Because he knew about the connection between our two families?'

'Possibly. Don't forget he used to visit Clockmaker Court too. Remember what Ben told us.'

'*Ben!*' we both say at the same time.

'Do you think he might remember Archie if he knew George?' I ask hopefully. 'He'd only be young if Archie went missing in 1945. But it might be worth a shot?'

'When will you see him next?'

I think about this. 'He should be in Monday. I'll ask him then.'

'Great, let's hope he can help us solve this mystery.'

'It's hardly a mystery. We'd just like to know how they knew each other, that's all.'

'And maybe what their relationship was?' Adam says to remind me. 'I've a feeling that small detail might become quite important too.'

★

Adam and I do as much sorting and boxing-up as we can for the rest of the afternoon, and then we call it a day at around 6 p.m.

'I don't know about you, but I'm exhausted,' Adam says, stretching his arms above his head as we lift the last of the boxes for today into the hire van. 'I think I'll take a hot shower, grab something to eat and head to bed if it's going to be like this again tomorrow.'

A brief vision of Adam in the shower slips into my mind and I hastily shake it away. *Where the hell did that come from?* I arrange the boxes and items in the van so they don't fall during my journey back to my lock-up. I can't deny that Adam is an attractive man … if you like that type – cocky, confident and likely a bit too fond of looking at themselves in the mirror. Adam is certainly not what I look for in a man – if I was even looking, of course. Which I'm not. Not after the last time.

'Are you all right in there?' Adam calls from outside the van. 'You've gone a bit quiet.'

'Yes, yes, I'm fine.' I come back out to the doors again. 'Just sorting a few things.'

'Who's going to help you lift all this out at the other end?' Adam asks, looking behind me at the inside of the van.

I didn't realise when we started this morning that there was going to be quite as much stuff for me to take back to the lock-up tonight. 'I'll manage.'

'Come on,' Adam says. 'Even you aren't going to be able to move all this stuff on your own, Superwoman! I'll help you.'

'No, you've done enough already – really, you have.'

'I know you don't think much of me, Eve. But I'm not going to leave a damsel in distress. Come on, let me drive back with you and help you offload.'

I have to admit the thought of having to unload the van on my own is quite daunting – especially when I feel as exhausted as I do right now.

'All right, thank you. I'll accept your kind offer. If you're sure?'

'I never say anything I don't mean,' Adam says firmly. 'You'll soon learn that about me. Now, am I allowed to help you down from there? Or is that incredibly chauvinistic of me?'

I smile. 'Sure.' I hold out my hand, Adam takes it and I jump down.

'There,' he says, still holding my hand. 'That wasn't too bad now, was it?'

I assume he means holding his hand. But when I don't immediately respond, he adds, 'Letting someone help you?'

'Er, no, it wasn't.'

'Are you sure you're all right?' he asks. 'You look a bit flushed?'

'I'm fine. I was just thinking about when I would be likely to see Ben so I can ask him about your great-grandfather,' I reply quickly.

'I thought you said it wouldn't be until Monday?'

'Yes … I was just wondering if he might be in tomorrow, though. Ben doesn't have his shop open anywhere near as often as the other shops in the court. But sometimes he'll come in if he feels like it on days he's not due to be open.'

Well recovered, I think to myself.

'It doesn't sound like the best way to run a shop,' Adam says. 'How does he make a profit?'

'No one knows.' I smile as I think about Ben. 'It's one of the great mysteries of Clockmaker Court.'

'You're very lucky to work somewhere like that,' Adam says as I close the back doors of the van and check they are secured. I look at him in case he's being sarcastic, but he appears genuine.

'Yes, I am lucky. They're all really lovely people.'

I climb into the driver's seat of the van while Adam locks up the house. Then, carrying a leather holdall, he returns from the house and hops into the passenger seat.

'Please put your seatbelt on.'

Adam grins and does as I ask. Then we begin the short journey back to the lock-up garages where I keep my excess stock.

'I meant what I said earlier,' Adam says after we've sat quietly for the first couple of minutes of the journey, which I much prefer. I don't like driving at the best of times and this van is so much bigger than I'm used to, so I'm happy just to concentrate on getting us there safely. 'About you being lucky with your work – you clearly enjoy it.'

'I do, yes. It's not what I set out to do in life, but I'm happy how it has turned out.'

'What did you set out to do?' Adam asks, and then he remembers. 'Oh, yes, you said you did a history degree at university. Did you want to be a historian?'

'It was social history,' I say. 'I'm not sure what I thought I was going to do with it, really. I only knew I wanted to work with history in some way. Maybe work for English Heritage or for the National Trust. Or maybe as an advisor in TV or film – when they make period dramas, that kind of thing.'

Adam nods. 'So what changed? How did you end up running an antiques shop?'

'Now *that* is a very long story.' I carefully manoeuvre the van around a mini roundabout. 'One this journey is far too short for. How about you?' I deftly turn the subject away from me, something I have become expert at doing over time to avoid discussing my past. 'How did you end up on the road with bands?'

'I told you that earlier, didn't I?' Adam asks, turning his head to look at me.

Luckily, I'm driving, so I don't have to look back at him. *Of course, he told me that when we were having lunch. Damn!*

'Yes, you did, sorry. I'm just trying to concentrate on driving – this van is bigger than mine. I'm not used to it.'

I hope this might quieten him, but annoyingly it doesn't.

'Did you really forget or were you just changing the subject away from you?' he asks astutely, still looking at me.

'Maybe a bit of both?' I answer honestly, deciding I don't have the brain power currently to think of clever answers at the same time as driving this van safely with so much stuff in the back. Stuff that I'm desperate to keep in one piece.

'Why don't you like talking about yourself?'

'I didn't realise that I didn't.'

'Yeah, right. You know exactly what you're doing when you change the subject or turn a question around. Have you got secrets hidden in one of your antique wardrobes you don't want people to find out about?'

'Don't be silly.' I take a corner a bit too fast and the van tips a little to the side. Adam doesn't know it, but he's getting far too close to the truth and it's unsettling me.

'Whoa, steady!' Adam holds on to the armrest. 'No need for that. I'll stop probing.'

'I didn't do it on purpose,' I reply, after I've taken a couple of steadying breaths. 'My little van would have taken that corner easily at this speed. I told you, I'm not used to this one.'

Adam doesn't reply and I know what he's thinking.

I snap at him. 'I didn't, all right!'

'OK. OK.' Adam holds on to the dashboard now. 'I forgive you. Now please just concentrate on the road.'

The rest of the journey – thankfully only a few minutes – is silent.

I pull up in front of a line of yellow garage doors.

'Is this it?' Adam asks as I reverse up to number twelve.

'Yep. I've only recently rented one of these,' I say, relieved the silence has been broken. 'I used to use the garage I keep my van in for overflow from the shop. But recently I've had a few slightly larger clearances, so I rented a proper lock-up. I'm glad I did now – by the time we've finished at your grandfather's house, this will be full.'

We climb down from the van and I unlock the back doors.

'All of it?' Adam asks, looking reluctantly inside.

'No, I've marked what I want in here and what I want taken to the shop.'

'Good. Very organised of you.'

'Look, before we begin, I'm sorry,' I say, knowing I must address what happened before. After all, Adam was good enough to offer to help me when really he didn't have to. I am the one doing the clearance.

'What for?' Adam asks, one foot on the back step of the van.

'Snapping at you earlier.'

'Oh, that? I've forgotten it already.'

'Really?'

'Really what?' Adam grins at me. 'Look, we all have our secrets. Why should you tell yours to me – a perfect stranger?'

'I'd hardly call you perfect,' I reply, and now it's my turn to smile as I slip past him up and into the back of the van.

Adam shakes his head. 'I think we'd better get this van emptied before I change my mind and leave you to do it all on your own.'

I turn back to him, but he's grinning as usual. 'How about you pass everything down to me and I put it in the lock-up?' he says. 'No point two of us being up and down all night.'

Our eyes meet and he blinks innocently at me. 'Yes?' he asks, wide-eyed.

I challenge him. 'You know exactly what you said just now, don't you?'

'That time was completely *un*intentional, actually!' he says earnestly. 'But if you've chosen to *interpret* it differently, Eve, then that's on you, I'm afraid …' His bright blue eyes look reprovingly at me. But then he can't help them twinkling, and immediately I spy mischief hiding behind his innocent façade.

'Nice try.' I shove the box at him. 'Now just get moving. We've got a lot to do.'

But I can't help smiling to myself as I go back for the next box. I really shouldn't find Adam amusing with his often schoolboy-like humour. But incredibly annoyingly – to me, at least – I do.

73

7

Eventually, we move everything that I want to keep in the lock-up from the van, stacking it neatly and in an order I can find things easily, then we climb back inside and drive towards the shop.

'At least it's after seven,' I say, glancing at the clock on the van's dashboard. 'So we can get close to the shop now. The barrier that prevented you driving through on your motorbike yesterday will be lifted now.'

I find my way back to King's Parade and pull up in a loading bay, putting my badge in the windscreen to inform any eager traffic wardens that happen to be passing that I have a business nearby and therefore I'm allowed to park for a short time.

'Right, then,' I say, looking across at Adam. 'Last push!'

'Last push it is!' Adam looks like this is the last thing he wants to be doing on a Saturday night.

'I did say I could manage. You could have stayed at the house.'

Adam shakes his head. 'No chance. Let's do this.'

Getting stock to the shop has never been easy. Clockmaker Court is situated down a small pedestrian path that leads off King's Parade, making direct access with a vehicle impossible. So it takes a number of trips back and forth to the van to unload the rest of the furniture and boxes. While we're on one of them, Orla pokes her head out of one of the leaded windows above her shop.

'Oh, it's you, Eve,' she says, looking relieved. 'I thought I heard some commotion down there, I wondered what was going on.' She glances at her watch. 'It's quite late for you to be here, isn't it?'

'We're just bringing some bits and pieces back to the shop,' I tell her. 'We'll try not to disturb you too much – we're nearly finished for today.'

'Oh, don't you be worrying about it,' she says dismissively with a wave of her hand. 'Now, tell me how you are getting on. Did you find much at Adam's grandfather's house?'

'Almost too much, if I'm honest. But it's been a productive day, hasn't it, Adam?'

Adam reappears empty-handed from the shop. He waves up at Orla.

'Oh, you're here too, Adam?' she says, looking with interest between the two of us. 'That's good …'

'Yeah, I'm just helping Eve move some of the stuff,' he says. 'Not that she needs help, of course.' He grins. 'But I have to make it look good, don't I?' He takes the box I'm carrying from me and heads back into the shop.

'Yes, indeed,' Orla says, smiling. 'That's good to know it's going well …' She gives me a wide-eyed knowing look.

I hurriedly shake my head and check that Adam hasn't seen. But he's already in the back room of the shop with the box.

Orla just smiles. 'Right, I'll be leaving the two of you to it. Don't do anything I wouldn't do!' She winks at me before closing up her window.

'This place really is too cute,' Adam says, emerging from the shop again and looking around him. 'It's like something from a children's fairy tale – all these old buildings in a little courtyard and people calling out of their lattice windows. It feels like we've gone back in time. Like it's a world away from the hustle and bustle of daily life.'

'I suppose it does a bit,' I say, looking around me at the court. 'But we're not too set in the past – we have telephones and the internet, and sometimes you might even get a 5G signal if you're lucky!' I carry my last box into the back room of the shop and Adam follows me inside.

I pull the green velvet curtain back across the doorway of the little room as I emerge back into the main shop.

'I'll sort all this out on Monday when I'm in again,' I tell Adam. 'I'd better leave Barney a note for tomorrow, though. He knows not to touch anything until I've sorted through it, but if it's quiet he likes to find himself something to do.' I search for a notepad and pen behind the solid oak shop counter that my grandparents bought in an auction, along with the big old-fashioned till I still use.

Adam is looking in the tall glass display cabinet where I keep some of my smaller items for sale. 'When you said you give everything a story, you really meant it.'

'Of course. Each item has its own tag with its price and as much history as I can give it. It's not always easy, but I do my best to give everything I have here at least some provenance.'

'This really is a cool little place,' Adam says, turning from his inspection of the cabinet to gaze around the shop. 'I like it. It's warm and welcoming, not dusty and gloomy like some antique shops are, and you've managed to pack a lot of stuff in here without it seeming crowded.'

I'm glad he's noticed. 'Thanks, I'm pretty proud of it.'

'How long have you been here?'

'I've been working here about ten years. But it wasn't until after the pandemic that I took over the running of the shop. My grandparents owned it originally,' I say, knowing he'll only ask. 'When my grandfather passed away, I helped my grandmother out, then, eventually, when she went, the shop became mine.'

'Family business, then,' Adam says, picking up a Moorcroft vase and looking at the base. 'Nice.'

'Yes, it always has been – for as long as I can remember anyway.'

'Your parents weren't involved, then?' Adam asks, moving on to examine a watercolour painting of two ladies being punted along the River Cam by a man in a straw boater and a striped jacket.

'No. They had their own careers. My father was detective in the police force and my mother was a teacher. She was never that interested in the shop, she grew up here – I think she was happy to get away when she could, to be honest.'

'So it was all down to you then to keep it going?'

'Yeah, I guess.'

Adam glances at me, but he moves on to look at the next painting hanging on the wall.

'Did you want to – take on the shop, I mean?' he asks casually while he continues to examine the wall of paintings. 'You said you took a history degree. No offence to this place, but you don't need a degree to run it.'

'It's harder than you think running a little shop like this,' I say, at last finding the notebook Barney and I always kept under the desk so we could leave messages for each other.

'I'm sure it is. I just wondered why you wanted to do it. Did you feel a sense of duty to keep it going because no one else was interested?'

'Something like that.'

'What do your family think now?'

'Not a lot,' I say, beginning to write in the book. 'Both my parents are dead now.'

'Oh,' Adam says, immediately turning to me. 'I'm sorry, I had no idea. Were you very young when they passed away?'

I didn't mean to say that so abruptly. 'Not that young.' I look up at him. 'I was twenty-four when it happened.'

Adam doesn't say anything. So I continue writing in the notebook.

'It seems like we have yet another thing in common,' I hear him say softly. 'I lost both my parents when I was quite young.'

'Your dad died too?' I say, surprised to hear him say this. 'You only told me about your mother.'

'I don't know if he's alive or dead, to be honest,' Adam says, picking up a statue of a dog but not looking at it. 'But he left not long after my mum died, so it felt like I'd lost both parents.'

I want to say something profound and comforting to him, but I find I can only nod silently.

Another connection between Adam and I has suddenly and unexpectedly appeared, and I want to tell him

I get it. I want to tell him I know exactly how he feels. But instead there's a slightly awkward pause as we stare at each other.

'Shall we get that clock in now, and then we're done for the day?' I hear myself saying. 'I don't know about you, but I could do with a bath, some food and an early night.'

Adam looks gratefully at me. 'Yes, the grandfather clock. I'd forgotten we still had that in the van.' He glances around the shop. 'Are you sure it will go in here? This shop is already full to the brim with stuff. I can just take it back to the house if you like?'

'Nice try!' I say, relieved the atmosphere between us has lightened once more. 'But I'm certain I can sell it if we can get it in. I'm not saying it will be easy, but I'm sure you're up to the task.'

'How did I ever get into this?' Adam says, shaking his head. 'I used to spend most of my Saturday nights either at rock gigs or down the pub – now I'm spending them trying to fit gigantic grandfather clocks into tiny timber-clad shops.'

'Don't worry, it's only this Saturday. Once we get the house cleared, your Saturday nights will be all yours again.' I finish scribbling the note to Barney, then I head towards the door.

But Adam hesitates behind me.

'Are you coming?' I ask, standing in the open doorway waiting for him.

'Yes… yes, of course,' Adam says, giving a little shake of his head as though he's waking himself up. 'I was just thinking about something, that's all.'

'I don't need thinking right now, I need muscle,' I reply, flexing my bicep at him. 'And unfortunately for me, right now you're all the muscle I have.'

Adam gives me a wry smile. 'Thanks! Right, come on then, let's see if we can move this clock.'

With one of us at either end, and with great difficulty, we manage to carry the full-size grandfather clock from the van back to the shop, and then we attempt to manoeuvre it inside.

'Are you absolutely sure you want to keep this?' Adam asks, awkwardly holding the face end of the clock as we try to move it through the door. 'Like I said, I can always take it back if it won't fit.'

'It will fit … if we can just … get it … round this corner,' I reply, slightly out of breath. The clock is cumbersome and awkward, but not as heavy as some I've lifted before. 'You're lucky, this is a particularly light model. Most are much heavier than this. That's it, now if we can just get it around that table … and then over this chest of drawers … we're nearly there.'

'Watch out!' Adam cries out as I nearly knock over the vase he was admiring earlier. 'Phew, that was close!'

'Not at all. I had it all under control,' I say, my heart racing a bit faster.

'Hardly, you nearly took that vase out.'

'I did not.'

'I'm going to let that go because I'm holding an incredibly large clock right now. But unless you want to wipe out half your stock, you need to go a bit more carefully.'

'Fine! Maybe if you lifted your end a little higher, we wouldn't even be discussing it.'

With ease, Adam lifts his end of the clock higher in the air and with one last effort, we manage to get it to the back of the shop, where I've already made room for it in a little alcove against one of the side walls.

'There,' I say triumphantly as I help Adam to push the clock upright against the wall. 'I knew it would fit in this alcove if we could get it back here.'

'Just as well.' Adam stands back to look at the clock. 'I wouldn't have wanted to take it back out to the van again. It looks as if it were made to go in there, doesn't it?'

'It's a good fit. Sorry for the bickering before,' I say. 'When we were moving the clock just now.'

'You call that bickering?' Adam grins. 'I call it banter. Forget it.'

I nod and turn my attention back to the clock again. 'I just need to get this working now and then I might be able to sell it on to the right buyer.'

'You know how to mend clocks?' Adam asks, looking impressed. 'That's quite a skill.'

'No, sadly not, but I know someone who can. I usually take any clocks or watches to him, but I'm hoping he might come to me since this is so big. It's a beautiful example for its time and the engraving on the front is magnificent.'

I crouch down and run my hand over the carved wooden tree on the door at the clock's base.

'Is that unusual?' Adam asks. 'To have a tree like that carved on the door? It's quite a simple design, isn't it?'

'I don't know that much about clocks, to be honest. I'll have to ask Freddy when I see him. I'm sure he'll be able to tell me.'

'Freddy?'

'He's my clock expert. I do hope he can fix it; it's such an unusual piece. It's big, but it's not weighty. I think because it's made from a light oak and not a heavy mahogany. Colour makes such a difference to the saleability of wooden furniture, and light wood is definitely in right now.'

Adam yawns.

'Am I boring you?' I ask, raising my eyebrows. But I smile. I know just how he feels – exhausted.

'Sorry, no, not at all. It's just been a very long day.'

'Yeah, I know. Shall I drop you back at the house now?'

'Do you fancy something to eat first?' Adam asks. 'I'm starving.'

'To be honest, I'd rather get a shower first and then some food.'

'Great, let's do that, then?'

'Erm … what?' I ask, confused.

'A shower first, and then food?' he says. 'I brought a change of outfit – that's what I have in my bag. That's if you don't mind?'

'Don't mind what?' My exhausted brain simply isn't following this.

'If I take a shower at yours before we go for some food? I mean, I don't have to if it makes you uncomfortable?'

'Oh …' *Oh, no, how do I get out of this?* Entertaining Adam is the last thing I want to do right now. I just want to go back to my little house and be on my own with a cup of tea and some buttered toast before I collapse into my bed.

But I just haven't got the energy right now to argue with him and he has been so helpful to me tonight. 'All right. You can shower at mine and we'll get something to eat – takeaway, though. I'm not going out to eat tonight. Plus you'll have to find your own way back to your grandfather's house later. I'm not driving you back to Grantchester once I'm all settled for the evening. How does that sound?'

'It's a deal.' Adam extends his hand to me and reluctantly I shake it. 'Now lead the way, my good friend! I'm intrigued to see Chez Sinclair in all its glory!'

8

'Wow, do you live down here?' Adam asks, looking at the row of higgledy-piggledy whitewashed houses that make up one side of the narrow lane where my home is. On the other side, black railings separate the houses from the church of Little St Mary's and a churchyard full of trees and gravestones. On this March evening, the row of buildings is lit only by the old-fashioned wrought-iron lamps that hang outside each house.

'I do.'

'You really are living in a fairy tale, aren't you? What with Clockmaker Court and now this fab little house.'

We've stopped outside one of the terraced houses. 'Hardly,' I say, pulling my keys from my bag and unlocking my navy-blue front door. 'But I'm lucky to have a house like this in the centre of Cambridge.'

'Wow,' Adam says, again looking up as we step inside onto the Victorian black-and-white floor tiles and he sees the long, tall, winding staircase, with its black iron banister, running up through the house. 'I thought it was just a tiny cottage from the outside. But this looks massive. How many floors?'

'Three. The main living area is up on the first floor.'
I flick on some lights. 'It also has a little roof terrace up
there too. This floor has a couple of smaller bedrooms
and the main bathroom, and at the very top is the main
bedroom.'

'It's amazing,' Adam says, his head almost swivelling
360 degrees as he follows me up the stairs to the next
floor. 'Who would have thought all this would be hidden
inside an adorable little terraced cottage? It's an incredible
place and I love what you've done with it. It's modern
and chic, and I can see you've got some of your favourite
antiques dotted about the place too, which makes it feel
warm and inviting. It's very you.'

I'm surprised to hear this rather lovely compliment
from Adam. And I'm pleased my face is turned away from
him as we climb the stairs, so he doesn't see my delighted
expression.

'Thanks,' I say quickly. 'I'm glad you like it.'

We arrive at the first floor of the house with its open-
plan living area. There's a cream shaker-style kitchen at
one end, leading to a small outdoor terrace with views
over the city's rooftops. On the other side of the kitchen
island is the lounge area, where I have a long, green
leather chesterfield-style sofa I bought at auction, an
armchair in a similar style but in a deep burgundy-red
velvet, a wooden coffee table, and some antique Tiffany-
style glass lamps.

'And this was your grandparents' place?' Adam asks. 'I
bet they were some pretty cool dudes.'

'They were pretty cool, yes. But this house didn't look
like this when I inherited it; it was a bit more old-fashioned
back then. I've done a fair bit of work on it since.'

'I can tell. A place like this would cost a crazy amount to rent in London. May I take a look outside?'

'Sure,' I say, unlocking the door to the terrace. I don't know why but I'm secretly really pleased to have Adam's approval.

'Nice,' he says, stepping outside and looking around. 'Is there another outdoor space above too?'

'Yes, the main bedroom has a little balcony too.'

'I think I'd better get into the antiques business,' Adam says, smiling. 'I'd love a place like this.'

'Antiques is the wrong game for you if you want to make a lot of money, I'm afraid,' I say lightly. 'We do it for love, not money.'

'You really get a sense of satisfaction from it, don't you?'

'Yes, I do. Don't you get satisfaction from your job, then?'

'I used to – not so much now, though. I've been trying to figure out for a while what I want to do instead, but nothing has come to mind as yet. So I just keep doing what I do.'

'When you sell the house you'll have some extra money, surely? Perhaps you could do something new with that?' I say.

'There's the house and what you give me for the clearance. There's some money in a couple of bank accounts too. Not a lot, but it all adds up, I suppose.'

'There you go, then.' I shiver a little in the cool night air. 'Shall we go back inside? It's pretty chilly out here tonight.'

Adam follows me back inside and I close the door behind him.

'Would you like to get your shower first, or shall I?' I ask a little awkwardly. 'There's two bathrooms here – the one downstairs and an en-suite upstairs. But the hot water doesn't always do too well if you try to use both showers at once. It's an old building.'

'You go first,' Adam says, putting his bag down on one of the kitchen stools. 'It's your house; I'm just an interloper. I wouldn't want to use all your hot water. I know what old buildings can be like – I've lived in a few in my time.'

'You're a guest,' I say, correcting him. 'But if you're sure?'

Adam looks pleased at my choice of word. 'Yeah, you go for it. I'll just chill here for a bit.'

'All right, then … Well, help yourself to anything you fancy. There's tea and coffee over there by the kettle, and cold drinks in the fridge.'

'Will do!' Adam wanders over to take a look in the fridge.

'See you in a bit, then.' I leave him looking inside my fridge and continue up to the second floor of the house where my bedroom and en-suite bathroom are.

As I remove all my dusty, dirty clothes and pull on my robe, I think about the situation I now find myself in. I met Adam just two days ago and now he's downstairs helping himself to the contents of my refrigerator while I'm about to have a shower up here. I really should be a little more wary about inviting strangers into my home.

Usually, I would be much more careful. But I trust Adam. I don't know whether it's because our great-grandparents clearly knew each other, or whether it's because we've spent much of the last thirty hours together? But I feel comfortable in his presence, and even though he irritates me at times, he is also very relaxed and fun to be around, and it's been a long while since I've found someone's company this easy.

Still pondering these thoughts, I have a quick shower, put on some clean, comfortable clothes – a sweatshirt and leggings – then head back downstairs.

Adam is standing in the sitting room with a glass of water in his hand, looking at my bookcase.

'All done,' I tell him. 'There are some clean towels in the bathroom downstairs for you when you're ready.'

'Thanks,' he says, turning towards me. 'I was just admiring some of your books. They're first editions, aren't they?'

'Some of them are, yes. I used to buy them from the shop next door until it closed down. Gerald was very good at putting things he thought I might like aside for me.'

'Is anything else opening in its place, do you know?'

'I doubt it. When shops close down in Clockmaker Court, they rarely open up again. The building is usually sold and then rented out as offices or sometimes flats.'

Adam nods. 'Right, I'll go get my shower then, shall I? Any thoughts about food?'

'Do you like Indian?' I ask hopefully. 'There's a really good one not far from here.'

'Love it!' Adam says, picking up his bag and heading for the stairs.

'Great, I'll find us a menu.'

After Adam has showered, and we've ordered and then eaten our food, we sit in the lounge together – me curled up in the armchair and Adam on the sofa.

I'm currently in that contented sort of daze you get when you're full from a really good meal, tired from a long day, but incredibly comfortable. I let out a long yawn.

'Sorry,' I tell Adam as I stretch my arms out. 'I can hardly keep my eyes open now we've eaten.'

'I know the feeling,' Adam says, blinking hard. 'That was really good food. I'm impressed.'

'Glad you liked it.'

'Do you have the number of a local taxi firm?' Adam asks. 'Or shall I call an Uber?'

I look at him sprawled out on my sofa and I know I'm going to regret in the morning what I'm about to say next. But we've had a couple of beers that Adam found in my cupboard and stuck in the fridge while I was showering, so the alcohol has only added to my hazy, comfortable feeling.

'Why don't you just stay?' I say, looking at the discarded boxes and empty beer bottles on the coffee table in front of me. 'We've already agreed on an early start tomorrow morning. It seems pointless you going back to the house tonight when I can just take you in the van in the morning.'

Adam looks surprised.

'One of the spare rooms is already made up,' I add, in case he's got the wrong idea. 'It's no trouble.'

'If you're sure? Then, yes, that would be great. I'm glad I packed my toothbrush now.'

'You packed a toothbrush?' I ask, about to kick off about him being incredibly presumptuous.

'Yes, I threw it in my bag with my change of clothes so I could freshen up. I didn't expect to be staying overnight or anything.'

I narrow my eyes at him.

'Honestly!' He holds his hands up. 'I know exactly what this looks like now you've invited me. But truly, I didn't expect to be staying. I'll admit I hoped we might go some-where after we'd moved all the boxes and stuff, and I knew

I'd want to freshen up before going out. No one likes the smell of sweaty armpits over dinner, now do they?'

'That is true,' I say, trying not to smile.

'But, please believe me, the toothbrush was just part of that. Otherwise this just makes me look like some sort of sleaze who made assumptions about what might happen and packed his toothbrush just in case he got lucky. And I know you don't think much of me. But I'd be mortified if you thought that.'

Adam looks genuinely worried as he awaits my answer.

'What make you assume I don't think much of you?' I ask.

'I just get that feeling from you. Am I wrong, then?'

I think carefully before answering. 'I can't deny I do find you a little annoying at times. Actually, not annoy-ing … irritating might be a better word.'

'What's new?' Adam shrugs. 'Most people do.'

'But that doesn't mean I don't think much of you – quite the opposite, in fact.'

Adam looks genuinely surprised. *Really?* Or are you just saying that to be nice?'

'I never say something *just to be nice,*' I say. 'If you've got the impression I don't like you, it's probably because I have trouble letting people get close to me. Luca is always tell-ing me I need to drop my guard and let people in more.'

'Why don't you like people getting close to you – have you been hurt in the past?'

My hazy state suddenly sharpens. *I nearly relaxed a bit too much there …*

'Honestly, Adam, I don't dislike you.' I stand up, and begin to collect the packets and plates from the table. 'You seem like a really nice guy,' I add quietly, not looking at him. 'You know, underneath all the bravado and silly jokes.'

I glance at Adam now and I'm pleased to see he's smiling.

'Eve, you don't know how glad I am to hear you say that.'

'Really?' I ask – albeit a tad quietly. I'm about to continue, but Adam hasn't heard me.

'Then you won't have any objections if I investigate the possibility of renting the shop next door to yours in the future?' he asks brightly.

I nearly drop the plates on the floor; I certainly hadn't expected to him to say that.

'Whoa, steady,' Adam says, jumping up to take them from me. 'It's not that much of a shock, is it?'

'Why would you possibly want to rent the shop next door to mine?'

'Because – like I told you earlier – I need a new challenge in life and owning a little shop in Clockmaker Court seems like a fun idea.'

'I can assure you owning a shop is not fun. There's a lot of hard work involved and often very little profit. And … what would you sell?' I'm still trying to process the thought of Adam in Gerald's old shop. I just can't imagine him in Clockmaker Court.

'Books,' Adam answers without missing a beat. 'Like the last owner. I already have a whole library at Past Times House to get me started and I couldn't help noticing when we were in Clockmaker Court today that the shop has been left with all its fixtures and fittings.'

'But … what do you know about books?'

'I know enough to get me started. I've been wanting a new challenge for some time, but it wasn't until I came here to your house tonight and looked at your bookshelves over there that I knew what I wanted that challenge to be.'

9

End of May 2024

Winter turns to spring, and delicate white snowdrops are replaced by bright yellow daffodils bursting into life all over Cambridge. As the cheery flowers cascade down over the sprawling lawns from the colleges towards the river, Easter comes and goes, and a new term begins at the university. Students take their final exams and even more tourists pour into the city's streets as spring now turns into summer.

It's one of the busiest times of the year for the city, and, in Clockmaker Court where nothing much ever changes, Adam is getting ready to open his new shop, almost three months since he first came up with the idea.

Even though I told him how hard it was to make a success of a little business like this, Adam was insistent.

'I want to do this, Eve,' he told me when we finished clearing his grandfather's house at the end of our very tiring weekend. 'I've decided. I want to honour not only my grandfather by doing something worthwhile with his estate, but my mother too. Being around books with my mother is one of my happiest childhood memories and when you don't have any close family any more, you suddenly realise that those memories are precious and you want to hold on to them.'

I knew exactly how he felt.

So from that moment on, I did everything I could to help him make his dream a reality. Which wasn't all that much to begin with – I was of little use when it came to dealing with solicitors, surveyors and estate agents – but now he was actually about to move in, I hoped I could be of some help in successfully getting his shop open to the public.

We discovered quite quickly that it was the whole building that was up for sale, not just the shop, so it wasn't quite as easy as simply renting the shop premises. But, to his credit, Adam only saw this as a bonus, as it meant he would also acquire the little flat over the shop in which to live. He managed to find a buyer for Past Times House pretty quickly, so once the sale went through, he was able to complete his purchase of both the shop and the flat without too many hold-ups.

Over the last few months, Adam has mostly been in London sorting out his life there and I've been getting on with things in Cambridge. But on the occasions Adam was in Cambridge overseeing the sale of Past Times House or the purchase of his new building, we would sometimes have a coffee or even lunch together, either at my shop or, now that the weather was getting better, in the little garden in the centre of Clockmaker Court.

Today is a warm sunny day at the end of May, and my fellow shopkeepers and I are hoping the spring bank holiday weekend will bring lots of visitors to Cambridge and therefore increase sales for all our businesses. Adam has chosen this weekend to move into his new shop, now the painters, electricians and carpenters he hired to give the shop a facelift have completed their work.

Last night, after we all closed up, a few of us in the court helped him transfer the many boxes of books that he'd acquired from his grandfather – along with others he bought both at auction and online – from storage into his shop, and, today, while we all trade as normal, Adam is attempting to fill the shelves.

'How's it going?' I ask at lunchtime on Saturday, sticking my head around the open doorway.

Adam's head pops up from the fortress of boxes that surround him.

'Slowly.' He grimaces. 'You were right when you said having a shop was hard work, and I haven't even opened yet.'

While I would have been anxious about how long contracts were taking to come through or how much time the builders were taking to do their work, Adam let it all wash easily over his head and hasn't shown the least bit of stress. In that time, I've seen how much he cares about this new project, and how much effort and care he's put into both renovating the shop and choosing the books that went into it. My opinion of him has only grown as each stage of his project has come to fruition.

Even now, with a mountain of work in front of him to get his shop ready to open, he is still relaxed and chilled, and his grimace quickly changes into his usual grin.

'Don't say I didn't warn you!' I say good-naturedly.

'I would never dare!'

'I'm just going to grab some lunch – do you want anything?' I ask.

'Ooh, yes, please – anything will do. I'm easy.'

'I know. I'll just go to M and S, then, shall I?'

'You know what I really fancy …' Adam says, his eyes lighting up.

'Don't tell me!' I know exactly what he is going to say. 'A Chelsea bun from Fitzbillies?'

'You know me too well, Eve!'

'Would you like a coffee to go with it?'

'My usual, please.'

'All right, just don't tell Harriet and Rocky we're buying lunch from one of their rivals, OK? I'll be back in a bit.'

'Do you want me to watch your shop?' Adam asks, knowing we never close our shops in Clockmaker Court during a weekend in the summer unless we absolutely have to.

'No need, Barney is in with me today.'

'Of course. I'll go back to my children's books, then. I'm currently knee-deep in some vintage Enid Blyton. Give me a shout when you're back – lunch alfresco?'

I nod. 'Of course. See you in a bit.'

I head out of the relative quiet of Clockmaker Court into what feels like another world – the hustle and bustle of King's Parade on a Saturday lunchtime.

Today, it's full of tourists enjoying the dry, warm bank holiday weather. I queue up at Fitzbillies – a popular Cambridge bakery – and buy two of its famous Chelsea buns and two coffees to go with it. Since he's been spending more time in Cambridge, Adam has become quite addicted to the bakery, and in particular their Chelsea buns. Just as I'm leaving, I recognise a familiar figure also heading in the direction of the shop. I pause on the pavement outside to greet him as he comes slowly and carefully along the pavement.

'Ben!' I say, delighted to see him again. 'How are you?'

Ben was struck down with a particularly bad virus the same weekend Adam and I cleared out Past Times House. We were all really worried about him, so Orla went to look after him, and while she was away, we all did our best to look after her shop. We offered to open Ben's shop for him too, but Ben declined, telling us we didn't need to worry ourselves, everything was in hand, and he'd return when the time was right.

'I'm very well now, thank you, young Eve,' Ben says, pausing to rest. He leans heavily on his stick with both hands. 'Much improved, as you can see. Orla did a fine job in taking care of me when I was at my worst. And you all took care of her too. Just as it should be.'

'That's wonderful news,' I tell him. 'Will you be able to return to your shop soon, do you think?'

'I do hope so. I thought I'd let the rush of the bank holiday crowds die down first. I'll be back as usual next week, though, to see how you're all doing.'

Most shop owners would be super keen to open on a bank holiday weekend in a tourist city like Cambridge, but Ben never did anything that was expected of him.

'Good, I'm pleased to hear it.'

'I hear that your friend Adam has taken on the bookshop next door to you.' Ben raises his bushy white eyebrows at me. 'You must be pleased.'

'Yes, it's good someone has taken it on. We don't want another empty shop in Clockmaker Court, do we?'

'No, indeed not. How is he getting on setting up the shop? Has he made many changes to the interior?'

'Er, no, I don't think so. I mean, he's had people in to spruce the place up a bit. But I think it's pretty much the same. He can't do too much, can he – all the buildings in

Clockmaker Court are listed and you know what a pain that can be when we want to do anything.'

'Change isn't always good, my young friend. Sometimes keeping things the way they are can be very beneficial in the long run.'

'That's true when it comes to places like Clockmaker Court. Most of our business comes from tourists keen for an Instagram snap or two in front of the old buildings.'

'Instagram?' Ben asks, his forehead furrowing.

'Don't worry, Ben,' I say, smiling at him. 'It's nothing you need to worry about. It's a social media site on the internet where people share their photos. Actually, that reminds me, Adam and I would like to have a little chat with you sometime now you're well again. We've been meaning to ask you about this for ages, but then you got ill and we didn't want to bother you about it.'

'Bother me about what?' Ben tips his head quizzically to one side.

'We found some photos when we cleared out Adam's grandfather's house and we wondered if you could shed any light on them.'

'Oh, yes?' Ben wobbles a little on his stick.

I put my hand out to steady him. 'Don't worry about it now. We'll pop over when you're back in your shop. It's nothing that can't keep.'

'You'd both be more than welcome, my dear.' Ben's dark eyes glance into the shop behind me.

'Chelsea buns?' I ask knowingly.

'Why, yes, they're my favourite. Just don't tell Harriet and Rocky, though, will you?' He winks and turns to look in the shop window. 'When they first opened, it was their sponge cake they were famous for, not their buns – they came much later. But I do have fond memories of joining queues outside here after the war hoping to get one of their juicy buns; I was just a boy then, of course.'

'Of course.' I smile at him. 'Fitzbillies is a Cambridge institution, that's for sure.'

'It certainly is. Now I mustn't keep you any longer.' He looks at the two cups of coffee I'm holding. 'Lunch date, is it?' he asks, his eyes twinkling mischievously.

'Hardly, this is for Adam. He asked especially for a Chelsea bun for lunch.'

'Did he?' Ben nods knowingly. 'That makes sense. His grandfather used to love them too.'

I'm about to ask him more, but I spy a large group of overseas students crossing the street and heading in the direction of the shop. 'You'd best get inside before this lot are queuing out of the door,' I tell him, looking over his shoulder.

'I had indeed,' Ben says, turning and seeing them too. 'I'll see you soon, my dear.'

I take a wide berth around the students and walk back towards the shop. Cambridge is always heaving with people on a Saturday, but now the peak of the summer is fast approaching, the streets around the university part of the town will be packed, not only with tourists, but by many students from overseas, here for the summer to better their English. Gradually, they will replace the university students as graduation ceremonies take place and the streets are filled with graduates wearing mortar boards and gowns, alongside their proud families and friends.

Summer in Cambridge is always hectic and busy, so as I return to Clockmaker Court, the change in both the level of noise, the amount of people, and also the temperature, is like transitioning into a different world.

I liken it to visiting a cathedral in the centre of a busy city. Outside is all hustle, bustle and noise, while inside is peaceful, calm and cool.

As I head to the centre of Clockmaker Court, to a little grassed area with a wooden bench surrounded by black railings, I pass both my shop and Adam's.

In Rainy Day Antiques, Barney is with a customer, but he lifts his hand and waves as I pass, and in the bookshop, Adam is standing up and stretching as I pass his window. He gestures that he will see me over at the bench in a moment.

I enter the little garden and sit in the cool shade of the large oak tree that grows in the centre of the court, happily sipping on my coffee while I look around at everyone in their shops.

Luca has a couple of customers in his shop right now looking at some of his vintage jewellery. Orla is showing a customer her range of dreamcatchers, and I can see Rocky take money from a couple who leave his shop looking pleased with whatever is in their white paper bag – no doubt something delicious for their lunch.

Harriet appears, looking every inch the old-fashioned waitress as she clears one of the little tables that they have outside their shop in the warmer months. She's wearing the black dress, white frilly apron and little white hat she always does when she's waiting tables. She sees me watching her and waves, so I hurriedly try to hide the coffees – all too obvious where they have come from in their unique turquoise paper cups.

'Don't worry about it,' Harriet calls good-naturedly as she loads empty glasses and plates onto her tray. 'I know Adam is partial to a Chelsea bun or two. I'll let you off this time.'

'How do you know they're for Adam?' I ask, relieved she's not upset we haven't bought lunch from her shop today. I do occasionally, but Harriet and Rocky special-ise in old-fashioned baking in their vintage tea room, with cakes and recipes from the past. It is quite unique in Cambridge and the tourists love it. It is the sort of place you go for a treat or a special occasion, not everyday for lunch.

Harriet looks surprised. 'Who else would you have bought lunch for? I know the two of you like to lunch together when you can.' She gives me a knowing look.

'It's not that often,' I say hurriedly. 'I was just popping out and offered to pick something up for him, that's all.'

Harriet nods. 'Yes, of course, dear. It must be nice for you now he's moved in properly.' She lifts her tray. 'Now you can eat lunch together every day!'

I watch her head back into the tea room and I shake my head. *Typical!* When I visit a rival bakery to buy Adam his lunch, it's perfectly acceptable. If I went to Fitzbillies just for me, Harriet likely wouldn't have spoken to me for a week!

When I first told the other shop owners that Adam was going to be taking over the bookshop, they were all delighted. Adam was welcomed into Clockmaker Court like a long-lost family member returning to take over the family business.

'Uh-oh, did Harriet spot you'd been to Fitzbillies?' Adam asks as he sits down next to me on the bench. 'I saw her talking to you just now.'

'Yes, but she was fine about it.' I hand Adam his coffee. 'Luckily it was for you, otherwise I'd have been in the mire.'

'You do yourself an injustice. Everyone thinks the world of you here.'

I'm touched, but a little embarrassed by his kind words. 'Perhaps. But somehow you seem to get away with more. Tell me, how do you do that? I've been here for years and it took ages for them to fully accept me running my grandparents' shop, yet you waltz in as a newcomer and everyone loves you immediately.'

Adam grins. 'My charm and good looks, obviously!'

'*Obviously* everyone else is seeing something I'm not, then!' I take a sip of my coffee.

'Ha ha, touché! Seriously, though, I know I haven't opened yet, but I really am so pleased I made the decision to come here,' he says, taking in the buildings around him. 'Everyone has been so welcoming to me. It feels like a whole new beginning, like I'm moving on to the next stage of my life. I think my grandfather would have been proud this is what I'm doing with my inheritance.'

'I think you're right – he would be very proud.' I put my coffee down on the bench between us. 'Talking of your grandfather, I saw Ben when I was getting lunch. He's much better now and he's coming back to his shop soon.'

'Great, that's good to know.'

'I told him we wanted to have a little chat with him about those photos we found when he is back.'

'What did he say?'

'Not a lot, but then Ben never does.'

'Good,' Adam says, nodding. 'It would be great if he knew how Dotty and Archie knew each other. Is it all right if I have my bun now?' he asks, sounding like a little boy asking for his sweeties.

'Of course.' I take a bun myself before handing him the bag.

Adam takes a bite of his Chelsea bun. While he happily munches on the sweet fruit-filled cake, he looks around Clockmaker Court.

'Have you ever noticed the buildings are a little odd here?' he asks in between mouthfuls.

'In what way?'

'Well, why isn't there a number seven?'

'What do you mean, there isn't a seven? Your shop is number seven, isn't it?'

'No, I'm number eight.'

'Are you sure?' I ask, looking over to Adam's shop. 'I always thought the bookshop was seven.'

'Of course I'm sure. I've just bought the building. It says it's eight Clockmaker Court in all the paperwork. I only knew yours was number six because I picked up some post for you one day from Orla's.'

Over time, many of the buildings within Clockmaker Court have been split into flats and shops, making delivering letters and parcels a bit of a nightmare. So, instead, any deliveries are now always left at one of the shops at the entrance to the close, and every day we all take it in turns to collect each other's mail and deliver it around the court.

I look at the buildings that surround us. 'There must be twelve buildings – it begins at number one and ends at number twelve over there where the solicitors' is.'

'Weird, isn't it,' Adam says, finishing off his bun. 'I just wondered if you knew why?'

I look around at the buildings again and begin to count them. 'There's only eleven buildings here!' Finding this hard to believe, I count them again just to be sure.

'Is there?' Adam asks, finishing off his coffee. 'That's odd. Why is it called Clockmaker Court then, if it doesn't have twelve buildings? I'd have thought that was a given.'

'Me too. I can't believe I've never noticed it myself. I know we all have shop names we go by, because of the buildings being split now it just seemed easier. But I always just assumed there were twelve.'

'The buildings are pretty old, and they're all different shapes and sizes; it's not surprising you didn't notice. I just thought it was odd there wasn't a seven.'

'Yes …' I look back at our two shops that stand side by side. 'You know, it's funny, when I was younger, I always wondered why Rainy Day Antiques wasn't bigger inside.'

'How do you mean?'

'Look at it. On the outside of our shops, we both have a door and one window.'

Adam turns to look. 'Yes, like most of the shops here.'

'But in between there's that large bit of wall.'

'Uh-huh.'

'So, it follows that one or both of us should have a similar amount of space inside our shops that equates to that wall space.'

'I suppose.'

'Do you have that amount of space in your shop?'

'Er … no, I don't think so. The inside wall of the shop runs fairly close to the doorway.'

'If you look in my shop, you'll find the same. Where the window ends is where the interior wall of the shop runs. It's the wall where I have those shelves with the vintage toys on.'

Adam looks at the wall that runs between our two shops, then he looks at all the other buildings in the court. 'All the other buildings sit really close to each other, don't they?'

'Exactly. When these buildings were originally built, there wouldn't have been the luxury of spacing them out; they were all built close together to utilise space to the max.'

'So, if the space isn't in your shop, and it's not in mine, then what exactly is behind that brick wall?'

10

We quickly collect up the remnants of our lunch and head back over to the shops to examine the buildings more closely.

Adam immediately begins knocking on the outside of the wall.

'What are you doing?' I ask, watching him with interest.

'I'm knocking on it.'

'Yes, I can see that. But why?'

'I dunno, really. It's what they always do on TV and in films. I think it's to hear if it's solid or if it's hollow.'

'True, but that's usually on an inside wall, not an outside one.'

'Oh, yeah.' Adam looks a tad embarrassed. 'You might be right there. Shall we try inside, then?'

We head into Adam's shop first. After he has moved a few boxes, we begin knocking on the interior wall this time.

'Still doesn't sound hollow, does it?' I say, pressing my ear to the wall.

'What are you doing?' a voice asks from the doorway of Adam's shop. 'I thought I was hearing ghosts with all the knocking. Either that or the builders were back.'

'Barney, hi,' I say, feeling a tad awkward. 'We were …
were …'

Adams fills in for me. 'Seeing if the walls were hollow.
Hi, Barney – we haven't met yet. I'm Adam.'

Adam goes over to Barney, who is still on the other
side of the doorway, and holds out his hand. Barney
reaches up and shakes it.

'I'd come in, but you've got a little step,' Barney says,
looking down at Adam's doorway. 'Makes it a bit difficult
with the wheels.'

'Oh, God, yes, I hadn't thought,' Adam says anxiously,
looking from Barney's wheelchair to the step at the
entrance of his shop. 'I'm sorry, I'll have to get that
sorted.'

'Don't worry about it,' Barney says good-naturedly.
'I'm used to it with old buildings, they weren't built for
wheelchairs. Back when Clockmaker Court was built,
people like me would have been hidden away from soci-
ety. Either that or put in a freak show somewhere.'

Adam looks quite shocked, but I'm used to Barney's
honesty. When it comes to his disability, he never holds
back and he always says it exactly how it is, and I admire
him for that.

'You wish you were that interesting!' I say, winking at
him. 'Who's going to pay to see you in a show?'

'Rudeness!' Barney says, pretending to look offended.
'I don't know, Adam, is she this rude to you?'

'She is, actually,' Adam says, suddenly getting it and
joining in. 'I thought it was just me.'

'You poor men with your delicate egos!' I sigh
dramatically. 'Sorry, I forgot you needed pandering to
twenty-four hours a day!'

Barney grins. 'So what are you really doing in here?'

'Did you know there isn't a number seven Clockmaker Court?' I ask him. 'I didn't until just now. We're number six and Adam is number eight.'

Adam and I join Barney outside and he looks back at the antiques shop. 'What, so you reckon number seven is behind that wall?'

'It could be. Why are we called Clockmaker Court if there's only eleven buildings? There should be twelve, surely. If seven is missing, it should be right here between our two shops.'

'Might just be solid behind there,' Barney says, looking at the brick wall now. 'It happens. Or it could be housing some old plumbing. When these shops were built, plumbed water wouldn't have been around. Maybe they took a building out at some stage to accommodate all the pipes and stuff when it became more common to have plumbed toilets. Either that or it could have been a privy for the whole court. There was often only one for a number of buildings like this.'

'Privy?' Adam asks.

'It's an early form of toilet,' I say. 'An actual privy was just a hole in the ground filled with ash with a wooden bench over it. Then the term has been used as a nickname for an outdoor toilet, before indoor ones became more popular. You really think it might be where all the sewage and stuff went?' I wrinkle up my nose.

Barney shrugs. 'Might have been. It would explain a missing building, and there must have been twelve at some stage – otherwise, like you said, why would it be called Clockmaker Court?'

'But how can we find out without physically knocking a hole in the wall of one of our shops?' Adam asks.

'Don't look at me.' I shrug. 'I was quite happy with my shop until you brought all this up. Now it's suddenly become this big mystery.'

'But how can you *not* want to know? It's interesting. It's *history*.' Adam raises his eyebrows. 'You love history, you told me so yourself.'

'I love the history of objects, not buildings,' I say, folding my arms. But I have to admit I am a little intrigued.

'Think about all the people who have been in these shops and buildings previously …' Adam says, trying to sound mysterious to pique my interest. 'All their *stories* … Aren't you at least a tiny bit interested in what the people inhabiting these buildings have got up to in the past?'

Barney laughs. 'He knows you pretty well already, Eve!' Barney winks at Adam, and Adam smiles.

'All right!' I agree mostly to shut them both up. 'We'll see if we can find out. But exactly how we do that, I'm not too sure.'

'If we could view the original plans,' Barney says, 'that might help. I wonder if they even kept architectural plans back when Clockmaker Court was built?'

'They might not have back then, but any more recent updates over the years would have to have planning permission. I guess we could try to have a look online.'

'Customers!' Barney says, wheeling himself back to our doorway. 'See you in a bit.'

'I'd better go too in a minute,' I tell Adam. 'I'll take a look online later if I get a chance. You need to get on with sorting your shop out if you want to open next week.'

'Next week? I want to be open by Monday if I can.'

I look behind Adam at all the boxes of books still to be unpacked. 'Good luck with that! You'll have to go some today and tomorrow to achieve that goal.'

'Ye of little faith,' Adam says, grinning as usual. 'Just watch me!'

I smile and leave him to it, heading back to my own shop. But I can't help looking at the brick wall between our two shops as I pass and wondering what might be behind it ...

With a busy bank holiday Saturday, and an even busier Sunday, the shops on Clockmaker Court have been full of customers, and even better, all our tills have been constantly ringing too. So my fellow shopkeepers and I are hopeful for once that we might actually make a profit this weekend if the good weather continues into tomorrow.

'It's looking great,' I tell Adam as I call in at his shop late on Sunday afternoon to find him still working away. 'You've done really well.'

Although Adam has completely overhauled and redecorated Gerald's quite dated second-hand bookshop, he's not gone too far. He's managed to retain the look of a traditional old bookshop with dark wooden shelves and a delicate neutral wallpaper. But he's added touches of green and red in the form of Tiffany-style lampshades and a few green bankers' lamps with brass bases perched on little side tables, to allow people to browse the books with ease in comfy leather chairs, and I'm actually quite impressed.

'Not well enough to open up tomorrow, though,' Adam says, his back to me as he empties a box of books onto the shelf in front of him. Unusually for him, he sounds quite deflated.

'But that might be for the best,' I say, trying to find a positive spin. 'You want to open when you're properly ready, not when you're still in a bit of a pickle.'

Adam puts the final book from his box on the shelf and turns around, and I'm shocked to see just how exhausted he looks.

'Gosh, you do look tired,' I say without thinking.

'Thanks. You might as well say I told you so.'

'How do you mean?'

'You told me I wouldn't be ready to open on Monday and you told me it would be harder work than I realised. You were right on both counts.'

'Why don't you stop for today and carry on tomorrow?' I say gently, realising this is not the time to agree with his statement. 'You really do look exhausted.'

'Why are you being so nice?' Adam looks at me suspiciously. 'It's not like you at all.'

'Gee, thanks! Any more of that and I *will* say I told you so.'

Adam grins. 'There it is.'

'Fine, if you want to be like that.' I turn towards the door and I'm about to stomp out of the shop when I catch my foot on a yet-to-be-emptied cardboard box. I stumble and topple to the floor.

'Are you all right?' Adam asks, rushing over.

'Yes, yes, I'm fine,' I reply, humiliated.

'Let me help you up.' Adam offers me his hand.

I'm about to take it when I notice something. 'What's that?' I ask, squinting across the floor.

'What's what?'

'On the wall over there. Some of the wallpaper has peeled away under the shelves. It looks like something metal.'

'I thought that decorator had finished quickly. If the paper is peeling away already, he must have done a shoddy job. Where exactly are you looking?' Adam bends down to try to see where the paper is peeling.

'He might have done us a favour, actually,' I say, pointing. 'Look, under the shelves just above the skirting board. It looks like there's several layers of wallpaper that are all peeling off, not just the latest one. But behind them it looks like there's some metal.'

'So?' Adam is now down on his hands and knees, trying to see what I can see.

'So … it's on the wall between our two shops. There shouldn't be metal there – there should be either brick or board, or even plaster, depending on when the wall was erected. Why would there be metal?'

'I don't know,' Adam says, sighing as he sits down on the floor next to me. 'I'm too tired for trivia questions tonight.'

'It's not a trivia question, it's a genuine one. There shouldn't be metal there. Not that sort of metal, anyway. I'm not talking a metal pipe, I'm talking a heavy, thick piece of metal like you'd get on a safe or something like that.'

Adam looks wearily at me. 'You're not going to let this rest, are you?'

'Considering what we were talking about yesterday, I'd say this is a rather interesting development.'

'I'd probably agree with you if I wasn't so damn tired.' He looks down at his dusty T-shirt. 'Well, I don't suppose I can get much dirtier today.' He rolls down onto his stomach and pulls himself towards the shelves. Then he reaches under the bottom shelf and taps the wall. 'You're right – it is metal.' As he reports back, I hear a tearing sound. 'And it seems to go further up the wall too.' He pushes himself out again.

'Shall we try to find out what's behind there?' I say excitedly.

Adam, still laying on his stomach, wearily rests his forehead on his arms and mumbles into the floor. 'I knew you were going to say that. Can't you go back to your "I'm not that bothered in finding out what's behind the wall" mood?' He turns his head to look at me again.

'What's happened to all your excitement? You were the one super keen to solve the mystery yesterday.'

'That was when I still had an ounce of energy in me. The only way we can find out what's behind that wallpaper is to rip it down, and to do that we would need to take all the books off the shelf, so we can move it away from the wall.'

'Look, I can see you're tired, so if you don't want to, I can stay and do it.'

'Yeah, right, like I'm going to let you do that on your own while I disappear off upstairs for a hot bath. What sort of guy do you think I am? And that's not me being sexist. I'd say the same if you were a man.'

'I thought you might say that,' I say, grinning at him and jumping up. 'Right, let's get started, then.'

Adam, still on the ground, shakes his head and sighs. 'I think somewhere back there I was conned and the worst thing is I'm too tired right now to figure out how.'

We spend the next half an hour or so removing all the books from the shelves and piling them up in order so they can be easily replaced. Then, after we've pushed the book-shelf to the side, we begin to carefully tear as much of the wallpaper away as we can without damaging too large an area.

'I can't believe I only paid last week for this to be redec-orated,' Adam grumbles as we stand side by side, gently peeling large strips of wallpaper from the wall. 'Why couldn't we have discovered this before the decorator came in?'

'Don't worry, I'll help you repair it. I'm a dab hand with wallpaper paste. This is a bit like a vintage pass-the-parcel, isn't it? There are so many layers of paper, and each one tells you so much about the era it was put up in, just from the pattern and the colour scheme.' So far we've seen the muted plain magnolia of the nineties, the bright, bold primary colours and prints of the eighties, the nausea-inducing orange and brown of the seventies, a sharp black-and-white print from the sixties, and now we are moving on through the floral chintz of the fifties into a fairly dull cream-and-green utility print that could equally be from the 1930s or forties.

'I'm glad you're enjoying this.' Adam pulls quite a large chunk of paper away from the wall. 'I can't say this lists very highly on my ideal way to spend a Sunday evening.'

'Look!' I say as his last effort begins to reveal a large piece of hardboard nailed to the wall. 'It's about the size of a door. Why would someone board up the middle of the wall like this if there wasn't a door behind it? The rest of the wall is plaster behind the wallpaper – it's only this bit that has a board covering it.'

As we pull off more paper, we find that the wood is rotting at the base, which has allowed whatever metal is behind it to begin to show through.

'Gerald did have a flood here a number of years ago,' I say. 'I remember him telling me about it when I first took over my shop. That would explain why the wood has begun to rot away – it must have got wet and never dried out properly.'

'We're going to need something stronger to get this wood off. It's nailed all the way around the edge and these nails look old. They've been in here a long time.'

'Do you have a toolkit? I think we need a hammer.'

'Of course I do.' Adam goes over to where his new cash desk will be and reaches underneath. 'Here,' he says, passing me a hammer. 'I have two, luckily for you.'

With the claw part of the hammer, we spend the next few minutes painstakingly removing each nail one by one until the hardboard begins to come away from the wall.

'Stand back,' Adam says. 'I'm going to try to break the last part out.'

I move away from the wall, still holding my hammer. Adam gets some safety goggles and thick gloves from his toolkit, and pulls them both on. Then he goes back to the hole we've created in his new wallpaper and grabs hold of the wood. He begins tugging on it, so it slowly comes away from the wall, only breaking at the bottom where the wood is rotten.

'Well …' Adam says, still wearing his goggles and holding the wood in his hands. 'That I did not expect.' He leans the broken wood against the bookshelf we've removed and lifts his goggles, and we both stand staring at what has been revealed. 'You were right, there is a door there … At least, I think that's what it is?'

I continue to gaze at the huge piece of metal we've uncovered in the wall. There are hinges on one side and a combination lock on the other. 'But it looks so heavy, doesn't it? And so thick. I said it looked like the sort of metal you use on a safe, but I didn't expect it would look like the biggest safe door I've ever seen. Why would someone put a door like this up in your shop, then hide it away?'

'Absolutely no idea. But if you need to put a door up like this, then what on earth are you hiding behind it?'

11

To our immense disappointment, we were unable to open the door on Sunday evening and find out what's on the other side.

Just like a safe, the combination lock on the huge metal door has been secured, and, after a few attempts where Adam pretended to 'listen' to the lock like they do in movies to try to open it, we realised that without the right combination of numbers, there was no way the door was opening.

'What do we do now?' Adam asked as we sat on two full boxes of books, feeling deflated.

'I don't know.' I felt immensely frustrated by this whole situation. 'If we don't have the combination, I can't see how we're ever going to get the door to open.'

'I'm hoping to open this shop in a day or two – I can't leave it like this with a great huge metal door in the middle of all the books. It's hardly the aesthetic I was going for.'

'But we can't just cover it all up again. Then we'll never find out what's behind there.'

Eventually, with no permanent solution, we agreed to tidy the shop up a bit and sleep on it overnight. Adam looked immensely relieved that at last he would be getting some rest as he headed up the stairs to his flat, while I went back to my own house, the mystery of the door still weighing heavily on my mind.

Now it's bank holiday Monday and, as I wait for Barney to arrive at the shop so I can go next door and see Adam to discuss what we do next, I find myself thoughtfully munching on an apple while I think about the events of yesterday.

First, there was the missing building. Then the subsequent discovery of the metal door – which really could only be described as some sort of heavy-duty security door. But a door securing or protecting what? It was approximately adjacent to where I had placed the grandfather clock in my shop – and then, annoyingly, I then made an unwelcome discovery about the clock. I was going to call Freddy, my clockmaker friend, as planned, and ask him if he would come and take a look. But when I opened the front door of the clock to find out some more information about the maker and model, I discovered that there was no mechanism inside. Instead it was completely hollow.

'Great!' I had told it, closing the door. 'Presumably one of your previous owners used you for display purposes only and took your insides to use on another, more deserving model. Luckily for you, I have a soft spot for broken and unwanted things, so I won't chuck you on the rubbish heap just yet!' And there the clock stayed – its time frozen at half past two. Customers would occasionally look at it or ask the price, but when I told them it wasn't working, they would quickly move on to something else. So, it seemed for now that we were stuck with each other.

'Morning,' Barney says as he expertly wheels himself up and over the small ramp I have installed in the doorway of my shop. 'How's life with you today?'

'Complicated,' I reply honestly, throwing my apple core in the bin behind the shop counter. 'Complicated and confusing.'

'How so?' Barney puts his rucksack out back and returns to the shop.

I tell him what had happened last night.

'Ooh, the mystery deepens,' he says. 'People don't put doors like that up unless they've got something extremely valuable behind it, or something they want to hide …'

'I know, that's what I thought. But what? I don't know much about tools of the past, but I'd definitely say the nails we pulled out of that wood were old, and the first layer of wallpaper was likely from the thirties, maybe forties. It's difficult to say when exactly, because nothing much changed in interiors during the war years.'

'So you just need to figure out the combination, then?'

'If only it were that easy.' I sigh. 'Where do we even begin?'

Barney grins. 'No offence to you, Eve, but you don't really have a mathematical mind, do you?'

'Whereas you do, I suppose? I thought science was your thing?'

'Close enough.' Barney shrugs.

'So where *would* we start, then?' I ask, half smiling at him.

I've adored Barney since the first time he wheeled himself boldly into my shop, asking me for a job before I even realised that I needed anyone. There was no messing with him – he was matter-of-fact and he always told you the truth, even if you didn't want to hear it. He had a confidence about him that I envied and he never let his disability get in the way of anything he wanted to do.

'We can't just sit at the door trying all the combinations, can we?' I tell him. 'It would take for ever.'

'You could. But you're right, it would be a long and frustrating process. I guess you need to know something about the person who had the shop when the door was likely to have been installed. Maybe then you could figure out what combination they might have used.'

'I only know of Gerald owning the bookshop before Adam. I'm not sure how long he'd been there, though. I wonder if Ben might know?' I look across to his shop. 'He's been in Clockmaker Court longer than anyone else.'

'Why don't you go and ask him?' Barney says. 'He was in his shop when I came in just now.'

'He said he wasn't coming back until next week.'

'You know Ben – he does things when he wants to. In Ben-time, not everyone else's.'

'That's true. I'll pop over and see him now, before I go and see Adam. You'll be all right, will you?'

'When am I not?'

'I know, but I don't want to keep leaving you here on your own on a bank holiday weekend.'

Barney waves his hand at me. 'Just go. I know you, Eve – you won't settle when something is on your mind or there's a mystery to solve.'

'Ben?' I call as I push open the door of his shop and step inside. The *Closed* sign is still turned on the door, so I'm not sure if he's actually open or not. His back is to me as I enter the shop.

'Hello, Eve,' he says, turning around. 'How nice to see you again.'

'I didn't think you were opening up until after the weekend?'

'I'm not. I just popped in to sort some stock out. What can I do for you?'

'I was wondering if you knew anything about some of the past owners of the shops here – particularly the bookshop next door to mine.'

'Why in particular that one?'

I begin to tell him the story of what happened over the weekend.

Ben simply nods as I talk. Not seeming particularly shocked by anything I tell him.

'It doesn't surprise me,' he says when I've finished. 'This court has been here so long, it was bound to have secrets somewhere within it.'

'Do you have any idea who might have owned that shop back in the thirties or the forties?'

Ben thinks. 'Hmm … I was actually around in the forties, although I was just a young boy back then. But I remember the court well.' He nods thoughtfully. 'I think it was around the early forties that the bookshop changed hands. I know that because we used to buy our comics there – the *Beano*, the *Dandy*, that sort of thing. But the new owner started to get some American imports in too, like Marvel comics – where he got them from, I'm not sure, maybe one or two of the GIs stationed here in Cambridge during the war would bring them over for him.' Ben pauses to think for a moment. 'But as young boys back then, we were very excited to see them. I still have some of those comics, I bet they're worth a bit now. Maybe I should fish them out sometime?'

'Yes, you probably should. Barney is into all that stuff – you should speak to him about them. But the owner,

Ben,' I say, prompting him. 'You said the shop changed hands. Do you remember who owned it back then?'

'Oh, yes, of course I do – the second owner, anyway – it was Archie.'

'Archie? Wait, do you mean the same Archie that's Adam's great-grandfather?'

Ben nods. 'Yes, that's partly how I got to know George. He used to hang around the shop. Archie didn't run the shop as such – he just owned it. Someone else ran it for him – it was Gerald's father, Oswald, Ozzie, we used to call him. Gerald took over from him when he passed away, and I think he might have took over the owner-ship then too? Anyway, I digress. I'm not sure if it was Archie that got the comics or Ozzie? But we were happy – Ozzie would let us read them before they were sold … We thought we'd died and gone to heaven.'

While Ben reminisces about his past, my mind is racing. Did Archie and this Ozzie put that door in, or did the previous owner? Suddenly this was incredibly important.

'They sound like happy times for you,' I say gently, bringing him back to the present once more.

'There were indeed,' Ben says, smiling. 'Very happy.'

'The shop sounds wonderful, I can just imagine you and George happily reading comics together. But I don't suppose you have any recollection of the door being put in, do you? Was it Archie who installed it?'

Ben thinks. 'I don't remember seeing it when I used to go there with George as a young boy. But you said it was hidden, so I suppose I wouldn't have noticed it, really.'

'That's true. I hoped that if I could find out something about the owner around that time, it might help us to figure out the combination to open the door. I wonder if there's anything actually behind there? I mean, there must be, or why would someone put up something akin to a vault door?'

'There is something behind there,' Ben says to my surprise. 'Don't get too excited, though,' he adds, seeing my face light up. 'I don't know if there's anything hidden there – but you were right when you first mentioned a building was missing from the court. There used to be a building between your antiques shop and Adam's bookshop originally. That's your missing number seven.'

'How do you know – do you remember it?'

'Oh, no, I'm sure it was removed before my time. But I do have a really old plan of Clockmaker Court, and on it you can see all the original buildings.'

'Can I see?'

'Of course.' Ben looks vaguely towards the back of the shop. 'You'll have to give me a little time to locate it, but I know it's here somewhere.'

I leave Ben in his shop about to begin his search and I head over to see Adam. I feel I've got so much to tell him already.

'Adam!' I call, knocking on the door. I wait for a bit, then I try again. 'Adam! Are you in there?'

Eventually, Adam appears. He waves as he comes towards the door and as he unlocks and unbolts it, I notice he's wearing pyjama bottoms and a T-shirt.

'Why are you all locked up this morning?' I ask. 'Is everything OK?'

'Yes, everything is fine. I slept a bit late, that's all.'

'Oh. OK. Look, I've got something really exciting things to tell you. It's about Archie.'

Adam looks at me with a puzzled expression. 'That's odd. Because I've got some rather interesting things to tell you too – funnily enough, also about my great-grandfather.'

12

We both simply stare at each other for a moment.

'Come upstairs,' Adam says, moving back from the door so I can come inside. 'I could do with a coffee – I've only just woken up. I was up really late last night.'

'You looked so exhausted,' I say as Adam bolts the shop door again behind me. 'When I left here last night, I thought you'd be asleep within minutes.'

'After you left, I found something interesting, and that led on to other even more interesting things, and before I knew it, it was 3 a.m.'

'What sort of things?' I ask as I follow him to the back of the shop and then up the stairs to his flat. I've been in both Luca and Orla's little flats before, so I know what to expect as I get to the top of the stairs.

But Adam's flat looks nothing like theirs do.

'What *have* you done up here?' I ask, looking around me as Adam walks through to the kitchen part of an open-plan living area.

'Not an awful lot. A bit of decorating to modernise it, that's all. Most of it was like this already. There's not a lot I can do to the building when it's listed, is there?' He begins to fill the water container of an expensive-looking coffee maker. 'I have to say I was inspired by what you'd managed to do with your place when I was designing it. Even if it's probably a third of the size.'

The large open-plan room is light and airy, with a pale modern kitchen and cream-coloured walls. At the front of the large space is a comfortable lounge area that over-looks Clockmaker Court. It has a large AirForce-blue velvet sofa with an extension at one end for putting your feet up. This sits alongside a mix of solid-wood furniture and newer IKEA-type flat-pack.

'I'm honoured,' I say, meaning it. 'This flat must have been opened up at some stage from what was here origi-nally, though. They've left all the original mouldings up on the ceiling and around the doors – perhaps that's how they got away with it. It's much more open-plan than either Luca or Orla's flats above their shops. They seem tiny and cramped in comparison to this.'

'Looks like I struck it lucky, then. Obviously it's noth-ing compared to your place. But I don't have a lot of stuff and I've been able to get everything I need in here with ease. Coffee?'

'Yes, please.'

Adam starts up the grinder on the coffee maker, so our conversation is paused momentarily. I look around the room again. In the corner there are a few unpacked moving boxes next to a table covered in a pile of books. There are some photos in frames standing on an elegant mantelpiece above an open fireplace. I go over and take a look at them.

'These are lovely.'

Adam looks across at me as the grinding ceases and the first cup of coffee begins to pour. 'The newer frames are a few of the old photos we found when we cleared the house out. There's one of me and some friends one New Year's Eve, and the last photo I have of me and my mum before she passed away. The new one of me and Mum we found in the suitcase is there too.'

My gaze lingers on the photos of Adam as a child. He has the same cheeky grin and look of mischief in his eyes as he has now.

'I'm glad you got all the photos we found framed. They look good.'

Adam nods as the coffee grinder starts up again and a second cup of coffee pours into a new mug.

I walk over to the window and glance out at the view of the court below, and, as I always do when I first enter an old building, I wonder who might have stood here before me, in this same spot, looking at the very same view.

'Your usual?' Adam asks.

'Yes, please.'

'Did you never want to live over your shop?' Adam begins frothing milk for the coffees. 'It's an amazing commute!'

Adam's kitchen is separated from the lounge by a sort of breakfast bar with stools underneath. 'The opportunity never came up,' I say, walking over to it and pulling out a stool to sit on. 'It had already been developed into offices by the time I took over. I moved in with my grandparents at the house I live in now when I began helping them out with the shop, and I just stayed there as things … well, as things changed.'

'What were you doing before you came to Cambridge?' Adam expertly pours frothy milk over the top of the two coffees.

'Er … not a lot. After I finished university, I was doing some odd jobs and stuff. Trying to find my way in the world – you know?'

'Yeah.' Adam passes me a beautiful-looking coffee. 'Been there. But you would have finished uni in what … 2009, 2010, if you're thirty-six?'

'2010. I had a gap year after my A levels.'

'What did you do – anything exciting?'

'I went travelling with a friend. Boyfriend, actually,' I say, thinking about Jake for the first time in ages.

'Cool – where?'

'European cities, mostly. Neither of us were quite the backpacking kind so we stayed in B and Bs. We'd both saved a bit working part-time beforehand, and we found bits and pieces of work while we were moving around.' *Happy times,* I think to myself. *If only we'd been able to have many more years of them …*

'I used to enjoy the travelling part of my job. I saw a lot of the world that way,' Adam says, leaning on the countertop while he sips his coffee. 'So, after uni, what did you do? You said you'd only been in Cambridge for about ten years, so what happened between 2010 and 2014? Did you stay with this Jake?'

I feel my heart begin to beat hard and I swallow. 'Lovely though this trip down memory lane is,' I say hurriedly, stirring my coffee as I swiftly change the subject away from these particular years, 'you still have a great big metal door in the middle of your shop. I think we should talk about Ben and what kept you up into the early hours of the morning, don't you?'

Adam nods. 'We probably should, yes. Especially if you don't want to talk about yourself …'

I ignore this. 'So, what have you found?'

'This.' Adam goes over to the table at the side of the sofa and lifts some of the books, then carries them over to where I'm sitting and puts them on the worktop in front of me. 'When I packed these up for the shop, I thought they were just leather-bound volumes of the classics. I'd brought a few of them up here to sort through and read, so after you left last night, I had a shower and made myself some food. There was nothing on TV, so I thought I'd maybe start reading one of them before I went to bed.'

The image of Adam sitting up here reading a literary classic before bed is not one I ever expected to pop into my head. It just doesn't sit with the image I have of him. Although the juxtaposition of these two images is confusing to me, for some reason I also find them comforting too.

'But when I picked up this copy of Charles Dickens' *A Tale of Two Cities*, and opened it expecting to read about Paris and London during the French Revolution, I was surprised to find this ...'

He opens up the leather-bound book and lays it in front of me. But instead of the usual pages full of prose, there's a series of what look like mathematical equations.

'They're on every page,' he says when I glance up at him for an explanation. 'There's also diagrams too. I can't make head nor tail of them. So, I went to *Great Expectations* instead.'

'Was that the same?'

Adam shakes his head. 'Nope, that was just a book with the actual story inside. I looked in some more Charles Dickens books and there was nothing unusual in any of them. So, I went downstairs and pulled out some more of these 'classics' in case there were any others like this. I almost gave up looking when I didn't find anything after a few minutes, but then I stumbled upon a series of Shakespeare volumes in similar leather covers, and when I opened a copy of *Twelfth Night*, the same thing happened. It was full of handwritten mathematical equations and hand-drawn diagrams.'

'But why hide them in the covers of these books?'

'It gets better,' Adam says, laying the copy of *Twelfth Night* out in front of me. 'To cut a long story short, eventually I found eight more books exactly like them. All classics, but instead of the actual book between the covers, they all had handwritten notes hidden inside.'

'That must have taken you ages – no wonder you were up so late.'

'I would probably still be doing it now, if I hadn't figured out the link between them.'

'Other than them being classics?'

Adam nods. 'The link is they all have numbers in the title!'

'Really?'

'Uh-huh, and after I'd been through things like *Twenty Thousand Leagues Under the Sea* and *Catch-22*, and they were just the books with no notes in, I realised that not only were the titles numeric, but they were specifically the numbers found on a clock.'

'Why a clock?'

'I don't know, but look.' He lifts a book from the pile. '*One, Two, Buckle My Shoe* by Agatha Christie. Took me ages to find that one, I can tell you.'

I nod. 'Not one of her more well-known novels if you're not a Christie fan.'

'Usual cover on the outside, but inside, no book, only more notes. I've already shown you *A Tale of Two Cities*, so next is *The Three Musketeers* by Alexandre Dumas, then *The Sign of Four* by Sir Arthur Conan Doyle.'

As he puts each book down in front of me, I quickly open the cover to find the similar diagrams, equations and handwritten notes in each one.

'A couple of children's classics next – which again took me a while to find, because I wasn't looking for children's books to begin with. *Five Children and It* by E. Nesbit, and *Now We Are Six* by A. A. Milne. Then we have *Seven Pillars of Wisdom* by T. E. Lawrence. *Around the World in Eighty Days* by Jules Verne – that was one of the last ones I found – the eight disguised in the eighty really threw me off the scent. And, finally, in a similar vein, *The Thirty*-Nine *Steps* by John Buchan.'

'I can't believe you found all these books on your own,' I tell him, looking at the pile in front of me. 'I'm seriously impressed by your literary knowledge.'

'Thanks. I had a little help from Google, of course, but I nearly got them all.'

'So what are we missing?' I check the books again. 'Just numbers ten and eleven?'

'Yep, they've got me stumped.'

I think for a moment. 'Ten … ten …'

'I couldn't think of one,' Adam says. 'Not what I'd call a classic anyway. Titles with ten in them are nearly all modern books.'

I look at the books on the counter again. 'These are all old books, aren't they? When they were published, I mean. What's the newest – the Agatha Christie?'

'Yeah, I think so,' Adam says, looking at the books again.

'Hmm …' I say, trying to recall classic novels. 'Nothing is springing to mind for me either.' I begin to run through some classic authors and the titles of their books – Dickens, Austen, the Brontë sisters … 'Wait! I might have one …' I say, as a title pops into my head. 'I'll be right back!'

I rush downstairs and search the shelves, and, just as I hoped, I find it. 'I have it!' I tell Adam as I breathlessly enter the kitchen again brandishing a hardback copy of a book.

'What is it?' Adam asks with his brow furrowed. 'You've done better than me if you've found our missing ten.'

'*The Tenant of Wildfell Hall* by Anne Brontë!' I say triumphantly, like someone giving the right answer on a television quiz game. 'And it has all the handwritten notes again like the others do.'

Adam takes the book from me and thumbs quickly through it.

'Amazing! Well done. Now if you can come up with the answer for our missing eleven, we've got the full set.'

I think again for a few moments, but infuriatingly nothing springs to mind.

'No, sorry. I'll have to come back to you on that one. I can't think of anything off the top of my head.' I look at our pile of books. 'So, what are all these notes that have been written inside? Can you understand them?'

'I think from my limited knowledge and memory from school, they might be physics equations. There's talk of relativity and mass – those names ring a bell from science classes.'

'They do for me too. But science wasn't really my thing at school either. I do know who might be able to help us, though – Barney. He works in physics at the Cavendish Laboratory!'

'So he does!' Adam says keenly. 'Shall we go and show him the books when we've drunk our coffee?'

'Worth a shot. But I must insist on something before that.'

'What?'

'You have a shower and get dressed first?'

'Oh, yeah,' Adam says, running his hand through his ruffled hair, making it look even more dishevelled instead of tidier. 'I completely forgot in all our excitement. I must look like a right mess!' He grins apologetically and pulls a sort of puppy-dog expression asking for forgiveness. 'You stay here. I'll be right back.'

'No need to apologise,' I murmur under my breath as Adam jogs off, presumably towards the bathroom. 'No need at all.'

Seeing Adam in his nightwear looking dishevelled and a bit sleepy this morning made, for some silly reason, my stomach do weird things and my mind go to places that I've been desperately trying to get it back from ever since. And now, seeing him run his hands through his hair like that has brought me right back to square one again.

Why is Adam so damn attractive to me right now? He really isn't my type at all.

I take a few deep breaths as I sit at the kitchen counter finishing my coffee.

There's far too much going on right now to be thinking the kind of thoughts you are, Eve, I try to tell myself sternly. *The last thing you need right now is to stumble into another relationship.* But as hard as I try to shake Adam out of my mind, he just keeps popping right back again – with that same silly grin he's had on his face since he was a child, and those same deep blue eyes that twinkle in such a way that my heart beats that little bit faster whenever he's near …

13

'Quantum physics,' Barney says as he flicks through the pages of one of the books.

Adam and I have carried the books from next door for Barney to have a look at in the antiques shop.

He looks up at us when we don't immediately answer.

'From my limited knowledge, these look like quantum physics equations, and the notes and diagrams would suggest that too.'

I glance at Adam, but he looks no wiser than I do.

'What's *quantum* physics?' I ask.

'Now there's a question!' Barney says, smiling. 'One that would take me a *long* time to answer properly. To keep it as simple as I can, it's the study of matter. Usually, but not always, tiny matter, like atoms and molecules, and how they behave.'

'Right … and you think that's what all these books contain. Just stuff about atoms and molecules?'

'I'd have to have a good look through them all, but, yeah, I'd say so. Remember I'm not a scientist, though. I just work at the lab helping the real scientists out.'

'But you must have picked up some knowledge working there,' Adam says. 'I'm sure you do all the hard graft while the students and professors take all the credit.'

Barney smiles. 'Something like that. They'd have to do their own donkey work if it wasn't for us. We set everything up for them so they can do all their experiments and teach and stuff, then we clear everything up afterwards.'

'Why would someone hide twelve books of notes away, and so cleverly too, if they don't mean anything?' I ask. 'They must mean something or why hide them?'

'Hi!' A female voice calls from the doorway. It's Orla. 'I don't suppose you have any change, do you, Eve? I've had nothing but notes this morning, and I'm desperate for some pound coins.'

'Sure,' I say. 'Come in – we've some out back.'

I go into the back room where I keep a small safe.

'Oh, hello, Adam,' I hear Orla say as she enters the shop. 'I didn't expect to see you here. How's the shop going?'

'Yeah, all right, thanks. Getting there, you know?'

'Grand. And how are you today, Barney?'

'Good. Yeah, really good, thanks,' Barney says quickly, in a slightly high-pitched voice, not sounding at all like his usual laid-back self.

'I'm pleased to hear it. So, what are you all up to? You look like you were in deep discussion when I entered.'

'Nothing,' Barney says guiltily.

'Just having a chat, really,' I hear Adam say.

'Right …' Orla doesn't sound too convinced. 'Oh, Barney, I've got that crystal in the shop you were asking me about the other day. Why don't you pop in later when you can.'

'Sure, thanks, I will,' Barney says in the same strange voice. I hear him clear his throat, then say in a deeper tone, 'Much appreciated, Orla.'

I come back into the shop with a bag of pound coins. As I hand Orla the bag, I notice how red the back of Barney's neck has gone.

'Ah, Eve, you're a star,' Orla says, handing me a twenty-pound note. 'Right, then, I'll leave you all to your gossiping!' She raises her blonde eyebrows, gives Barney a quick smile, then walks towards the door just as Ben is about to enter the shop. 'Ben! Grand to see you back in Clockmaker Court at last.'

'If it hadn't been for your healing ways, Orla, I'm sure it would have taken a lot longer for me to get back here.'

Orla smiles and pats him on the arm as she leaves. 'Good to have you back where you belong.'

Ben stands in the shop doorway. 'Is this a good time?' he asks, glancing at Adam and Barney.

'Of course,' I say, going over to escort him in. 'We've no secrets here. Did you have any luck?'

Ben holds up a roll of paper. 'I certainly did. Can I lay it out somewhere?'

We clear a bit of space on the cash desk and while Ben sits on a wooden chair, Adam unrolls the map.

'It's a plan of this area of Cambridge, including Clockmaker Court, drawn up in 1938,' Ben says. 'Just like you thought, there was another building between your two shops originally.'

Adam and I pore over the map, where the missing building is quite clearly marked.

'When do you think it was boarded up?' I ask. 'Obviously sometime after 1938.'

'You'd have to find some more up-to-date maps show-ing the area. I might have something, but again I'd have to look through my stock. I don't recall that shop being here when I was a young boy, so I doubt it was much after 1938 that it changed.'

'Sometime during the Second World War then?' I ask.

'It's possible. The thing is, during the war a lot of indus-tries changed their production for the war effort. I would have thought street plans would have been one of those things. Also, we didn't want anything circulating that could help Hitler plan his bombings and possible invasions.'

'So if it changed between 1939 and 1945, it's unlikely we'd know exactly when?'

Ben nods. 'But like I said, I don't remember it being there during the war when I used to come and read the comics with George in Archie's shop.'

'Wait, what?' Adam asks, confused. 'What do you mean, Archie's shop?'

'Didn't Eve tell you?' Ben looks at me in surprise.

'I was going to,' I say hurriedly. 'And then we were caught up in the book mystery.'

'Book mystery?' Ben asks.

'Hang on,' Adam says. 'Let's not get distracted again. What do you mean, Archie's shop?'

I gesture to Ben to explain.

'As I explained to Eve earlier, Archie owned the book-shop in Clockmaker Court during the forties. Your grandfather George and I used to spend a lot of time in there when we were young.'

'But I thought he was a professor at the university?' Adam looks completely bewildered now.

'He was. He only owned the bookshop – someone else ran it for him. His name was Oswald; we called him

Ozzie.' Ben pauses to remember what are clearly happy memories for him.

'But why would Archie buy a bookshop?' Adam asks.

'A side hustle, maybe?' Barney says.

'I doubt it. Didn't university professors get paid quite well back then?'

'It does seem a little odd, doesn't it?' I say. 'Perhaps he just wanted it as a hobby?'

'Hmm …' Adam is clearly unconvinced. 'This just isn't adding up for me. What you're saying, Ben, is that not only did my grandfather used to hang out here in Clockmaker Court when he was young, but that my great-grandfather at one stage actually owned the shop that I do now?'

Ben nods.

'That's crazy. I didn't even know of this place until a few months ago.'

'It's like it's meant to be,' I say, secretly pleased that this strange twist of fate was in part due to me. 'Like you were always meant to own the shop next door.'

'What sort of comics were they?' Barney asks while Adam and I are still ruminating on this.

'In Archie's shop?' Ben's bushy white eyebrows draw together as his brow furrows. He must be wondering, like me, what this has to do with anything.

'Yes.'

'Erm … the *Beano*, the *Dandy*, that sort of thing.'

'Anything else? Any American comics?'

'Yes, as a matter of fact, there were. I was just telling Eve earlier that there were some American imports. I think they must have come over with one or two of the GIs stationed here during the war.'

'Marvel?' Barney asks.

'Yes, although they weren't called Marvel, they were called Timely Comics back then, if I remember correctly. Archie loved a comic and so did George. I think that's one of the reasons they stocked them, so George could read them.'

'Why are you asking, Barney?' I say. Barney is into comics and superheroes, and he helped me value many of the items from Past Times House we brought from the cabinet in George's office. He actually bought a few bits off me before they went on sale in the shop.

'Because there's some references to Marvel in the books you showed me,' Barney says.

'The equation books?' I ask doubtfully.

'Yeah, look.' Barney reaches for *Twelfth Night*. 'While you were poring over the map, I continued to look at the books. It was difficult for me to see the map up there.'

'Oh, Barney, I'm sorry,' I say, feeling immediately guilty. 'We should have put it on the lower part of the desk so you could see it too.'

Barney shrugs good-naturedly. 'No worries. It's probably a good thing, because although I couldn't understand all the equations and formulae in the books, what I did see at the back of a couple of them are references that only a Marvel geek would understand. I'm a Marvel geek,' he says when none of us respond. 'Well, a comic-book geek, really, but Marvel is my favourite.' He looks at Ben, who nods approvingly.

'What sort of references?' I ask.

'All sorts that could mean anything, but one in particular might be relevant. It says *EARTH* in big capital letters inside a doodle of Captain America's shield.'

'I'm sorry, Barney, but you'll have to explain further?'

'In the Marvel universe, Earth is referred to with three numbers – 616. It's complicated,' he says quickly. 'But the doodle of the shield is inside what looks a bit like a combination lock.'

'Like the one on the door?' Adam is piecing all this together much faster than Ben and I.

'Exactly.' Barney points at him.

'But the combination has six digits,' I say, not really catching on.

'I know, but what if three of those digits are 616. If you can discover the second three, you might be that little bit closer to unlocking the secret of what's hidden behind that door.'

14

In between customers, we pore over the rest of the books looking for a clue to three further numbers, but we don't find anything that immediately makes any sense. According to Barney, there are more comic-related clues doodled within the pages, but nothing that gives us any numbers. What we do discover, though, is that the doodles are always drawn in a different pen than the rest of the notes within the books.

'The notes were all written in black ink with a fountain pen,' Ben says. 'While these doodles are done with a more modern ballpoint pen, it would seem.'

'They must have been added later,' I say. 'When did people start to use ballpoint pens?'

A quick internet search suggests they first became popular in the 1960s.

'So do we all agree then that the main body of notes were written pre-sixties and the added doodles sometime afterwards?'

'Not necessarily,' Ben says. 'Some people still use fountain pens today.'

'But the novels all date from pre-1960, don't they, so it's more than likely.'

Adam takes a quick look through all the books again. 'Yep, they are all published before 1960; the latest one is the Agatha Christie in 1940. The editions we have here are all dated before 1960, too.'

'Even though the comics began in the forties, some of these references are from much later,' Barney says. 'Earth was not referred to as 616 until the eighties.'

I know Barney is an expert on comic books, but I had no idea how much of an expert until today. He knows every fact and hasn't looked anything up on the internet.

'So we're thinking that the original notes were written in and hidden in the books before the sixties, and the doodles were added post-eighties, then?' I ask.

Barney nods. 'It seems likely.'

'It certainly seems to narrow it down to those dates,' Ben says.

'If only we could figure out what the missing book is,' I say. 'I feel like there's going to be something really relevant within its pages.'

'The elusive book number eleven,' Adam says, sighing. 'Knowing our luck, that one will likely hold all our answers.'

Ben yawns. 'Excuse me,' he says, stretching in his chair. 'I'm not used to being in company for this long since my illness. Perhaps I had better go.'

'I'm sorry we've kept you, Ben,' I say. 'You've been incredibly helpful, though.'

'I wish you all every success with your endeavours.' Ben leans on his cane as he slowly rises to his feet. 'It's a conundrum that I have a feeling you might be close to solving. Perhaps there's other branches you could explore than just the books? That might help you find what's between your two shops.'

'I guess,' I say. 'But the books are all we have right now.'

'In my experience, taking a break and standing back from the problem sometimes allows the brain to think new thoughts, and the eyes to see new solutions.' He begins to walk towards the door of the shop. 'Nice clock,' he says, passing the grandfather clock. 'Is that the time already?'

'No, it's ...' I glance at my watch. 'Ten past one. The hands have been stuck at half past two since I got it.'

Ben nods. 'What a shame. It's a fine-looking clock.'

'Yes, I might be able to sell it if it actually worked.'

'Perfection is rarely interesting, Eve. Sometimes, it's the fault in something that makes it that extra bit special.'

After a bit more discussion, Adam eventually goes back to his shop, and Barney and I go about our business in Rainy Day Antiques. It started to rain a little while ago, so the shop immediately became busier while people found shelter, but now the rain has set in, the flow of customers is rapidly diminishing.

'He's all right, Adam, isn't he?' Barney says as we decide where to hang some new paintings on the wall. We recently sold a couple of large watercolours, so we are trying to fill those gaps without having to move too many of the other paintings.

'I suppose, yes.'

'You clearly like him.'

'Do I? What makes you say that?'

'I've known you long enough by now, Eve, to tell when you *like* someone.'

I look down from the little wooden trestle ladder I use for reaching things down from high shelves and hanging paintings on the wall, at Barney's grinning face.

'You can talk,' I say, not answering his question. 'I know when you *like* someone too.'

'What do you mean?'

'Orla?' I climb down the ladder with a watercolour painting of a riverbank in my hand.

Barney's neck immediately begins to flush again.

'See? Two can play that game. I noticed you get all flustered when she was here earlier and it's not the first time.'

'Orla is very pretty,' Barney says shyly.

'You're a similar age. Why don't you ask her out?' I say, about to try a different painting against the wall. 'She might say yes.'

Barney looks at me like I'm crazy. 'Yeah, right.'

'Why not?'

'As if someone like Orla is going to be interested in me.' He looks down at his legs.

'You underestimate Orla, if you think your disability is going to bother her. It made no difference to me when you came asking for a job here, did it?'

Barney grins. 'I'd have had you for discrimination if it had!'

'I know you would!' I climb the ladder again with the new painting, an oil this time of two King Charles spaniels curled up in a basket. 'But seriously, Barney, you're kind and funny, and you're honest – too honest sometimes! But people value honesty. I think Orla in particular would think you were quite the catch!'

'Quite the catch!' Barney grins. 'What am I – a fish!'

'You know what I mean.' I hold the painting up to the wall to see what it looks like. Happy, I hang it on the hook already in the wall.

'Giving someone like me a job and dating someone like me is very different,' Barney says quietly.

'True,' I say, descending the ladder again. 'But I think you should give Orla the chance to make that choice for herself.'

'I'll think about it. Now, that painting isn't straight.' He looks up at the wall. 'I'd offer to do it myself, but me and ladders aren't really a good match.'

'Excuses, excuses,' I say, pretending to grumble as I climb up the ladder again with one of the oil paintings from Past Times House.

'So you and Adam, then?' Barney says. 'I'm sure that's how this conversation began before you changed the subject.'

'There isn't a me and Adam,' I say firmly. 'There, is that straight now?' I adjust the painting of the dogs a little.

'Perfect. But you like him, right?' Barney continues.

'He's pleasant enough.'

'Pleasant! Is that what you old guys call it?'

'Hey, enough of the old. We're hardly ancient. I'm barely ten years older than you!'

'Twelve, actually. Adam must be older, though – what is he, forty-five?'

'Don't tell him that,' I say, hanging the next painting – a modern-looking oil, almost abstract in its composition. 'Adam is forty. He was born on the same day as me.'

'Another leap-year baby.' Barney wheels himself back to look up at the new painting. He gives a thumbs-up. 'What are the chances?'

'I know. It's quite the exclusive club.' I descend the ladder again and take a quick look at the painting to check it is straight. I then choose another smaller picture to hang in the last small gap. 'I was very impressed with your knowledge earlier today about the comic books.'

'Thanks,' Barney says, looking pleased. 'It's been a hobby of mine for a long time. That's why I was so excited when you brought those bits from Past Times House. It's a dream of mine to own my own shop selling all that kind of thing one day.'

'Really?' I say, climbing the ladder for the last time. 'I thought you liked working at the university.'

'I do. My background is in science, but my passion is comic books and their heroes.'

'Well, you just never know. I didn't set out to own an antiques shop and yet here I am, and Adam didn't set out to own a bookshop and look what's happened to him this year.'

'True – and he's taken on a lot more than that, it would seem, with all these mysteries hanging around everything.'

'Yeah, I know. We'll probably end up unlocking that door and find nothing behind it.'

'But what if there is something? It might be something really exciting.'

'I'll believe it when I see it. But, you're right, there is something going on here – there's just been too much happening to believe it's all a coincidence.'

'More than the books and the door?'

'Oh, yes, so much more.'

I climb back down the ladder and quickly explain to Barney everything that's been going on that he doesn't already know.

'So, let me get this straight,' Barney says slowly when I've finished telling him. 'You're saying this family not only wanted you to do their house clearance, but they also had some strange photos of *both* your great-grandparents hidden in the attic that you and Adam just *happened* to discover?'

I nod.

'Adam has taken on the bookshop that his great-grandfather once owned – yet he didn't know that when he bought it,' Barney continues, wide-eyed. 'And subsequently you've now discovered not only a locked door hidden away behind many layers of wallpaper, but a set of novels with notes, equations and diagrams that are clearly supposed to tell you something important, but as yet you don't know what?'

'Yes, that about sums it all up. Sounds a bit crazy, doesn't it, when you put it like that.'

Barney shakes his head. 'It doesn't sound crazy, it sounds very much like you and Adam were meant to discover all this. Like it's been the plan all along.'

The rest of the afternoon is quiet so I tell Barney he can go early, which he gratefully accepts.

I tidy up the shop, pausing to look at the pictures from Past Times House we hung this afternoon.

Is Barney right? Has it been the plan all along for Adam and I to find everything we've discovered so far?

But if that is the case – why? What possible reason could there be?

The particular painting I've paused in front of is the abstract one. It's nothing like any of the other pictures that hung on the walls of Past Times House, but something about it spoke to me so I added it to the others in the hope it might be to one of my customers' tastes.

Depicted in the oil painting is a tree standing in the middle of a garden. There's a pile of books in front of the tree, with a single apple balanced on top of them. Inside the trunk of the tree is a clock, and dotted about in the branches are lots of random objects, including, very oddly, a black-and-white-spotted dog.

I'm about to move away from the painting when I stop and take a closer look. Something about it is familiar …

What is it? I look closely at the artwork. *Is it the tree?* But really it could be any tree, it's depicted in such an abstract way. *The books?* Again they could be anything. I count them – there's exactly twelve. And the objects – they are such an odd assortment they could mean anything. And the red apple balanced on top of the books looks like any other apple. *Perhaps it's the clock?* I stare at it for a moment and then it hits me – the time! The time reads half past two, just like the broken grandfather clock.

I look across at the clock face and then down at the carving on the door underneath. The tree on the door looks exactly the same shape as the one in the painting! But why do the two clocks say exactly the same time? Is it simply a coincidence or does it actually mean something? And what is so special about the time half past two?

15

I close up my shop at five o'clock, still none the wiser what the time on the painting and the clock might mean, and I head next door to see Adam.

'Gosh, you have made some progress this afternoon,' I tell him, looking around the shop at all the neatly stacked bookshelves. 'It looks like you're almost ready to open. The whole place looks amazing.'

'All except that wall,' Adam says, looking at the wall with the metal door in. 'If we can't find out how to unlock it, I'm going to have to put the bookcase back again.'

'I know. It's so frustrating, though – I feel like we're so close to finding out what's behind there. Oh, I need to tell you about the picture Barney and I hung this afternoon in my shop.'

'That's odd,' Adam says when I've explained. 'I remember that picture in my grandfather's study; he often used to point it out to me, but I wasn't really interested in art when I was young. It was so different to all the other artwork he had in the house, though – that was much more traditional. Do you know who did the painting – is there a signature on it?'

'No, I've looked. Which is odd in itself. I wonder where your grandfather got it from?'

'Absolutely no idea. So you think the tree in the painting might be the same as the one engraved on the front of the grandfather clock?'

'It is very similar.'

'You know I've looked around at all these books today,' Adam says wearily. 'And there's none with an eleven in the title. That's incredibly frustrating too. Where is eleven when all the others were clearly on show on my grandfather's bookshelves?'

'Do you think we're thinking about this too hard?' I say. 'Is the answer staring us in the face?'

'Probably. Do you fancy a drink?' Adam asks. 'I could murder a pint.'

'Sure, why not? Maybe it will help us relax so we can begin to think clearly.'

'You'd better hope so. Otherwise that door is going to have to go back into hiding until we have some more clues.'

After Adam has insisted on cleaning himself up, we head out of Clockmaker Court and across to the pub where we both celebrated our birthdays back in February.

'Seems quite apt, doesn't it?' I say as we head through the door.

'What does?' Adam asks, holding the door open for me.

'The name of this pub – The Timekeeper – with what's happening with the books and the clocks.'

'Yeah, I guess it does. This is a bit busy tonight,' Adam says, looking around the packed and unusually noisy bar.

'Bank holiday, isn't it, that's why. There's some more seating outside. Shall I see if there are any tables free?'

'Why don't you see if there's any tables free?' Adam says, obviously not hearing me above the chatter. 'And I'll get the drinks in. What would you like?'

'I'll have a lager, please.'

Adam nods. 'Half or pint?'

I smile. 'Half will be plenty, thanks.'

While Adam goes up to the bar, I head out of the back door to the little beer garden. On first glance there don't seem to be any tables free, but then I spot Luca at one of them with a couple of people I don't recognise.

'Hey, Eve!' Luca says, waving. 'Over here.'

'Hello.' I walk over to him. 'Great minds think alike.'

'Are you here on your own, my darling?' he asks.

'No, Adam is trying to get served at the bar. It's busy in there tonight.'

'It is the beautiful weather this evening, *bella*! It's brought everyone out again after the rain earlier. Do you wanna sit with us? Or would you prefer just the two of you?' He wiggles his eyebrows suggestively.

'Luca!' I shake my head. 'Joining you would be great if you don't mind.' I look at the other two people at the table.

'Go for it,' a man with an American accent says, pulling out a chair for me. 'We're about to head back to our hotel soon anyway. Early flight tomorrow.'

'This is Annie and Ed, friends of mine from America,' Luca says, introducing them. 'This is my Eve. She owns one of the shops in Clockmaker Court.'

'Oh, which one?' Annie asks, also with an American twang to her voice.

'The antique shop.'

'I've been in! It's wonderful – you have so many amazing things in there. You weren't there when we visited, though – there was a young guy?'

'Yes, that's Barney; he works with me.'

Annie nods eagerly. 'All the shops in that little court are so quaint. Like something time forgot.'

'Yes, they are a bit.'

'When Luca first sent me photos of his little clothes shop, I squealed, didn't I, Luca?'

'That's what you said, darling,' Luca says calmly.

'I never thought I'd hear the end of it until I agreed to come here while on our holiday, to England,' Ed says, rolling his eyes. 'We must go and see Luca's little shop, was all I got for at least a year!'

'I'm not that bad,' Annie says reproachfully. 'We've had a wonderful time, though. We've been all over England over the last few weeks; you have so much fabulous history here we don't have in the US.'

'And we ended up here in Cambridge,' Ed says. 'My family come from here originally.'

'Really?'

'Yeah, I'm going back many years, though. My grandfather was stationed here during the Second World War at Duxford. He met my grandmother here, and, after the war ended, he stayed in England and they moved around to various airbases where US troops were stationed. My father was born here and it wasn't until he met my mother that they decided to move back to the States.'

'Gosh, my great-grandmother was stationed at RAF Duxford during the Second World War too.'

'Holy moly! That's amazing. Maybe they knew each other?'

'Maybe they did,' I say, smiling at him.

'What did she do after the war?' Ed asks. 'Did she continue to serve?'

'Sadly, she died in 1944.'

'Oh, how sad,' Annie says. 'Was she killed by a bomb? A lot of Brits were killed in air raids, weren't they?'

'Luckily, Cambridge didn't get too many bombing raids during the war. When I say she died, she actually went missing.'

'Missing? Like behind enemy lines?' Annie asks excitedly. 'Ooh, was she a spy?'

'No, nothing as exciting as that, I'm afraid. She was stationed here in Cambridge for the whole of the war, I believe. She was, however, one of the first female engineers at Duxford.' I'm surprised at how proud I feel saying this. I've been thinking a lot about Dotty lately since we found that photo of her. Ed and Annie aren't the only ones keen to know more about her story.

'So how did she go missing?' Ed asks, appearing genuinely interested.

I explain as quickly as I can what I know about Dotty.

'Gee, that's quite the family mystery you have there,' Ed says. 'And sadly one I doubt you'll ever solve all these years later. I thought I'd uncovered some twists and turns in my family – Annie and I have both been tracing our family trees. That's how we met Luca.'

'Oh, yes?' I turn to Luca. 'I didn't know you'd been doing that. Are you guys related, then?'

'No,' Luca says, shaking his head. 'But that's how I met Annie – on a Facebook group for finding families. When she said she was coming over to England, I said she should pop in if they were ever in Cambridge.'

'And here we are!' Annie says. 'I'm sorry about your great-grandmother, Eve.' She pats my arm. 'But the internet is a wonderful place for trying to trace people. Maybe you should try sometime. I can see it bothers you not knowing what happened to her.'

I look down at Annie's hand on my arm. And, for some reason, her kind gesture touches me. 'Funny thing is, it didn't bother me too much before. It wasn't until recently that I started thinking about it and wondering. It was just one of those stories passed down through the generations.'

'What happened recently to change your mind?' Annie asks gently.

'Change your mind about what?' Adam asks from behind me and I turn to see him deftly holding a bottle of lager and an empty glass in one hand, and a pint of beer in another.

'Adam!' Luca leaps up from his seat. 'Come and sit by me here – there's room for two on this bench.'

'Nonsense,' Ed says. 'Annie and I will share. You take my seat, Adam.'

Much to Luca's disappointment, we have a little shuffle around, so now Luca, Adam and I have our own seat, and Annie and Ed share the little bench Luca was perching on.

'Right, now all that's done. Shall we begin again,' Luca says. 'This is Adam. He owns the bookshop next door to Eve's antique shop.'

'As yet unopened,' Adam says, smiling at Annie and Ed. 'I hope to open soon, though.'

'Luca met Annie and Ed when he was tracing his family tree,' I say to Adam. 'Ed had family in Cambridge too. His grandfather was stationed at RAF Duxford during the war.'

'Really? What a small world,' Adam says, nodding. He casts a purposeful glance in my direction before turning to Ed. 'Did your grandfather see any action in the war?' he asks.

'Yes, we believe he flew a few successful missions over Germany,' Ed replies. 'He never really spoke much about it to anyone, though. People back then didn't, did they. Not like now when people share everything about themselves on social media. In those days it was a stiff upper lip and all that.' He tried, unsuccessfully, to do an English accent and apologises as we all smile. 'Bombing another country wasn't something he was particularly proud of, I'm sure. But I guess it had to be done. I'm sure many of the German pilots felt the same. You said before, Eve, that Cambridge didn't get bombed too much during the war? How come? I thought all the big cities were hit.'

'I'm not really sure.'

'Some say it's because we didn't have many big factories or major transport links back then,' Luca says to my surprise. 'But there's another theory, that Britain and Germany made a pact – the Germans wouldn't bomb Cambridge or Oxford, if we spared two of their big university cities in exchange.'

'Really? That's incredible if it's true,' Ed says.

'There was only one major bomb dropped on the city,' Luca continues keenly. He really seems to be enjoying sharing his knowledge with us. 'That was on Vicarage Terrace in 1940. They think the bomber mistook the light on a nearby church for the lights on a control tower. Nine people died that night.'

We all go quiet.

'You guys suffered a lot in that war,' Annie says softly. 'It was the Blitz, wasn't it, when you were most hit?'

'I believe so, yes,' I reply. 'London in particular, but all the big cities suffered a lot of damage.' I turn to Luca – he seems to be the expert in all this. I had no idea before now he was interested in any type of history other than that of vintage clothes.

Luca nods. 'Yes, there was huge loss of life during the Blitz. Whole cites were decimated and people's lives torn apart.'

'Unimaginable for us, isn't it?' Annie says. 'Imagine one day just going about your daily life and then, boom, just like that, your house and your whole life are gone in an instant.'

We all nod sombrely.

'I've studied quite a lot about the Second World War,' Luca says. 'It's a bit of a hobby of mine. I've read accounts of people who were trapped for days under the wreckage of their houses. And there are amazing stories of people and animals just about giving up hope of ever being rescued, when someone randomly heard them calling out. Sometimes it took days to get people out safely.'

While we all think about this, I hear Adam ask, 'Another drink, anyone?'

I turn to him and frown.

'No?' he asks when no one responds. 'Well, I need another one.' He finishes off the last of his pint and slams the empty glass onto the table. 'Back in a bit.'

'Did we say something wrong?' Annie asks, looking concerned as Adam strides across the little beer garden.

'I don't think so.' I turn back from watching Adam stomp back towards the pub. 'He isn't usually abrupt like that.'

'Does he have trouble hearing in busy environments like this?' Annie asks gently.

'No, I don't think so …' I reply, thinking that was a strange thing to say.

'It's just that I noticed he has a hearing device in his right ear.'

I stare blankly at Annie.

'Most people wouldn't notice it; they can make them so tiny these days. But I have one.' She taps her left ear. 'And sometimes I have trouble hearing in busy places. I often go back to old-fashioned lip-reading if it's really bad.'

'I … I didn't know he had anything in his ear,' I say, as a few things suddenly begin to make sense. The times I thought Adam was staring intently at me when we first met … was he lip-reading? Then there had been a couple of times when I spoke to him when his back was turned and he didn't hear me properly, even though I was quite close to him – and just now in the busy pub …

'I have to admit I hadn't it noticed either,' Luca says. 'And I notice everything about a person's appearance.'

'I'm sure Adam would be pleased to know it,' Annie says, smiling kindly. 'No one who wears a hearing aid particularly wants people to notice. But we often notice each other.'

I feel awful. Adam and I have spent a lot of time together since we met in February – how can I not have noticed he had a problem with his hearing?

'Do you think it's to do with him spending so many years in loud environments?' Luca asks. 'You know, at rock concerts and things.'

'Maybe, I don't really know,' I say, shaking my head as I try to process this news. 'I think I'm going to pop to the ladies. Back in a bit. I won't be long.'

I head quickly across the garden to the pub, but instead of turning in the direction of the toilets, I walk towards the bar with the intention of finding Adam.

But he doesn't seem to be anywhere at the bar, so I take a quick tour around the rest of the building, eventually returning to the toilets. But when Adam does not appear after a couple of minutes, I pull my phone from my bag. I'm about to call him to see where he is, when I notice I have a new text message. It's from Adam.

Sorry, had to go. Please pass on my apologies. A x

I look at the text for a moment. *Should I just leave him be? Maybe something has come up?* I'm about to put my phone back in my bag, but a nagging feeling in my gut stops me. What if something is wrong? So I press reply, then I hesitate with my finger hovering over the blank screen before I type.

Where are you? Are you all right? E

I hesitate again, then I quickly type a kiss. *It doesn't mean anything; everyone puts kisses in text messages.* Then I press send.

Clockmaker Court comes the reply before I've even had time to put my phone back in my bag. Under the tree. X

I think for a moment, then I text Luca.

Sorry, something's come up. Please pass on my apologies to Annie and Ed, and tell them it was great to meet them. Fill you in tomorrow. Eve xx

Then I head quickly back to Clockmaker Court and find Adam, as expected, sitting under the old tree on the bench. But he's hunched over with his forearms resting on his thighs as he stares at the ground in front of him.

His appearance stops me in my tracks. He looks so different from how I'm used to seeing him. Nothing like the Adam I'd always known before, full of bravado. He looks ... *broken* is the only way I can describe it.

'Hi,' I say quietly as I approach him. 'Are you OK?' Then I remember what Annie had said, and I repeat it in a slightly louder voice.

As Adam slowly turns his head towards me, I can see immediately that he's not; his face is drawn and pale and his eyes look tired and heavy.

'Why are you shouting?' he asks.

'Sorry.'

'If anyone should be the one apologising, it's me. I'm sorry I ran out on you. Did you make my apologies to the others?'

'Sort of. What's going on?' I ask, sitting down next to him. 'You don't look too good.'

'Thanks,' Adam says with a half-smile that vanishes as quickly as it appears. He sits back on the bench and sighs. 'There's probably something I should tell you. But it's not something that comes up easily in conversation. It's also something I don't like talking about unless I have to.'

'It's all right, I already know,' I say confidently. 'It's fine, don't worry about it. No one would ever notice.'

Adam looks at me strangely. 'OK ...'

'Honestly, I'd never even seen it until Annie mentioned it just now. Is it because of all the loud music you've been exposed to over the years?'

'Eve,' Adam says, tilting his head a little to one side with a puzzled expression. 'What are you talking about?'

'Your hearing aid.' I look at his right ear. 'Honestly, I can just about see it now. But I'd never noticed it before. You shouldn't feel bad about having to wear one. I'm sure lots of people do.'

Adam's puzzled expression slowly changes to one of amusement. Then, in complete juxtaposition to the way he looked a moment ago, he throws his head back and laughs.

'Why is that so funny?' I ask, totally confused by his reaction.

'It's not,' Adam says, shaking his head. 'Wearing a hearing aid isn't funny in the slightest. What's funny is I wasn't talking about that. I was talking about something completely different. Something much more serious. But you've just managed to lighten an awkward moment for me and for that I'm extremely grateful to you.'

'What do you mean?' I ask, still confused. 'What *were* you talking about, then?'

Adam's amused expression fades and he becomes sombre once more. His eyes wander over my face, as if he's deciding whether to tell me or not. He looks so lost, so concerned about his next words, that I actually feel a bit scared.

'If you don't want to tell me, that's fine,' I say. 'You really don't have—'

'There's something I need to tell, you,' he says slowly. 'No, there's something I *want* to tell you.'

'OK …'

'It's something that happened to me a long time ago, but still affects me today.'

'Go on …' I try to sound encouraging. But I'm actually quite worried about what he's going to say. 'In your own time. There's no hurry. I'm here.'

I hesitate, but then I reach out and put my hand on his arm, as Annie did for me, hoping it will have the same comforting effect.

Adam looks surprised at my gesture and he gazes at my hand. But then he looks gratefully up at me. 'It's nothing. Silly, really. I shouldn't be bothering you with it.'

'If it's made you look like this, then I'm pretty sure it's *not* silly and it *is* worth bothering me about.' I continue to hold on to his arm.

Adam nods slowly and deliberately. 'You're right,' he says, and he takes a deep breath. 'The thing is … I have PTSD,' he says quickly, as though he's allowing it to escape from him. 'It's not due to anything brave or heroic. I've never been in the armed forces or anything like that.'

'You don't have to have been in a battlefield to have PTSD,' I say knowingly.

Adam looks at me. Right at me, as though he's looking deep into my soul. For a moment I think he's going to ask me how I know, but to my relief he doesn't. He turns away and stares in front of him as if he's watching something play out on an invisible screen.

'It should have been me,' he says. 'Not her.'

I wait, but he doesn't immediately continue. 'What should have been you?' I ask gently.

Adam turns his head slowly towards me.

'It should have been me that died that day. I shouldn't be here now. I should be dead.'

16

For a moment I simply stare at Adam, trying hard to comprehend what he's saying.

'What happened?' I ask gently.

Adam shakes his head. 'Aargh, I feel so stupid after what you were talking about with Luca, Annie and Ed.'

'Why?' I continue in the same gentle voice. 'What's that got to do with it?'

I'm desperately trying to piece all these events together in my head. *What did we talk about that triggered this level of reaction in Adam? This is obviously why he left the pub so abruptly.* I'm just trying to run through our conversation in my head when Adam says, 'It wasn't a Second World War bomb or anything dramatic like that. It was still an explosion, though.'

Ah, right, now it's making a little more sense.

'It was when I was in the band,' Adam continues. 'We were on a UK tour as the support band for another group. We'd played a huge arena gig in Newcastle the night before. And I'd had this one-night stand with a girl I barely knew – pretty standard for me back then, I'm ashamed to say. I'd met Kate the night before in a bar. I'd stayed the night at her house, which was in a quiet little place just outside of the city. I wanted to get away as quickly as possible the next morning so I didn't get in trouble with our management. But right before I left, we had an argument ...'

He pauses to remember, so I sit quietly and wait for him.

'She caught me trying to sneak out early. She didn't see it quite the way I did – as a one-off – and quite rightly she was upset and angry. I was furious she'd called me out on my behaviour; I thought I was God's gift back then because I was in a band.'

He glances at me to see my reaction, but I remain silent.

'Anyway, I stormed out with the intention of catching a cab. I was used to London, where you could step outside and hail a taxi immediately. This was of course before the days of Uber.'

He looks at me again. I nod.

'But I'd forgotten we were in a little village in the middle of nowhere. So there was nothing, not even a bus back to the city, for a few hours. Kate followed me, trying to make it up with me. She said she was going to work soon anyway and if I came back inside, she'd give me a lift back to my hotel on her way. I agreed and went back to her house. Kate went upstairs to get ready for work and told me to help myself to anything in the kitchen. I was going to make some coffee, I wasn't big on breakfast then. But there was a smell in the kitchen that turned my stomach. I thought I was just hungover so I called up to her that I was going to have a cigarette outside instead – I smoked then, but I was trying to give up.'

He thinks for a moment.

'But before I could light up, Kate called down to me from the upstairs window to ask if the kettle was on.

When I said no, she said she'd pop down and put it on herself. So I headed to the bottom of the garden where there was a little bench. Her little dog had come outside with me ...'

Adam stops again. 'Sorry,' he says after he's paused for a moment. 'This is the tough part.'

'Take your time,' I tell him. And I put my hand on his arm again. This time I pat it gently with my fingers.

This small gesture seems to encourage Adam. 'But before I could sit down on the bench, there was this tremendous booming sound and I remember being thrown backwards against a garden shed. I hit my head and I think the glass from the shed window must have smashed, because I was covered in tiny shards of glass. When I sat up, I saw that the whole of the top of the house had disappeared in front of me; it had simply collapsed in on the ground floor, and there was smoke and flames beginning to come from the inside. I could hear a whining sound from under some of the rubble that was now in the garden, so I just went into a sort of automatic pilot. I pulled myself up and shook as much of the glass off me as possible, then I ran towards the whining. Somehow the dog had got trapped underneath some of the timbers that had been part of a wooden pergola attached to the back of the house. How he wasn't crushed, I don't know – they seemed to have fallen in a sort of crisscross pattern that had protected him instead of crushing him. I began pulling the timbers carefully away from him – it was like doing a gigantic Jenga, but one that meant life or death if it collapsed.'

He pauses, but I simply nod for him to continue.

'I pulled away the last timber I could safely without it all collapsing on him and I was trying to encourage him to crawl out through a gap I'd made, when suddenly there was a second explosion and he was sort of blown towards me. I remember grabbing him and shielding him in my arms like you would a child. We fell to the ground and everything went dark around us. The second explosion meant what little was left of the house had been blown out and now we were both trapped under the wreckage. I don't know who or what was looking out for us that day, but this time a steel lintel from the house had fallen over both of us and was holding a hell of a lot of bricks and rubble inches away from our bodies. If the lintel had given way, that was it for us both.'

Adam's breathing has become fast and shallow, so he stops to take in a few deep and calming breaths.

'Are you all right?' I ask. 'You don't have to continue if it's too much.'

'No, I need to tell you everything,' he says resolutely. He takes a final deep breath. 'As we're lying stuck underneath the back of a house that is now on fire only metres away from us, not really knowing whether we were going to live or die, it dawned on me I might have saved a dog, but what I really should have done was try to save his owner. I thought if Kate was lucky, she might be in the same situation we were. Maybe she'd been protected in some way when the house caved in – but I knew if she wasn't …' He swallows hard. 'Then she was in trouble. But there was nothing I could do; the dog and I were trapped, and we had no choice but to stay there and hope help came quickly, before anything further happened.'

'How long were you there?' I ask quietly. I hate interrupting his painful memories to ask questions, but I know if Adam is to let everything out, which he clearly wants and needs to do, then I may have to prompt him occasionally.

'Just over four hours. The rescue services turned up quickly, but it felt like for ever before I heard anything other than the scream of neighbours witnessing what was happening and the crackle of the flames from the house. The smell was rancid too.'

'You mentioned a smell before – was it a gas explosion?'

'Yeah, the smell was like rotten eggs. I should have realised, maybe if I had …' He shakes his head. 'Anyway, they got the fire under control first and once they'd got the right equipment to lift all the debris off us, they began what felt like an incredibly slow process to get us out.'

'You must have been really scared.'

'Yeah, it was pretty horrendous. Not so bad once people came, and they said everything was under control and we'd be fine. But in those minutes before anyone turned up, it was just me and Lucky – that's what I called him, the dog. His name was actually Loki, but Lucky seemed more appropriate. I adopted him afterwards, when Kate's family couldn't look after him. Lucky lived with me for another five years before his luck finally ran out.'

Adam looks down at the ground again.

'There was photo of a hairy black dog in your flat,' I say. 'With the others on the mantelpiece. Was that him?'

Adam nods. 'Yes, that's Lucky. Great dog, he was. We had many good times together. He pretty much saved me when we were trapped together. Having him to focus on got me through it, when otherwise I think I'd have gone to pieces.'

'It sounds like you both saved each other.'

Adam smiles. 'Yes, I suppose so. Not only that day, but in the weeks and months afterwards too; we were everything to each other.'

I remove my hand from his arm and take hold of his hand instead.

Adam doesn't look surprised this time; he only looks grateful again for this simple, but meaningful gesture.

'Kate didn't survive the blast,' he says quietly.

'No.'

'The impact of both the first explosion and the top floor of the house collapsing killed her immediately. They tried to tell me she wouldn't have suffered; it would have all been really quick. But how could they have known that?'

'I don't know.'

'No one knows, do they? Not really. It took ages for the investigation to take place into what caused the gas leak. There had been some works on the gas mains further down the road a few days previously – I found that out afterwards. The final report said the gas board was at fault and they had to pay out compensation to all the residents in the street that were affected. They tried to give me some. To begin with, I refused, I didn't think I deserved it. But then I decided to donate it to a charity that looks after animals when their owners die and they have no one to take care of them.'

'Why didn't you think you deserved it?'

Adam looks at me as though I should know this. 'Really?' he asks.

'Yes, tell me.'

'Kate wouldn't have been downstairs turning the kettle on if it hadn't been for me. That's what triggered the first explosion, they told us afterwards – the simple act of flicking an electrical switch on a kettle. If I hadn't gone out for a cigarette, I would have done it and she would have been upstairs.'

'Adam, you must know you can't blame yourself.'

'That's what my therapists told me – all of them. And my friends. "It isn't your fault. You mustn't blame yourself. You weren't to know. It was the gas company's fault." I heard it all over and over again. Until I stopped listening. I dropped out of the band and I withdrew myself from everyone, so it was just me and Lucky. He didn't tell me it wasn't my fault. We both knew what had happened. We both knew what we'd been through. We were the only ones who understood each other. And then eventually he left me, just like all the others had before him. The only living creature who understood. The only one who would listen unconditionally.'

I squeeze Adam's hand. I want to tell him so much more right now. That I understand. That I get that level of trauma. That I know how it feels to have your whole world flipped upside down in an instant and when it lands again, nothing is ever the same.

'Was it the blast that affected your hearing?' I ask instead of saying all those other things, as I notice Adam absent-mindedly rubbing at his right ear.

Adam nods. 'Yeah, I didn't realise to begin with, but I'd perforated both my eardrums in the blasts, so everything sounded muffled for a while. The hearing eventually returned fully to my left ear, but this one never worked properly after that.' He taps his right ear. 'That's why I have this. It helps me a lot.'

'What other injuries did you have – was it pretty bad?'

'Surprisingly not a lot. Some cuts and grazes, mainly from the glass, a few broken bones in one arm, and a cracked rib. But in the greater scheme of things, it was incredible neither Lucky or me were hurt more.' He smiles. 'The dog was out for walks a lot faster than I was, that's for sure. He certainly lived up to his name.'

'It sounds like you were both pretty lucky that day.'

'It was twenty years ago today,' Adam says. 'Since it happened. That's one of the reasons it hit me so hard tonight at the pub. It was what you guys were talking about that reminded me. But the thing I was upset about was the fact that, for the first time ever, I'd forgotten the date. I remember every year. Every year since it happened. But this year, for some reason, it completely slipped my memory and that's what I couldn't handle – the fact I'd forgotten.'

'You've had a lot on. You can't blame yourself.'

'Yes, I can, Eve.' He pulls his hand away from mine as he stands up. 'I can't forget. I must never forget. Otherwise it was all for nothing. I need to remember. I need to remember her.'

Again, I know exactly what he's feeling right now. His hurt is stirring within me all sorts of painful memories and feelings, most of which, just like Adam, I suppress all the time too, because no one I know gets it. But I know I must choose my words carefully right now. This is about Adam, not me.

'Remembering those dates is important,' I say instead. 'But just because you might forget occasionally doesn't lessen the importance of the event. It just means you've moved on a little with your own life – which can only be a good thing, surely?'

Adam looks at me, his face still holding all the anger and hurt, and I think for one moment he's going to have a go again. But then his expression softens.

'You're very wise, do you know that?'

I shrug.

'What you said is exactly it. All these years I've never had the opportunity before to forget that date. Nothing and no one have ever been more important to me that

I've been able to forget. Then I came here to Clockmaker Court, I met you and your friends, I bought my little shop, and, for the first time, my life has moved on from that day. It may have taken twenty years, but now I feel like I'm ready to move on with the rest of my life.' He sits down again on the bench and takes hold of my hand this time. 'And it's all thanks to you, Eve.'

'Not just me,' I say, feeling a tad embarrassed. 'Perhaps you should thank your grandfather too for wanting to hire me?'

'Perhaps, but if you hadn't knocked on my door that day, telling me it's your birthday and that we both shared such an unusual and important date, I might not be here now telling you all this.' He prompts me when I don't immediately respond. 'Eve?'

'Oh, sorry, yes,' I say. 'You're totally right. Something just occurred to me, that's all.'

'OK …' Adam says, clearly a little put out that I haven't responded in a way that matches his own enthusiasm.

I feel his grip on my hand loosen just a little, so I quickly explain. 'I was just thinking when you were talking about remembering significant dates, and then you mentioned our birthdays are both on quite a significant date too.'

'Yes …'

'What if the missing numbers on the combination lock in your shop are also from a significant date?'

Adam thinks about this. 'It's a possibility. You think our birthdays could be relevant? The twenty-ninth of February is pretty unusual, but why would it be used for the combination? That would have been set years before we were born.'

'True …' My mind whirs again. *We're so close; I can feel it.* I look back across Clockmaker Court at our two shops. *There has to be something we're missing* … 'I've got it!' I suddenly say. 'How have we not thought of this before?'

'What?' Adam asks eagerly. 'What have you got?'

I explain as calmly as I can while my insides are doing a dance of excitement. 'Not only do our birthdays both represent the numbers 292, but the grandfather clock in my shop, and the clock in the painting, have both stopped at just before two-thirty …'

Adam looks lost now, so I fill in the last pieces for him.

'Otherwise known as twenty-nine minutes past two …'

17

We both leap up from the bench and rush over to the bookshop. Adam hurriedly unlocks the door.

'I can't believe you've figured this out, Eve,' he says excitedly as we go inside.

'Let's wait and see if these new numbers work first,' I reply, trying to remain calm as Adam locks the door behind us and we head over towards the metal door. 'We might have got a bit carried away.'

'This is going to work,' Adam says firmly, putting his hand over the dial. 'I know it is. So we're going for 292, right? What about the other digits? Shall I try 290284? That's my date of birth.'

'But it's not mine. Mine would be 290288.'

'We'll try both.'

Adam agonisingly turns the dial on the combination lock using both our dates of birth. His first, and then mine. But as I hold my breath in anticipation of the door opening, each time it's a sigh of disappointment rather than jubilation that I have to let out when the combination fails.

He then tries the year first followed by the day and month, but again it doesn't work.

'Worth a try,' he says, turning back to me. 'Maybe we're overthinking this. Maybe whatever is going on isn't quite as complicated as we think it is.'

I turn away from the door and look around the shop. My eyes rest on some vintage children's annuals that Adam has displayed face-out on the shelf and I cry out as I suddenly realise what we've forgotten.

'We forgot the comic connection!'

'What do you mean?'

'Archie, your great-grandfather, used to sell comics here, didn't he? Ben told us all about it. And George, your grandfather, used to collect superhero stuff too – he had it in his house. And then Barney discovered that doodle – the circles with the star.'

'Captain America's shield ...'

'And he said he thought the word Earth written in the middle represented three numbers ... Can you remember what they were?'

Adam shakes his head.

'Argh!' Frustrated, I bury my head in my hands. 'What did he say they were?'

We both think.

'He said it was something to do with Marvel comics, didn't he?' Adam says, his forehead furrowed as he tries to remember.

'Yes!' I pull my phone from my bag and quickly google the words *Marvel*, *Number* and *Earth*. '616!' I tell Adam, almost dropping my phone in excitement. 'Try 616 with 292. Both ways round.'

Adam tries 616292 first, but infuriatingly the door stays locked. Then he tries 292616. 'If this doesn't work, we really are back at square one again,' he says as he's about to turn the last digit. Slowly he turns the dial to the final six, and we both hear a very clear and a very satisfying clicking sound.

Adam turns back to me. 'It only bloody worked!' he says, his eyes wide with excitement. 'I think we're in!'

'Now to find out what's on the other side of this door …' I say in barely a whisper. 'It had better be worth it after all this time.'

18

Adam slowly and carefully swings open the door as if we might find something from a horror movie behind it, biding its time to jump out and scare us.

'You're not afraid, are you?' I ask, grinning as he opens the door a few centimetres at a time.

'No, of course not!' he says, standing up straight and pulling his shoulders back.

But as we open the door further, it only reveals a darkened room with no obvious windows or doors to allow any light in.

'Is there a light switch?' I ask as Adam tentatively steps forward into the dark.

'I don't know, do I?' he says, pulling out his phone and switching on the torch. 'Yes, look – there on the wall.'

Adam reaches for an old black Bakelite light switch, but when he clicks it, nothing happens. 'Looks like there was a working bulb once,' he says, directing his torch up to the ceiling from which a single bulb hangs from a cord. He shines the light further around the room.

'It's more like a big corridor, than a room,' I say, peering over his shoulder. 'It doesn't look like there's anything in here.'

'You can see where the entrance to the building would once have been.' Adam holds the beam of light on the same wall where the exterior doors to both our shops are. 'It's all bricked up now, though. The window too.'

I switch on the torch on my phone now as well, shining it over the walls.

'There's another door!' The light falls on a panelled wooden door at the end of the room. 'Shall we see what's in there?'

'Wait,' Adam says as I take a step forward. 'We need to wedge this heavy door open first. Otherwise, we could be trapped if it swings shut.'

'Or if someone tries to shut us in!' I joke in a silly ghostly voice. 'That's what always happens in *scaaary* movies.'

'You're making this sound like an episode of *Scooby-Doo*,' Adam says seriously. 'Do you want to be trapped in a building with – as far as we're concerned right now – no other way out than this door?'

'All right, Velma.' I grin at Adam, but then I remember. 'Oh, God,' I say in an anguished voice. 'I'm so sorry. Is this difficult for you – the dark and the chance we might get trapped? I didn't mean to make a joke out of it. After everything you've just told me, too. I'm such an idiot.'

Adam smiles. 'Thanks for having my back – I appreciate it. But really, I'm absolutely fine. Do I like the dark – not particularly, especially if it's teamed with a confined space. But I'm just being sensible, that's all.'

'Oh, good.' I breathe a sigh of relief. I can't believe I've been so thoughtless. I'm so touched that Adam shared what he had with me outside that I want him to know I understand. I'm just so used to making light of everything with him. This feels like new ground between us. 'I'm glad you're OK.'

'Right, then, let's wedge the door open first,' Adam says. 'Then we can be those meddling kids and explore a little further ...'

We prop the metal door open with a couple of cardboard boxes filled with books and then, still using our phone torches to light our way, step back inside the room. The space is completely empty, devoid of any fixtures or fittings that might originally have been a part of an old shop or even a home. Except for some old wallpaper peeling away from the walls, there is nothing inside to date it to any particular year as we make our way slowly towards the heavily varnished wooden door on the far wall.

'Do you want to open it or shall I?' Adam asks, holding his phone in my face.

'Careful.' I hold my hand over my eyes. 'You'll blind me. You go.'

'Sorry,' Adam says, turning back towards the door. He reaches for the black doorknob, again turning it agonisingly slowly as he carefully pulls the door towards him.

'Can you see anything?' I ask from behind him.

'No, it's dark again.' He feels around on the wall next to the door and I hear the click of another old light switch. This time the bulb works, and the yellow light that fills the area is slightly diffused by a single old-fashioned lampshade hanging over the bulb.

'It's a staircase,' I say unnecessarily as we both see wooden steps descending down into more darkness. 'Shall we go down?'

'I guess we'd better.'

'You go first,' I say, standing back a little.

'Thanks,' Adam says, looking back at me. 'That's good of you. What happened to ladies first?'

'I believe in equal opportunities,' I say, grinning at him.

Adam rolls his eyes, but he begins to take the stairs slowly, with me following close behind.

When we get to the bottom, Adam shines his torch around the walls and we find yet another black light switch. Adam flicks the switch down and another single bulb lights the room in front of us, but this time the bulb is covered in a green glass lampshade.

But it's not the lampshade that interests us as we gaze around in amazement.

'What is all this stuff?' I ask as we both step fully down into the room.

'I have no idea.' Adam spins around so he can take everything in.

Although there are again no windows, this room is definitely not empty. The walls are covered in old maps, and next to them, cork pinboards with brass drawing pins hold up sheafs of both typed paper and handwritten notes.

Underneath the pinboards, two wooden chairs sit behind two solid wooden desks. On top of the desks are blotting pads, an old typewriter, pots with pencils in, and fountain pens sitting neatly next to tiny bottles of black ink. On the same wall as the stairs there are two large olive-green metal filing cabinets.

It's like we've walked into a museum, the sort where they stage rooms to look like they would have in a certain era – and the era we've stumbled into is very definitely the 1940s, of that I have no doubt. One of the desks still has a cardboard box with a gas mask half falling out of it.

'It's like time stood still here.' Adam walks around trying to look at everything at once.

'In the forties by the look of it,' I say, standing in one spot but still trying to take everything in. 'All the furniture fits, the typewriter, even the gas mask over there.'

'The maps are definitely old,' Adam says, looking closely at one. 'It's been a long time since some of these countries have been known by these names. What's this?' He picks up something on one of the desks that looks like brass. 'It has numbers on it – I think they might be dates? And a sun and a moon too.'

I go over to see what he's holding.

'It's a perpetual calendar,' I say, taking the flat, circular piece of brassware from him. 'It's a pretty old one too by the looks of it. These dials here turn so you can make dates, months and years. Often there's a limited amount of years you can make up, but this one seems like it might be infinite, looking at how they've done the numbers in Roman numerals.' I put the calendar back down on the desk and go over to one of the filing cabinets. I expect it to be difficult to open, but to my surprise the drawer easily slides out. Inside there are rows of Manila files. I pull one out and open it.

It's a typed report dated May 1942. I skim-read it quickly.

'What have you got there?' Adam asks.

'I don't know – it seems to be a report about a visit someone has made. There's talk of a successful trip and it mentions a few streets I recognise in Cambridge, but then ...' I feel my forehead crease as I try to understand what the report is saying. 'There is talk about 1912 and some difficulties getting back because a door or something was obstructed?' I look at Adam. 'It doesn't really make sense? It's almost like it's coded.'

'Is the other cabinet full of the same thing?' he asks.

I pull open another drawer and randomly lift a file.

'Yes, this is very similar. But the date at the top is earlier – January 1942. But this time ...' I trace my finger down the page a few lines. 'Yes, at the same point it mentions 1896 instead of 1912.'

I pull out a few more files, passing the previous one to Adam each time, and I find similar reports all written in code, but all mentioning different dates at the same place on the page.

'Have you noticed something else about these reports?' Adam asks after we've looked at six or seven files. 'They are all stamped exactly the same at the bottom of the last page.'

I look at the last page of the report I'm currently reading. *PROJECT EDEN* is stamped in red ink at the bottom.

'What's Project Eden?'

'I have no idea,' Adam says, looking around the room again. 'But if this room was used in the forties, I'd hazard a guess that anything called project something around then was something to do with the war.'

'I wonder if it's something to do with Anthony Eden?' I say, still looking at the stamp.

'Wasn't he a prime minister?'

'Yes, but much later, in the fifties. During the Second World War, I think he was in the cabinet. I'd have to check.' I pull my phone out of my pocket. 'No signal. These walls are obviously quite thick.' I put my phone back and lift another report from the cabinet.

'Whatever we've discovered hidden away down here, it was obviously top secret,' Adam says. 'There's another door over there. It's probably just a cupboard, but we should take a look.'

'We've come this far,' I say, walking towards it. 'Why stop now?'

With Adam following me this time, I gently open the door. I feel for a light switch on the wall like Adam did previously, and flick it on. The bulb works, but only provides just enough light for us to see what's inside.

'Why is it so dark?' Adam asks from behind me.

In front of me is a tiny, narrow room – more like a large cupboard. There's a long table covered in trays, and above it what looks like a washing line with pegs on. 'It looks like a photographic developing studio.' I strain my eyes to see properly. 'Yes, there's still a few negatives over there on the table and some photographic paper.' I manoeuvre myself into the tiny room and pick up the negatives. 'The paper is still blank,' I tell Adam as I look quickly through it. I carry the negatives back out into the light and hold them up.

'What can you see?' Adam asks impatiently as I go silent.

'You're not going to believe this,' I say as I examine all the photos one by one.

'I bet I do,' Adam replies. 'After what we've discovered tonight, I don't think anything is going to surprise me any more.'

'This might. It's a series of photos of my great-grandmother, Dotty.'

'What? Are you sure?'

'Yes, it's definitely her,' I say as I continue to look through the photos. It is a really strange feeling to see her in these negatives. Unlike the more formal photos I've seen of her before, she looks so alive in these pictures – like she's really living her best life. She's smiling and I can see she's genuinely enjoying herself.

'What's she doing?' Adam leans over my shoulder to try to see the tiny strip of photos for himself.

I turn towards him to pass him the photos and I find our faces are suddenly inches apart. In the dim light we lock eyes for what feels like an eternity, but is likely only a few seconds as we both hold on to one end of the strip of photos.

'S-sorry.' I hurriedly let go of my end. 'Here, you take a look.'

I step aside and wait for Adam to hold them up to the light like I did. But he doesn't. Instead, he simply continues to gaze at me.

'They're a bit like the photos of Archie we found,' I say quickly, hoping this will encourage him to break his gaze. 'Remember? Of him in different outfits from different decades.'

As if he's been in a hypnotic trance, Adam suddenly seems to remember where he is and what he's doing. '*Yes* …' he says, blinking. 'Yes, of course I remember.' He turns away and holds the negative strip up to the light. 'Why is it your great-grandmother that's dressing up in costumes now?' he says to my relief. 'Wartime was hardly the time for fancy-dress parties.'

'If she is in fancy dress?' I reply, pleased everything is back to normal between us. 'Look behind her – you can see ordinary men and women going about their daily business again, just like in Archie's photos. They look like they're also dressed in the clothes from the early twentieth century, like she is – probably late Victorian, I'd guess.'

Adam squints at the negatives again. 'Just what have we stumbled upon here, Eve?' he says, turning back from the photos to look at me. 'A secret room that looks like it was last used in the Second World War. Photographs of both our great-grandparents looking like they were taken in years they couldn't possibly have been in. Cryptic notes hidden in classic novels, a clock that's stopped on a time representing both our birthdays, and a painting that seems like it could have all the answers if we could only figure it out!'

'The answers to what, though?' I ask, completely lost. 'What's going on here, Adam? And why are you and I seemingly at the centre of it all?'

19

The next morning, I walk towards Clockmaker Court feeling physically and emotionally drained from the events of the night before. Both from our latest discovery down in the basement between our two shops, and also from what Adam shared with me about his past.

After we met, I knew quite quickly that Adam and I shared a connection. I thought at first it was because of our great-grandparents. But as time ticked by, I realised there was something else, something much deeper. Until last night, though, I didn't know what it was. The question I now had, among the many others that were swirling around in my mind, was: would I ever be brave enough to share with Adam the secret from my past too?

As I walk through the streets of Cambridge, I don't, unusually, notice the historic buildings I pass or the early-morning cyclists that pass me. Instead, as I make my way towards my shop, my mind is firmly focused on what happened last night.

Adam and I eventually left the secret room carrying both the strip of photos and as many of the files as we could manage between us. With the agreement we would both go home and read as much as we could manage, in the hope we could work out what was being described within the reports.

But after I read five reports and still couldn't make head nor tail of what they were saying, I decided to look some things up on the internet, beginning with Project Eden. But everything that came up only referenced the Eden Project in Cornwall. Even when I eliminated Cornwall and gardens from my search, and put in *Project Eden, Second World War*, nothing of any relevance appeared. Eventually all I was getting were reports about primary school projects dedicated to the biblical Garden of Eden.

It was only after I gave up and got ready for bed that lightning finally struck, and after that I lay awake tossing and turning as my mind went into overdrive.

Is Project Eden actually a reference to the biblical Garden of Eden, and does that mean Adam and I, with our biblically matched names, are more involved in this than I first thought? No. I quickly tried to talk myself out of that theory. *It's just coincidental, surely? But then our great-grandparents clearly knew each other …*

My mind went round and round until, finally, around 3 a.m., I nodded off, only to be woken again by my 7 a.m. alarm.

But now, as I walk through the market square with most of the stalls already set up, and the traders having a chat and a gossip with each other before their first customers arrive, my mind is still whirring. Not only about Project Eden, but about Adam too.

I couldn't shake what happened down in the office between us – the *moment*, I was calling it. The connection wasn't only the strip of negatives we were both holding.

When we held each other's gaze, something stirred inside me, something that I thought was buried a long, long time ago. Did Adam feel it too, or did I just imagine that? After all, there was a lot going on. Maybe I got confused? This felt like more than simply finding him attractive – it felt deeper, and it felt stronger. Much stronger.

I glance across at the bookshop as I arrive in Clockmaker Court and unlock the door to my shop, but there is no sign of Adam just yet. So I head inside and begin setting up for the day ahead. But I've barely set the till up when Barney comes wheeling through the door.

'What are you doing here?' I ask, surprised to see him. 'You're not working today … are you?' With everything going on, it wouldn't surprise me if I had got mixed up.

'No, I'm just on my way to the lab and I wanted to call in on you first. Those books you gave me to look at? I think I know what they are.'

'Go on.' I wonder what he's going to say. I had a couple of thoughts as to what might be happening, but they were so far-fetched that I quickly pushed them to one side. So I'm keen to know now what Barney's theory might be.

'OK, now hear me out first, all right,' he says, looking a tad anxious. 'Don't shut me down before I've had a chance to explain.'

'All right …' Now I am getting worried. *What if Barney has come to the same conclusion as me? A conclusion that simply can't be true, however much the evidence is mounting by the minute to make it seem that way.*

'The diagrams and the equations seem to relate in physics terms to the theory of time travel,' Barney says, confirming my worst fears. He waits to gauge my initial reaction to this.

'Go on,' I say calmly.

Barney hesitates, clearly not expecting this reaction from me.

'I don't know if you know, but the theory of travelling into the future is actually well documented in modern quantum physics. The *theory* behind it, obviously. I'm not suggesting anyone has actually attempted it successfully.'

'Of course not.'

'But if you look on YouTube, you can actually find people like Professor Brian Cox explaining for the lay person how time travel into the future could be achieved.'

I nod.

'So it's not just for science-fiction films and television shows. It's actually a proven ... well, not actually proven, but a well-known theory.'

'OK ...'

'You're taking this a lot better than I thought you would,' Barney says suspiciously, tilting his head. 'Are you all right?'

'I'm a bit tired today, but nothing to worry about. Go on.'

'Right, so as far as I can see, the notebooks are trying to prove the same theory, but with the addition that time travel into the past might be equally as possible.'

I swallow hard. 'And do any of the notebooks actually prove this theory? Or is it just conjecture?'

'That's it – I don't think they could prove it. All the equations are trying to, but they never quite get there.'

'I see.'

'All right, what's going on?' Barney folds his arms. 'I've just told you that someone was trying to prove that time travel could be achieved in some secret notebooks you and Adam discovered, and you're not even a little bit shocked? I expected sceptical at the very least.'

'As strange as this may seem, Barney, I think you might be right.'

I explain to Barney what happened last night. About us figuring out the combination, and then getting into the room, and finally what we found.

'This is insane,' Barney says when I'm finished. 'What *have* you both uncovered?'

'I really don't know, Barney. Whatever it is, I'm getting more and more worried by it all as each day passes.'

'Morning,' Adam says, putting his head around the open door. 'What are you two discussing so intently?'

I quickly catch Adam up on Barney's theory.

'I hate to admit it,' Adam says, like me remaining much calmer than expected. 'As crazy as it sounds, the thought has crossed my mind too.'

Barney looks between the two of us. 'I can't believe this,' he says, shaking his head. 'I thought when I came here today, I was going to be laughed out of the shop. But instead I find the two of you are agreeing with everything I say!'

'The whole thing is mad – yes,' Adam says, looking at me. 'But I don't think either of us can deny the evidence. Can we, Eve?'

I shake my head.

'The question is, what are we to do with all this information? We have the notebooks that you've deciphered for us, Barney, the combination to the lock on the hidden room, all these reports – that didn't really make any sense to me – did they to you, Eve?' he asks, turning to me.

'Not a lot.'

'And finally some strange photos of both our great-grandparents. So what do we do with all this information?'

184

'Do we have to *do* anything?' I ask. 'You know I love history, but sometimes things are better left alone. We've found out what is behind the locked door now. Perhaps we should leave it be.'

'But what about the *story*, Eve?' Adam says. 'You told me you loved the story behind items from the past. This has more of a story here than in one of your old tea sets over there. In fact, there's not only a story, there's a whole great mystery. Don't you want to find out what it is and put the story to that painting over there, and that clock.' He gestures to them both. 'And what about the hidden room – there must be tons of stories of things that went on down there. It was clearly something top secret. Everything we've discovered has been related to the Second World War or earlier.'

I think about this.

'Did you say before that the numbers to open the locked door were both your birthdays, plus the 616 I'd told you about?' Barney asks suddenly.

'Yes, they were,' Adam replies. 'You were spot on with that comic-book reference in the doodle.'

'But I told you that Earth wasn't referred to as 616 in Marvel comics until the eighties. So unless those numbers are referencing something else, that combination can't have been set on the door until then, maybe even later.'

Adam and I both think about this.

'And,' Barney continues, 'if you remember, we discussed the doodles in the notebooks were drawn in ballpoint pen, likely much later than the original notes written in black fountain-pen ink.'

'So that means,' I say, still thinking, 'that even if the room was used in the forties and the reports we found last night were typed then, someone much later set up the combination lock on the door and added to what was already in the notebooks.'

'Someone that wanted someone else in the future to discover what was going on, and so left them a trail of clues so that they might discover the room.' Adam looks at me, as everything crazily begins to drop into place.

'And it appears,' I say quietly, 'that that someone wanted the people who discovered it to be us.'

20

Barney reluctantly heads off to his job at the university, while Adam and I grab a coffee and some breakfast from Harriet and Rocky's café.

We go in for bacon rolls, but surprisingly come out with pastries. An apple turnover for Adam, and a cinnamon and apple tart for me.

'So, what next?' Adam asks as we're about to enjoy our breakfast while leaning over the counter in my shop, which luckily for us is quiet today after the bank holiday weekend. Not good for my takings, but it does give us the space to be able to think.

'I have no idea,' I reply honestly.

'I feel like a lot of the answers we're still searching for can be found in this painting.' Adam goes over to look at the bold, brightly coloured artwork on the wall.

'And this clock,' I say, doing the same to the grandfather clock.

'What do they have in common?' Adam asks, examining the painting. 'Other than the fact they both came from my grandfather's house and the time is the same on both clocks? And why is this piece of artwork so different in style than all his other paintings? There has to be something else, something we're missing …'

'What about the matching trees?' I say.

'Yeah, they're the same shape and they both have the exact same number of branches – twelve. Argh, this is all so frustrating,' Adam says, his brow furrowing. 'I feel like the answers are all there, but we just can't see them!'

'Let's have our breakfast. Maybe some food and some coffee will help our brains to think a little more clearly.'

We begin to tuck into our pastries. But something else from last night is still bothering me.

'Adam?' I say, when Adam has just taken a huge bite of his apple turnover.

'Mmm.' He tries to reply politely with his mouth full.

'When you opened up on the bench outside yesterday about what had happened to you, I was really touched you shared that with me. It meant a lot – really, it did.'

Adam finishes chewing. 'I don't tell many people about it. Only those that matter.'

'Thank you. Then it means even more in that case.'

'Maybe one day you'll share all your dark secrets with me too?'

My heart stops. *How does he know?*

'You don't need to pretend to look shocked,' Adam says, taking a gulp of his coffee. 'I know you're far too pure to have any deep, dark secrets to share…'

Oh … he's joking with me.

'So we'll have to reserve our lovely old tree outside for lunches and coffee breaks only from now on.' As Adam glances out of the window at the little garden, his amiable expression changes and he frowns.

'Is everything all right?' I ask.

He suddenly cries out, 'Oh, my God, that's it!'

'What's it?' I ask, confused.

'The tree!' Adam says, rushing to the doorway of the shop. 'The tree in the middle of Clockmaker Court. It's the same as the tree in the painting and the same as the tree on the grandfather clock!'

'What?' I mumble, for a second not following.

'It's only been staring us in the face, Eve!' He turns back towards me. 'I can't believe I've only just noticed it. Look.' He looks out through the open doorway again. 'One, two, three …' He quickly counts the branches of the tree. 'Twelve – just like in the picture and on the clock.'

Adam heads outside towards the tree, so I follow him, pulling the door of the shop closed behind me.

'How long do you think this tree has stood here?' he asks, standing underneath the branches and looking up. 'Oaks have long lives, don't they?'

'I believe so.'

'So what would you guess with this one?'

'I don't know. It looks pretty old, though.'

'She's a beauty, isn't she?' Rocky calls out from across the court and we turn to see him clearing one of the tables outside his café.

'She sure is,' Adam says. 'Do you know how old she might be?'

'I read once that oaks grow for three hundred years, live for three hundred years and die for three hundred years,' Rocky says. 'Some even live for over a thousand years. That one looks pretty old to me. It's a wonder her roots have never disturbed any of these old buildings, really. They must be pretty big.'

I'm just about to ask Rocky if he knows anything else about oak trees, when Harriet appears.

'What's going on?' she asks. 'Why are you all staring at the tree?'

'Just admiring it, my love,' Rocky tells her.

Harriet looks at us suspiciously.

'Hmm … probably be for the best if the damn great thing was cut down,' she says to my surprise. 'It casts a ridiculous amount of shadow over all the buildings. It would be nice to get some more sunshine in here occasionally.'

'Oh, no, love,' Rocky says in protest, disagreeing with Harriet for once. 'That's history right there. Just imagine all the things that tree has seen over the years. It was probably here before any of these buildings were. Maybe that's why Clockmaker Court was built like this in a circle. It was built around this old tree.'

A woman with a baby in a buggy wants to enter the café, so Harriet hurriedly ducks back inside to allow them to enter.

'Well, I think it's pretty awesome,' Rocky says, now Harriet is out of earshot. 'It would be a travesty if it was cut down.' He smiles at us as he lifts his tray of empty dishes and heads back into the café.

'I wonder if this tree *is* older than Clockmaker Court,' I say, looking back up at its gnarled, twisty old branches.

'And almost more importantly right now, does it have anything to do with our hidden room?' Adam asks, doing the same.

'Do you think it might, then?' I turn and look at Adam. 'I mean, it is similar to the trees on the clock and in the painting, but are we reading too much into this?'

'Trees do seem to be a theme, though, don't they?' he says, meeting my gaze. 'The clock, the painting and now this one.' He walks forward and places the palm of his hand on the sturdy trunk. 'I bet you've some stories to tell.' He strokes the rough, knotted bark. 'I bet you know the answers we're searching for.'

'Something else is bothering me,' I say as I look up at the old tree and wonder if Adam might be right. 'I'm sure I've seen another tree like this somewhere before.'

Adam turns back to face me.

'I don't mean I've seen oak trees before,' I continue. 'Of course I've seen them many times. But it's the emblems – something about the simplicity of how the trees have been depicted in the painting and on the clock. It seems familiar.'

'What in the name of Mary are you two up to?' Orla asks from her shop doorway. 'You'll be hugging it there next, Adam. I thought tree-hugging was much more up my street than yours.'

'We were just wondering how old the tree was?' I answer quickly. 'Any idea, Orla?'

Orla looks up at it. 'Pretty ancient, I'd say. Our tree has a lot of wisdom in its branches, that's for sure. You know, in Celtic mythology it's said an oak tree is a door to ancient wisdom or knowledge, possibly even entry to the otherworld, the realm of the fairy.'

'I'll give you ancient,' Adam says, smiling. 'But I have to draw the line at fairy. Surely even you don't believe in fairies, Orla?'

'It's not a case of believing,' Orla says serenely. 'It's a case of knowing. The Celtic word for the oak tree is *daur*, which is where it is believed we get the word "door" from today. So it makes perfect sense an oak tree is the door to somewhere new. Are you all right there, Eve? You look a little unnerved by what I'm saying?'

'Not at all, Orla. It all makes perfect sense to me.'

Orla looks surprised I've taken what she's said so easily, and without question.

I calmly turn to Adam. 'Adam, I've just remembered where I've seen that other oak tree before … In fact, we both have.'

21

'Are you sure it's in there?' Adam says. 'Maybe we left it in the house?'

'I'm certain of it,' I reply from behind a pile of boxes. 'I have an inventory of everything I brought from your grandfather's house, I remember clearly noting it down.'

I closed up the shop a little early tonight, and Adam and I travelled to the lock-up in my little van. Now, while Adam waits, I'm scrabbling about behind a load of boxes trying to find it.

'Yes!' I exclaim as I see a flat piece of oak wedged behind the frames of some large oil paintings. 'I've found it.' I tug at the wood, but it's stuck tight. 'Argh! I can't shift it.'

'Do you want me to try?' Adam says.

The area behind the boxes is small, cramped and also very dark without the use of a torch, and after what Adam told me yesterday, I'm worried about asking him to go in there. But if we don't get the piece of oak out this way, we will have to move all the boxes and then the paintings before we can get to it, and it will take ages.

'If you're sure?' I ask hesitantly. 'The area behind here is quite … snug.'

'Claustrophobic, you mean?' Adam says, knowing exactly what I'm suggesting. 'Don't worry, I'll be fine, Eve. Now let me help you back over the top.' I climb back over the boxes and Adam offers me his hand as I'm about to jump down.

His gesture is very sweet and gallant, and once more, as I take hold of his hand, I can't help but like it. 'Thank you,' I say, feeling a little shy, as what can only be described as a warm glow spreads right through me.

Is it my imagination or is Adam holding my hand for a little longer than is strictly necessary now I'm back down on the ground?

I glance up at him to see if he might be feeling something similar. But as our eyes meet, this seems to jolt him back into action and he quickly drops my hand.

'Right, then,' he says with a brief nod of his head. 'My turn!'

Adam, looking incredibly athletic, leaps effortlessly up onto the boxes and then does a sort of vaulting movement down over the other side, looking like a gymnast doing the perfect dismount from the pommel horse. Whereas when I climbed over, I sort of grappled myself up on top of the boxes, then rolled, or rather fell, inelegantly over the other side.

'Can you see it?' I ask, holding my phone torch high in the air so he's not in the dark for too long.

'Yep, I can see something that looks like what you described, wedged behind these paintings.'

'Yes, that's it. Can you get it out?'

I hear some tugging sounds and Adam grunting.

'Christ, it's wedged tight,' he says. 'Right, one … last … *pull*!'

I hear a sort of scraping noise. 'Have you got it?'

'Yep! I'm going to pass it over the top to you.'

A thick piece of oak appears from behind the boxes and I carefully lift it down over the other side. It's followed by Adam, looking a little more red-faced than before, climbing carefully this time over the top of the boxes.

'You were right,' he says, standing back to look with me. 'There is a tree carved on there that looks just like the others. So now we have three trees – four if you include the one in the middle of Clockmaker Court.'

What we're both looking at is a small door carved in solid wood. It has a bronze handle and bronze studs around the outside, and, just like the door on the grand-father clock, in the middle there's the simple carving of a tree.

'It's small, isn't it?' I say, looking at the door. It can't be much more than five feet tall. 'If this is a standard door, it's going to be pretty old. People were much shorter in the past, so they didn't need such tall doorways as we do now.'

'Why would my grandfather have this in his house, though? It definitely wouldn't fit any of the door frames there – they were all standard height. Remind me where you found it again?'

'Tucked behind some of the other furniture in his study – the bookcases, I think. It was the day when the company came in to remove the big bits of furniture I couldn't take. They took the bookshelves after we'd emptied them and this was behind one of them.'

'Right, so, along with a modernist painting, a grand-father clock and an actual living tree, we also now have a tiny door carved of... oak?' Adam asks.

'Yes.' I rub my hand over the door. 'I think so.'

Adam shakes his head. 'This mystery just gets stranger and stranger as each day passes.'

'But with no apparent solution… yet.'

'Only Barney's idea.' Adam suggests this as if he doesn't really want to.

'That it's time-travel related? We both thought that – it wasn't just Barney. Do you *really* believe that?'

'I don't know what to believe any more.' Adam sighs.

'Why don't we take this door back to my house tonight, get some food and think some more about it. There's nothing more we can do here.'

'Good idea!'

After we've driven back towards my house and safely parked up the van, Adam carries the door from the garage to my house. When we get inside, he props the door up in the lounge against the wall next to the fireplace. When he's finished, I open two bottles of apple cider and pass him one.

'Thanks,' he says, taking a swig. 'That hits the spot on a warm day.'

I do the same. 'So, what do you fancy?'

'To eat?' he asks, his blue eyes twinkling.

'Yes,' I reply, hurriedly pulling open a drawer and rummaging about inside. My stomach does that flip-flop thing again, like it's on a rollercoaster, only faster. It seems to be happening a lot around Adam recently. 'I should have some menus in here somewhere.'

'Sure,' Adam says, sitting down on the sofa. He takes another sip of cider while he looks thoughtfully at the door in front of him.

'Er… I can offer Chinese, Mexican, Thai, burgers and kebabs, pizza or good old fish and chips. Any of those sound good?' I ask, choosing my words carefully this time.

'I'm easy,' Adam says, leaning back on the sofa and resting his elbow casually on the arm. 'What would you like?'

I'm shocked when I find myself having to fight hard against the voice inside me that's shouting, *'Say* you! *Say* you!'

I swallow hard and take another gulp of my cider. *I have to get a grip. I just can't stop staring at him. Why is Adam so incredibly attractive?*

I mean, I've always known that he's attractive. He's a very good-looking man. But just lately he's become… hot. And him doing that stupid twinkly thing with his eyes isn't helping either. And now he's running his fingers through his hair. Oh, God – stop!

'Eve?'

'Er …' Annoyingly my cheeks flush and I quickly turn away on the pretence of selecting one of the menus. 'Chinese?' I say, grabbing the menu from the side.

'Sounds good to me.'

I pass Adam the menu from my local Chinese takeaway and take another sip of my cider. While he browses the dishes, I kneel down and take a closer look at the door.

'What are you looking at?' Adam asks, glancing up.

'I don't remember seeing an apple on the tree before, when we pulled it out of the lock-up,' I say, putting my drink down on the coffee table behind me. 'Look, there's a tiny apple carved there on one of the branches.'

Adam kneels down next to me and inspects the carving. 'So there is. I guess we could have missed it before; it wasn't the best light in there.'

We both turn to look at each other and our eyes lock once more. There's no doubt in my mind this time – Adam's expression completely mirrors my own feelings of desire. Like an incredibly strong magnet pulling me towards him, I find myself unable to do anything else other than lean forward and kiss him.

For one awful moment I think Adam isn't going to respond to my advance, and my impulsive feelings rapidly begin to subside as another feeling begins to emerge – humiliation. I'm about to pull away and apologise, to say I don't know what came over me, when I feel his hands gently cup both sides of my face. His lips don't need words to express what he's thinking – their message is crystal clear...

22

Later that evening, I'm lying in my bed gazing at the ceiling and feeling extremely naked underneath the duvet, and, for the first time in a very long time, there's a man lying next to me, equally bereft of clothing.

But surprisingly, to me at least, I don't feel worried or regretful. I just feel... happy.

'Well, that was a surprising turn of events this evening.' Adam is turned towards me, his bent arm supporting his head while his elbow rests on the pillow.

I glance up at him and see a kind and concerned face looking down at me. I smile at him. 'It certainly was. A rather nice surprise, though, don't you think?'

'Absolutely! How do you feel about it?' he asks a little hesitantly. 'Honestly?'

'Honestly... I feel completely fine.'

'No regrets?'

'No, none at all. Why, do you?'

'Of course not. I just didn't think you were that into me, that's why I ask. It all came as a bit of a shock when you kissed me.'

'It was a bit of a shock for me too. I don't usually behave like that.'

Adam smiles. 'I'll take that as a huge compliment, then. So, what changed?' He slides down onto the pillow so he's level with me.

'I really don't know. Something just came over me, and, well, you saw what happened next.'

'I sure did.' Adam grins. 'I had a ringside seat!'

'Aw… stop. You're embarrassing me.'

'You're so cute.'

'Am I?'

'Yeah, I love that you're all coy now and I adore it when you blush. You go pink just here.' He leans forward and lightly kisses my cheek. I close my eyes at the touch of his lips. 'And here…' he says in a whisper, about to kiss my other cheek. But something makes me pull away before he does.

'What's wrong?' he asks, as I try to do that thing they do in movies when the woman elegantly pulls a sheet around her as she leaves the bed to hide her modesty. Except I have an extra-thick, king-sized duvet, half of which is over Adam right now. So instead I simply end up naked at the side of the bed, while the duvet remains firmly covering Adam's modesty instead. I quickly reach for the blanket that hangs over the back of my dressing-table chair and wrap that around me instead.

'Nothing is wrong. I just need the loo, that's all.'

I hurry to the en-suite bathroom, drop the blanket and sit down on the toilet seat to think. A wave of uncertainty has suddenly washed over me.

Oh God, what have I done? Has sleeping with Adam messed everything up? I bury my face in my hands. *But it isn't like Adam is doing his best to leave immediately, is it? He seems quite happy about the situation. In fact, he seems* very *keen to stay…*

A vision of Adam lying naked under the duvet floats back into my mind. His muscular chest covered in just the right amount of hair. His kind blue eyes that twinkled like sapphires when he was enjoying himself. His dishevelled dark hair that he has a habit of running his fingers through, making my stomach do silly things when he did. The stubble on his square jaw that I felt gently brush against my face and my body when he kissed me with his incredibly soft lips...

I shake my head. *Right, stop that right now! You're getting distracted. You need to think clearly about this.*

It feels like there's a little white angel on one shoulder and a little red devil on the other having a rather heated argument.

The angel speaks now. *Getting into a relationship with Adam is asking for trouble. He works next door to you. If you break up, it will be really awkward, not just for you, but for everyone else on Clockmaker Court too.*

The devil pipes up. *You aren't even in a relationship. You've just had a one-night stand – a little bit of fun. And it was really good fun, wasn't it? Why don't you go back through that door for some more... It's been a while, Eve, and he is really handsome...*

'Enough!' I hear myself saying out loud this time and I immediately clap my hand over my mouth.

'Are you all right in there, Eve?' Adam calls from the bedroom.

'Yes, yes, I'm fine.'

'Would you like me to leave?' he asks now.

This time I don't have to think. I jump up, forgetting I don't have the blanket around me any more, and pull open the door.

'No, I don't want you to leave.'

Adam looks me up and down and smiles. 'You don't know *how* pleased I am right now that you said that.'

When we finally extract ourselves from the bedroom, it's too late to order any food, so instead Adam insists on making me cheese on toast. Which he does extremely well.

'This is lovely, thank you,' I tell him as we sit together on the sofa. I'm now wearing the very unsexy items of pyjama bottoms and a T-shirt, and Adam has pulled his jeans and shirt back on. But his shirt is only half buttoned up, leaving the incredibly arousing view of his rather lovely chest partially on view, and I have to keep averting my eyes to prevent a repeat of before happening.

'I'm glad you like it. Do you want to talk about what happened earlier?'

'Which particular time?' I ask, grinning.

Adam raises his eyebrows suggestively. 'I actually meant what happened when you rushed to the toilet. That wasn't just because you needed to pee, right?'

Adam said he could read me like a book.

'No, it wasn't just that. I panicked.'

'Why?'

'It's been a while since I've been in that situation with a man,' I answer honestly. 'And I wasn't sure what I wanted.'

'I think you made that pretty clear when you came back to the bedroom!'

'Funny. No, I mean... look, I just overthought every-thing, that's all. I'm fine now.' I take another comforting bite of my cheese on toast.

'I don't make a habit of one-night stands, if that's what you were wondering?' Adam says. 'Maybe in the past that suited me. But not now. As I said earlier, tonight completely surprised me. But I'm glad it happened – really I am. Clearly I find you attractive, that goes without saying.'

I feel myself beginning to blush once more.

'But I didn't want to act on it before, because I didn't think you felt the same way.'

'I didn't know how I felt until this evening. Actually, no, maybe it was earlier today when we were having our breakfast in the shop.' I think again. 'Or maybe even earlier than that. I thought we might have had a moment last night when we were down in the office together.'

'You felt that too, then?' Adam asks. 'Over the negatives?'

'Yes, exactly then. I mean, clearly you are a very attractive man. I've known that from the moment I met you.'

Adam smiles. 'You didn't let on.'

'Because you were also very annoying back then too,' I say, grinning. 'And full of yourself.'

'Steady,' Adam says, but he's still smiling. 'Don't ruin it.'

'I don't want to ruin anything,' I say. 'I feel like I'm living in a very strange fairy tale right now with everything that's been going on, and like in all good fairy tales, I've just kissed the handsome prince!'

Adam grins. 'I'm pleased I got cast in that role in your fairy tale. A while ago you'd have cast me as a troll or a gremlin, or something equally as annoying.'

'Nah, I wouldn't do that. Maybe an ugly sister ...?' I grin at him.

'I knew it was too good to be true,' Adam says ruefully. 'I should have quit while I was ahead. Talking of fairy tales, I couldn't help but notice your collection of children's books up in your bedroom when I was getting dressed. Some of those editions look quite old.'

'You're not having them to sell in your shop if that's what you're thinking!' I say, still joking with him. I'm really enjoying being with Adam tonight, not just when we were upstairs but now, simply sitting on the sofa with him eating toast and having a laugh.

'As if. Have you collected them over time?'

'Some of them. But most were my grandmother's. She used to read them to me and my sister when we were younger and we came to visit her and my grandfather.'

'That's nice. Happy memories?'

'Of course. I loved coming here to Cambridge to visit them.'

'Did you live far away?'

'Brighton.'

Adam nods, but still presses on with his questions. 'Big family other than your sister?'

'No, not really.' I can feel myself beginning to close up as I always do when my family is mentioned. Like a turtle retreating into its shell for protection when it senses danger, my instinct is to immediately hide away from this difficult subject. But at the same time, I also want to confide in Adam as he confided in me yesterday. 'There was only my mum, my dad, my sister and me,' I say, remaining out of my shell for a tad longer than usual. 'We were very close.'

Adam nods. 'You were lucky. I didn't have any brothers or sisters to be close with. It was just Mum and me. I was never that close to my father when he was actually around. But I'm sensing you don't like discussing your family too much – am I right?'

I nod. 'Sorry, I know you've shared a lot with me, but I just find it really difficult.'

'That's OK. I understand. It takes time.' Adam looks around the room for something else to talk about. 'So, of those children's books upstairs, what's your favourite?' He's deftly changed the subject and I'm grateful to him.

'Hmm... good question,' I say, relieved. 'I don't know... I was always quite keen on Enid Blyton as a child.'

'Lashings of ginger beer and all that!' Adam says, smiling. 'Yes, I remember them fondly too. I used to read them with my mother.'

'What was your favourite to read with her?'

'You'll laugh,' Adam says, looking a little sheepish.

'No, I won't.'

'It was *The Hundred and One Dalmatians*. I loved it. I remember asking my mother constantly if we could have a Dalmatian dog after that. I used to watch the Disney movie, too, on repeat. That was in the days of VHS, of course, and it was changed to *101 Dalmatians*. Why they thought the original title wasn't good enough, I'm not sure ... Eve, what's wrong?'

I blink at Adam as my mind spins.

'My grandmother had a copy of that book too,' I reply slowly, my brow furrowing as I remember. 'But she wouldn't let me look at it for some reason. It always sat up on a high shelf, annoyingly just out of my reach – which was odd because both my grandparents always let me touch stuff. I helped out in their antiques shop, for goodness' sake, so they knew I could be trusted with delicate things.'

'Why didn't your grandmother hide the book away if she didn't want you to touch it? It seems a bit harsh to have something on display teasing you like that if she didn't want you to read it.'

'Unless she *wanted* me to know it was there – to be aware of it so I'd remember it.'

'Like my grandfather did with the painting from his study. He was always pointing that out to me for some reason too. But why would they do that?'

My brain races. 'There has to be a reason why both these things were made known to us. We know why the painting was now, but why the book ...?' This is so frustrating. I just can't put my finger on the answer ... 'Oh, my God!' I stand up, just catching my plate in time before the toast crumbs go everywhere. I shake my head. 'No ... it can't be ...' I stare blankly in front of me.

'What can't be?' Adam asks. 'What are you talking about, Eve?'

I turn and look at Adam. 'I think we might have found our missing book.'

'What missing book?'

'The books with the hidden notes inside. The books with titles numbered one to twelve?' I say to remind him. 'We're still missing eleven, aren't we?'

'Yes?' Adam says, not understanding.

'*The Hundred and One Dalmatians*, Adam. Or more commonly known these days as *101*. That's two ones ...'

'But I don't have a copy of that book any more and neither did my grandfather. I know what I put in my children's section in the shop and Dodie Smith was definitely not one of the authors.'

'You might not have a copy of it,' I say, smiling triumphantly. 'But I do ...'

23

'*The Hundred and One Dalmatians*!' I say triumphantly,
holding up a copy of the book. We had to search through
several boxes of my grandparents' things before we finally
found it. And now we have, I am ecstatic. I just know this
is going to mean something significant. 'Now we find
out if my theory is correct!'

Slowly I open up the cover of the vintage hardback
book, but, to my surprise, I don't find pages of text inside,
but a small, flat box.

'It's a fake book!' Adam looks as amazed as I am by
what we're seeing. 'I've heard about these, but I've never
actually seen a vintage one like this.'

'I've had a few pass through the shop,' I say. 'But
they tend to be generic leather-bound volumes, used by
people to hide important and valuable things. Definitely
not children's books.'

I lift out the plain wooden box, then try to open the
lid.

'It's locked,' I say, looking at Adam.

'Then there really must be something inside that no
one else is supposed to see. What sort of a lock is it – not
a combination again?'

'No, it needs a key this time.'

'Any idea where the key might be?' Adam asks hopefully.

I think about it for a moment before my face lights up.

'Yes, as a matter of fact, I do!' I race back up the stairs and pull open the bottom drawer of my chest of drawers. Then I lift my grandmother's old jewellery box out from under some winter jumpers. I quickly open the lid to see if what I'm looking for is inside, then I hurry back down the stairs.

'It's in here,' I say, opening up the jewellery box again. 'My grandmother used to wear a silver key on a chain around her neck. I bet it fits this box.' I lift a silver chain with a tiny key hanging from it and try it in the lock. There is absolutely no doubt in my mind that this is going to fit and my thoughts are confirmed when we hear a satisfying click. I lift up the lid of the box to see what's inside and find a neat stack of three identical envelopes.

'What do they say?' Adam asks excitedly as I lift them from the box.

'The first one is addressed to Sarah,' I tell him. 'Do you think that's my grandmother?'

'It must be, if it was hidden in here with her things? What about the other two?'

I pause on the first envelope for a moment, before putting it down.

'The next one says *Eve* on the front, and the third is addressed to you.' I show Adam the envelope with his name on. 'They're all in different handwriting, though.'

'Why would there be one addressed to me?' Adam asks, looking puzzled. 'Your grandparents didn't know me, did they?'

'Not that I'm aware of.' I stare at the three envelopes. 'Should we read them, do you think?'

'They are addressed to us.'

'But which one first? Oh, there's a tiny number on the back of this one and the other two as well. So there's clearly an order in which we're to read them.'

'There you go, then,' Adam says. 'What are you waiting for?'

I hesitate with the first envelope in my hand. It's the one addressed to Sarah.

'I don't know. What if it's private?'

'Eve, you must see we've clearly been led here to this moment? Someone wanted us to read these letters – otherwise why would they have all been hidden together like this, and two of them addressed to us?'

I nod. 'You're right. Of course you're right.' Carefully I open the first envelope that has *Sarah* handwritten on the front in black ink, and I read aloud.

'*My beautiful Sarah. If you are reading this letter, my darling, then I am not with you any more. Please never think for one moment I did not care for you or love you. I absolutely adored you – you were my whole life and I would have done anything for you.*

'*But I had to put right our mistake. I had to give another mother the chance to love and care for her own child, just as I did mine. It was my fault that the chance was taken from her and I had no choice but to try to right a terrible wrong.*

'*You will grow up not knowing me, only your father. Remember, he is a good man and nothing that has taken place is his fault, so please don't blame him. The fault lies entirely with me. Sometimes the right thing to do in life is not always the easiest. But I hope by now you understand that.*

'*I wish with all my heart that you have a wonderful life filled with love and happiness, and that one day you can forgive me and know that what I did was the right thing to do, for us all. Your ever-loving mother, Dorothy xx.*'

'It's from Dotty,' I say quietly as I stare at the letter. Suddenly this person, who I've only ever heard about from others, or seen black-and-white photos of, is real. Her words are real. Her love for her daughter is real. It's as if she's here in the room with us, telling us how much she loved her child, and how she didn't want to leave, but she had to – but why?

'May I see?' Adam asks. He prompts me when I don't reply. 'Eve?'

'Sorry, yes, of course,' I say, passing him the letter.

Adam quickly reads through Dotty's letter. 'What's this bit about giving another mother the chance to love and care for her own child? And righting a terrible wrong?'

'It sounds like she was trying to put something right – something that she thought she'd caused to happen. I knew she must have gone missing. I knew she hadn't simply died in some random accident never to be found again. It was all too easy to say that, to make that excuse.'

I can feel myself getting angry now on Dotty's behalf.

'I must admit I thought the same thing,' Adam says. 'It all sounded a bit dodgy from what you told me. But I didn't like to say anything. It's your family.'

'Yes, it is,' I say with conviction as I make my mind up about something. 'And I'm going to find out exactly what happened. I'm going to uncover Dotty's real story. Instead of all this murkiness surrounding her name, future generations of my family will know exactly what happened to her.'

'I really admire your determination,' Adam says. 'Truly I do. But we've still got two more letters to read yet. They might be of more help to us than you charging off on your own personal crusade – as admirable as that is, of course.'

I nod, realising that he's absolutely right.

'Why don't you read the letter addressed to you next?' Adam says. 'I wonder who it's from?'

'I know who wrote this letter before I even open it,' I tell him, lifting the second letter up. 'This is my grand-mother's handwriting.'

Again I carefully prise open the envelope and begin to read out loud.

'*This letter is for Eve. If you are not Eve, and for some reason this letter has fallen into the wrong hands, then please put it back where you found it, for what I have to say next is of no interest to anyone but Eve Sinclair or Adam Darcy.*' I look up from the letter at Adam. 'She did know you … but how?'

'I've a feeling we're going to find out,' Adam says. 'If you keep reading.'

'*My darling Eve,*' I continue. '*If you have found this box and matched it with the key, then it's likely what I'm going to tell you next will make some sense. If, however, you have simply stumbled upon the contents of this copy of* The Hundred and One Dalmatians *and somehow paired it with the right key, then I suggest you lock the box and wait until the time is right to open this book again. You will know when.*

'*What I'm about to tell you has to be written in a sort of code. A code that, if you're my Eve, you will easily be able to decipher, of that I have no doubt.*' I pause to look at Adam again. 'Not another code …'

Adam looks equally as disheartened by this news.

'*If everything has gone to plan and you have met Adam, you will by now have many questions. Some of which may have been answered, but I suspect many will not. You may even suspect that your chance meeting with Adam was not chance after all and you would be correct. It was always the plan – you two were always destined to be the ones.*' I glance at Adam again to see how he's receiving all this.

'The ones?' he asks.

'Let's find out,' I say, looking down at the letter again. *'As you know, I grew up without my mother, your great-grandmother. She disappeared towards the end of the Second World War. In 1945, my father took me to the USA to be with his family and then later decided to settle back here in Cambridge, the area he was stationed in during the war.*

'What you do not know is how my mother disappeared. That I cannot tell you here, in case this is read by someone other than yourself and Adam. This is a secret that once you uncover, you can tell no one else – unless you trust them with your life.

'What I can tell you now is:

'Look out for Venus and Mars – they will guide you to what you need to know.

'Ask Freddy to come and visit.

'There is someone close who will have many of the answers.

'The Romans knew their numbers.

'Hide-and-seek, Eve.

'Put right the mistakes of others only. You are here to help those that are lost, not yourselves.

'Your heart will guide you. When your mind says it's not possible, trust your feelings.

'I'm so sorry I cannot be clearer about any of this. But you will soon come to understand why. And please remember, even though you may feel like it at times, you are never truly on your own. GG xx.'

I gaze at the letter in my hand. My grandmother died so many years ago that having this letter here in my hand feels like she is right here with me again. Every word I can hear in her soft, gentle voice. A voice that was never raised, but was always listened to by everyone. Because what she said always meant something. Her words were always worth listening to. Just like they are now. But what is she trying to tell us and why is everything so secret?

'Are you all right?' Adam asks. I carefully place my grandmother's letter next to Dotty's on the coffee table in front of me and it feels like I'm reuniting them once more.

'Yes,' I say quietly. 'It's just so odd hearing them both speak like that. Obviously I didn't know Dotty, but that letter sounded just like my grandmother.' I touch both letters again as though I'm making sure they're comfortable – like a mother putting her baby to bed. And once again I feel the pull not only towards Dotty's loss, but to my own mother as well, whose touch I haven't felt for such a long time either, and the strength of feeling and connection I suddenly have to all three of these women is so powerful, it's almost frightening.

'It was definitely written by your grandmother – you're sure of it?'

Adam's voice breaks my spell. But I'm not annoyed – I'm simply grateful to have him here with me as I discover all this. 'Yes, it's definitely her handwriting,' I tell him. 'I always called her GG – it was a nickname. I couldn't say her name properly when I was small so I called her GG instead.'

'I can see that reading those letters have really affected you,' Adam says. 'Do you want to go on?'

'Of course I do. This has made me even more determined to find out what's going on here – I owe it to *all* the women in my family. Plus, we still have your letter to read.'

Adam lifts the third envelope from the box. 'It's incredible how certain people were that we'd meet one day,' he says as he looks at his name written on the front.

'I know. That would be strange enough on its own, but it's only *one* of so many odd things happening to us.'

Adam opens his envelope and begins to read aloud.

'Adam, it's your grandfather here.' Adam smiles. 'This already sounds like him. He was always to the point.

'When you read this, I will likely be dead. Don't spend time mourning me, dear boy. You have far more pressing things to attend to.

'If you haven't done so already, make sure you give plenty of time to a young lady called Eve. She will be performing my house clearance if all goes to plan. Eve is very important to what happens next.' Adam glances at me. 'None of these letters have dates on them. I wonder when they were written?'

'Go on,' I say.

'If you are reading this letter, you will likely also have discovered the special books from my bookshelves, and, if Gerald plays his part correctly, now be in possession of the bookshop too. He knew?' Adam looks shocked. 'So much for my own free will. It seems I was always destined to have the bookshop!

'The bookshop will do more for you than touring around with those popular music bands ever did. And if she's anything like her grandmother, so will Eve.'

Adam glances at me and I feel my cheeks begin to flush.

'You both had to be told, but in a way that no one else would understand. So my apologies for all the puzzles and clues, but hopefully this will allow you to discover the truth without others finding out.

'Sarah helped me concoct this whole plan. She was definitely the brains of the whole thing. Without her to help me, I'd have been quite lost. Both Lily and Bill were unaware of what was going on, and when I say going on, I don't mean any funny

business, you understand — I mean in terms of the plan. Bill?' Adam asks.

'He was my grandfather. Was Lily your grandmother — George's wife?'

Adam nods. '*I believe Sarah will give you the rest of the clues you both need to succeed. So it's just for me to wish you both the very best of luck. I never said this when I was alive, Adam. But I was and still am very proud of you. Warmest wishes, your grandfather, George. P.S. Always remember the apple doesn't fall far from the tree.*'

'Are you all right?' I ask as Adam continues to stare at the letter.

He looks up and I notice his eyes look a little misty. 'No one ever said they were proud of me before. I mean, maybe my mother, but I can't really remember now.'

I squeeze his hand. 'Your grandfather was obviously very proud. He seems to be entrusting something quite important to you.'

'To both of us, it would seem. But what is that something?'

24

The next afternoon, Adam and I are waiting for Freddy, my clockmaker friend, to arrive at the shop.

I phoned him this morning and asked if he could call in at the shop as soon as possible, and he promised to come this afternoon.

Adam's plans to open his shop have had to be postponed. He planned to open today, but, after what we found out last night, he decided to delay the opening and concentrate on the latest instalment of our mystery.

'Saturday is a good day to open anyway,' I told him. 'More people around.' I wasn't happy. I didn't want him to delay opening a business he's already put so much work into. But Adam was insistent.

While we wait for Freddy to arrive, we go through the contents of the letters once more. I thought a bit about it last night before falling asleep. But Adam stayed the night and having someone sleeping next to me in my bed, when I was so used to sleeping alone now, felt very strange indeed.

'*Venus and Mars* ...' I say, reading from my grandmother's letter as I lean up against the wooden cash desk. 'It rings a bell. Isn't there a painting called that?'

'I assumed it meant the planets,' Adam says, sitting in a Lloyd Loom chair.

'It could well do ... I'll check online.' I look around and lift my phone from the counter. 'Yes, it's a painting by Botticelli. *Venus and Mars* is also a studio album by Wings. Could that mean something, do you think, with your music background?'

'Paul McCartney's band after the Beatles,' Adam says, thinking. 'Hmm ... I don't think so. But I can't say I'm particularly familiar with it.'

'We'll go back to that clue, then. So hopefully we'll know about the Freddy reference when he arrives. What about: *There is someone close who will have many of the answers?*'

'Someone in Clockmaker Court, perhaps?' Adam glances out of the window.

'Possibly, but who? Ben, maybe – he knew your grandfather.'

'Yeah, he'd be a good place to start. How about we try to talk to him later, when we've seen this Freddy. Now, what's next?' Adam stands up from the chair, walks around the desk and puts his arm around my waist while we read the letter together. Although it feels a little odd to have him this close to me in the shop, I can't deny his touch feels incredibly comforting.

'Erm ... *The Romans knew their numbers.*'

'Roman numerals, perhaps?'

'Yes, that's what I thought too. Have you seen any lately?'

'They're everywhere, aren't they? Even the grandfather clock over there has Roman numerals on its face.'

'True. Perhaps it is another clock reference. It would make sense. Now ... *Hide-and-seek*. I really have no idea what that means at all.'

'It says Eve, so I really think it's aimed at you.'

'True. Hmm …' I rack my brains trying to think what that could mean. 'I can't think of anything right now. And the last two seem like they are guidance of sorts. Let's hope Freddy can shine some light on it all when he arrives. Otherwise I think we're going to be stuck once more.'

'Freddy!' I call from the doorway as I see him walking towards the shop a while later. 'Thank you so much for coming at such short notice.'

'Anything for the Sinclair family,' Freddy says, kissing the back of my hand in greeting. 'You know that.'

Freddy is a tall man, with white hair and wire-rimmed spectacles perched on the end of his nose. He carries a black cane with a silver tip, and he wears what I can only describe as dandyish clothing – velvet jackets, ruffled shirts, that type of thing.

Today he is sporting a navy-blue smoking jacket with a white shirt, a brightly coloured cravat perfectly tied around his neck, and emerald-green trousers.

'And who may this be?' he asks, looking Adam up and down.

'This is Adam. He owns the shop next door.'

'Adam …' Freddy looks surprised. 'And you have the shop next door now?'

'I do,' Adam says, holding out his hand to Freddy. 'Pleased to meet you.'

'The pleasure is all mine, dear boy,' Freddy says, shaking his hand, then mumbles almost to himself: 'You were right, then, Sarah. Good on you both.'

'What are you saying, Freddy?' I ask.

'Oh, nothing, my dear. Nothing you need to worry about, anyway. Your grandmother always said she'd match you up with an Adam one day, and it would seem she was right.'

'Oh … Adam and I aren't …' *Actually we kind of are now.* 'You see, we …' I glance at Adam. He just nods.

'And you'd be right, Freddy,' I say, surprised how good this feels to admit. I look at Adam again, and he smiles.

'Can I get you anything, Freddy?' Adam asks, as Freddy sits elegantly down on the chair Adam had been sitting on earlier. 'Tea, coffee … juice, perhaps?'

'Kind of you, dear boy, but no. I stopped for a cup of tea at Fitzbillies on the way here. Charming as always.'

'Adam is very partial to their Chelsea buns,' I tell him.

'And why wouldn't you be? They perfected that recipe over a hundred years ago when they first opened. It should be the best and it still is. Anyway, enough talk of cake,' Freddy says. 'Wonderful though that is. What can I do for you today?'

'I was hoping you could tell me, actually. I found a letter,' I say carefully, 'from my grandmother, and she said to ask you to come and visit the shop.'

'Did she now … for what purpose?'

'I'm afraid I don't really know.'

'I see … well, let me take a look around.' Freddy scans the shop from his chair, his hands resting on the top of his cane. He does this slowly, taking in everything on view in the shop bit by bit. Finally, his gaze rests upon the grandfather clock on the wall opposite.

'Where did you get that?' he asks, pointing his cane at the clock. 'Quite the beast. I don't think I've ever seen such a large specimen.'

'In a house clearance,' I reply, not wanting to lead him at all.

'A house clearance … where?'

'In Grantchester. It was Adam's grandfather's house.'

'I see.'

'I was actually going to call you about it when I first got it, but then I found out it wasn't working because it has no mechanism inside.'

'Really … open, please.' He gestures to the door of the clock now.

I go over and open it up. 'See, nothing.'

Freddy nods knowingly. 'That door is not the original,' he says. 'It's been replaced.'

'This door,' I say, swinging the door to and fro on its hinges.

'It's not a revolving door, my dear, be careful with it.'

'Sorry, how do you know it's not the original door?'

'I just do. The wood is not the same grain, for one thing.'

Both Adam and I examine the door.

'He's right.' Adam kneels down next to the clock. 'It is slightly different.'

'How did I not notice this before?' I ask, annoyed at myself.

'No one other than an expert would notice,' Freddy says. 'Don't reproach yourself too much, my dear. In fact, I'd say that was never supposed to be the door of a clock case; it's far too thick. Clock-case doors are much more delicate usually. There's no need for them to be great chunks of wood like this one is. Far too heavy.'

'I did think it was a funny weight when we carried it into the shop. It makes sense now you've said that.'

Freddy leans forward in his chair. 'Do I spy something on the other side of that door? Some detailing. Engraving, perhaps.'

I open the door of the clock as wide as it will go. 'Yes, there is! Look, Adam.'

Adam comes over to the other side of the clock and I open the door as far as its hinges will allow.

'It's only another tree again!' he says. 'Perhaps a bit fainter than we've seen before, but it's definitely there, carved into the wood.'

'Yes, I can see it too,' I say. 'It looks like half a tree, though, this time, and there's another carving at the side. What is that? It looks like an arrow. Is it pointing at something?'

Freddy stands up and comes over to inspect the carving with us. He leans down by supporting his weight on his cane so he can peer more closely at the door. 'I'd say that's the Greek sign for male you've got there,' he says, pointing with his cane again. 'You see there – the arrow looks like it's coming out of the side of the circle. This side would have been the front of the door when it was first used. There are still marks where the original hinges would have been. Can you see?'

Adam and I both look closely, and I can just make out some marks at the side of the door, which are partly covered by newer, much smaller hinges.

'This would have been part of a pair of small doors originally, and this door was the right one.'

Freddy returns to his seat.

'I don't suppose you have the other one to make up the pair, do you?' he asks while Adam and I still look at the door. 'Did you see anything else like this at your grandfather's house, Adam?'

'No,' Adam says honestly, looking at me now. '*I* didn't see one at all. But Eve has a door that looks *extremely* like this one, don't you, Eve?'

Adam returns to my house to collect the door while I see Freddy off, promising to keep him updated on our progress. Then, while I wait for Adam to return, in between customers, I sit and think about everything that has happened so far.

'You OK, my lovely?' Luca asks a few minutes later, making me jump as he pauses in the doorway of the shop. 'You looked away with the ... how you say, er ... the fairies, just now.'

'Hi, Luca, yeah, I'm fine. Just got a lot going on right now, you know?'

'You should never have so much going on that it puts a frown on your pretty face!'

I smile at him. 'Thanks.'

'Where is Adam? I thought he was opening up his shop today?'

'He's postponed it for a few days.'

'How so?'

'He's got some stuff going on, too.'

Luca narrows his eyes. 'The same stuff as you, by any chance?'

I can't help smiling. Suddenly I want to share my exciting news with someone else, and who better than one of my best friends. 'Perhaps ...' I grin.

'I knew it! Tell! Tell!' Luca rushes into the shop and hops up on the counter.

'There isn't really that much to tell. Things sort of escalated last night when he came back to mine for some food.'

Luca nods approvingly. 'And?'

'And ... I'm not going into details, Luca.'

'Once. Twice?'

'Three times, actually,' I say quietly, a tad embarrassed.

'Really? My goodness, we've got ourselves a stallion!'

'I hardly think I'd call Adam a stallion!'

'I don't know,' Adam says, grinning in the shop doorway. 'I think it kind of suits me.'

'A strong stallion too!' Luca says, glancing admiringly at Adam's biceps bulging under his shirt as he comes into the shop carrying the oak door. 'You lucky, lucky girl.'

I turn my back to Adam and pull a face at Luca. 'Was there something you wanted, Luca?' I ask, my cheeks burning bright red.

Luca winks. 'Ah, yes, I bring a message! Well, an invitation, really. We are all going for some drinks tonight at the pub, if you'd like to join us? It's for Rocky's birthday.'

I turn to see what Adam thinks.

'Sure, sounds good,' Adam says. 'What time?'

'Six,' Luca says. 'No, I stand corrected. It's six-thirty.'

'Six-thirty it is,' Adam says. 'We'll see you there.'

'Great!' Luca hops off the counter. 'Then I shall leave you lovebirds to it! Don't do anything I wouldn't do! Ciao for now, darlings!'

Luca skips out of the shop.

'Well?' I ask Adam, immediately turning my attention back to our door.

Adam turns the door around and I see the remnants of another carving just like the one on the clock door. 'It's very similar,' he says. 'It's like a mirror image of the other door, so both sides hung together would make up the whole tree. The only difference is this one has a different symbol at the side. It's the Greek symbol for a woman this time. I looked it up before I left your house.'

I kneel down in front of the door to examine it more closely.

The engraving of the tree has faded over time, like the engraving on the inside of the clock door. But you can definitely see it, and next to it this time is a circle with a cross underneath. Like someone has drawn a stick man without legs.

'It is the same,' I say, looking across the shop at the clock. 'We should put them both together.'

'Do you have a toolkit? If you have, we could remove the door from the clock and properly stand them both together.'

I fetch the toolkit I keep behind the desk, and, using a tiny screwdriver, we remove the screws that hold the hinges onto the clock case. Then we stand the two doors together.

'It's a perfect match,' Adam says, looking at the doors. 'Freddy was right. These doors were once a pair.'

'But why are there symbols for a man and a woman either side of the tree?' I ask.

'Could they be ancient toilet doors?' Adam asks. 'What?' he says when I laugh. 'I'm serious.'

'I highly doubt it. These doors look like they're a lot older than the invention of men's and women's toilets!'

I have a couple of customers come into the shop, so Adam steps outside while they look around. They browse for a few minutes, but don't buy anything.

'Venus and Mars,' Adam says as he comes back into the shop.

'What?'

'The two symbols. That's what they originally represented. I've been looking it up. In ancient astrology they symbolised Venus and Mars. It was the Romans who named their gods after them. Venus, the goddess of love, and Mars, the god of war. Eventually they came to represent woman and man. There's a lot of theories on the internet, depending on your point of view, how they came about. But this is the most common consensus.'

'Venus and Mars will guide you to what you need to know …' I say, staring at the doors again.

'Who knew it would be a pair of wooden doors,' Adam says, doing the same as me. 'The question is, what were they originally attached to? I'm sure they're too small to be regular doors.'

We both look at the doors, hoping something will spring into either of our minds, but frustratingly nothing does.

'I feel like we're *so* close to this,' I say in an exasperated voice. 'So close, we're in touching distance of figuring it all out.'

'I know.' Adam puts his arm around my shoulders. 'I'm as frustrated by this as you are right now.'

'We can't let this delay the opening of your shop any longer,' I say, turning towards him and putting my arms around his waist. 'You've worked too hard.'

'Yes, I have, but—'

'No buts! You open tomorrow. I know you don't want to cover up the door in case we need to go down there again. But if we do, we'll move the bookcase. We've done it before and we'll do it again.'

Adam smiles. 'You're very sexy when you're bossy, you know?'

'Good, I'm glad you like it.'

We lean forward to kiss, but just as our lips meet, there's the noise of someone clearing their throat.

'I'd ask if I'm interrupting,' Barney says, grinning in the open doorway. 'But I think I already know the answer to that.'

Adam and I immediately pull away from each other.

'Barney!' I say, surprised to see him. 'What are you doing here?'

'I have news!' Barney says. 'I've been doing some digging in the university's records and I think I've found out something you both might find very interesting …'

25

'Barney, you've not done anything illegal, have you?' I ask, immediately concerned he's been up to things he shouldn't.

'Eve!' Barney says in protest. 'Is that really your first thought? Doesn't think much of me, does she?' he says to Adam.

Adam smiles.

'Let's just say,' Barney continues, 'I'd probably be in trouble if I was found to be searching through secret files, but it was totally worth it.'

'Why are they secret?' Adam asks.

'All in good time,' Barney says, clearly enjoying his reveal. 'Now, are you going to put the kettle on or shall I? This isn't a quick story, but I think you're going to think it's very worthwhile listening to.'

I quickly make three cups of tea. Adam and I pull up a couple of chairs and then Barney begins his tale.

'So, I've been doing some detective work about the time that Archie owned the shop next door. I don't know if you know, but all Cambridge professors have records kept about them – they include what they achieve while they are part of the university and usually what they get up to after they leave.'

'I thought they just stayed on in the job until they croaked it,' Adam says. 'Like a perk of the job.'

'Many of them do,' Barney says. 'But for those that leave, their university usually likes to keep a record of what they go on to do. You can access pretty much any information on the university's database about any staff member – that's the point of it being there. All the old records that were kept on paper have been copied and uploaded too. But when it came to Professor Archibald Darcy, the records just stopped in 1940.'

'How do you mean, stopped?' Adam asks, frowning.

'It said he'd been seconded by the government to work on a top-secret project and he would return to his job at the university after the war was over. That was nothing unusual in 1940, I'm sure.'

'But he never did go back, did he?' I say, looking at Adam. 'You said he went missing.'

'I said it was likely he had a breakdown. That was the story passed down in my family, that he'd gone a bit mad after the war. Barney has sort of confirmed that now. Poor old chap.'

'I'm not finished,' Barney says. 'There's more. When his records just stopped abruptly, I tried to do a bit more digging. So I found my way to where the old paper files are stored – they've never been destroyed even though most of the information has been uploaded onto the database. It's an old building at the back of the university – no one really knows it's there. It's just an old prefabricated hut, really.'

'How do you know about it, then?' I ask.

Barney taps the side of his nose. 'People underestimate us support staff. We know everything that's going on in the university and if we don't, we usually know someone who does. Everyone thinks it's the professors and the deans who are the clever ones, but it's the people doing what they'd class as the menial jobs that actually run the place.'

'Go on,' I say to encourage him.

'So, anyway, I decided to head out to this building and see what I could find. I'd managed to obtain the keys too.'

He raises his eyebrows at me, but I just shake my head. I don't approve of what he's done, but I can't deny it is quite intriguing so far.

'I was just about to go inside when this old fella stops me,' he continues. 'I guess I wasn't as stealthy as I thought in my chair. It does make doing things secretly quite difficult − you tend to stand out in a crowd instead of blend in.'

'What did the guy want?' Adam asks.

'This is where it gets a bit weird.' Barney frowns. 'He asked what I was doing, so I said just looking for some files. I held up the keys as if I was supposed to be there. He said some files on who? I debated whether to lie or tell the truth, but there was something about the old guy that made me want to tell him, so I did. I said I was look-ing for information on Professor Archibald Darcy, and I thought the guy was going to pass out on the spot.'

'Goodness, why?' I ask.

'He just went totally white. Then his expression changed from shock to relief. He said he'd been waiting for so long for someone to turn up asking for information on that person. And he couldn't believe it had finally happened.'

'Blimey,' Adam says. 'What happened next?'

'He asked why did I want to know more about the professor and I said it was do with something called

Project Eden, and I swear his legs almost gave way. Then he looked around him like they do in movies to check if anyone was watching us. When he seemed happy the coast was clear, he asked did I know an Adam and Eve?'

'Whoa, he didn't?' Adam says, looking shocked, and I notice he's barely touched his tea.

'He did. I said that's who I'm here for, and he looked like he might cry. I was a bit worried for the old guy, to be honest, so I said would he like to get a cup of tea somewhere? He agreed and so we went to a café.'

'Then what happened?' I ask eagerly.

'Once we'd got a cup of tea each, Ernie – that's the old guy's name – told me all about how Roger, his father, knew Archie during the war. Roger had worked at the university with Archie, before Archie had left to work with the government on something top secret. But they had stayed in touch, often going for a drink at the pub together. Archie would never say what his top-secret project was. But Roger knew that Archie met Dotty at RAF Duxford when he'd gone there to scout for an assistant to help him. He'd been very impressed with her, and had secretly enlisted her to help him with his war work.'

'We wondered how Archie and Dotty had met, didn't we, Adam?'

Adam nods.

'Ernie said he'd also met Dotty.'

'*Really?*' I'm amazed that Barney has spoken to someone who actually knew my great-grandmother.

'Yes. Archie enlisted his friend Roger's son as a sort of runner for him when he was working in Clockmaker Court. Ernie was a young boy at the time, and he would carry messages to and fro for both Dotty and Archie when they were working, and sometimes fetch them things. He said he often worked alongside George, Archie's son.'

'Ernie knew my grandfather too?' Adam asks in amazement.

'Apparently. I asked where in Clockmaker Court Dotty and Archie were working and Ernie said they would meet him or George in the bookshop, but he wasn't sure where exactly they did their work, because it was just a bookshop as far as he was concerned. He assumed there must be a room at the back of the shop. But in the war there were a lot of secret things going on, so you learnt not to ask too many questions.'

'So the office was a secret, then?' I say, looking at Adam. 'I mean we thought it might be, but, hearing this now, it definitely was if Ernie didn't know where they went.'

'It would seem so,' Adam says, and I can see he's trying to piece together what all this means as Barney talks, just like I am.

'Ernie said this secret project continued through the rest of the war, even after the funding was withdrawn in 1944,' Barney continues. 'Apparently Archie was still committed to the project, even after the war ended, which Ernie thought was strange because he'd assumed it had been for the war effort, so why continue after the war? Anyway, Ernie said it wasn't long after that Archie became a little odd – as he described it – and he started to say some strange things before he disappeared. But by then Ernie was older and he had a new job himself, so he didn't think too much about Archie, Dotty, or his time in Clockmaker Court. That was until his father came to the end of his life about twenty years ago, and began talking about Archie and the war again. It was then his father said – and *this* is the important bit ...' He pauses for dramatic effect, looking between the two of us.

'Come on, Barney!' I say when he holds his pause a bit too long. 'We need to know.'

'Ernie's father told him that one day an Adam and an Eve would come asking questions at the university about Archie and a Project Eden, and if Ernie came across them, he must tell them to find the *timekeeper*. The timekeeper in Clockmaker Court will have all the answers.'

Barney stops talking and looks at both of us expectantly, as though we might now be able to fill in all the missing answers.

'Who or what is the timekeeper?' I ask.

'How the hell should I know?' Adam replies, holding up his hands in despair.

'Could it be the pub?' Barney asks. 'That's called The Timekeeper?'

'Oh, yes,' Adam says excitedly. 'So it is!'

'It's not actually in Clockmaker Court, though,' I say. 'Is it? But it's worth bearing in mind,' I add when their faces fall. 'It might be related. Did he say anything else, Barney?'

'Not really. That's all Ernie knew. I think he was just glad to be able to tell someone after all this time.'

'But he knew about us, Barney?' I ask. 'You said he mentioned an Adam and Eve.'

'He did. He asked me how I knew you and I told him I worked at the antique shop with you, Eve, and Adam had the bookshop next door, and he seemed more than happy to hear that.'

'But how did he know you'd be turning up at the records place at that exact time if he'd been waiting for a long time for this?'

Barney smiles. 'Now this is the really clever part. He'd got one of his grandchildren to put some sort of tracker on Archie's name on the database so that if someone started looking him up suddenly, Ernie would get an alert and know to go to where the paper records are kept – and that's exactly what happened when I was checking the database before work this morning. I couldn't get out to the shed until this afternoon because of work, so goodness knows how long he'd been waiting there for someone to appear.'

'And Ernie definitely thought this timekeeper was in Clockmaker Court?' I ask, trying to clarify everything in my own head.

'He was adamant about it.'

'So,' I say, looking at Adam again. 'No biggie. If it's not to do with the pub, all we need to do is discover which of our neighbours here might be otherwise known as the timekeeper.'

26

Barney joins us at the pub that evening, after we've filled him in on everything else that's going on.

Adam quietly pulls me aside before I tell Barney, reminding me what my grandmother's letter says about only telling people I fully trust. But I quickly reassure him that I 100 per cent trust Barney. He's already been there with us when we've made many of our discoveries, and he's been super helpful, so he deserves to know everything.

We hope at the pub we might be able to surreptitiously question our fellow shopkeepers while they are having a drink and discover who might be the infamous time-keeper. But instead our questions are expertly evaded at every turn. So we leave the pub even more confused than before, and decide to go back to Adam's flat to try to make sense of everything.

To my surprise, Barney declines the offer.

'Oh, God, it's the stairs, isn't it?' I say, suddenly realising, and I'm annoyed with myself for not considering Barney before deciding to go to Adam's.

'It might be a factor,' Barney says in his usual matter-of-fact way.

'Then we'll go somewhere else,' I say. But my house also has the main living area upstairs, so that won't be any better. We've just come from the pub and that's far too busy tonight to discuss the kinds of things we need to.

'Really, it's fine.' Barney shrugs. 'I'm used to it.'

'No, it's not fine!' I say crossly. 'You're as much a part of this as we are now. I want to hear your take on everything. It's not fair if you miss out.'

'I don't know if this is the right thing to suggest,' Adam says quietly. 'But I can carry you up the stairs, Barney, if that would help. Or would that be totally condescending and wrong?'

I close my eyes, fearing what Barney might say. But I'm surprised to hear him respond favourably. 'On this occasion, Adam, that would be great, thanks.'

So I watch as Adam carries Barney – who isn't a particularly large young man, but still must weigh plenty – effortlessly up the stairs to his flat, where he places him carefully on the sofa.

'Cheers, Adam,' Barney says, arranging himself more comfortably. 'That was good of you.'

'No problem, mate. You're no heavier than some of the equipment I used to lug around in my touring days.' Adam winks at Barney and then nips downstairs again to lift Barney's wheelchair up the stairs too.

'You can at least be independent up here,' Adam says, putting the chair next to Barney. ''Cos there ain't no way I'm carrying you to the toilet, fella!'

Barney laughs and I breathe a sigh of relief as the atmosphere in the room relaxes.

'Did you notice how they all evaded our questions tonight?' I say to them both, when Adam has got us all a bottle of beer and we're sitting in the lounge waiting for yet another takeaway to be delivered. I feel like I'm living on takeaways right now, but there always seems to be something going on that prevents me from eating my usual healthy-ish meals. Maybe one day Adam and I might be able to go out to dinner in a restaurant, just the two of us, and talk about the sort of things that normal couples did – but then, when was it any fun to be normal?

'I did notice that,' Adam says. 'Do you think that was deliberate? Or were we reading things into it that weren't really there?'

'Difficult to say?' Barney says. 'But we did the right thing by pressing them. How else are we going to find this timekeeper?'

'I actually thought at one point they might be questioning us?' Adam says. 'Or was that just me.'

'No, I thought that too,' I say. 'But why would they do that?'

'How about we go through everyone one by one,' Adam says. 'See if we can rule anybody out of the equation.'

'Worth a go, I suppose.'

'So we definitely think the timekeeper is someone who lives here in Clockmaker Court?' Adam asks.

Barney nods.

'Yes,' I say. 'It must be. Well, at least someone who has a shop.'

'Why not the others who use the buildings as offices and flats?' Adam asks.

'They come and go,' I say. 'But the shops have all been here for … well, as long as I can remember.'

'What, all of them?'

I think about this. 'When I started helping my grand-parents out, Harriet and Rocky were here, and Luca too.

Orla had been here for a while, I think, and Ben has been here for ever, as we all know.'

'So the shops haven't changed much, then?'

'No, not really. Actually, not at all. Gerald owned the bookshop next door before you did, and Ben said before that, Ozzie, Gerald's father, had owned it. So that's been here ages too.'

'Right then, so what do we know about all these people?' Adam asks, sounding like a detective in charge, summing up the case so far with his team. 'Do any of them have families?'

'Not that I know of ...' I say, suddenly realising that I don't know that much about any of my fellow shop-keepers. 'But they must do, I guess. Do you know, Barney?'

'No, come to think of it, I don't remember any of them ever talking about families. But then I'm not here as much as you, Eve.'

'Harriet and Rocky are married ... but don't have any children,' I say, trying to add something useful. 'I think Orla's family must live in Ireland ... not that I remember her actually saying that, though. Luca ... I mean, I know he has partners, I've met some of them before, and we both met some friends of his from the States, didn't we, the other night at the pub?'

Adam nods. 'Yes, they were friends, weren't they, not family?'

'I guess. And I don't think Ben has family either ... when he was ill a while back, Orla went to look after him because he had no one else.'

'So not one of us has ever heard any of the others talking about a family?' Adam says, his eyebrows raised.

'But that doesn't necessarily mean anything,' I say quickly. 'I mean, you and I don't have any direct family still alive, do we?'

As what I'm saying begins to register in my brain, I stare at Adam, and he, looking equally as surprised, gazes back at me. I turn to Barney.

'Barney, please tell me you have family somewhere?' I ask desperately.

Barney slowly shakes his head. 'Not blood relatives, I was adopted when I was a baby. So I've only ever known my adoptive parents.'

As we sit silently trying to take in exactly what this means, the doorbell rings, making us all jump.

'That must be the takeaway downstairs,' Adam says. 'I'll be right back.'

'What's happening, Eve?' Barney asks. 'I'm getting a really weird vibe about this.'

'I don't know, Barney. I wish I did, but I don't.'

Adam comes back up with the Indian takeaway we've chosen tonight and after we've plated everything up, we sit back down to eat.

'Do you want to continue our discussions?' Adam asks. 'Or shall we wait until after we've eaten?'

'I don't know about you two,' I reply. 'But it's all I can think about right now.'

'Me too.' Barney picks up a poppadom. 'I don't know how we can't continue to talk about it.'

'Right, then.' Adam takes the lead once more. 'So apart from the family thing, which we don't know is relevant yet, what else do we know?'

'What about these doors you have in the shop?' Barney asks. 'Should we discuss them a bit more?'

'The Venus and Mars doors,' I say. 'With the tree in the middle of both of them. We've had a lot of tree symbolism and this is just the latest one.'

'Do you have the letter from your grandmother?' Barney asks. 'The one with the clues on it?'

'Not on me. I thought it best if we keep it safely locked away in the shop safe. But I took a photo of it. Here.' I pass him my phone.

Barney quickly reads through the letter. 'Do you think *There is someone close who will have many of the answers* could be the same person as the timekeeper?'

'I think it's more than likely.'

'So the only clues you have nothing on is *The Romans knew their numbers* and *Hide-and-seek, Eve*?'

'We think the first one is Roman numerals of some sort.'

'But you've no ideas on hide-and-seek?'

I shake my head.

'Did you used to play hide-and-seek as a child?' Barney asks.

'I guess I must have.'

'Don't you remember?'

How could I tell Barney I blocked many of my childhood memories a long time ago. Remembering what I once had is too painful.

'Not really.'

Barney glances at Adam.

'Could you try, Eve?' Adam asks softly. 'I know it's difficult for you, but it might help?'

'All right, I'll try.' But after a few moments, I shake my head. 'Nope. I'm sorry. Nothing.'

Adam glances at Barney this time, and I snap at them.

'You two can stop with all the looks. I am trying. Really, I am.'

'We didn't say you weren't,' Adam says calmly. 'You're the one who seems a bit jittery when we talk about hide-and-seek.'

'I just don't remember, that's all. And even if I did, what connection could those two small doors have with my childhood? It's not as if I used to play hide-and-seek in a cupboard with those two doors on it. I think I'd remem — I stop suddenly. Something is jolting in the back of my mind.

'What is it, Eve?' Barney asks. 'Have you remembered something?'

'Give me a minute,' I say, thinking hard.

I close my eyes. My mind doesn't want to go back … but I force it to. 'I did used to play hide-and-seek …' I say as a distant memory begins to swirl in my head. 'With my grandmother when she was younger and more agile …' I can feel my face screwing up as I push my mind to go deeper. 'I used to hide in a sort of half-dresser thing … no, it wasn't a dresser … it was a cupboard with two doors and it was built into the wall … a bit like a cupboard under the stairs. Actually, that's exactly what it was – a cupboard under the stairs.' My eyes fly open. 'I used to play hide-and-seek with my grandmother in a cupboard under the stairs. That's it, I'm afraid.'

'Were the doors wooden with engravings on them, by any chance?' Barney asks excitedly.

'Not that I remember.'

'Oh.' Barney sounds disappointed. 'That's a shame.'

'Not necessarily,' Adam says slowly. 'If your grand-mother was trying to tell you something by mentioning hide-and-seek, do you think she was hinting at something similar – a cupboard recessed into a wall or a cupboard under some stairs?'

'Perhaps. But where would that be? We used to play hide-and-seek in her old house – not the same house I have now, but their previous home.'

'What about if it was here?' Adam says, thinking again. 'In Clockmaker Court. What about down in our hidden office? You have to go down some stairs to get to that, don't you?'

'But we didn't see any cupboards when we went down there,' I say. 'Only filing cabinets and desks.'

'What if the cupboard was hidden by one or two of the filing cabinets? They were big enough.'

It takes a moment for what Adam is saying to sink in, then I cry out excitedly, 'Let's go take a look! This could be it!'

'Now?' Adam asks, sounding remarkably calm.

'Yes, now. Why not?'

Adam glances at Barney.

'Don't worry about me,' Barney says. 'I'll stay here if there are stairs involved. You two go.'

'No way, José,' I tell him. 'You're coming too.' I look at Adam and he nods.

'Too right you are. That's if you don't mind me lifting you again?'

Barney grins. 'Of course not. Come on, then! What are we waiting for?'

'It's like I've stepped into the forties,' Barney says in awe, looking around the office. 'Either that or a really good museum.'

We got downstairs to the little office in stages.

First Adam lifted Barney down into the bookshop, and then he went back for his chair. Then we opened up the metal door and I went first into the darkened room, and then down the stairs to switch the lights on. Adam then followed carrying Barney, and again went back for his chair, in which Barney is now sitting, looking around the room in amazement.

'Now to see if we were right,' Adam says, looking at the filing cabinets in the office. 'Come on, Eve, I might need a hand moving these.'

Adam and I begin to push one of the large metal filing cabinets away from the stair wall. 'Blimey, this is heavy,' I say, struggling to push. 'It's just as well we've brought the muscle with us. Eh, Barney?' I wink at him.

'Indeed,' Barney says. 'Although, I'll sit this one out if I may. You two look like you've got it covered.'

Although I am helping to heave the huge filing cabinet away from the wall, I'm sure it's really Adam who's doing most of the work.

'There is a door!' I shout out excitedly as one side of a pair of doors is revealed. 'Look!'

Adam puffs. 'Let's get this other cabinet moved first, then I'll look.'

We both push the second filing cabinet in the opposite direction and again we find another small door concealed behind it.

'Right,' Adam says, still puffing a little. 'Shall we see what's inside?'

'Do it!' Barney says encouragingly.

Adam pulls on one of the doors, but it doesn't open. He then pulls on the other. 'I don't believe this. Now these doors are locked too. Why is everything locked all the time!'

I look around to see if there's keys hanging anywhere. Then we all start opening drawers in the desks and the filing cabinets to see if we can find one.

'Here!' Barney triumphantly holds up a large key and wheels himself towards the doors. 'It only bloody works!' he says as the key turns easily in the lock. Barney gives a tug on the first door, then reverses back a little to fully open it.

'What can you see?' I ask.

'Nothing. It's just dark.' He pulls open the second door. But the same greets us – only darkness. 'It's just an empty cupboard,' he says disappointedly shining his phone's torch around. He wheels himself forward a little, until he's able to get all the way inside. At Barney's height in his wheelchair, he doesn't need to bend his head. 'Yep,' he says. 'It's a hell of a cupboard, but there's just a wall here at the end.' He reverses himself back out again. 'Now what?'

'Why would someone hide this cupboard behind these filing cabinets if it wasn't important?' Adam says. 'There are other walls these cabinets could have stood against that didn't block it.'

'Do you think your doors would fit this opening?' Barney asks, his head tilted to one side. 'I only saw them briefly today, but I reckon they look a similar size to these ones.'

'They might,' I say, trying to size them up in my mind. 'Should we try them, do you think?'

'What would be the point?' Adam asks. 'Nothing is going to change if we attach two new doors to this empty cupboard.'

'That is where you are wrong, I'm afraid.' A familiar voice comes from the top of the stairs. 'Things *will* change, and dramatically so. For us all.'

27

'Ben?' I walk to the bottom of the stairs to greet him. 'What are you doing here? And Orla!' I say as I spot her standing next to Ben. 'Why are you here too?'

'I'm just here to support Ben,' Orla says in her usual calm manner. 'This is a big day for him.'

I wonder what she means.

'I see you've all discovered the office,' Ben says, looking as far into the room as he can from his viewpoint.

'We have, but what do you know of it?'

'Probably a lot more than I should. Could we possibly continue this conversation up here?' Ben asks. 'These stairs look a bit uneven for me, and as you've probably noticed, I'm not as steady on my feet as I used to be.'

'Of course.' I look back at the other two.

'Let's go up to my flat,' Adam says. 'I don't want to have to carry Ben up the stairs if he gets stuck down here.' He winks at Barney. 'No offence, Ben!' he calls up the stairs.

Ben calls back to him, 'None taken, young man! Good thinking.'

Luckily the stairs up to Adam's flat are much newer and deeper than the uneven, narrow stairs down to the basement office, so Ben is able to make his way slowly, but safely, up them. 'I hope you don't mind, Adam,' he says as he arrives at the top. 'I let myself into the shop downstairs before. I still have a spare key from when Gerald was here.' He hands a bemused-looking Adam a brass key as he makes his way through to the lounge area.

'So,' Ben says, as finally we all get settled back in Adam's flat. Ben and Orla on the sofa, Barney in his chair, and myself and Adam sharing one of the armchairs. 'You're probably wondering what I have to do with all this, and as I said before, the answer is a lot more than I should.' Ben smiles at us all. 'It's a long story.'

'We've got all night,' Adam says. 'Take your time.'

'Should I begin, Orla?' Ben asks, turning to her. 'Or would you like to? I'm afraid my voice might give up before the end otherwise.'

'Shall I fill them in on the history side of things and you do the other bits?' Orla asks gently, leaning towards Ben and putting her hand on his arm.

I look between the two of them. What is going on here? What has Orla to do with all this now?

Ben nods. 'That's a good idea.'

'Right, then, let's give it a go.' Orla looks around at us all. 'As you probably know, Clockmaker Court has stood on this spot in Cambridge for many hundreds of years. It was built around the old oak tree that stands in the middle of the court out there. That ancient tree, and its predecessors before it, have stood here for many more centuries than this court has.' Orla pauses to see if we're taking all this in, then, happy we are, she continues.

'The court was built with twelve buildings originally. Even more than it is now, the number thirteen back in the day was considered extremely unlucky, so twelve buildings were built, and because they resembled a clock face, it was eventually named Clockmaker Court. Twelve is also a very common number for units of measurement – have you ever stopped to notice just how many things are counted in twelves?'

She looks around at us all.

'For example, a dozen eggs, the twelve days of Christmas, twelve inches to a foot, twelve months in the year and even, historically, twelve ounces to a pound. They are all measured using the number twelve.'

'So why is there a building missing?' Adam asks. 'Why are there only eleven buildings now if there were originally supposed to be twelve?'

'For as long as anyone can remember, building number seven has been missing. But there's a reason for this – because building number seven marks the exact spot of a portal.'

She pauses to judge our reaction to this word.

Adam looks immediately sceptical. Barney's eyes light up. Ben's expression doesn't change, and I … well, I'm just wondering what on earth is going on.

'The portal,' Orla continues, 'has been on this very spot for millennia. Before the buildings, possibly even before any of the oak trees. The current oak tree was planted to mark the spot when the previous tree died away.'

'What are you talking about when you say a *portal*?' Adam asks suspiciously.

'A portal is a gateway into another world,' Orla says without a hint of hesitation. 'Like I suggested to both you and Eve when you were outside examining the oak tree, remember?'

'How could I forget,' Adam says, raising his eyebrows. 'Is everyone else hearing this like I am? Eve?' he asks, looking at me.

'It does sound a little strange, Orla,' I say almost apologetically.

Orla nods. 'That's because it is strange. It's a phenomenon few get to experience.'

'So where do we all come into this *phenomenon*? And Ben too?'

Orla looks to Ben. 'Would you like to come in here, Ben?'

'I think I'd better. You've done a great job at explaining it so far though, Orla, thank you.'

Orla smiles serenely.

Ben looks around at us all. 'My name is actually Benjamin Johnson, and I was born in 1894 during the reign of Queen Victoria.' He pauses to get our reaction to this.

Poor Ben, I think immediately. *Is he getting a bit confused? Maybe Orla should have carried on for him for a while longer.* But something about Ben's face suggests he knows exactly what he's saying and I feel the hairs on my arms begin to prickle.

'I know you're old, Ben,' Adam says, his eyes shining. 'But you look damn good for ...' He quickly does the maths. 'One hundred and thirty years old!'

Ben just nods calmly. 'Like I said, I was born in Cambridge in the Victorian era.'

'I'm sure you told me once you were just a boy after the Second World War ended ...' I think about this for a moment. 'Yes, you did! You said you could remember queuing up outside Fitzbillies for Chelsea buns when you were young.'

'That is correct; I did do that,' Ben says without hesitation.

'But you just said you were born in 1894. If that's true, then you'd have been fifty-one at the end of the Second World War.'

'Why don't you let Ben tell you his story, Eve,' Orla says gently. 'All will become clear in time.'

'Sure.' I sit back in my chair with Adam. I feel Adam's arm go protectively around me and I'm really glad he's here.

'I came to Clockmaker Court in 1944 when I was just ten years old. Where I met my soon-to-be best friend, George, who was *your* grandfather, Adam. I also met Archie and Dotty too.' He turns to me. 'You remind me so much of her, Eve. Not only your looks – you both have the same kind yet determined spirit and you're fiercely protective of what is important to you.'

'Thank you,' I reply, a little taken aback by this. *Ben knew Dotty too? All this time and he's never said anything to me before. But why?*

'Archie and his wife, Violet, kindly took me in when I arrived and I grew up alongside George, who was a little older than me at the time, but still a young boy. As I've told you before, George and I used to spend a lot of time here in Clockmaker Court when we were young. At first we'd come to Archie's shop to read the comic books when he was working with Dotty. And then when Archie disappeared, and Violet, his wife, continued to care for us both, we would still visit, and Ozzie, who you remember I told you about before, would look after us. Both George and I loved our comic books.'

He pauses to remember.

'Hang on a minute,' Adam says, interrupting his memories. 'Those dates just don't add up.'

'Please, Adam,' Orla says. 'It's important you all listen and understand. Ben will explain everything to you if you're patient.'

Adam sighs with frustration, so I put my hand on his leg and give it a squeeze. In turn he rubs my shoulder to show he's understood. I'm desperate too to find out more about Dotty and what Ben knows. But we must all be patient with him while he tells us in his own way, and in his own time.

'When I became old enough,' Ben continues, 'I too took a shop here in Clockmaker Court. It had become clear by now that it was simply a waiting game and I wanted to be close by when it happened.'

Adam opens his mouth again, but Orla silently puts her finger to her lips.

'George by then had his career at the bank – he wasn't interested in being in Clockmaker Court. I think after what happened to his father, he wanted to get away from it, to be honest, and I can't say I blame him. His family still owned the bookshop, of course, but, by now, Gerald, who you knew, Eve, had taken it over from his father. Sarah, Eve's grandmother, came shortly afterwards, opening her antiques shop. We were the only ones who knew the secret and as we all grew older, we knew we had to put in place plans in case we all passed away before the time came. Your parents had sadly passed by then, Eve. So your grandmother was the only one in your family that knew, and your mother had also left us by then, Adam.'

Adam and I glance empathetically at each other, while Ben pauses to take a sip of the whisky Adam poured for him earlier.

'So,' Ben continues, 'we set about planning a series of clues and guides that would, we hoped, lead you to uncovering the secret when the time came. We had to be secretive – no one else could uncover this accidentally. It would be catastrophic if they did. I'm the only one left now of the four of us and it's wonderful to see that everything George, Sarah, Gerald and I put into place has led you both here to this moment – the books, the letters, the grandfather clock, and the painting. George did that, you know. He was quite talented artistically, but he loved his numbers more.' He stops to remember again.

Adam holds up his hand. 'Can I please ask a question now?'

'Yes, of course,' Orla says. 'I'm surprised you only have the one, though, at this stage?'

'I don't,' Adam says. 'I have many, because I'm not really following exactly what Ben is saying. But my main question is, what have Eve and I to do with all of this? You haven't explained that yet?'

'Ben, should I continue for a bit?' Orla asks, and I notice Ben is looking a little weary. Adam is right. So much of what he's saying isn't quite adding up and I'm beginning to wonder again if he's getting a little mixed up with his memories.

I'm also wondering just what Orla has to do with all this. But her steadying influence does create a sense of calm, when so much of what we're hearing right now seems like utter nonsense.

Ben nods his agreement.

'Our portal,' Orla says, taking up the story again – 'if we can go back to that – has always been guarded by someone who is close to this area. Someone who can be trusted with the secret. Before this was Clockmaker Court, there would have been a person who had a dwelling nearby, who would act as the protector. It was never something that anyone chose to do – they were the chosen ones. It's not known exactly when the carvings on the two doors you now have in your possession appeared, but what was immediately clear was what they both meant. The symbol for the planet Mars, and the symbol for the planet Venus, either side of a tree. It was quickly interpreted that these two symbols meant man and woman, and this over time understandably evolved into the story of Adam and Eve, and the tree in the middle of them was said to be the tree of knowledge, often known as the tree of life in Celtic folklore. Once these rumours began, it was of course hard to stop them and, through the following generations, whoever was the keeper of the portal passed this information down to the next in succession and so on, until it became widely known that on a particular date a boy and a girl would be born, who were to be called Adam and Eve.'

I turn to Adam to get his reaction to this news.

He simply shakes his head disbelievingly. 'Come on, Orla. Are you telling us that it's been predicted for hundreds or maybe thousands of years that Eve and I would both be born on this particular date? I know you believe in all this –' he waves his hands in the air – 'spiritual, airy-fairy nonsense, but even for you this is taking it a bit far, isn't it?'

'I didn't say I necessarily believed in the hearsay, I am simply telling you how this particular myth began. All myths and legends have to begin somewhere, with the smallest grains of truth. How they evolve usually depend on how much people believe in them.'

'Orla, what was the date?' I ask quietly. While Adam has been doing all the questioning for both of us, I've been thinking. 'You said this boy and girl were to be born on a certain date?'

Orla turns to me. 'That's correct. On each side of the doors you found, hidden within the tree trunk are carved two dates in Roman numerals. They both read the twenty-ninth of February – which of course is an unusual date in itself. How much do you both know about leap days?'

'They only come around every four years,' I reply.

'Exactly. Leap days are so much more than simply odd blips in our calendars,' Orla says. 'They serve a vital purpose in harmonising our earthly rhythms with vast celestial movements. They are a cosmic recalibration to ensure our calendars stay in perfect harmony with the cosmos.'

'If you say so,' Adam says, raising his eyebrows again.

'But what were the *exact* dates?' I ask again. 'Including the years.'

Orla nods. 'On the woman's side, it's twenty-ninth of February 1988 and on the man's, twenty-ninth of February 1984. And in the middle of the trunk is carved the date twenty-ninth of February 2024. The day the woman and the man would first meet.'

'And you're saying that these dates are carved into the bark of the tree on the two doors we have?' I ask, while both Adam and Barney can only stare wide-eyed at Orla as they register the significance of these three particular dates.

'Yes, but not only the doors,' Orla says. 'Those dates were added much later to the tree carvings – by who, we don't know. But the originals are carved into the trunk of the tree that stands in the centre of Clockmaker Court. This tree is where the wood for the two doors was originally sourced.'

Adam and I both look towards the window at the end of Adam's lounge.

'Why don't the two of you go and take a look?' Orla says. 'You'll find the carvings hidden around the back of the tree. The side that doesn't face out towards the majority of the court. They're very small, so they're barely notice-able, but if you look hard, you'll find them.'

'Would you like to, Eve?' Adam asks.

'I suppose we should.'

Leaving the others in Adam's flat, we both go down-stairs in silence as we try to comprehend everything both Orla and Ben have told us so far.

The cool of the clear night air is just what I need right now as we emerge outside into Clockmaker Court, and I pause for a moment to take a few deep breaths.

'Phew,' Adam says, after he's done the same. 'That's crazy what's being said up there. I need a moment just to try to get my head around it all.'

'Me too. What's going on, Adam? None of it makes any sense, and yet so much of it does?'

'I know, I feel exactly the same. My rational mind is just not believing any of it. But my gut is saying what they're telling us is true.'

I look across the court towards the oak tree.

'I don't know why we're looking, really,' Adam says, taking my hand. 'You know those carvings are going to be there, don't you?'

'Yes. But at least we'll be able to see how old the carv-ings appear. Which, with everything else we're being asked to believe right now, seems quite important.'

We walk across into the little garden at the centre of Clockmaker Court and then around to the back of the oak tree.

'Here,' I say, spotting the carvings after we've searched for a few moments.

'Where?' Adam asks, squinting.

'Look, just there, in the bark. They're really hidden. You wouldn't know they were there unless you knew what you were looking for.'

'But these look like the bark of the tree has grown around them over the years.' Adam squats down to examine the Roman numerals. 'I thought they would look like someone had carved them into the tree.'

'Like a vandal?'

'Yes, exactly that. Or when two people carve their initials inside a heart. These look like they've been here – for ever.' Adam runs his fingers over the carvings and then he looks up. 'What the hell is going on, Eve?' he almost whispers.

Unlike the Adam who was full of bravado and questions up in his flat, this Adam looks anxious and a little scared. I crouch down next to him. 'I don't know,' I whisper back. 'I wish I could tell you otherwise, really I do.'

I do something then that I've never done before with anyone else. I cup Adam's face with my right hand and gently stroke his cheek with my thumb. 'I'm as lost as you right now.'

Adam closes his eyes at my touch.

'I'm so glad this is you, Eve,' he says, opening his eyes again. 'I trust you. I'm not sure I trust everyone else up in my flat right now, but I love you.'

Adam stares at me, immediately registering what he's just said.

'Love or trust?' I ask quietly, not letting my hand drop.

'Both. Is that all right?' He matches my gesture by gently cupping my face with his left hand. 'I know we haven't known each other all that long but—'

'Of course it is,' I say, putting my finger on his lips. 'I feel exactly the same about you.'

We both lean forward and underneath the protective branches of the ancient oak, I have possibly the most romantic kiss of my entire life.

It doesn't matter for now the chaos that's ensuing just a few metres away from us up in Adam's flat. What matters is that we're together.

28

Eventually, after we can put it off no longer, Adam and I walk hand in hand back up to his flat and join the others.

'The carvings are there,' Adam tells Barney. 'Just like Orla said they would be.'

'Did you look at the doors in the antiques shop too?' Barney asks. 'Did they have the same markings on them?'

'Oh, no, we got a bit ... distracted,' I say. 'The bark of the tree was very interesting, though.' I glance at Adam. He smiles.

'Are we all ready to continue?' Orla asks, from the sofa. 'Ben, would you like to begin? Perhaps go back to explaining what happened in the war years?'

Adam and I take our place in the armchair again as Ben begins.

'As I'm sure the two of you have guessed by now, your great-grandparents were working together on a secret project during the later war years. It was called Project Eden, for all the reasons that Orla has explained already. I'm assuming you are all familiar with the biblical story of the Garden of Eden?'

We all nod.

'When war broke out in 1939, Archie of course already knew the secret that lay between his bookshop and the shop next door. Dotty's sister, Amelia, ran that shop as a dressmaker's at the time, but she was fully onboard with everything that happened in Clockmaker Court. Both your families have been keepers of the secret for many centuries and that's what they intended to continue doing – keep it a well-guarded secret. But when the war continued for longer than anyone expected, and Hitler and his forces continued to advance across Europe, Archie decided that they might be able to use the powers of the portal to help defeat the Nazis.'

Ben pauses to see if we're all keeping up, then continues.

'Archie stepped back from his work at the university and decided to fund himself in his own war effort – Project Eden. He needed help, so he enlisted Dotty, who, because she was the youngest in the family, knew nothing of the secrets of Clockmaker Court, only that her sister had a shop there. Dotty was in the WAAF at RAF Duxford – the Women's Auxiliary Air Force,' he adds, in case we don't know.

'I did know that,' I tell him. 'She was one of the first female engineers there. But I thought Project Eden was funded by the government at the time?'

'Who told you that?' Ben asks, his dark brow furrowing.

'A source,' I reply cryptically, not looking at Barney.

'I think that's what Archie told people who asked,' Ben says, not bothered in the slightest. 'He couldn't divulge the secrets of Clockmaker Court, in case, like I said before, they got into the wrong hands. So he funded the project himself and paid Dotty to come and work with him. Dotty had joined the WAAF thinking she'd just be doing clerical work at Duxford, but she quickly ended up in a more skilled hands-on role mending the aircraft. Dotty was bright and clever – the perfect partner for Archie. So the two of them began their secret war work in the basement of the old bricked-up building. The perfect hiding place. Very few knew they were there, and anyone who noticed their comings and goings was told it was for the war effort and they asked no more. That's what people did back then. So much was at stake, no one questioned someone else doing something secretive. It's just the way it was. Archie entered their office from the bookshop and Dotty from the dressmaker's. So they were rarely seen together.'

'Wait a moment,' I say, interrupting him. 'You're saying there was an entrance to the basement from my antique shop as well as the bookshop?'

Ben nods. 'It's probably still there.'

'Whereabouts?'

'Funnily, exactly where you positioned George's old grandfather clock.' He smiles. 'You must have sensed it.'

'Perhaps …' I think about the wall behind the clock in the shop. There is a recess there – that's why I stood the clock in it. Was that once a secret door?

'What exactly was this secret project they were both working on?' Adam asks. 'You said it was called Project Eden. But we still don't know what this big secret is that's down in the basement. Only that we shouldn't put the two doors back on the cupboard down there.'

Ben glances at Orla. She nods for him to continue.

'I'm surprised you haven't already guessed from what we've told you tonight. Maybe your rational minds don't want to believe, hmm?' He looks first at Adam, then me, and then Barney. 'They were attempting to perfect the art of time travel,' he says, pausing to get our reaction. 'Using the ancient portal that has always been in Clockmaker Court.'

'Wait, this portal is a *time* portal?' Barney asks, a mixture of awe and excitement on his face. 'But that's only in movies and books … isn't it?'

'Most would assume so. But it seems these things actually exist. Like Orla says about the ancient tree, our portal is a gateway into another world.'

'But how can that be?' I ask, finding my voice. 'Time travel can't really happen. Everyone knows that. It's impossible.'

'Ordinarily I would probably agree with you,' Ben says, nodding. 'If I hadn't experienced it myself.'

'You've travelled in time, Ben?' Barney asks, his eyes even wider. 'Oh, my … that's incredible. Where did you go back to, what year? What was it like?'

Ben turns to Barney. 'I didn't go back,' he says. 'I came forward.'

Again, sensibly, he waits for us to absorb this nugget of information.

'I came forward when I was a ten-year-old boy, from 1904.'

'But you just confirmed to Eve a while ago you were a young boy at the end of the war,' Adam says. 'Look, guys, if you're going to spin us this crazy tale, at least get your facts right. There are far too many flaws to this already.'

'This is correct,' Ben says. 'I was ten years old in 1904, when I met Eve's great-grandmother, Dotty. It was she who brought me forward in time to 1944.'

There's absolute silence as everyone tries to process this.

'Wait, if Dotty brought you forward in time,' I say, 'that means she must have gone back?'

Ben nods. 'That is exactly what happened. Archie and Dotty's secret project was time travel. They were trying to perfect the process of travelling to exactly the right place and right time in history. They thought if they could do that, they might be able to influence the outcome of the war.'

'That's crazy,' Adam says. 'You can't do that.'

'We know that now,' Ben says. 'But you must remember that people were desperate back then. Hitler was far too close to invading this country. People would have done anything to stop him.'

'When you say they were trying to perfect the process – I'm assuming they didn't?' I ask.

Ben shakes his head. 'No, they tried everything. They both travelled back – usually together to begin with, for safety purposes, I think. But later they began to go independently, in case there were difficulties. They tried to control where they went to and when, but the portal seemed to have a mind of its own. I think they might have got it down to the year, but that was it. Most of the time they could only travel back to Cambridge, and if they did end up somewhere new, then it wasn't the right year. The time portal, as far as we know, can't be controlled. It seems to be a natural phenomenon created by ... well, we don't know exactly why it's there and how it was created. All we know is, it's definitely there in the basement of number seven Clockmaker Court.'

'But why did Dotty bring you here?' I ask. 'You said she brought you here from 1904?'

'She wasn't supposed to, of course – it was a sort of accident. When I met Dotty, she and Archie had been experimenting with the portal for a number of years. But as much as they tried to figure it out using scientific means, they simply couldn't control exactly where or when you travelled to when you opened the portal and walked through.'

'Is that what all those notes and equations were?' I ask. 'In all the books we found? All their different ideas on how to control this portal.'

'I said they were quantum physics equations, didn't I?' Barney says triumphantly. 'I said they related to time travel, but I don't think you really believed me at the time.'

'I did believe you, but it was hard to process,' I tell him. 'Just like all this is now, hearing that our great-grandparents were apparently time travellers!' I suddenly exclaim, turning to Adam. 'Oh, my goodness – the photos! The photos we found of Archie and Dotty. We thought they were in fancy dress, we couldn't explain it, but they weren't – they were actually in those years ...'

Adam looks a bit white. 'Christ,' he simply says. 'That's mad.'

'When they travelled together, they took the photos for proof, should they ever need it, that it could be done,' Ben says. 'You can imagine what it was like trying to disguise a fairly large camera from the forties in Victorian London, for example. People would have been immediately suspicious. It's not like they had telephones like you young people do today, that they could easily slip into their pockets and then take secret photos on.'

'That's why there's a darkroom downstairs – so they could process their own photos without anyone seeing them,' I say, as so many things begin to make sense.

'Exactly,' Ben says. 'They had the proof should they ever need it, but it was their secret.'

'But how did you end up here, Ben?' I ask. 'You said it was by accident. What happened?'

'Dotty travelled back to Cambridge in 1904 at a time when I was a bit of a rapscallion.' Ben looks a little ashamed. 'I had got myself in trouble with some ne'er-do-wells and I was running from them. I was a decent pickpocket back then, so I'd been recruited by a gang to work for them. But when they found out I was keeping some of my trophies for myself, they got a tad annoyed, shall we say?'

'You sound like the Artful Dodger, Ben!' Barney says in delight. 'Did you find your Oliver Twist, by any chance?'

Ben smiles as he remembers. 'Not quite. Those Dickens chaps were orphans; I actually had a mother.' His expression changes as he remembers. 'She wasn't of good health, so she struggled to find work; the colour of her skin didn't help either back then. My father had died in battle in the Boer war, so it was up to me to keep us both by doing whatever I could to get money for food and rent. Otherwise she'd have ended up in the workhouse and I would have gone too – except in those days we'd probably have been split up; the welfare system wasn't what it is today. I know people moan about today's system of benefits, but people in my day would have bitten your hand off for the sort of help you get given now if you're out of work or a single parent, especially if you're disabled in some way.'

He glances at Barney.

Barney nods. 'I know. The system isn't perfect these days by a long shot. But,' he shudders, 'the thought of living as I do now back then is something I can hardly bear to think about. There's no way I'd have the opportunities I do now.'

'And you'd be right,' Ben says. 'The poor disabled folk then.' He shakes his head. 'Oh, I saw some terrible,

terrible things.' He pauses for a moment to remember. 'I'm sorry,' he says, coming back to the present once more. 'I keep getting distracted. Where was I?'

'You were telling us how Dotty brought you here?' I feel bad for prompting him. Some of Ben's memories are clearly very painful. Especially those about his mother.

'Ah, yes. The chaps that were chasing me that day were big, angry fellas. I was just a little scrawny fella back then and, boy, was I scared! As I was running from them, I crashed right into Dotty crossing the road. Dotty, as you can imagine, tried to keep a low profile whenever she was out of her own time, so to have me nearly bowling her over was the last thing she wanted. Anyway, she quickly recovered from our collision and realised as quick as a flash what was happening. She grabbed my hand and pulled me into this side alley, away from the thugs chasing me across the market square. But as they ran past, one of them caught a glimpse of me and followed us into the alley, which also happened to be a dead end. Dotty bravely tried to shield me from the thug, but he demanded she get out of the way. When she wouldn't, he went to strike her, but Dotty ducked and pushed me into what I thought was a beer cellar, but to my surprise, as I went through the doors, I didn't fall. Dotty quickly followed me, closing the doors behind her. She grabbed my hand and pulled me along this dark corridor. When we got to the other end, she pushed two more doors open and I found myself in the same office where I found you all earlier. The only difference was I was now in 1944, when only moments ago I'd been firmly in 1904.'

Ben takes a break to have sip of his whisky and to allow us to absorb all this.

'And you'd just gone down a corridor?' Barney asks. 'It was as simple as that? There was no noise or funny sensations, or anything?'

'This isn't time travel in a TV programme or a film, Barney,' Ben says. 'It's time travel in real life. Not quite as dramatic, but equally as disconcerting when it happens to you.'

'What happened next?' I ask, both amazed and intrigued by the incredible tale Ben is telling us. If it was anyone else, I'd already be questioning its validity. But I've known Ben a long time; my grandparents were friends with him too. I don't believe for a moment he is making any of this up, as crazy as it sounds.

'You can imagine the shock that Archie got when Dotty appeared with a little boy in tow,' Ben continues. 'I didn't know then what had happened, I thought I'd only gone through a tunnel. But I remember being really surprised by what Archie was wearing – he looked very different to what I was used to seeing men dressed in. Dotty was still wearing her Edwardian clothes so looked no different, of course. Dotty explained to Archie what had happened and said she would take me back when I was likely to be safe from the men who had been chasing me. So we waited a few minutes and then we went back where we'd come from, through what looked like a cupboard from the office side, back down the same tunnel. When we came out at the other end, we were back in the same alley, but, unfortunately, we quickly discovered it was a different year. So we tried again, and again. I can't remember how many times we went back through the tunnel that day, but each time we'd come out in a different year, decade, or even century. It was always Cambridge, but it was never 1904. In the end Archie told Dotty just to leave me in whichever year was closest. He wasn't an unkind man,' Ben says, looking at Adam. 'I think he just panicked at the situation they'd found themselves in.'

Adam nods.

'Dotty argued with him and said she couldn't just leave a young boy on his own. Eventually, we had to stop trying because it had got late. They explained to me that I'd have to stay with Archie until I could go back again, but they weren't sure when that would be. Which I just accepted. I knew something had happened, but I didn't really know what – I was just a ten-year-old boy, and, to be honest, when I got to Archie's house that night, it was like nothing I'd ever seen before – it was huge! Remember, I lived in what we'd now describe as squalor, in two tiny rooms with my mother, fighting for every morsel of food. The size of the meals that Archie and Violet gave me – even with rationing – I thought I'd gone to heaven instead of 1944.'

'So you never returned?' I ask. 'They couldn't get you back to 1904?'

Ben shakes his head. 'They tried – numerous times. But they simply couldn't find a way of pinpointing the exact date and Dotty wouldn't just leave me anywhere. By this time, I'd got used to living with Archie, Violet and George in Past Times House. It was a world away from where I used to live, and I'm ashamed to say most of the time I didn't want to go back. I had a full belly every day and a warm bed. They even enrolled me in the local school – and even though I was the only black child in my class, I loved it there. If it hadn't been for my mother, I think I'd have been glad it happened. But I couldn't forget that she'd been left alone and I daren't think what might have become of her without me.'

Ben's head drops and he looks down into his glass.

'Are you all right to continue, Ben?' Orla asks gently. 'I would take over, but obviously you know this part of the story best.'

Ben lifts his head and nods. 'Yes, I'll be fine.' He takes a deep breath. 'Eventually the war ended. By that time Dotty had disappeared, followed a little while after by Archie. They were the only ones who had any idea of how the portal worked, so there seemed no possibility of me ever returning. I had no choice but to stay with George and his mother, and that became my life. I knew I'd come from 1904. I knew I'd travelled forward in time. And I knew that Dotty had disappeared trying to get me home. But everyone had drummed it into me from the beginning how top secret that knowledge was, and that I should never share that information with anyone, other than those that already knew – which after the war was George, his mother, Violet, and Dotty's sister, Amelia. I wasn't going to go around saying what had happened and where I'd come from, or back then I'd probably have been locked up in an asylum. So I kept quiet. I missed my mother, of course, but I never went back, so I never knew what happened to her. I just continued to live my life from that point onwards, and here I am now.'

'So even though you were born in 1894, you just aged from when you were ten years old in 1944?' I ask.

Ben nods. 'This year I turn ninety years old. You can imagine the problems I've had over the years registering my date of birth. I had to pretend I was born in 1934. Luckily for me, records and birth certificates could go missing back then, and births weren't always registered. So I've got away with it and, in time, I've built up records and trails of my own, so I've used that as proof when it's been needed. Ben Johnson – as I'm now known – was born in 1934, but Benjamin Johnson was born in 1894.'

I glance at Adam; he's been quiet for a while. But he appears to be trying to piece all this together, as am I.

'So what exactly happened to Dotty?' I ask. 'You said she disappeared trying to get you home?'

'Ah, yes. Sorry, the details. My old brain forgets to fill in the gaps sometimes. Dotty blamed herself for what happened to me. I don't think she could ever forgive herself for bringing me back here – she'd separated a child from his mother. Dotty was a young mother herself; she had a baby with one of the American GIs who was stationed here in Cambridge during the war. His name was Harry, I believe?'

'That's right – he was my great-grandfather,' I say.

'Dotty, unusually for the time, had continued to work with Archie through her pregnancy. She considered her work too important to stop, although Archie wouldn't let her time travel during her pregnancy, of course – that was his one rule. Even when her baby – your grandmother – was born, she continued to work part-time. Amelia looked after baby Sarah the rest of the time, when she wasn't in her shop. But Dotty just couldn't accept that she'd separated a mother from her child and would get very upset about it on occasions. I tried to tell her not to worry and that I was having a grand old time living in 1944, but she wouldn't have it – she was determined to reunite me with my mother. Unfortunately, this determination is what led to her disappearance.'

Ben pauses again, and I get the feeling he's beginning to tire with all this talking. He has said more tonight than I think I've ever heard him say in the entire time I've known him. But I can also sense how much this unburdening, of all these secrets he's carried with him for so long, is helping him to heal.

'What happened to her?' Adam asks now.

'No one knows exactly,' Ben says. 'And of course what I do know is only what George and I gleaned at the time of her disappearance. Once Archie had gone too, no one was left who knew exactly what happened. All we knew was she tried to travel back to 1904 and got stuck there.'

'How do you know she got stuck in 1904?' Adam says. 'Maybe she just upped and left – it happens, you know.'

I know Adam is referring to his father now.

'Because I was there,' Ben says. 'We both went down the tunnel together that night. Archie and Dotty would mostly do their experiments in the day, but on this particular evening it was just Dotty and me. Dotty placed four envelopes on one of the office desks. We found out afterwards one letter was addressed to Archie, telling him what she was attempting to do. One was to Harry, telling him how much she loved him and to look after their daughter should anything happen to Dotty. One was to Amelia, instructing her what she wanted to happen to baby Sarah in the event Dotty didn't return, and the last was to Sarah herself to be read when she was older.'

I gasp. 'I think we've seen that letter, haven't we, Adam? It was in the box disguised in the *Dalmatians* book.'

Adam nods. 'It must be the same one.'

'I don't know what happened to the other letters,' Ben says. 'But Archie told us that Dotty had worded them all so no one would understand what she was really saying, just in case they got into the wrong hands.'

'So what happened next, Ben?' Barney asks. 'To you and Dotty?'

'After we'd both gone through the doors and down the tunnel together, Dotty told me to wait inside this time. She stepped through the doors as she always did to check what year we were in. This often involved finding someone with a newspaper if the period looked like it might be correct, which usually didn't take too long back in those days. Dotty returned quite quickly this time; I was used to her saying at this point we were in the wrong year or the wrong place. But that night she said we were finally back in Cambridge in 1904. The right place *and* the right time. She looked ecstatic ... so happy.' Ben smiles as he remembers. 'She told me to wait on the other side of the doors while she checked if my mother was in the lodgings I'd told her she lived in, and she'd be right back. So I waited and I waited, but Dotty didn't return. I think eventually I must have nodded off in the tunnel, because the next thing I knew, Archie was kneeling down next to me calling my name. He asked me what happened and where Dotty was. When I told him, he opened the doors, but there was nothing there. Only a brick wall. He took me back into the office and then he tried again to go back down the tunnel himself, but when he returned he said the same thing was happening. Eventually, after several attempts, he took me back to the house, and it was the last time any of us ever saw Dotty.'

There's silence in the room.

'You mean she never came back?' Barney asks quietly.

Ben shakes his head. 'No. Archie tried to get her back. He worked day and night in that office trying to find a way. But nothing worked. I think it was that that drove him off the rails in the end. He'd always been a healthy, robust sort of chap before, but, after Dotty disappeared, he lost weight and he didn't sleep. He had great dark circles under his eyes – I remember that very clearly. And he started to ramble about things, muttering under his breath. Eventually one day he disappeared too.'

'Did he get stuck in time as well?' Barney asks. 'Like Dotty?'

'No, he was found wandering the East Anglian fens by a farmer out tending his fields. But by that time, he really wasn't well. He was immediately taken to hospital and he never came out again. Violet went to see him, but there was nothing she could do. He'd had a breakdown and unfortunately the things he was saying made him seem like he'd truly lost his mind. I'm sure after what you've been told tonight, you can imagine the type of subjects he was ranting about.' Ben raises his bushy white eyebrows. 'Archie never got over Dotty's disappearance – they were great friends. In the end, the portal was his downfall as much as it was Dotty's and it was all my fault.'

As Ben's head drops once more, large tears begin to fall down his cheeks. 'As much as Archie couldn't forgive himself for what happened to her, neither could I.'

'Ben,' I say, immediately rushing to his side. 'It wasn't your fault. You mustn't blame yourself.' I put my arm around his old shoulders and he looks gratefully up at me.

'Just like your great-grandmother Dotty and your grandmother Sarah,' he says, his eyes misty from his tears. He reaches into the pocket of his jacket, pulls out a clean white handkerchief and dabs at his eyes. 'They cared just like you do – too much sometimes. But now you're here at last, Eve. You and Adam. We've waited a long time for this. Now you both know everything, you can help us to put right what once went wrong.'

29

After we've comforted Ben and he's calmed down a little, Orla asks if we'd all like to continue.

'There's more?' Adam asks. 'How can there be?'

'I'd like to hear more from you, Orla,' I say. 'We know Ben's role in all this. What is yours? How do you know so much about all this?'

'Oh, that's quite simple, really,' Orla says. 'Ben confided in me when he was ill, didn't you, Ben?'

Ben nods and looks gratefully at Orla. 'I don't think any of you realised quite how ill I was. Nasty, nasty virus, it was. I was worried I might not live to see you discover everything and be able to tell you my side of things. So I confided in Orla. I trusted her completely to keep a secret, and I knew with her background and her beliefs she'd be open to hearing the truth. You kept our secret beautifully.' Ben pats Orla's arm.

'Thank you, Ben,' Orla says, putting her hand over his. 'I'm just glad you're here to tell your story. I'm not sure they would have believed me if I'd had to tell it.'

'Nonsense, you would have been fine. Now, if you'll permit me to continue the story a little further?' Ben asks the rest of us.

'If you feel up to it,' I say. 'We don't want to tire you out too much.'

Ben smiles. 'That's kind of you, Eve. But I'll be just fine. Now, after Dotty disappeared and then Archie was hospitalised, nothing happened in Clockmaker Court for a good while. No one visited the office, of course, and life after the war went on. Everyone was too busy trying to get their own lives back on track to worry too much about a room underneath a bricked-up shop, and not many people even knew it was there. Eventually, Violet passed away, and Amelia, and then it was only myself, George, Sarah and Gerald who knew. Sarah had taken over the shop from Amelia, and Gerald had taken over from his father, Ozzie. The doors that led down to the office and the portal from the shops weren't sealed exactly, they were simply disguised behind furniture. To be honest, we rarely talked about it. George began his career at the bank and the others continued with their own businesses. That was, until it began to happen again ...'

'What do you mean?' Barney asks, open-mouthed. 'It happened again?'

'People began to appear behind the doors that led up from the office,' Ben says. 'It was random at first. Gerald or Sarah would hear knocking from behind one the doors, they'd move the furniture out of the way, and when they opened the door, there would be a very confused person on the other side. We had no way of getting them back again, we didn't know how to control the portal, so they simply had to stay.'

'You mean there's *more* people like you?' I ask, aghast. 'People from a different time, living here as if nothing is strange or unusual.'

Ben nods. 'There seemed to be no reason for it at first, but then we noticed a pattern. They would all appear in leap years, just like I had in 1944, and, not only that, they were always leap days too – the twenty-ninth of February, to be exact. It kept happening until George decided to pay to seal up not only the office, but the tunnel too. He removed the two doors with the tree carvings from the portal in the office, boarded up the doors at the other end of the tunnel that led outside, and finally the doors that led down from each shop – he used the sort of secure door they used in his bank's vaults for that. He didn't want to take the risk that if we weren't here one day in the future to protect the gateway, someone might accidentally discover the office and then the portal. We all knew that if someone unscrupulous discovered what we knew was there, it could unleash a whole world of trouble. So the secret had to be kept with us until …' He pauses, as if he's choosing his words carefully. 'Well, until the day when Venus and Mars would appear as predicted on the doors and the tree, and then the secret could be revealed once more.'

'When you say Venus and Mars, you actually mean Eve and Adam, of course,' Adam says defensively.

Ben nods.

'And for argument's sake, just what are we …' Adam gestures between the two of us with his hand. 'What are Eve and I supposed to do now we are here?'

'Firstly, protect the portal, and, secondly, help those who wish to return go back again,' Ben says, as if it's the most natural thing in the world. 'Everyone that's come through that portal did so because they were in trouble in some way.'

'How do you mean, Ben?' I ask.

'They were all fleeing from something – persecution, violence, injustice, discrimination.'

'Why would they want to go back if that's the case?' Adam asks. 'They'd be better staying where they are, wouldn't they?'

'Some – perhaps. But some, like myself, would like to go back and find their loved ones again. To check on them. To see if they are all right.'

'Even if we could find a way to get you back,' I say, 'would you go back like you are now? Or would you revert to your previous age again?'

Ben shrugs. 'No one knows. But a few of us might like to try.'

'When you say a few of us,' Adam asks. 'Are you still in contact with all these others?'

Ben smiles. 'Many still live close by.'

'How close?'

'Right here in Clockmaker Court.'

'What?' I say. 'How can they possibly? Do you mean people that live here now?'

'Yes,' Ben says calmly.

'Who? Harriet? Rocky?'

'Harriet is from 1952 originally,' Ben says. 'Not Rocky – he doesn't know anything of Harriet's past. Harriet is …' He chooses his words carefully. 'A little touchy about the subject when it's mentioned.'

'She said she thought the oak tree should be cut down,' I say, remembering. 'I thought that was odd at the time. Is it because she doesn't want the portal to ever open up again?'

Orla nods. 'She doesn't want to go back and leave Rocky.'

'That's totally understandable. But why did she come through the ...' I hesitate. It seems odd saying the word. 'The portal in the first place.'

'She was in a violent and abusive marriage in the fifties, when it was very difficult to leave your husband,' Orla says. 'She escaped and arrived here in Clockmaker Court in 1980. She eventually met Rocky, who is nothing like her previous husband was.'

'Rocky *is* lovely,' I say. 'No wonder she doesn't want to return. I still can't believe she's from the fifties, though that does explain their old-fashioned tea shop and the type of baking she specialises in, I suppose.' I consider this for a moment. 'Who else is there that I would know? It can't be Luca, surely?'

'Luca escaped from France during the Second World War to avoid being persecuted by the Nazis,' Ben says. 'Originally from Italy, he was a well-known costume designer in French theatres during the thirties. He arrived in Clockmaker Court in 1972.'

I stare at Ben for a moment in disbelief. 'I ... I just can't believe that,' I say, shaking my head. 'Luca is my friend. How can he have kept this hidden from me all this time?'

'He had no choice,' Ben says. 'Remember, we can trust no one with this secret until we know they can be trusted.'

'But hold on a minute,' Adam says, interrupting. 'Ben, you said that you'd aged from the moment you arrived here at ten years old. If Harriet and Luca arrived in 1980 and 1972, they'd be much older now than they currently are.'

Ben nods. 'It does seem like a bit of an anomaly. But we have a theory on that, don't we, Orla.'

'Yes, we think that when you come through the portal, you possibly age to the point when you would originally have passed away if you'd stayed in your own time. So Ben, for instance, would have lived a long life. Even though he was originally living in poverty in 1904, we think he must have changed his life around at some stage to enable him to live many years.'

'But Harriet and Luca wouldn't have lived such long lives?' I ask.

'We don't know this, but because Luca hasn't aged too much at all since he arrived, it's possible he might have been detained by the Nazis. Many gay people were sadly imprisoned in detention camps and of course, as we know, died there too.'

'Oh, God, that's awful,' I say, clapping my hands over my mouth. 'Poor Luca.'

'I must stress we don't know this for certain, but, since that's what Luca was escaping from, we can only guess that's what might have been his fate had he stayed in France.'

'And Harriet?' I ask.

'Harriet has aged a few years since she's been here, but we think she may have died at the hands of her abusive husband had she not escaped from him and come here.'

'So they both only survived because they came through the tunnel?'

Orla nods. 'The portal, yes.'

'How many more are there, other than Ben, Luca and Harriet?'

'Not many we've been able to keep track of,' Ben says, glancing at Orla. 'Most of the people who came through before George finally sealed up the tunnel in 1981 didn't want to stick around and hear our explanations

– they simply ran. Just glad to have escaped from whatever they needed to.'

'So which of them want help to go back?' I ask. I don't know how Adam and I are supposed to achieve this. But if my friends want to go home to their families and I can help them in some way, I'm going to do everything I can to be of assistance to them.

'Harriet definitely doesn't,' Ben says, smiling. 'She's adamant she's staying right here.'

'What about Luca?' I ask, hoping he says the same. I don't want to lose my friend.

'He comes and goes between desperately wanting to stay here, and going back to find out what happened to his friends and family during the war. He's tried to trace some of his family and got answers, but not all of them.'

'What about you, Ben?' I ask. 'What do you want?'

'I want to go back,' Ben says without hesitation. 'I've had a happy life here in Clockmaker Court – I'm not going to complain. But if I could just see my mother one more time, even if she doesn't know who I am, and check she was all right without me, then I'd die a happy man.'

I nod. More determined than ever to figure this out, if only for Ben.

'The portal would be a wonderful tool to help those in peril, if only someone knew how to get them back when their particular danger has passed,' Orla says. 'But that's the problem – nobody does. That's why they end up stuck here.'

'I wish we did have some answers for you,' I hear Adam say while I'm deep in thought. 'But neither Eve nor I have any ideas of how to control this so-called portal. Do we, Eve?'

I shake my head. 'Sadly, no. Not at the moment. But if I could help you, Ben, you know I would.'

'I'm in no doubt about that,' Ben says knowingly. 'You're a Sinclair woman.'

'You guys might not have any brilliant suggestions,' Barney says cryptically. 'But I might have a few ideas we could try …'

30

'Are you sure about this, Barney?' I ask the next day when we're back down in the office. We've attached the two carved wooden doors to the cupboard – checking first whether they too have the same dates engraved on them as the tree, which of course they do – and now we're trying Barney's various ideas about how we might pinpoint specific years to travel to.

'No, but we have to try everything. Time travel is an incredibly complicated process. If it was easy, everyone would be doing it.'

'Would they, though?' Adam asks from the corner of the desk where he's currently perched. 'In every movie I've ever seen about it, something always goes wrong. I'm not sure I'd want to risk getting stuck in the past.'

'No one is getting stuck in the past,' I say to reassure him. 'All we want to do is to be able to choose just where and when those doors open out to. We're not actually going to go back there ourselves. Just see if we can get Ben back to see his mother.'

'Fine, but so far we've been down here all morning and we haven't even been able to get this portal working again. Let alone choose where we want it to take us.'

He was right. Every time we've tried one of Barney's ideas – which all seem to be based on time-travel philosophy from TV programmes or movies – all we find when we open the doors at the end of the tunnel is the same brick wall that faced Archie when Dotty disappeared.

Adam refused to go down the tunnel each time we tried something new. I knew why that was, of course – it was dark and cramped, and must immediately remind him of a time he didn't ever want to return to. So it was just me checking the doors, because Barney's wheelchair was currently upstairs in Adam's shop.

As I anticipate, Barney's latest idea – involving some very complex equations, along with some strange chemicals, a test tube and a Bunsen burner – fails once more.

'Let's give this a rest for now, shall we?' I say as Barney's face, currently covered in some sort of sooty ash, looks desperately disheartened. 'Perhaps some fresh air might help?'

Adam carries Barney back up the stairs and reunites him with his wheelchair. Then we all head outside to sit on the bench in the middle of the court.

I haven't spoken to any of my fellow residents of Clockmaker Court since last night's revelations by Ben and Orla, but I know I'm going to have to at some stage.

Even though I know why they've kept their past lives a secret from me, it still feels like they've been lying to me all these years. I know I'm not exactly great at sharing my secrets with anyone, but the difference is they all know my backstory. They knew from the minute I arrived in Clockmaker Court to work with my grandparents. But I still can't shake the feeling of being let down by those I trust.

Now that we know Ben's story, so much of what has been going on kind of makes sense – if stories of a time portal and people travelling from the past can ever really be fully believed or understood.

'So, what's next, then?' Adam asks as we sit in the lunchtime sunshine drinking takeaway cups of coffee from Fitzbillies. Neither Adam nor I want to see Harriet and Rocky today, knowing what we now know. We are both worried about putting our foot in it with Rocky, as he knows nothing about Harriet's past. 'Any more bright ideas, Barney? Should we be considering strapping the shop to the back of a DeLorean car and driving it at eighty-eight miles per hour through a thunderstorm until it gets hit by lightning?'

'Hilarious,' Barney says flatly. 'I think you'll find I've mostly based my ideas around scientific formula, rather than Hollywood special effects.'

'Maybe that's where we're going wrong,' I say, sipping on my coffee as I think. 'Perhaps we're basing our attempts too much on scientific reasoning like Dotty and Archie did. Maybe there's another way …'

'Like what?' Adam asks. 'Should we just stand in the tunnel and request what year we want to go back to? Do you think it's listening to us …' He makes a sort of spooky gesture with his hands, then grins.

'If you're not going to take this seriously,' I tell him, 'then perhaps it should just be Barney and me trying to make the tunnel … *the portal* work.'

'Sorry. But we have to keep this light, otherwise when you think about the seriousness of the situation and some of the things these people were running from, it gets a bit heavy.'

'I know. I think I've been through some trauma in my life, but when you hear these stories, it puts a lot of things into perspective.'

Both Barney and Adam look expectantly at me, waiting for me to say more.

'It doesn't matter,' I say lightly. 'You don't need to hear about my past troubles. We've got enough of our own right now.'

'Perhaps we do,' Adam says. 'I told you about my own trauma and I have to admit, it really helped me at the time to talk to someone new about it. Someone who wasn't a therapist, but a friend. I was caught up in a gas explosion many years ago,' Adam tells Barney. 'I was trapped under the side of a house for hours with only a dog for company. It doesn't sound much now, but it messed me up a bit – guilt that I'd survived when others hadn't, you know?'

'I do know, actually,' Barney says to my surprise. 'I wasn't always paralysed from the waist down like this. It was only after the fire that this happened.'

'What fire?' I ask. 'You never told me that before.'

'There's a lot you don't know about me, Eve. When I was four years old, the house that I lived in with my real parents caught fire – electrical fault, not gas this time,' he says. 'They managed to throw me out of my bedroom window, to neighbours below, who were supposed to catch me in a sort of blanket thing. They did catch me, but not firmly enough, so I sort of twisted badly as I landed and I tore my spinal cord. Apparently I never walked again after that. I don't actually remember it, to be honest, which is probably just as well.'

'What happened to your parents?' I ask, knowing from what Barney told us before about being adopted that it was unlikely to be good.

'Both they and my baby brother perished in the fire. I was adopted by a lovely family, though, and I grew up not knowing anything different. It wasn't until they told me when I was older that I'd been adopted, that I realised I'd ever had another family.'

I'm shocked to hear this from Barney. We've known each other for a number of years now and until today I had no idea how he'd come to be in a wheelchair. He never said anything to me before and I didn't want to appear nosey, so the subject never came up.

'So you don't remember anything about your first family?'

'Not a thing. But when I found out what happened, I always wondered, why me? Why did I survive when they didn't?'

'That's exactly how I feel,' Adam says. 'Why me? Why did I survive that explosion with no permanent injuries, other than my hearing' – he taps the hearing aid in his ear – 'when another person had to die? It just doesn't seem fair.'

'I know exactly what you both mean,' I murmur quietly, unable to prevent my own trauma from being forced to the front of my mind. 'Why did I survive?'

'What happened to you, Eve?' Barney asks, looking surprised to hear me say this. 'What's your story?'

I look at them both, and see two kind faces gazing back at me with worried and concerned expressions, and, for the first time ever, I want to share my story. I want to unburden myself to these two people I've become so close too.

'I was in a car accident,' I tell them. 'My whole family was – including Jake, my then fiancé.' I glance at Adam to see if he remembers me mentioning Jake to him before. He nods to let me know he does. 'I was twenty-four at the time and we were on our way to visit my grandparents here in Cambridge for Christmas. It wasn't like we were even packed into one car or anything. I was driving with Jake in my car, and the rest of my family, including my younger sister, Ruth, were in the family car. A lorry was going too fast on the opposite side of the road. He lost control on some black ice, jack-knifed and skidded into us both, pushing us off the road and crushing our cars between his vehicle and an incredibly strong drystone wall that held its own even with all the force thrust upon it.' I shudder as I remember both the force of the blow from the lorry, which sent us spinning across the road, and then the awful sounds that followed, of hot metal buckling as the cars were crushed between the weight of the lorry and the rocks the other side. 'My father and my sister were killed on impact, my mother died on her way to the hospital, and Jake died after an emergency operation – one I didn't even know he was having until they told me afterwards. I was rescued and taken to hospital, but with only a broken bone in one hand and a few cuts and bruises. The paramedics and the police couldn't understand how I'd managed to be in the same accident and come out so unscathed. I might have been relatively unscathed physically, but the mental trauma of what happened lived long after the physical scars had healed.'

Although I told them quickly and without drama, I realise that what took only seconds for me to say has suddenly and powerfully unburdened me of the years of anger, anxiety, sadness and guilt that have weighed heavily on me for so long. I can't believe how much lighter I immediately feel. When people talk about the weight of the world being lifted from their shoulders, I now know exactly what they mean.

'Christ,' Adam says, taking my hand. 'That's bloody awful. Losing *all* your family in one accident? I just don't know how you'd ever come back from something like that. I knew you were a strong woman, Eve, but I had no idea how strong. You're amazing. Really you are.'

'I'm so sorry, Eve,' Barney says, looking shocked. 'At least I was too young to remember what happened to me. You were twenty-four. No chance of forgetting.'

'It messed me up, that's for sure – for a long time. That's how I came to live here in Cambridge with my grand-parents. They were my only remaining family. I was in such a bad state that I couldn't look after myself. So even though they were going through their own grief, my grandparents cared for me just like they had when my sister and I would come to stay with them when we were young. They loved me and listened to me, and did every-thing they could to try to help me – even when I didn't want to be helped.'

'Is that why you stayed here and never went back to your previous life?' Adam asks. 'You felt you owed them something for looking after you?'

'Partly, and partly because living here in Cambridge, and working in a little antiques shop, was easy and just what I needed to begin healing. I don't know if you've noticed, but Clockmaker Court is a very calm and healing place. I've always felt safe here, nestled among the buildings, with this strong oak tree protecting us from above. So I decided to stay and to give back to both them and Clockmaker Court what they had given back to me – my life.'

'That's really beautiful, Eve,' Barney says. 'You're right – this place does feel special. I think that's one of the reasons I've always enjoyed working here with you so much more than my other job at the university.'

'Thank you for sharing your past with us.' Adam squeezes my hand. 'It seems like we've all had far too much trauma in our lives and yet I suspect we've all come out the other side stronger because of it. We survived when many of those around us sadly did not.'

'It's almost like we were saved,' Barney says, considering this. 'Saved because we had a greater purpose to fulfil.' He hesitates. 'I hardly dare say this, but do you think that purpose was protecting this time portal?'

'Whoa, that's a bit deep, man,' Adam says, his brow furrowing. 'Suggesting we were saved from death because we had a greater purpose in life than those around us.'

'Sorry.' Barney's face reddens. 'I didn't mean it like that. It's just what it sounds like, though, when we all tell our stories, don't you think?'

'If what Orla and Ben were saying last night is true, maybe we were saved?' I say quietly. 'It seems an awful coincidence that all three of us survived different life-changing events when those around us didn't.'

We all stare at each other as the enormity of what I'm suggesting begins to sink in.

'You don't really believe that, do you?' Adam asks just as quietly, as though we're all party to a huge secret that no one else knows about.

'I really don't know what I believe any more. So much has happened over the last few weeks and months since I met you at your grandfather's house back in February. Some of it good.' I squeeze his hand now. 'But a lot of it very strange and extremely odd.' I shiver, and I realise the sun has moved in the sky so we're now bathed in shade from one of the branches of the tree. I glance up to see exactly how far the shadow is being cast – across the court and between our two shops, so it completely covers the missing building, the one that was bricked up, the one that hides the secret office and the time portal ...

'Oh, my God!' I leap up, letting go of Adam's hand.

'What is it?' Adam asks as I stare at the tree above us. 'What's wrong?'

'Nothing ... Nothing is wrong at all. In fact, everything could be all right from now on.' I look down at Adam and Barney still staring at me. 'I think us sitting out here might just have allowed me to figure out how the time portal actually works ...'

31

'It's a sundial,' I say to the two of them as I walk around beneath the tree. 'This oak tree above us. That's why there's always been a tree planted here, so it can work as a sundial – the earliest form of telling time.'

Adam and Barney still stare at me as if I've lost it.

'The sun moves around in the sky above and therefore, at different times of the day, the tree casts its shadow over the buildings in Clockmaker Court like a sundial does. On a sundial there are twelve markings, like the markings on a clock that allow us to tell the time. I think the portal only works when the tree casts a shadow over number seven, the missing building.'

'I get your theory,' Adam says, not sounding as enthusiastic about this idea as I am. 'But Ben said when Dotty went missing it was the evening, so there would be no sun then to cast a shadow. Unless it was seven o'clock in summertime, I suppose. But I got the impression it was later at night than that.'

'No, you don't understand. This particular sundial doesn't tell time, it simply tells the exact moment when the portal is open. Look, the tree is casting a shadow over the missing building now, but it's not seven o'clock.' I look at my watch. 'It's just gone midday.'

'Moonlight also casts a shadow if it's bright enough,' Barney says. 'To cast a shadow, you only need a source of light and something blocking it. So, in theory, when the tree casts shadow from moonlight onto the building, it could also happen at night too.'

'You see,' I say, gesturing my hands between Adam and the bricked-up wall. 'Our hidden building could be picked out twice a day. That must be when the portal comes alive – when it's hit by shadow from the sun or the moon!'

'*Technically* …' Barney says. 'I don't want to poop on your party, Eve. But it would only happen if the sun wasn't covered by cloud or if the moon was full enough to provide enough light to cast a shadow.'

'Yes, agreed. But it *could* happen.' I look up at the tree again. Although it's currently casting a shadow over our hidden building, the sun's rays are fully on the antiques shop right now, bathing it in a warm glow. 'What if it's not shadow that causes the portal to open?' I ask, as another theory forms in my mind. 'What if it's sunlight or moonlight that makes the magic happen?' I look at the other two, who again don't look quite as convinced as I sound. 'Think about it. Before time was invented – or recorded, really, I suppose – how did people tell what time of day it was or even what time of the year? By using the position of the sun for the time of day and the position of the moon during its lunar cycle for the time of year.'

'You're right,' Barney says. 'The sun rises and sets in a very similar position every day, only changing slightly as we on Earth orbit it over the year. But the moon's position changes over the period of each lunar cycle. If this portal is as old as Orla was suggesting yesterday, it would make sense that anything to do with it would be measured in terms of the sun and the moon – rather than what we know today as the familiar way to measure the passing of time, in minutes and hours, and days and months.'

I turn to Adam.

'I guess,' he says, still looking unconvinced.

'I don't know if you've noticed since you've been here, Adam,' I say, 'but we get a lot of sun here in Cambridge. This part of East Anglia is known for its dry climate. Compared to the rest of the UK, we get a lot less cloud and rain. Therefore more opportunities to view both the sun and the moon, without cloud blocking them.'

'OK, I'll buy it,' Adam says, giving in. 'For now we'll go with the portal opens when the sun or the moon shines directly on number seven. But it still doesn't tell us how to control the portal so we can choose the dates in history for it to open on to. That was Dotty and Archie's main problem in getting Ben back, remember?'

I think about this. He's right, of course. Even with my new theory, we still don't know how to actually control the portal.

'If we're going as far back as the sun and moon controlling when the portal opens, rather than a set measurement of time or dates, then we're looking as far back as pre-Roman times,' Barney says. 'The way of measuring days, months and years that we use today is in line with the Gregorian calendar introduced in 1582, if I remember rightly. Before that, they used the Julian calendar introduced by the Romans. This was the first to include leap days as part of a calendar year, which seems to be relevant in this case after what we heard last night. But, before that, recording the passage of months and years was mainly based on solar and lunar cycles, just like Eve suggested.'

'How do you know so much about all this?' I ask, amazed at Barney's knowledge on the subject.

'I've just always been interested in time,' Barney says. 'How we tell it now, how they did in the past. How we move through time, and of course the possibility of time travel. I've watched countless TikTok and YouTube videos about it.'

'Ah, the modern way.' Adam grins. 'So, Einstein, how do you propose we control the sun and the moon so we can choose exact dates and years, then? Because unless you know some NASA astronauts willing to help us, I can't see how we're going to get up there to do that.'

'You said the Romans brought in the modern-day way of us measuring the passing of time?' I ask Barney, as yet another idea begins to spark in my mind.

Barney nods.

'Remember that perpetual brass calendar we found down in the office when we first went there?' I ask Adam.

'Yes …'

'It was in Roman numerals, wasn't it?'

'Er, I think so.'

'It was, *and* it had a sun and a moon on it too. What if we could use that to control the portal, to request a date to travel to?'

'Wouldn't Dotty and Archie have tried using that when they were trying to get Ben back originally? I kind of thought that's why it was left there.'

'Oh. Yes,' I reply a little despondently. 'I guess they would.'

'Nice idea, though,' Adam says, trying to sound encouraging. 'You'll get there, Eve. I have no doubt about that. Why I've been roped into all this, I have no idea. But I can see why you have.'

'What do you mean?'

'It's like Ben said – you're determined, you don't give up. Dotty clearly never gave up trying to get Ben back to his right time, even though it was to be her downfall in the end. You're the same as Dotty. It must run in the family – you won't quit until you've got to the bottom of it all.'

Hearing Adam say that makes me immediately proud. I only knew hearsay of my great-grandmother before all this, stories passed down through the family of what she was like and what she did based on assumption and conjecture – including that about her disappearance. But every day now, I was feeling closer to her and what she stood for. What Ben told us last night had only furthered my need to find out more about her, and to finally discover exactly what happened to her when she went missing in 1904.

'Thank you for saying that, Adam. It's such a compliment to me that people think I'm like Dotty. She sounds like a bit of a hero, doesn't she? I'm definitely not that, far from it. I'm sure I could never be as brave as she was. But your words have made me feel a lot better, when really I feel a bit useless right now.'

'Don't be daft,' Adam says. 'You're the one who's got us here to this moment. I wouldn't have figured it all out on my own. I'd have given up as soon as it got difficult. But you kept pushing until we found ourselves where we are now. I might not like the thought of a tunnel under that building that you can time travel in, and to be fair, until I actually see it working, I can't fully believe it's true. But I know you do, and I'm absolutely certain you will be the one who will get us to where we need to be in the end.'

I smile lovingly at him.

Next to us, Barney begins to applaud. 'You two.' He sniffs, pretending to be moved to tears. 'You're so cute together. That speech.' He wipes an imaginary tear away. 'It's just too much.'

'Ha ha,' I say sarcastically. 'Very funny.'

'Actually,' Barney says, snapping out of his 'emotional turmoil' pretty fast to sound affronted now instead. 'I should be upset that you didn't mention me in that impassioned speech, Adam. I've been involved in working a lot of this stuff out too, you know.'

'You have indeed, Barney,' Adam says, pretending to be serious. 'Do you want a pat on the back instead? Or a hug, maybe?'

'Nah,' Barney says, switching back to his normal self. 'I'm good, thanks. You stay right there on that bench. I think you and me have had enough physical contact already since you've been carrying me up and down the stairs!'

Adam grins. 'Will do.' He looks up at the tree again. 'I still think this tree has something to do with how the portal works. It seems to be involved in everything else.'

'I definitely think it is,' I say, looking up with him. 'But how?'

All three of us stare up at the tree.

'You remember when we read those letters we found hidden in the book?' Adam says. 'It said in mine to remember that the apple doesn't fall far from the tree. I never really understood what that meant, but now I think my grandfather is telling us the tree is involved with how the portal works.'

'I think so too,' I reply. 'Wait ... what if the brass calendar doesn't work when it's down in the office, but it does work when it's up here in the light?'

'How do you mean?'

'Maybe rather than the building like I originally thought, the tree uses the calendar as a sundial? If we turned the dates on the calendar to where we wanted to go, and held it under the same light source that's shining on the building, we'd get a shadow on the calendar from the tree ...'

I look from Adam to Barney to gauge their reaction.

'You did say that little calendar thing looked really old when we first saw it,' Adam says. 'Do you think it could be Roman old?'

'It's very well preserved if it is. But I definitely think it could be. What if no one could fully control the portal until the Romans arrived here? But using the sun, the moon, this ancient oak tree and a rudimentary early calendar, they were able to for the first time?'

'You know what they say?' Barney says, looking excitedly at us both. 'When in Rome ...'

32

'Are you nervous?' Barney asks.

'Yes, are you?' I glance across at him.

The three of us are standing outside the brick wall between the antiques shop and the bookshop, waiting for the sun's rays to hit the hidden building, and the shadow from the tree to hit the brass calendar held firmly in my hands. We've set the calendar for a date earlier this year, to test it for the first time.

There was much discussion in the little time we had about when to set our possible first trip back in time, with the two men choosing all sorts of famous dates in history. But we eventually decided to attempt to go back just a little way, to see if this portal actually works, and not to try anything too radical.

'Of course I am,' Barney says. 'I'm bricking it.'

Adam grins at him.

The sun finally moves across onto the building. I don't know what we were all expecting to happen when it did, but nothing unusual happens as the sun's rays warm the honey-coloured wall and the heavy grey timbers.

'Hurry, Eve, get the calendar in the right place for the shadow,' Adam says anxiously.

'All right,' I reply calmly. 'I am.' I move the brass calendar around until the shadow passes over the dates that we've set, and again we wait.

'What now?' I ask when nothing happens. Everything happened so fast when we decided this might be worth a try. The sun was moving so rapidly towards the hidden building in Clockmaker Court that there was no time to discuss what we'd actually do once everything else was put into place. 'Should we go down to the office and see if anything has actually happened?'

'Yes, I think ...' Barney stops. 'Rocky, at ten o'clock!' he whispers urgently, looking behind me. 'You two go down there. I'll head him off.'

'Are you sure?' I ask.

'Yes, it will take too long to get me down there. Go! Go!' He swivels his chair in Rocky's direction. 'Tell me what happens later.'

Adam and I rush towards my shop. This morning, we found the entrance down to the office was actually easier taken from my side than his. Once we peeled back the wallpaper, we found the metal door was secured with the same six-digit code as the one in Adam's shop. But rather than the great huge bookcase that now covers the secret door in Adam's shop, in my shop we only have to move the grandfather clock.

'Look,' I gasp as we pass the clock, already moved to one side to allow us quick entry down to the office.

'What?' Adam asks.

'The clock's hands are spinning ... backwards!'

We stop for a moment to look at the grandfather clock, whose hands haven't moved since we originally dragged it into my shop back in early March. The hands are now spinning freely around its face ... but instead of going forwards, they're going backwards.

'Do you think this is a sign the portal might actually be working?' I say, looking nervously at Adam.

He nods. 'Let's go before it changes its mind and stops.'

We rush down to the office and pause for a moment in front of the two wooden doors. Which, now they're attached to the little cupboard in the wall, make up the two halves of an ancient carving of an oak tree. Before I can change my mind, I pull the doors open. With my torch lighting my way, I bend down, step through the doors and find myself in the tunnel.

'Come on,' I say excitedly to Adam when I realise he's not with me. 'We might not have much time!'

Adam hesitates in the doorway and suddenly I remember.

'Would you prefer not to?' I ask gently.

Adam forcefully shakes his head. 'No ... I'll be fine,' he says with determination. He looks fearfully inside the tunnel, as though he's trying to weigh up whether it's as bad as he's imagining.

'You stay here,' I say, making a quick decision. 'Someone needs to make sure I can get back, in case there's a problem.'

'No, I can't let you go alone,' Adam says with annoyance, at himself rather than me. 'I'm coming.' But as he bends down to step inside the tunnel, I can hear his breathing immediately become far too fast.

'I'll be fine, Adam. You stay here and if I'm not back in ten minutes, then you can come and rescue me. I might need someone to open the door at the other end.'

Adam steps back into the light of the office and nods.

'Good luck,' he says, looking very sheepish. 'Be careful, won't you?'

'I'm only going back to February. It's not like I'm going to the Middle Ages.' I smile bravely. 'I'll be just fine.'

I turn around and, to my enormous relief, I find that once I'm properly inside the tunnel, I can stand up straight. I call back to Adam, 'Shut the doors, in case that makes a difference.'

Adam looks reluctant, but does as I ask.

The tunnel is now fully in darkness, so I only have the light from my torch to guide me. It only takes ten seconds or so of cautious walking before I find myself at the other end in front of two more doors. There's a couple of thick wooden planks placed horizontally across the doors to prevent anyone accessing the entrance from the other side, so I lift them off one by one and lean them up against the wall. Then, taking a deep breath, I gently pull one of the doors open.

Daylight floods into the tunnel and I find myself staring out onto the little alleyway that runs behind my shop on Clockmaker Court. It's a dead end – probably used in the past for deliveries and such to the shops – so there's no one passing by to see me emerge from the tunnel.

I wonder whether I should shut the door behind me – I don't want someone stumbling upon the tunnel accidentally. But I'm very conscious that Dotty never returned from her last trip and I don't want the same to happen to me. I see some abandoned pallets from a delivery to one of the market stalls at the end of the alleyway, so, rather than fully shutting the door, I quickly stack a couple in front of the opening, which allows me to wedge the door open a little – just in case.

'Right,' I say, taking a deep breath. 'Let's see if this has worked.'

I walk out onto the market square in Cambridge, which looks just like it always does on a weekday. There are shoppers browsing the various market stalls with bored-looking stall holders waiting to see if their customer actually wants to buy something or if they're just looking. The only stall that looks particularly busy is the fresh fruit and veg stall. I shiver – it feels cold. *Of course it is, you numpty. It's supposed to be February now and you're in a short-sleeved blouse, jeans and flip-flops!* I notice then that everyone else walking about is well wrapped up for the cold in thick coats, scarves and gloves. *I need to be quick, before I either freeze or draw too much attention to myself for wandering the streets of Cambridge in summer clothing on a cold February day.*

I look for anyone carrying a newspaper, like Ben said Dotty did, but there's no one. I could just ask someone the date, I think, but that, along with my strange attire, might draw far too much attention. *I'll pop into WHSmith just off the market square, take a quick look at their newspapers and then go back. That should do it.*

I head quickly to WHSmith, find their stand of daily newspapers and lift one up – *February 29, 2024* it says at the top of today's edition of *The Times* newspaper.

We did it. I gaze at the newspaper for a moment. *We only went and actually did it! I've travelled back in time.* As I'm staring at the newspaper, someone passing by on their way to the exit catches my eye.

It's a woman wearing jeans, a long green coat and a patterned art nouveau scarf tied artfully around her neck. Her long dark hair is twisted up into a messy bun and she's in a hurry.

It's me.

I realise I've stopped breathing for a moment and I gasp suddenly to let in enough air.

I've just seen myself passing through WHSmith with a brand-new notebook, just as I did before I went to get the bus to Grantchester to meet Adam that afternoon. When we chose this date, I didn't think of the possibility I might actually see myself. It just seemed like a familiar and safe date we all knew what had happened on.

I quickly put the newspaper back on the shelf and follow myself to the door. *Little do you know how much your life is about to change.* I pause to watch my past self cross through the market. 'Good Luck ...' I whisper out loud as my past self disappears from view. 'You're gonna need it!'

I sigh. *Time to go back.*

I head back across the market and I'm about to turn into the alleyway, with the intention of returning down the tunnel to Adam, when I pause. I suddenly feel a very strong inclination to go and see what happened in Clockmaker Court that day ...

Without thinking about it any further, I quickly head around to the entrance of the courtyard. I lean stealthily up against one of the walls, where I hope I won't be seen by any of the other shopkeepers, but where, if I peek around the edge, I can still see what's happening within the court.

I look over to Rainy Day Antiques, with its *Closed* sign hanging in the window, just as I left it. Then across to the café – where I can see Rocky wiping down a couple of tables inside. Harriet appears from the café door, so I immediately retract my head as she passes by the entrance. When I take another peek again, I see she has walked across to Luca's shop, which is quite near to where I am, and they are both standing outside having a conversation. I listen hard to try to pick up what they're saying.

'You know where Eve has gone today, don't you?' Harriet says after they've exchanged pleasantries. 'To the grandfather's.'

'Is that today?' Luca asks, sounding shocked. 'I can't believe it's finally happening, after all these years of waiting.'

'If I'm honest, I wish it wasn't. I have no desire to go back, even if they really do figure this thing out.'

'What do you think the chances are of that?' Luca asks, sounding worried. 'I know that's what the predictions said. But it's been so long, Harriet. I quite like living here now.'

'Well, no one is forcing *me* to go back down that tunnel,' Harriet says stoutly. 'There is no way I'm leaving my Rocky.'

'We can't be forced to do it,' Luca says. 'I was under the impression it was always optional whether we wanted to return or not.'

'Ben wants to go back,' Harriet says. 'You know that, don't you. He's always been keen. Too keen for my liking. Why would you want to go back to Victorian times when you can live here with hot running water and central heating!'

'It was Edwardian by then, wasn't it, where he came from – 1904?'

'It's still not 2024, though, is it? It would feel primitive going back to those times again after you'd got used to living here now.'

'He wants to see if his mother was all right after he left,' Luca says. 'I can understand that. I left my friends just before Hitler invaded France in 1940. I have no idea what happened to some of them. Or some of my family in Italy. It is very tempting.'

'At least we know the truth,' Harriet says. 'We can make our choice *if* the portal ever begins working again and *if* they can control it. What about those who don't know where they came from?'

Luca pauses before answering and I can only assume he's nodding since I can't see him. 'Do you think they'll ever tell him?' he asks.

'No idea. But I wouldn't want to go back if I was him. It must be bad enough being in a wheelchair now, let alone back then. Probably best if he never knows. What you don't know can't harm you – that's what they say. And in Barney's case, I'd say they were right.'

My heart stops beating for a moment, like it had in WHSmith, and again I gasp. *Barney is from the past too? He can't be ... can he?*

I try to think quickly. *Harriet said he didn't know he was. If so, why doesn't he? He must have come through the portal when he was very young and he can't remember? That would fit with what Barney told us about him not remembering his real family, only his adoptive parents. Was he placed with a family when he came through the tunnel by someone?*

My mind is racing so much that I don't realise Luca and Harriet have stopped talking and have retreated back to the warmth of their shops. I shiver – from the cold or from the newfound knowledge I now have, I'm not sure. But I'm suddenly desperate to get back to May 2024 and to Adam.

But as I turn, about to rush back to the alleyway, I almost bump into Ben.

'Eve,' he says, smiling at me. 'What are you doing hanging around here in the cold?'

I can do nothing but stare at him.

'Are you all right?' he asks. 'You must be freezing out here dressed like that. Where's the lovely green coat you often wear? In fact, didn't I just see you wearing it a few minutes ago as you crossed the market square?'

'I ...' I'm lost for words. Partly at this sudden encounter with Ben and partly still at what I've just heard.

Ben narrows his eyes. Then, like a lightbulb going off, I see his expression change as his eyes light up.

'Don't worry,' he says, tapping the side of his nose. 'I get it. I can't believe it's going to happen at last, but you've obviously made it work. Now go. And I'll pretend this meeting never happened. OK?'

I nod hurriedly. Then I dash off towards the alleyway.

To my enormous relief, the pallets are still where I left them and the door is still wedged open. I clear the entrance, step back inside the tunnel and pull the two exterior doors closed behind me, replacing the wooden planks across them. Then I step quickly, but cautiously, down the tunnel and knock on the doors at the other end.

Adam immediately pulls them open. 'Thank God you're back!' he says, looking incredibly anxious. 'It felt like you were gone ages. I was just about to come and look for you.'

'Yeah ...' I say, not knowing quite where to begin. 'I got a little sidetracked.'

'What was it like?' Adam asks. 'Did it work?'

'Yes, it worked. I went back to the twenty-ninth of February this year. I checked a newspaper and I saw myself.'

'What? How?'

I tell Adam what happened.

'And then you came back?' he asks. 'When you left the shop?'

'Er, not immediately, no,' I reply hesitantly. 'I went to Clockmaker Court and I found out something quite interesting. No, not interesting, that's the wrong word. Something actually quite worrying ...'

33

'What should we do?' I ask Adam when I've finished telling him about Barney.

'Nothing,' Adam says. 'What he's never known he can't miss.'

'But he has the right to know he's one of the ... *time travellers*?' I say, for want of a better phrase.

'Why? Maybe he's better off not knowing. Then he won't have the dilemma of whether he should go back or not. If we really have found a way of controlling this portal, then it will open up all sorts of opportunities.'

'Then Barney deserves to have that opportunity too.'

'All right,' Adam says reluctantly. 'Don't say I didn't warn you, though.'

'Can you guys hear me?' We hear Barney from upstairs. 'I don't know if you can, but I've seen Rocky off and I'm wondering what's happening down there?'

I look at Adam. 'Not a word,' I whisper. 'To Barney. Not until I decide what's for the best.'

Adam nods. We close the cupboard doors and climb the stairs together.

After I've repeated my story – up to the WHSmith part – for Barney, we sit down in the shop together to decide what to do next.

'I still can't believe that actually worked,' Barney says, shaking his head in disbelief. 'Imagine actually being able to travel back in time … It's unbelievable.'

'It is quite exciting,' I say carefully.

'It's mega! When are you going to tell the others?' Barney asks excitedly.

'Today. There's no point in waiting, is there? Then they can decide what they want to do.'

'I'm sure I wouldn't want to go in time – not permanently, anyway – though a quick trip to see a few things might be fun. But in this thing' – he points to his wheelchair – 'no siree Bob! As I've said before, going back in time with a disability is never going to be a good thing.'

Adam and I exchange glances.

'Which of our time travellers should we tell first?' Adam asks quickly.

'Is that what we're actually calling them now?' Barney asks gleefully. '*Time travellers*. So what are we, then?' He thinks for a moment. 'What about *the guardians of time*? Or *the protectors of the portal*?'

'I'm not sure we need an actual title, do we?' I say, feeling uncomfortable. I'm not exactly lying to Barney, but I feel like I'm not telling him the truth either.

'We have uncovered a pretty major thing today,' Barney says, clearly still elated by our discovery. 'Personally I think it's the least we deserve. Ooh, maybe *we're* the timekeepers now, like Ernie said?'

'I'm going to see Ben,' I say, standing up. 'To tell him what's happened. He was in his shop earlier.'

'Shall we come?' Barney asks, still full of excitement.

'No!' I snap at him. 'No,' I repeat a little more gently. 'I'll tell him. There's a few things I want to ask him while I'm there.'

Barney opens his mouth, but Adam speaks first. 'I don't know about you, Barney, but I could do with something to eat. Shall we nip out and get some lunch while Eve speaks to Ben?'

I smile gratefully at Adam as I leave the shop, stopping immediately outside to take a few deep breaths. Everything is moving too fast right now – I just need some time to think. Both about what we've discovered and what's the right thing for Barney.

But time, ironically, is something I don't have enough of right now. Because Ben spots me from his shop window and waves me over.

'Eve, my dear!' he says as I enter the shop. 'Are you all right? You looked a little stressed outside your shop just now.'

'A little shellshocked might be a better description, Ben, and not only about what you told us yesterday.'

I tell Ben everything that happened this afternoon. From our ideas about the tree and the brass calendar, to me actually travelling back in time, and our meeting. But I leave out the conversation I overheard between Harriet and Luca.

'Oh, my,' Ben says, looking shocked. 'You actually did it?'

'But you worked that out already when I bumped into you in February?'

Ben smiles knowingly. 'It depends what timeline of events we're following. Remember, that meeting between us didn't happen originally.'

'It's very confusing.'

'The ability to time travel is, that's why it's only granted to those who can handle both the knowledge and the pressure. But you've learnt how to control the portal, Eve. The first person in … well, it could be centuries, for all we know. You are truly worthy of this honour that's been bestowed upon you.'

'It's very early days, but I think we might have a loose grip on it.'

'I think you are too modest. It really is truly incredible,' he continues, looking amazed and at the same time emotional. He shakes his head in disbelief. 'I can't believe that after all these years, not only were the predictions on the tree and the doors correct, but now there's actually a chance for me to return.'

'Why do you want to go back, Ben?' I ask, knowing the reason, of course. But I want to know more. 'I know it's to see your mother, but what else is making you want to take this enormous risk?'

Ben looks at me as if he doesn't quite understand.

'You don't know what will happen to you if you time travel. You might remain as old as you are now, or you could revert back to the ten-year-old boy you were when you came here. Will you have memories of what's to come in the future? How will it all work?'

'That's the beauty of it,' Ben says, smiling. 'I don't know. No one does.'

'Then why do it? Forgive me for saying this, but you're old, Ben. You're fragile. Being old at the turn of the last century isn't like being old now — it will be tough.'

'I know it will be,' Ben says sombrely. 'But I haven't got many more years on this earth, whether I decide to spend them here in the present time, or back then. If

I don't go back now, I'll never do it, and therefore I'll never feel truly at peace with myself.'

'But what if you didn't know *where* you came from? You didn't know you'd time travelled here and you had no memory of your original life. Do you think you'd want to know the truth?'

Ben gazes steadily but silently at me. Only breaking eye contact to blink.

'Barney,' he says eventually. 'Who told you?'

'No one told me. I found out earlier when I travelled back to the twenty-ninth of February. I overheard a conversation between Harriet and Luca that day.'

Ben nods, as though it doesn't surprise him the two of them would have been gossiping together.

'Barney doesn't know he came through the tunnel,' he says. 'He doesn't know he was actually the last person to do so as well. He was just a small child when he came through, barely walking. Actually, that was the problem. He wasn't walking – he couldn't.'

'Barney told me he couldn't remember his parents because they'd died in a house fire when he was four, and that was when he lost the use of his legs.'

'That part is true. That is exactly what happened to him. But it didn't happen in the year 2004 like he thinks it did, it happened in 1908.'

I try to process the dates as well as what Ben is telling me. 'How did he come through the tunnel if he couldn't walk?'

'We think someone put him there. Someone who thought they could help him by sending him into the future.' Ben waits to see if I understand.

'Dotty ...' I say immediately. 'It has to be. Do you think Dotty put him in there?'

'Who else knew the tunnel was there? And I don't think it was the only time she did it either. When George decided he was going to seal up the tunnel permanently, your grandmother and I weren't too happy about it. We worried that people might still appear in there on a leap day, and not have a way out. So every twenty-ninth of February after the tunnel was closed, we'd secretly go down and check on and off throughout the day from the antiques shop so George never became suspicious. That's one of the reasons the portal is more accessible from your shop than Adam's – it was opened more often and more recently than the other side. The day we found Barney on the twenty-ninth of February 2004 was one of those times. Whoever had left him had also left a note with him.'

'You've still got the note, haven't you?' I ask, knowing he will have.

'Of course.' Ben pulls an envelope from his inside jacket pocket. 'I took this from my safe when you and Adam were beginning to make some progress with the portal – or was it when I bumped into you at the entrance to Clockmaker Court …' He raises his eyebrows mischievously. 'I can't quite recall.' He passes me the note and I open it carefully. It's handwritten in black ink on yellowing paper.

To whom it may concern.

For whatever reason, I know that you have now closed off the tunnel at your end and I have not been sending anyone to you for some time.

However, this child is different. He deserves a good life and I hope whatever year he arrives in with you, someone can give him a better life than he will have if he stays here in 1908. The boy was orphaned in a house fire and his

*injuries mean he will never walk again. Although things
are starting to improve, most handicapped children are
still treated badly here and have a very poor quality of life.*

*I do not know what the future holds for children like him
but, even if he only travels as far forward as 1944, I know
he will have a better life than he will have in this time.*

His name is Barnaby and he is four years old.

Please look after him. I know you will.

'It's Dotty's handwriting,' I say, looking at Ben. 'I remember it from the letter we read that was in the *Dalmatians*
book, and she went missing in 1944, didn't she, so she
would know things were better up to that year.'

Ben nods. 'It seems that Dotty may have been sending us
people all along. Obviously I know my story with her, but
some of the others remember a mysterious woman guiding
them down the alleyway to the doors. Until Barney – or
should I say Barnaby – appeared, though, we never really
thought about it being Dotty.'

I consider this for a moment.

'But some of the others came from much later years
than Victorian and Edwardian times, didn't they?' I say,
thinking out loud. 'Are you suggesting she was doing this
for many years – decades, even?'

'There seems to be no correlation between when they
arrived with us and the year they came from,' Ben says,
remembering. 'All we know is that they came from leap
years and arrived in them, too, every four years. I don't
think Dotty, if it is her, knew what year they would appear
in once they went through the portal. But bearing in
mind that Harriet came to us from the fifties, one can

311

only assume that Dotty was trying to help people for a long time after she arrived in 1904 – that's if she really did stay there. We have no way of truly knowing.'

'So, you're saying even if she was guiding them to safety in order at her end, the order they appeared here in Clockmaker Court was random?'

Ben nods. 'I don't think the tunnel can be completely controlled. It seems to make its own mind up what year people are deposited in the future. It's as if it knows what's going to be best for them.'

'I can just about cope with the fact we've discovered an actual time tunnel, Ben. I really can't deal with the thought it might have its own mind too!'

'Fair enough. But you agree it might be Dotty at the other end helping people out of difficult situations?'

'Yes, I do. It sounds like her style.' I smile. Dotty is becoming more heroic and more wonderful to me by the minute. 'I wonder why she's never tried to come back herself, though?'

'I've wondered that too, many times. But as the time grew closer for both you and Adam to take the helm, I thought I would wait and see what happened.'

'You were all putting a lot of hope on the two of us working out, weren't you?'

'It was always going to work out,' Ben says, smiling. 'I had faith in the old oak tree. Every time I wavered and worried for the future, I just looked out of my shop window and saw it standing there, bravely weathering every storm, just waiting patiently for the day it would be proved correct. And here you now are.'

'Yes, here we are. But Barney,' I say, watching him come back through the court with Adam, carrying paper bags filled with lunchtime goodies. Adam glances across at Ben's shop and sees me watching him through the window. He mouths silently, 'You OK?'

I nod at him and then I turn back to Ben. 'Should I tell Barney he's from the past now I know?' I ask. 'I really don't like keeping secrets.'

'I think you'll know when the time is right,' Ben says in his usual calm, considered way. 'You now have a much bigger secret to keep, Eve. A secret that many generations before you have kept hidden. I don't think you need to be told why it must be kept a secret. Something like this in the wrong hands ... well, it could be disastrous.'

'I have seen the *Back to the Future* movies, Ben. I remember what happened when Biff got the *Sports Almanac*.' I smile at my joke – somehow making light of all this helps lift the burden a little.

But instead of joining in, Ben looks even more grave. 'This isn't a movie, Eve. This is real. You have been given an incredibly important task here, one people have been undertaking for hundreds, possibly thousands of years before you. You and Adam are the new timekeepers. You *must* keep the portal safe.'

'Of course,' I agree earnestly. 'I do understand, Ben, how important this all is.'

'Good. I'm glad you do.'

I feel bad now for making light of the situation and I want to make it up to him.

'You know, if you really want to go back to 1904 to see your mother, Ben, then I think I can help you do it. If you're absolutely sure, that is?'

Ben's dark brown eyes, that always seem to twinkle, suddenly shine that extra bit brighter. 'Eve, I've never been surer of anything in my whole life – all one hundred and thirty years of it.'

34

'Are you absolutely sure about this, Ben?' I ask him the next day as we wait for the moment when the sun moves onto the hidden building in Clockmaker Court.

'Perfectly sure,' Ben says, standing tall next to me. Adam and Barney are already down in the office waiting.

Yesterday was a tough one for many reasons.

After I returned from Ben's shop and reported our conversation back to Adam and Barney, I then talked to both Harriet and Luca separately on the bench under the oak tree, while Adam and Barney took it in turns to watch their shops. I told them what we now knew and asked whether either of them wanted to join Ben in attempting to return to their past lives.

Harriet's reply was simple – a very clear and adamant no. She told me she was incredibly happy living here with Rocky and she never ever wanted to go back again. But she wished us luck on our quest to help Ben.

'What you're doing is wonderful,' she told me before she returned to Rocky. 'If anyone deserves a last moment of happiness, it's our Ben. We'll miss him here in Clockmaker Court, of course – it won't be the same without him. But I know he's doing the right thing for him.' Then, to my surprise, she hugged me. Which was so unlike Harriet that it actually left me speechless as she walked back across the court to her shop.

Luca's answer to my question was undecided. He wavered between wanting to go and being scared to return. 'I need to think about it, darling,' he told me eventually. 'It's such a big decision. I'm just not sure yet.'

'That's absolutely fine,' I told him. 'I know it's a tough decision to make.'

'Are you cross with me?' Luca asked anxiously. 'Because I didn't tell you my secret?'

I hesitated. Even though I know why Luca and the others have never said anything, I couldn't help but feel a little upset by them keeping their past lives a secret from me.

'No, I'm not cross as such – how can I be? If you'd told me the truth, I'd have thought you were crazy. It's not your fault you had to keep it a secret. But it does feel like I don't truly know who you are any more.'

'Oh, beautiful, I'm so very sorry,' Luca said, taking both my hands in his. 'Of course you know who I am – I'm exactly the person you knew before. I'm just a few decades older than you thought! Look on it like I've had really good Botox, if it makes it easier!'

He was right, of course. These people are exactly the same people that I knew before. Their personalities aren't any different now I know where they came from – they are just older and they've been carrying the weight of a huge secret with them for many years. A secret that I already know is going to weigh heavily on my shoulders now I'm a part of it too.

'It might do,' I said, smiling at him. 'You know, I wondered why my Luca was such an expert on the Second

World War. I thought you were some sort of secret history buff. Little did I know you actually came from that era.'

'Ha, I nearly gave myself away that evening, didn't I? Annie and Ed were really impressed by my knowledge too.'

'It's a shame you weren't related to them. It would have been nice for you to find out something about your family.'

'Who said we aren't?' Luca raised his eyebrows mischievously at me. 'I found out Ed's grandmother is actually my second cousin.'

'What?'

'I couldn't tell them that, obviously. But it was good to know I have some family still in this life, even if I can't find out too much about what happened to my own from back then.'

'It's amazing the pull you feel towards anyone who might have been your family, isn't it?' I told him, thinking of Dotty and the incredibly strong connection I felt towards her.

Luca nodded. 'That's what I've always found lovely about Clockmaker Court. We're like a little family here. For whatever reason, we've all been orphaned from our original families, but because of that, we've all bonded and made our own unique little family right here.'

'Gosh, I've never really thought about it like that. That's really lovely, Luca, thank you.' Leaning forward, I gave him a big hug. 'You know, if you do decide to go back, I'll support your decision, of course. But I will miss you terribly.'

'Not as much as I'd miss you, my lovely.'

Now, as I stand waiting with Ben just in front of the oak tree, I'm reminded once more of those conversations.

For today is the day we are attempting to send him back to 1904.

We all gathered to say goodbye and it was a tearful few minutes as Ben bade farewell to everyone. Now we are all waiting for the minutes to tick by until the sun moves into the right place and it's the right time to instruct the portal to open on our requested year.

After my discussions with Harriet and Luca, I thought long and hard about whether to tell Barney or not. And I decided for the time being, it was best not to, even though it didn't sit well with me. Barney was happy here in Clockmaker Court – he'd told me that. Knowing his true story would surely only upset him and cause the sort of trauma that Luca is now wrestling with. So, for now, I've decided to keep quiet about it.

'I will miss you all when I go,' Ben says, looking around at the buildings and all the people waiting to see him off. 'But I know I'll be leaving Clockmaker Court in safe hands. It's time to pass this secret on to the next generation to keep it safe and secure. Just as our predecessors have been doing for thousands of years before us.'

I'm trying to be as brave as Ben is appearing, but I'm failing badly. 'I'm worried about you, Ben,' I say anxiously.

'Why, my lovely girl? I'll be absolutely fine.'

'I know you think you will. But the truth is, you're not getting any younger. How will you cope back then? It's not like it is now.'

Ben smiles. 'No, I know it isn't. But don't you worry, I'll be just fine. Our friend Luca has given me a good start with this wonderful attire,' he says, gesturing to his outfit. He looks like a fine Victorian dandy in his long black tailcoat, pinstripe trousers, burgundy-red cravat, and, to finish it all off, a shiny black top hat. He's also carrying a cane and some gloves, and tucked into his waistcoat, he has a gold pocket watch on a chain. 'I look just the part of an elderly man who hasn't quite left the Victorian era behind yet. I'll fit right in.'

'But what will you do for money?'

'Eve,' he says. 'I've been running a shop for over fifty years that sells antique maps, coins and notes.' He opens one side of his jacket and I can see a bundle of large banknotes tucked away in his inside pocket. 'And there's plenty more where that came from,' he says, lifting up a large brown suitcase. 'I'll be able to buy whatever I want with the amount of money I've got tucked away. Enough to live comfortably on, anyway.'

'Good, at least that's something. But you will be careful, won't you? I mean, is there any way you could let us know you're all right? Could you send a letter or something, and have it arrive next week?'

'How would I do that?'

'You could give it to a solicitors' office and ask them to keep it until the year 2024 and then have them deliver it?'

'Is this something you've once again seen in a movie, by any chance?' Ben asks, raising his eyebrows.

'Yes … but I think I might have read it in a book as well. It's a good idea.'

'Eve, this is real life – it's not as simple as some of those stories make out. There's far more complexities and things we don't know about.'

'Please?' I ask. 'Can you at least try?'

Ben nods. 'I'll see what I can do. No promises, though.'

'Thank you.' The sun is moving ever closer to the building, but more worryingly, there are now several large clouds drifting slowly across the sky as well. I'm praying they don't cover the sun just at the moment we need it to shine fully on the building.

'Can we talk about you for a moment,' Ben says. 'There's some things I need to tell you.'

'Of course, but we don't have a lot of time before the sun hits the building.'

Ben glances at where the sun currently is. Happy, he continues. 'Now you and Adam are the new timekeepers – I know you don't like that word, but that's what you are – it's down to you to both protect the portal and decide how it's used in the future.'

'What do you mean, how it's used? Once we get you back safely and any others that might want to return after you, that's it, as far as I'm concerned. We'll seal it all up again and keep it safe.'

Ben smiles. 'That would be the simplest plan. But remember, we sealed the building up when we couldn't control the portal. Now you and Adam know how, the temptation will always be there to go back to try to change things. I'm certain you've learnt from all your movies that the one rule of time travel is you mustn't change the past.'

'Of course, I know that.'

'But you *will* be tempted. Both of you. Especially with both your histories. There are things you don't know yet. Our tale is only one chapter of a much bigger story.'

'OK,' I reply, looking behind me. I am listening to Ben, but one of the clouds has just parked itself in front of the sun. I hear a sharp intake of breath from those behind us as the sun's rays are immediately blocked.

'I mean it, Eve,' Ben says sternly. 'It's only natural to want to right wrongs – especially if they're personal to you. But you must remember the portal is there for much greater reasons than we understand.'

'Ben, I get it, all right. Don't mess with time or it will mess with you.' I'm smiling again now, because the cloud above us has moved on quickly to allow the sun to shine once more.

'I'm serious, Eve. You and Adam have great power now, and with great power—'

'Comes great responsibility? Yes, I know that one. Are you the one quoting movies now?'

'Comic books, actually.' Ben visibly relaxes and I'm pleased to see him smile. 'That phrase is often attributed to one of my favourite comic-book stories. But it's been said many more times before that, by a great many people. Winston Churchill said something similar and I believe you will find it in the Bible too.' He thinks. 'Yes, Luke 12:48 – look it up sometime.'

'I will,' I tell him.

'It's true, though – you must not treat this responsibility lightly. You must treat it with the respect it deserves. If you do that, you will never go far wrong.'

The sun moves onto the outside of the building.

'It's almost time,' I say. 'Are you ready?'

Ben nods and we stand in silence for the next few moments as we watch the sun move to the centre of the building. I hold the brass calendar up so the shade from the tree passes over the Roman numerals set to the exact date in 1904 that Ben has requested to return to.

'It's time,' I tell him.

Ben nods at me, then he turns and gives one final wave to the others behind us, before we both enter the shop together.

The hands on the grandfather clock are spinning backwards as we pass, just like they did before. We go through the door and down the stairs to the office where Adam and Barney are waiting for us.

'Did it work?' Adam asks as we enter the office.

I nod silently. The emotion of this moment has suddenly got to me and I know if I don't hold it together, I'm going to burst into tears.

'Adam.' Ben shakes his hand. 'Your grandfather would be very proud of you. I'm very proud of you too. Look after yourself and Eve, won't you?'

'I will,' Adam says stoutly, but I can hear the emotion in his voice as he speaks. 'Good luck, Ben.' They embrace briefly, patting each other's back.

'Barney,' Ben says, reaching into his jacket pocket to pull out an envelope. 'These are the deeds to my shop. It's yours if you'd like it.'

'Really?' Barney says, looking shocked as he takes the envelope from Ben. 'Are you sure?'

Ben nods. 'Perfectly. Do what you want with it. But, if you'd like to open a shop that sells comics, that would make me very happy. And I think possibly you too?'

Barney grins. 'Oh, yes. That would be amazing. Thank you so much.'

Ben bends down and hugs him. 'You've grown into a fine young man. Clockmaker Court will continue to look after you, if you look after it in return.'

Barney nods. 'I will, Ben. I promise I will.'

'Eve,' Ben says, turning to me.

'Oh, Ben, I will miss you,' I say as tears begin to pour down my face as we embrace. 'You've been such a help to me since I came to Clockmaker Court, and not just recently, but all those years before, when I was simply trying to keep the shop going. I don't know if I could have done it without you.'

'You would have done,' he whispers, his voice breaking a little. 'You're a true Sinclair, Eve. You don't give up easily. Your grandparents were so proud of you. Dotty would have been proud of you too. Never doubt yourself. You are more than up to the challenge that lies ahead. Now, I must go,' he says, pulling away from me. He ducks his head to go through the wooden doors already open for him, using his cane to support him. Then he turns as he stands up fully in the space on the other side. 'I bid you all farewell, my friends. It's been an honour and a pleasure knowing you, and your families. I have a feeling we'll all meet again one day.'

With one final salute, Ben turns and walks away from us down the tunnel, carrying his top hat in one hand, and his suitcase and cane in the other, and he looks younger and more alive than I think I've ever seen him as he disappears into the darkness.

Once he's out of sight, Adam moves forward and silently closes the doors behind him. Then we wait.

After a moment or two, Barney asks, 'How long before we see if he's gone?'

'I don't want to look,' I say, turning away. 'I want it to have succeeded, of course I do. But I don't want to think he's gone for ever.'

Adam waits another minute, then opens the doors once more and calls into the darkness, 'Ben? Ben, are you still there?'

Silence fills the tunnel. Slowly it filters through to the office.

'I think he's gone,' he says, turning back to us. 'Back to his right place and his right time.'

35

A few months later …

I stand in the doorway of my shop and look out at Clockmaker Court. I can see Luca in his shop window arranging a new display of 1920s dresses and jewellery. He blows me a kiss and I wave back. Luca decided in the end to stay. I was so grateful to still have one of my best friends here with me that I made a vow to help him in any way I could to find out more about what happened to his family and friends during and after the Second World War. Progress is slow but we'll get there, I know it.

A couple of doors along, Harriet and Rocky are just closing up for the day. Harriet is wiping the countertops and Rocky is turning chairs upside down on top of the tables in their shop so he can sweep the floors underneath. Harriet is also a lot happier and more relaxed since she told us she wasn't going back, as though a worry she's been carrying with her for so long has finally been erased, and she can fully relax and enjoy her life here in the twenty-first century.

Across from me, I can see just Orla is in her shop, sitting behind the till and reading a book – I still haven't let her read my tarot cards, but Orla doesn't ask as much any more – she said she was happy that I was on the right path now. Next door to her is what used to be Ben's old shop. I still can't quite get used to the fact he isn't there now when I look out onto Clockmaker Court. Instead I jolt just a tad when I see the unfamiliar shop front of Barney's new comic-book store.

Barney gave up both his job at the university and working alongside me, and now runs his shop full-time, and I've never seen him happier. He called his shop the Geek Retreat and alongside the many vintage comic books he sells, he's filled his shop with an eclectic mix of other superhero merchandise that seems to attract quite the mix of new clientele to the court. Which in turn helps boost the sales of all the other shops alongside his.

Adam and I eventually took the difficult decision of telling Barney where he originally came from. But much to our surprise, Barney said he already knew, thanks to Ben telling him everything before his departure into the past. Barney, to my enormous relief, decided he was much better staying here, and I wondered if Ben's gift to Barney of his shop was a shrewd move on his part to encourage Barney to stay in the twenty-first century.

And that left Adam and me.

Adam was finally able to open his bookshop, and for a while, everything in the court, and our lives, calmed down and began to run a little more normally. Throughout the summer, both our shops were busy and profitable, and all the shops in Clockmaker Court began to flourish once more.

The shops weren't the only thing flourishing. My relationship with Adam went from strength to strength through the summer too. We were both busy with our shops, but made sure we always had time for each other, whether that was grabbing a quick lunch together under the oak tree or going on a proper date in the evenings somewhere, usually a pub for a drink or meal. Everything about being with Adam is relaxed and chilled, and I can't remember the last time I've felt this happy.

There is one thing that I sometimes allow myself to think about, even worry about occasionally, but I try very hard to put it firmly to the back of my mind. The last thing I want to do is rock the proverbial boat that is sailing so smoothly right now through the waves of my life. But today, those thoughts that I can usually nip in the bud before they turn to worry are particularly poignant and hard to control.

'Penny for them?' A voice makes me jump. And I realise that Adam has left his shop and is standing outside mine watching me.

'Not worth a penny,' I say, smiling at him.

'I'm sure they are,' Adam says, coming towards me and immediately pulling me into his arms. He tucks a piece of stray hair that's come loose from my ponytail behind my ear. 'Fancy telling me about them tonight over dinner?'

'Let's skip dinner and go back to mine.'

'How very forward of you, Miss Sinclair,' he says, raising his eyebrows. 'But I won't say no!'

'I actually meant let's get a takeaway and go back to mine. But there might just be time for the other thing afterwards if you play your cards right.'

Adam grins. 'I've already shut up my shop for the day. It's gone dead quiet since four o'clock. How about you do the same and we'll head off now.'

'Yeah, it has. Good idea.' I give Adam a quick kiss, then pull away from him to begin the process of cashing up for the day.

'Are you sure you're all right?' he asks.

'Yes, why?'

'Nothing, you've just seemed a bit preoccupied today, that's all.'

'I'm fine.'

'No, you're not.' Adam follows me to the shop counter. 'What's up?'

I sigh. I struggle to hide anything from Adam, as he does from me.

'It would have been Ben's birthday today,' I say. 'I miss him most days, but today in particular I've found myself thinking about him a lot.'

Adam nods. 'That's understandable. We always think about loved ones that little bit more on special days.'

'Yes.' I open my till and begin counting the cash. 'We do.'

'It's not just that, is it?' Adam asks perceptively. 'There's something else other than it being his birthday?'

It's no good. I'll have to tell him. I put the notes I'm currently counting down on the shop counter. 'I just find myself wondering what happened to him, that's all. We never heard anything from him. Anything could have happened when he went back.'

Adam frowns. 'Were you expecting to hear something from him, then?'

I shrug. 'Maybe.' *Damn, I've lost count now. I'll have to start again.* I pick up the notes.

'How?'

'I hoped he might send me a letter or something.'

'OK … You're going to have to fill me in a bit more, I'm afraid. How was Ben supposed to send you a letter from 1904, but it not arrive until 2024?'

I swallow hard. It was going to sound silly now.

'Remember the movie *Back to the Future* – actually, it was the second film in the trilogy.'

'Er, yes, vaguely.'

'Do you remember the part when Doc sent Marty a letter from where he was in the past, and it was delivered many years later?'

'Yes …'

'Like that.'

'You asked Ben to write you a letter to let you know he was OK. Then he was to arrange for it to be kept for nearly a hundred and twenty years, and delivered in 2024?'

'Yes.'

'And he hasn't?'

'No.'

'Does it surprise you? Even if Ben did manage to do that, the chances of someone actually keeping that letter for all those years, or for the company he left it with to still be in existence, is incredibly low.'

'I know it is. But if I had got a letter, at least I would know whether he was all right when he went back. I try not to, but I worry about him, Adam. I wonder what happened to both him and to Dotty. I worry about her too. It feels like we just got to know her a little better and then suddenly she was also gone. Now we don't talk about her any more.'

Adam sighs and joins me behind the shop counter. 'I'd love to say something reassuring to you, to let you know that they were both OK,' he says, taking my hand. 'But I'm afraid I can't. There's just no way of ever truly knowing what happened, to either of them.'

'That's not exactly true …' I reply coyly.

'No,' he says, shaking his head. 'No way!'

'You don't know what I'm going to say!'

'Oh, I do. You're going to suggest you use the portal to travel back and check on them – Ben, at the very least. You're going to say something like, "I won't stay long. I'll just pop back, find out what happened, then come straight back again."'

It is infuriating when Adam does this. But he is spot on.

'I could do, though, couldn't I?' I ask brightly. 'Just set the portal to a few days after when Ben returned, find him, check he's all right, then come back.'

'And there's no part of you that thinks that could be a tad dangerous?'

'I've done it before and I was fine.'

'You went back a few months to a date when we both knew what had happened that day. It's hardly the same as going back to the Victorian era!'

'Edwardian,' I say. 'Have you any better ideas?'

'Yes, leave the portal well alone. We've discussed this before.'

There's no point in arguing with him. So I begin counting my notes again.

'Eve? You won't do anything silly, will you?'

'No,' I say, innocently blinking at him. 'Of course I won't.'

'Promise me?'

'OK. I promise I won't do anything *silly*.'

Going back in time is never silly. It is only ever going to be deadly serious.

36

The next morning, I awake to an empty bed next to me.

Nothing strange in that. Even when Adam stays the night, he will often get up earlier than me to give himself time to go for a run before work and then take a shower, or sometimes he has to be at the bookshop early to receive a delivery. So I don't think too much about getting up alone and getting ready for the day ahead.

As I go downstairs to the kitchen, I'm still thinking about what we discussed last night. We didn't say anything more about the possibility of me using the portal to check on Ben. It didn't seem necessary to continue discussing it. I knew Adam's stance wouldn't change. In his opinion, it was just too dangerous for me to go back there – and that was the end of it.

But Adam should know me better than that. Once I decide to do something, no one is going to stop me, especially not my boyfriend.

I planned today, if the shop was quiet, to figure out a way I could go back without him knowing. *I might have to get Barney onside to help me*, I think as I shower and get dressed for work.

Time is getting on when I'm finally ready to leave the house.

I'll grab a coffee on the way to the shop. Maybe even a couple of Chelsea buns too, to keep Adam sweet. But I'll take some fruit with me to keep it a bit healthier.

I open up my fridge, meaning to grab a banana and a pear, but I stop dead as I see what's sitting on the shelf in front of me – a large red apple.

'How the hell did that get there?' I say, still staring at the apple. For some reason, I've completely gone off apples recently, after both eating and drinking quite a lot of them at the beginning of the year, so now I never buy them.

Maybe Adam put it there, is the only explanation I can think of. But it still seems strange. Adam didn't have any apples with him when he came back to mine last night. So why would he go out and buy one this morning, then leave it in my fridge.

The apples thing was very odd. It was almost like I couldn't get enough of them, or products that contained them, for a while, and I began to wonder if maybe I had a vitamin deficiency. Then, as quick as anything, around the time that Adam and I got together, I went completely the opposite way and now actually feel quite queasy at the thought of eating one. So much so that Barney had teased me mercilessly for a while, with jokes about the Adam–and–Eve effect, forbidden fruit, the Garden of Eden, and suchlike.

But now, as I enter Clockmaker Court with my coffee and buns, all thoughts of apples – good and bad – are forgotten. Because something doesn't feel right.

Unusually, a few of the shopkeepers are standing outside their shops.

'What's going on?' I ask Luca as I approach the group, consisting of him, Orla, Barney and Harriet.

'A couple of us had a break-in last night,' Luca says. 'Well, I say break-in – no one actually forced entry, but things were taken.'

'What things?'

'I had some clothes taken, and Barney some money.'

'Oh, no!' I turn to Barney. 'How much?'

'It wasn't my actual takings,' Barney says. 'I mean, it wasn't modern money. It was some of Ben's old notes that he'd left with me. I haven't got round to selling them on yet, so they were tucked out the back in a box.'

'That's odd. How did they know they were there? And they didn't take any of your stock or anything else?'

Barney shakes his head. 'Not that I can see.'

'The things they took from my shop were a bit odd too,' Luca says. 'Nothing particularly valuable, like my jewellery. It was a few bits from my rails.'

'What sort of bits?'

'Er, from what I can see, a tweed suit, a matching waistcoat, a white shirt, and a flat cap. I'm sure there must be more, but that's all I've noticed.'

Oh, God. My stomach feels like it's dropped down to my feet. *He hasn't, has he?*

'What sort of era are the clothes from?' I ask Luca, as an uneasy feeling begins to settle inside me.

Luca looks confused by my questioning. 'They're a mix, really. But put together, I suppose they might look like something a man would wear in the early part of the twentieth century. Not a city gent, but more of a working-class man.'

Of course that's what he'd choose.

'Has anyone seen Adam yet this morning?' I ask hopefully, looking over to his shop.

'No,' Orla says. 'He's not opened up yet. Why, what's going on, Eve? You've gone awfully pale.'

'Nothing. Everything is fine. Are you going to call the police about the break-ins?' I ask Luca and Barney.

Luca shrugs. 'Can't really, can we? It wasn't a break-in — somehow the thief got in without forcing an entry. It was almost like they had keys to open up the shops. They even locked up after they'd left. But the only people who have keys to my shop are you guys.'

'Same here,' Barney says. 'Clean entry. And the only other people who have keys to my shop are also you lot.'

'I'll be right back,' I tell them. 'I'll just go and check my shop in case the same has happened to me.'

I dash over to my shop and unlock the door. Then, unusually, I lock the door behind me before I dump the buns and coffee on the countertop. As I suspected, the grandfather clock has been pulled forward away from the wall; so I am able to easily open the door down to the office.

I head quickly down the stairs, knowing exactly what I'm going to find, but still feeling sick at the thought of it.

The light is already on in the office as I reach the bottom. I hurry over to the carved wooden doors and I'm about to pull them open when I notice there's a white envelope on the desk addressed to me. Next to that is the bundle of keys to all the other shops in Clockmaker Court that I keep hidden in my safe, and, next to those, the brass perpetual calendar we use to make the portal work. It looks like my fears were correct.

'What have you done?' I say, picking up the envelope. 'You … silly idiot!'

Eve is written in Adam's handwriting on the front of the envelope.

I rip it open and pull out a letter, also in Adam's handwriting.

Eve,

If you're reading this, then you know, and I've not been able to get back quickly enough without you discovering what I've done.

I have of course gone in search of Ben and Dotty for you. I know you'll be angry, but I couldn't let you go back to Victorian (sorry, Edwardian!) times alone – which both of us know you would have tried to do, whatever I had to say about it.

You wouldn't have been safe there on your own, and I simply couldn't have lived with myself if something had happened to you or if you'd got trapped there like Dotty. So, I'm facing my fears and going through the tunnel myself, and if all goes to plan, I'll come out the other side in 1904.

I have no intention of staying, so this isn't a goodbye letter – you can't get rid of me that easily! I will be back before breakfast, I PROMISE you.

But just in case I don't see you for a little while, for what-ever reason, always know I love you with all my heart, and NOTHING will stop me from returning to Clockmaker Court to be with you.

Adam xx

I stare at the letter, half angry with Adam, half in awe. He's faced his fears and gone into a possibly dangerous, dark and enclosed space, and he's done it for me.

'Oh, Adam. Please be all right,' I say, looking at the two wooden doors in front of me. 'Please come back to me.' With his letter still in my hand, I sit down on one of the office chairs and wait. Hoping desperately to hear the sound of someone coming back down the tunnel. But there's nothing – just silence.

After a while, I get up and pace around the office for a bit, stopping occasionally when I think I might have heard something. But again, all I can hear is just an awful, empty silence.

Eventually, after I can pace no longer, I sit again, alone with my thoughts, and they are all about Adam.

When we first met, I thought he was the sort of annoying cocksure man I usually went out of my way to avoid. I told myself I only had to put up with him until the house clearance was complete and then we'd never have to see each other again.

But to my utter bewilderment, Adam grew on me and he got under my skin – in a good way – and now, as I continue to stare at the two wooden doors in front of me, I can hardly bear to think that I might never see him again. 'What if what happened to Dotty happens to you?' I mumble to myself. 'What if you're stuck there and you can't get back again? I'd never forgive myself.'

I think back on our time together over the last few months. As each day passed and we uncovered more about this room and the mysteries of Clockmaker Court, I gradually began to understand there was much more to Adam than he let on. He, like me, suffered trauma in his life. The sort of terrible, scarring experiences that change you for ever, but ones that you choose not to talk about too often, because most people don't and can't understand. And that brought us so much closer.

But it isn't just that. Adam is kind and funny, and most importantly, he gets me. In fact, I'd go so far as to say he knows me, sometimes better than I know myself – which is incredibly annoying when we are having a difference of opinion, but at the same time incredibly comforting too.

I wondered, after Jake, if I would ever meet anyone I could feel that strongly about again. But in Adam, I have. I have totally fallen in love with him, I want to be with him and I just know he has to come back through those doors so we can spend the rest of our lives together.

'Adam Darcy,' I say in a loud, stern voice, standing up. 'You'd better come back through those doors in a minute, or … or … I will be coming down that tunnel to find you myself!'

'Oh, Christ, am I in trouble?' My heart leaps at his voice. 'Maybe I should have stayed in the past?'

I rush forward, fling open the two doors and a dishevelled-looking Adam stumbles towards me. Immediately I fling my arms around him.

'Adam! Oh, my God, I thought you might be gone for ever.'

'You don't know me very well,' Adam says, stepping out of the tunnel, 'if you thought I'd let that ever happen.'

Adam is wearing exactly what Luca described as missing from his shop. Unlike Ben, who returned to his past looking like a character from a Charles Dickens novel, Adam looks more like an extra from the television series *Peaky Blinders* – even though that is set a tad later than the era he's just come from.

We continue to embrace for a few blissful moments more.

'I see you found my letter,' Adam says, noticing it lying on the desk.

'Yes, what the hell were you thinking of?' I say, releasing him as my relief is rapidly replaced by anger.

'You were going to do the same,' he says, removing his cap and sitting down at the desk. 'Don't tell me you weren't?'

'Perhaps. I hadn't actually decided.'

Adam looks reprovingly at me, then he grins. 'You can't hide it from me. I know you, remember?'

Suddenly, I realise how exhausted he looks, as well as dishevelled. 'Forget that now. What happened to you? I assume you went back to 1904? Was everything OK? Are you OK? You look really tired. What about Ben and Dotty – did you find them? Are they all right?'

'Whoa, steady. One question at a time.'

'Sorry.' I pull up the other chair in the office and sit down next to him. 'Tell me everything.'

Adam takes my hand in his and immediately I fear the worst.

'I didn't find Ben,' he says, sounding utterly dejected. 'I tried – believe me, I tried. I searched and searched, and I asked so many people. A couple of them had actually seen a man matching the description I gave them, but they didn't know where I could find him.'

'Oh, please don't worry,' I say, putting my hand over his now. 'At least we know he probably got back there all right if people have seen him. I can't imagine there would be too many people matching his description walking around Cambridge back then – he cut quite the striking figure in his outfit when he left.'

'However … I did locate his mother,' Adam says, some sparkle returning to his eyes. 'And I spoke to her.'

'Gosh, did you? What did she say?' I ask eagerly. 'Had she seen him too?'

'Kind of. I mean, I know it was Ben from what Eliza – that's Ben's mother's name – told me, but I don't think she knew it was him.'

'How do you mean?'

'I think Ben must have gone back to 1904 before Dotty rescued him. Because when I went to visit Eliza, she told me a well-dressed man had come to her house asking about her son just over a week ago – which she thought was odd. She asked what did he want with her son? But the man wouldn't say. He simply told her not to worry and her son was absolutely fine. But he insisted on leaving her money – more money than she'd ever seen in her life. Eliza was suspicious at first and thought there might be a catch. But when nothing happened and the man didn't return for his money, she decided not to look a gift horse in the mouth. There's enough money, she told me, for her and her son to move out of the slum they are living in and to rent a little cottage on the outskirts of the city. They were moving out the next day – I only just caught her.'

'So our Ben went back early so he could give his mother money before the young Ben went missing?' I say, trying to follow this.

'Yes, it appears so. That's if young Ben actually did disappear this time?'

'I don't understand. What do you mean?'

'Ben told us he was pickpocketing back in 1904 to keep both him and his mother from going into the workhouse, didn't he?'

'Yes …' I say, not understanding where Adam is going with this.

'What if, by giving his mother money before the day he was rescued by Dotty and ended up in 1944, the young Ben was able to stop what he was doing, because they both now had plenty of money to live on?'

I stare at Adam as what he's suggesting begins to make sense.

'So he never got chased by the men?' I ask, slowly piecing this together.

Adam nods. 'And he never ended up here in Clockmaker Court.'

'But how can that be? We know he did?'

'In that version of events, yes. But there's a theory of time travel that says by travelling in time you can create new alternative timelines that branch off the main timeline and run simultaneously alongside the others.'

I frown at Adam, trying to understand. 'When did you become such an expert on time-travel theories?'

'I've been doing some reading,' Adam says. 'I didn't want us to take on the responsibility of the time portal without knowing exactly what we were taking on.'

I smile at him.

'What?' he asks.

'You're so amazing,' I tell him proudly. 'Not only did you face your fears and go into a dark, enclosed space so you could go through the portal for me, but you've taken all this time-travel stuff in your stride and now you're doing homework too! I love you so much for that.'

Adam grins. 'I'm pleased to hear it. You know I love you too – very much.'

He leans forward and kisses me.

'As much as I hate to stop you when you're kissing me like that,' I say, smiling at him as I reluctantly pull away. 'But this time-travel theory – the different timelines one. Is it like branches on a tree? They all come from the same trunk, but branch off to be very different?'

'That's it exactly. Ben's origin story started the same, but it may have branched into two different versions at the point in time Ben gave Eliza the money.'

'He's a sly old fox,' I say, smiling as I think about this. 'He told me not to mess with time, and there he is, creating new timelines for the better.'

'If that's what actually happened – it's only a theory.' Adam shrugs. 'I guess we'll never truly know.'

'But at least we know Ben was able to see his mother and make sure she was OK. Above all else, he wanted to make sure his mother was taken care of. Now he can live out his final years in peace.'

Adam nods. 'And hopefully you can find some peace too knowing that.'

'And Dotty?' I ask, feeling bad for doing so. Adam has already done so much for me in finding this information about Ben. But I want so much to know what happened to her too.

Adam shakes his head. 'I'm sorry, I couldn't find out anything about her. I tried – really I did. I may have only been gone for a few hours this end, but I spent days in 1904 Cambridge asking questions and searching – but nothing. No one knew anything.'

'It's fine,' I say brightly, attempting to conceal my disappointment. 'You did really well finding all that out about Ben. I'm so grateful to you.'

'But you really wanted to know about Dotty, didn't you?'

'I wanted to know about both of them,' I say. 'Obviously, I never knew Dotty like I knew Ben. But after what we discovered about her earlier in the year, I feel a real connection to her. I want to know she was all right too.'

'I understand,' Adam says. 'I did try, but—' He stops abruptly. 'Did you just hear that? That knocking sound?'

'Yes, I thought I heard something, but it sounded a bit muffled. I thought it might be coming from outside in the court.'

We both listen again, and again we hear knocking.

'Is that coming from the tunnel?' I look questioningly at Adam.

'I think it is,' he says. 'But it's not these doors someone's knocking on.' He gestures to the doors with the tree on them. 'It sounds like it might be at the other end.'

We stare at each other, neither one of us knowing what to do.

'Should we go and find out?' I ask.

'I guess we'd better,' Adam says. 'Come on.'

We walk warily together down the dark tunnel towards the exterior doors that we know lead out onto the alleyway at the back of Clockmaker Court.

We stop when we get to the closed doors. Adam removes the planks of wood, then he takes my hand.

'Ready?' he asks, reaching for the handle with his other hand.

I whisper back, 'Ready.'

Adam turns the door handle at the same time as the person the other side decides to knock again, and we both nearly jump out of our skins.

The door swings open and the person on the other side simply stares at the two of us, standing there openmouthed, then she smiles.

'Are you Adam and Eve, by any chance?' she asks in a rounded, polite voice, as though we're being formally introduced.

I open my mouth a couple of times, unable to speak. And then, in only a whisper, I reply.

'Are you … *Dotty*?'

37

Adam and I both stare at the woman standing in front of us.

She's wearing a long navy-blue dress in a heavy tweed-like fabric. It has a full skirt and a fitted bodice, underneath which she has a white, high-necked, buttoned-up blouse. On her feet she wears brown boots with buttons, and on her head a wide-brimmed hat with both flowers and feathers sewn onto it. The hat is pinned to her dark hair, which is arranged in a tight bun at the back of her neck. Her gloved hands are held neatly in front of her. And my first thought is she looks a bit like Mary Poppins as she stands there in front of us.

'I am indeed Dotty,' she says. 'And you are?'

'I'm Eve,' I say quickly. 'And this is Adam.' I give Adam a nudge – he too seems to have lost the use of his voice, like I had to begin with.

Dotty lets out a long sigh. '*That* is very good to know.'

'Would you like to come in?' I ask, sounding as though I'm calmly inviting her into my house for tea, when actually my mind is in complete turmoil at what's unfolding in front of me.

Dotty looks past me into the tunnel. 'It's a long time since I set foot inside the portal. I'm not sure it will let me.'

'What do you mean?' I ask.

'Let's see, shall we?' she says. Dotty seems much more in control of herself than we do – as if she's been expecting this moment for some time.

Adam and I stand back a little to allow Dotty to come through the doors.

She gingerly takes one step forward. When nothing happens, she takes a second. 'Well, that's already further than I thought I'd get,' she says, looking pleased. 'Shall we continue?'

'Yes, of course,' I say, trying hard not to stare at her. But I can't help it. *How is this happening?*

Adam and I lead Dotty all the way back to the office. Again she hesitates before stepping into the room.

When she does, she lets out another huge sigh of relief.

'You don't know what this means to me, to be back here again,' she says, looking around. 'This place has so many memories.' Dotty walks slowly around the room, occasionally stopping to touch a desk or a chair as her memories come flooding back to her.

Adam and I can do nothing but watch her. Both of us utterly astonished at what's happening in front of us. How can Dotty be here in this office with us? It's like we've watched an old black-and-white photograph not only colour itself in, but turn into a completely three-dimensional moving image at the same time.

Eventually Dotty turns back to us. 'Archie and I had many happy times here in this office,' she says. 'Many stressful times too, when we couldn't figure out why our experiments weren't working as we wanted them to. But overall, I have wonderful memories of my times here with your great-grandfather, Adam.'

I feel Adam jolt next to me at his name.

'You know who I am?' Adam speaks for the first time since Dotty arrived. 'I mean, I know you used our names before, but you actually *know* who we both are?'

'Of course I do. As I just said, you are Archie's great-grandson. Your grandfather was George. I remember George when he used to be our messenger boy here with his friend Ernie. We didn't pay him all that much and I think he spent almost every penny on comic books. But he seemed happy doing it and we were grateful to have him.'

'Yes, that's right,' Adam says in awe.

'You look a little like him,' Dotty says, smiling. 'Just around the eyes. And you're just as handsome as your great-grandfather was.'

Adam looks pleased and slightly embarrassed at the same time.

'There was nothing between Archie and I, of course,' she adds. 'Only friendship. Your great-grandfather was a fair bit older than me. He was more like a father figure to me than anything else.'

'Of course,' Adam says, as though the thought never occurred to him.

'And you,' she says, turning to me, 'are my great-grand-daughter, Eve.' For the first time since she arrived, Dotty's calm, almost clipped voice softens as she says my name.

'Yes, I am.'

'Your grandmother was my Sarah ...' Dotty's stoic expression suddenly changes and her face softens too. 'My baby.'

She wobbles a little and Adam immediately rushes forward.

'Here, have a seat,' he says, pulling one of the wooden chairs out for her.

'Thank you, dear boy,' she says, sitting down after smoothing her skirt carefully underneath her first. Then she reaches into the little velvet bag that's been hanging over her arm and pulls out a clean white handkerchief with a delicate lace frill around the edge. She dabs at the corners of her eyes.

'Would you like a cup of tea?' Adam asks.

Dotty looks like he's offered her the world. 'Oh, my goodness, would I? I haven't had a good cup of tea for … well, for far too long.'

'Will you be all right?' Adam asks me. 'If I pop upstairs and put the kettle on?'

'Of course,' I say. 'Tea is a great idea.'

'I'll be right back,' he says.

Adam heads out of the door and I hear him climb the stairs.

'Come sit next to me, Eve,' Dotty says. 'I have much to tell you.'

I pull up the other chair and position it next to Dotty.

'You know, I never thought I'd be sitting here in this office again. Let alone sitting here beside my great-granddaughter,' she says, looking proudly at me. 'You're doing a wonderful job so far, Eve. You and Adam. I've heard all about you and what you've done so far with the portal.'

'But how?' I ask, wondering how she knows any of this.

'From Ben.'

'You've seen him?' I exclaim. 'Is he all right?'

'He's absolutely fine. He's living quite the carefree, relaxed life now he's seen his mother and put things right.'

'Oh, good. I was so worried about him.'

'He said that you would be. He also said to tell you you mustn't worry about him. Although he misses you all greatly, he's happy where he is and he's so grateful to you for helping him.'

I can't help but let out a little sigh. It feels like a huge weight has been lifted.

'I would like to thank you too,' she says. She looks down at her gloves, then quickly but carefully removes them before taking my hand in hers.

The feeling that surges through me when she does is like nothing I've ever felt before. It's like a heady mixture of love, belonging and complete peace.

'You've turned into a fine young woman, Eve,' she says, looking into my eyes. 'You've not had the easiest of lives so far. You don't need to explain. I know all about your family. But despite all that, you've grown into a strong, independent, brave and deeply loyal human being. One I'm very proud to call my great-granddaughter.'

'Thank you—' I begin say, but Dotty pats my hand to stop me saying any more.

'Let me finish, dear. It's so important to me I tell you this while I have the chance. People say you remind them of me. And perhaps we do look a little alike, yes. Even I can see the resemblance.' She winks. 'But you are your own woman, Eve. Never forget that. You make your own decisions in this life. If you think something is right, then don't let anyone tell you otherwise. Trust your gut – that's what the young people say nowadays, isn't it?'

'Er, yes.' I wonder how Dotty knows this.

'I can tell you it's *always* the right thing to do. If you listen to yourself, you'll never go far wrong in life.' She pats my hand again. 'Now, would you like to ask *me* anything?' She lifts a small gold pocket watch fastened with a chain to her dress, and opens up the cover. 'Sadly, time is running short for me,' she says, snapping it shut again. 'But I'll do my best.'

'Er … yes,' I say, trying to sort all the questions I have for her into order of importance in my mind – but instead they all just come tumbling out randomly.

'Why did you always send people back on leap days?' I ask, realising as I say it that this is by far the least important question I have for her. 'That was you doing that, wasn't it?'

'It was. Because the twenty-ninth of February is a day when time doesn't really count. All bets are off, as they say. The additional time we have that day messes with the rules of time. So it makes it much easier to move people from one year to another with fewer repercussions – that's the simple answer, anyway. And for your reference, when we change the clocks forward and back – that works in a similar way too.'

'Right, got it,' I say, eager to ask my next question. 'When you first got stuck in 1904, did you try to return to 1944?'

'Of course I did,' Dotty says earnestly. 'I tried everything. There was no way I was leaving my little Sarah behind – she was my everything. I tried for years – different times, different days. But the harder I tried to return, the firmer the door to the portal stayed shut. Eventually I had to stop trying. It was draining me physically and mentally to the point it was making me very ill, and I almost didn't survive. But it's often when we're at our lowest points that we find the greatest strength. And that's when I decided if I wasn't allowed to go back, then I would stay and help others in peril, just like I'd helped

Ben. I had to hold on to the hope that one day I would be allowed to return – it's what kept me going.'

'But why didn't you try to come back through the portal when you sent the others forward in time?' I ask. 'Surely the doors must have been open for them?'

'Every four years there would be a window to help someone have a better life,' Dotty says wistfully. 'That sadly was the only time I ever saw the doors open. Except they weren't open for me, they were only open for the others. Whenever I tried to join them in the tunnel, the doors would immediately close up again and I'd find myself back in 1904 once more.'

'But why? The doors allowed you through today. That's why you're sitting here now.'

'Yes, I know. I haven't quite figured out why yet …' Dotty's pale brow furrows. 'It might be because you and Adam opened them for me. But then, I assume Archie tried to get me back when I first disappeared?'

'He did. I think he was very … frustrated,' I chose my words carefully, 'when he couldn't get you back. It made him quite ill, I believe.'

'Poor Archie,' Dotty says sadly. 'I thought that might happen.'

'So why did you come to the doors today?' I ask. 'February was months ago now.'

'I heard that someone was going around looking for me,' Dotty says. 'I've been in 1904 Cambridge for so long now, on and off, that I've developed a lot of contacts in the city. They let me know that someone had been asking after me, and also Ben. So I decided to investigate myself. I followed your Adam as he searched for Ben and visited with Ben's mother, Eliza, so it didn't take long for me to work out who he was. This morning, I followed him to the alleyway and saw him disappearing back through the doors into the tunnel. I thought about it for a while, before I decided to knock on the door. I didn't know quite what would happen. So when the two of you answered, I was overjoyed to see you both.'

'But that still doesn't explain why you haven't been able to come through the portal before today?'

'As I spent more time moving around in the past, I began to understand more about how all this ...' She waves her hand around the office. 'How it works. There are rules and regulations to it all, and I broke the rules of time, Eve,' she says sombrely. 'That's why I couldn't return.'

'What do you mean, you *broke* them? How did you do that?'

'There are many rules of time, Eve, which you eventually will learn for yourself. Unfortunately for me, I didn't realise I was breaking any when I tried to help Ben.'

'What happened?'

'I messed with the past and it affected the future,' Dotty says in a hushed tone, as though she's worried about someone hearing her. 'By sending Ben forward all those years ago, I changed what could have happened – it wasn't his choice to come forward, I decided it for him. We all have freedom of choice in this world, Eve. When either our freedom or our choice is taken from us, we have nothing. I took Ben's right to choose his future away from him, and so in exchange I had to give up my own.'

'But you were trying to help him,' I say indignantly. 'Just like you helped all the others afterwards. Some of those people are my friends now. Luca, Harriet, Barney. If you hadn't helped them – goodness knows what would have happened to them.'

'You said Barney?' Dotty asks, frowning. 'You don't mean Barnaby, do you? The small boy who couldn't walk?'

'Yes, he's one of my best friends now. If it wasn't for you, he definitely wouldn't be here now. He was one of the people who helped Adam and I figure out what was happening down here. We couldn't have done it without him.'

Dotty pauses to think, as if she's working something out. 'Maybe that's why?' she murmurs.

'What's why?' I ask.

But Dotty is deep in thought. 'Who would have thought it would have been young Barnaby who would be my saviour?' Tears have formed in the corners of Dotty's eyes and she reaches for her handkerchief again. 'Barnaby was very special to me,' she says as tears fall delicately down her pale face. 'I took such a risk sending him through the tunnel that day, not knowing what would become of him. But now I understand. You needed him. You both needed him to get to where you are now. Does he know?' she asks suddenly. 'That he came from the past?'

'He does now. He didn't until recently, though.'

'He doesn't want to go back, though?' Dotty asks anxiously.

'No, he knows he's much better off here.'

'Oh, good. That's such a relief.'

'You've done so much good, Dotty,' I tell her, determined she should know this. 'It doesn't seem fair you've been punished for doing so.'

Dotty smiles.

'But now you're here with us, Adam and I can help you to go back,' I tell her keenly. 'We know how to control the portal. We can help you to get to 1944.'

Dotty shakes her head. 'No, I can't do that, Eve.'

'Why? You've done so much for others – it's time you had something good done for you. You can go back, see your daughter again and pick up where you left off with Archie, except this time you can take with you the knowledge of how to control the portal. I can teach you. Think of what you'll both be able to do.'

'Stop!' Dotty says. 'I mustn't know. You and Adam were always the chosen ones. It's you who must go forward with this knowledge, not me.'

'But why? I thought you'd jump at the chance to see your daughter again. I'd do anything to see my mother one more time.' I swallow hard.

'Oh, my dear.' Dotty takes my hands in hers again. 'I know you would. I'm so sorry for how everything turned out for you – really I am. But what you must understand is every choice we make in life has a consequence. Sometimes that consequence is good, sometimes it can be bad. If I were to go back with the knowledge of how to control this portal, not only could it change my life and the people who come after me, it could change the course of history too. The way it is is the way it's supposed to be. You'll learn that soon enough. There is a plan for us all. It's helping people to stick to that plan that's the difficult part.' She smiles. 'There's a few of us, you know, doing what I do. This is *our* path in life. You and Adam, you have your path mapped out too. And if I can let you into a little secret? *Yours* is a very special path indeed.'

I don't know what to say. I desperately want to help Dotty, but I can't if she won't let me. 'Wait – the time-lines!' I say suddenly.

'Timelines?' Dotty asks.

'Yes, if you open up a new branch on the tree, the original one still exists,' I say, knowing I'm not explaining this very well. 'You could start a new timeline and the old one would still be there, so nothing would change.'

Dotty smiles. 'I know the theory you're referring to. Unfortunately, that's not exactly how that works,' she says kindly. 'It's a lot more complex. One day you will understand, Eve.'

'Are you absolutely sure we can't help you?' I ask her one more time. 'It just seems like it would be such a wonderful thing to do for you, to reunite you with your daughter and give you back your life.'

'I know. And I love you for wanting that for me.' She reaches out and puts her hand on my cheek, in exactly the same way I did with Adam when I realised how I truly felt about him. 'But sometimes it's the most difficult choices you make in life that are the most important ones.'

Dotty strokes my cheek.

'You're good girl, Eve. No,' she corrects herself, 'you're good woman. You and Adam are going to make a wonderful team. And when you're both ready, you too will do great things together with this portal. Just like we always knew you would do.'

Dotty pulls out her watch again and glances at it. 'And now I must go,' she says, standing up. 'I've a feeling after what's happened today that my many times on this earth are now coming to an end. It's time I found my peace.'

She heads towards the doors and I follow her. She takes one more look around the room. 'Can I give you one last piece of advice, Eve?'

'Of course.'

'You've been given a great gift here, you and Adam. Use it well and use it wisely, won't you?'

'Of course we will.'

'Because this is your time, Eve. Yours and Adam's. And you have all the time in the world.'

Dotty reaches out and gives me a long hug, and I feel the same feelings of love, belonging and peace surging through me once more, only a hundred times stronger this time as she wraps her arms around me. 'I'd wish you both all the luck in the world,' she says as she finally pulls away, 'but I don't think you'll need it. You two were destined for this moment and destined for each other. Always remember that.'

I follow Dotty into the tunnel and, using my phone torch, light her way to the end.

'Wait,' I say as she opens the external doors and is about to go through them again. 'I have photos of your daughter on my phone here – not only that, but photos of your granddaughter and your other great-granddaughter too.' I look down at my phone and begin scrolling through my photo app. 'Would you like to see them all grown up?'

'Eve, I don't need photographs to see them,' Dotty says quietly, her voice fading a little. 'I know exactly what you and all my family look like. I always have.'

'But how?' I ask, still searching furiously for the photos.

'Because I've been with you all along,' she says, her voice getting ever fainter.

I raise my head to see Dotty smiling serenely at me. The light from behind her at the end of the tunnel is making her look like she has a halo all around her.

'I was always with your grandmother, your mother, your sister, and now you, Eve. I never left any of you. And I never will.'

And then, instead of going through the doors and returning back to Edwardian Cambridge as I expect her to, Dotty simply fades away in front of me.

'Eve?' I hear being called down the tunnel from behind me. 'Eve, are you there?'

I call back to Adam, 'Yes, yes, I'm here. I'll be back in a moment.' I take one last look at where Dotty was standing moments ago, and then, very calmly, I walk the few steps towards the doors and close them up, securing them with the two planks before returning down the tunnel to Adam.

Adam is standing in the office waiting for me as I emerge through the doors. Behind him are three cups of freshly brewed tea, with milk and sugar all on a little tray. Next to that, where Dotty was sitting, is a single bright-red apple.

'Where's Dotty?' Adam asks, looking behind me into the tunnel as I step back into the office. 'Didn't she have time for a cup of tea in the end?'

'I think Dotty has always had *all the time in the world* to do everything she needs to do,' I say, gazing at the apple shining like a beacon of hope under the dim light of the office. 'And do you know something?' I say, smiling at Adam. 'Now *we* have that same, very precious gift too.'

Epilogue

Clockmaker Court, Cambridge. February 2044

Adam and I sit together on the bench underneath the old oak tree in the garden at the centre of Clockmaker Court. Some welcome winter sunshine is currently keeping us a lot warmer than we might have been if we were sitting out here in the shade.

'They're on their way,' he says, looking at his phone.

'You know they think you're almost antiquarian using that old thing now,' I tell him.

'I can't keep up with all the modern ways of communicating these days,' Adam says, putting his old iPhone in the pocket of his warm winter coat. 'I'm more than happy to continue using this for now. It suits me. Plus, we need to keep a few old gadgets around us, for when we need to look authentic.' He raises his eyebrows at me, reminding me of when we were both much younger and Adam would cheekily do the same thing when he was teasing me or winding me up.

Nothing too much has changed with the two of us in all the years we've spent together since. We still own shops next to each other in Clockmaker Court, with all our friends still close by. We still enjoy a takeaway and a quiet night in more than we enjoy eating out at a fancy restaurant, and we are still very much in love with each other after twenty years together.

What has changed, however, is we are both a bit older and greyer, with a few more lines and wrinkles now Adam is sixty and I'm fifty-six. And we've also spent seventeen of our twenty years together as husband and wife.

'If we'd kept all our old gadgets, I could probably sell most of them in the shop now as antiques,' I say, casting my gaze across to Rainy Day Antiques. The shop currently has its *Closed* sign hung in the window, while Adam and I wait snuggled together on the bench, and it's the same for Adam's bookshop next door.

Today is an important day for our family and we're currently waiting for our two children to arrive from the townhouse we all share not far away. The same house I lived in when I first met Adam, and the house that originally belonged to my grandparents.

'What do you think our grandparents would make of what we're about to do today?' I ask Adam, taking hold of his gloved hand with my mitten-covered one.

'I think they'd be very proud of us,' Adam says without hesitation. 'Our great-grandparents would as well.'

'Me too. We've had some adventures, haven't we?' I ask, resting my head on his shoulder. 'In the last twenty years.'

'You could call them that,' Adam says, smiling ruefully as he puts his arm around me. 'I'd call some of them lucky escapes.'

'That too. But we've guarded our secret well and used it only for good. Just like we promised we would.'

'Technically, you promised that. I don't actually remember having much of a choice in the matter.'

'You've loved every minute of it!' I reply, knowing he's just teasing me.

'I have. But it's not over, you know? We can't retire just yet.'

'No. We're not quite passing on the baton. We're simply training up the new team. Seriously, though, do you think they'll be all right with it? It's quite a thing we're entrusting them both with.' I turn to Adam, a worried expression on my face. I've been going back and forth about today for weeks.

'They will be absolutely fine. They're good kids. We'll let them make their own decision, of course, but I'm pretty sure they'll step up. Just as well they've inherited their mother's bravery, eh?'

Adam leans in to kiss me.

'Eurgh! Do you two have to do that on a public bench?' Benji, our youngest, asks as he walks towards us across the court.

'You are both far too old for PDAs,' Dot, our eldest, says, wrinkling up her nose as she walks beside her brother.

'I'll have you know your mother and I were sitting on this bench having PDAs a long time before you two were ever thought about!' Adam says, but he stands up to welcome his children by giving them a hug.

'So what's going on?' Dot asks, sitting down next to me on the bench. 'What's the big secret?'

'Yeah,' Benji says, sitting down the other side of me. 'What's going on?'

I glance up at Adam. 'Who said there's a big secret?'

'Eve,' Adam says warningly. Adam is very aware that I'm still hesitant about sharing our secret with our children. I want to protect them that little bit longer and keep them innocent. But they are fifteen and thirteen now, and they've begun to question far too often just where we went, when we often went missing for hours at a time. And just why they were never allowed in the basement of the shops.

'All right, there is a bit of a secret we have to tell you.' I put my arms around them both and pull them close.

'Oh, my God, you're not pregnant, are you?' Dot asks, looking horrified.

'No! Of course I'm not. Dot, I'm fifty-six and I'm in menopause. It's very unlikely I'd be pregnant again, now, isn't it?'

Dot shrugs. 'Fair enough.'

'What is the secret, then, Mum?' Benji asks quietly. Benji is by far the quieter and more sensitive of our two children. I suspected a while ago he thought something was going on.

'Yeah, why have you brought us out here on a freezing cold February day and made us sit on this old bench?' Dot asks. 'Can't we at least go in one of the shops where it's warm?'

Adam takes over. 'The reason we've brought you here to this specific spot today is because many of the most important moments for your mother and I have taken place on this very bench, underneath this old oak tree. It's where I proposed to your mum.' Adam looks lovingly down at me. 'And it's where she told me she was pregnant with you, Dorothy, and you, Benjamin.' I feel the children both sit up a bit straighter, as they always do when either of us use their full names. Because usually they're in trouble when we do.

'Yes,' I say. 'This bench and this oak tree have not only been a part of many important moments in our lives, they are also a part of the reason we've called you here today.'

I swallow hard as our two children – our whole world, and why Adam and I do many of the important and sometimes dangerous things we do – look up in anticipation at me, and I hesitate again.

'It's also a leap year this year,' Adam says, taking over once more. 'And now that it's February and we're fast approaching the twenty-ninth of this month, some things might start to happen that might seem a little odd to you.'

'What sort of things?' Benji asks.

It's Adam who pauses now. He looks at me.

'The thing is,' I say. 'Oh, where to start?' I look desperately at Adam once more.

'Mum, don't worry,' Dot says, taking hold of my hand. 'You can tell us. Whatever it is, we'll understand.'

'Yeah,' Benji says, taking hold of my other hand. 'Take your time – there's no hurry. I'm not going anywhere. Are you, Dot?'

'No,' Dot says. 'We have all the time in the world …'

Her familiar words tug at my heart and I feel tears spring into my eyes as I think of Dotty. Hurriedly I blink them away.

Of course my children will get it, of course they'll understand. They'll understand and step up just like I did, and Adam, and all the people who came before us.

I look around Clockmaker Court, lost for a moment in memories of both friends and family, past and present.

The secrets of the portal, and everything wonderful and noble it can be used for, will remain safe for generations to come. Of that I have no doubt.

Because the memories we create and the love we share, with our friends and with our family, is always going to be the most important time of all.

THE END

Acknowledgements

It takes a huge team of people to take the thoughts, imaginings and words of an author, and craft them into the book you have just (hopefully!) enjoyed reading.

So my endless appreciation and thanks goes out to:

— Darcy, Maisie, Sophie, Faye, Amy, Abi and all the amazing team at Bloomsbury for all their help and guidance with this book.

— Hannah, my always steadfast and wise agent, for her never-ending words of wisdom and advice.

— Jim, Rosie and Tom, my wonderful family, for listening, supporting and always being there for me.

And to you my fabulous readers, for loving, reading and buying all of my books! Whether you've been there with me from the start, or you are new to my novels, I appreciate you all very much.

Until the next time…

Ali x

Note on the Author

Ali McNamara's debut novel *From Notting Hill with Love... Actually*, the first of three Notting Hill books, was published to much acclaim in 2010 and became an instant bestseller. She now writes feel-good fiction with a magical twist, a unique combination that has proved very popular with readers around the world. She has been nominated for the Romantic Novel of the Year four times. Ali lives near Cambridge in the UK with her family and her beloved dogs. She has the chronic illness ME and is a disability & invisible disability advocate.